M.K. GIBSON

Villains Academy

By M.K. Gibson

www.mkgibson.com

Story, cover design, and layout by: MK Gibson

ISBN: 979-8-950162-10-7

2nd Edition

NOTE FROM THE MAIN CHARACTER

This one will be short and sweet. Thank you to all the idiots of the world. Your colossal dimwittery, self-centeredness, and mob-like behavior have fueled my rants for all these many years. I am so, SO thankful to have profited from your general stupidity.

From the bottom of my black heart, thank you!

~ J. Jackson Blackwell, The Iconoclast Titan

BLACKWELL

TABLE OF CONTENTS

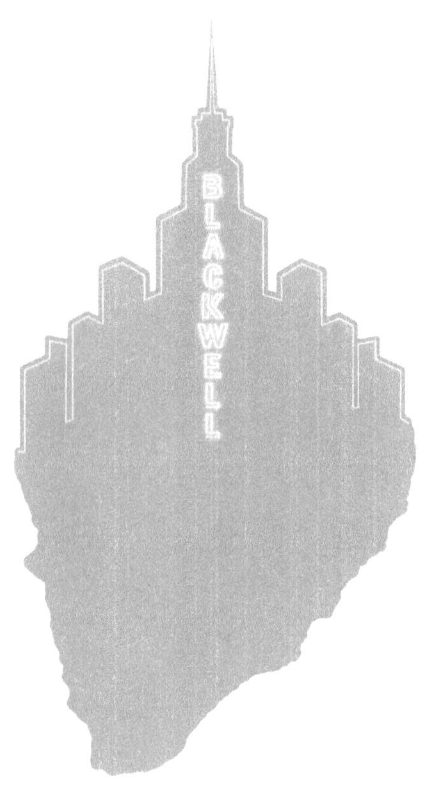

BLACKWELL

CHAPTER 1

WHERE I SIDESTEP STANDARD INTROS, SHINE A SPOTLIGHT ON WEALTHY ORPHANS, AND GIVE A QUICK RECAP

Across the vastness of space and time, an infinite number of worlds, universes, and planes of being exist. And tucked away in a tiny, almost inconsequential fold of the multiverse was a certain pocket dimension.

There was nothing special about the space itself. It was, after all, just one of literally countless micro-universes. Yet this rather contentious piece of interdimensional real estate was a locus for change. The battles for ownership over said dimension helped to shape the cosmic narrative.

Almost as if it had been by design. Which, in fact, it was.

It was in this nameless micro-dimension that the Iconoclast Titan, Jackson Blackwell, the grand TiT himself, sat contemplating—

"Nooooope!" I said, my voice rippling through the Cosmos. "We're not doing this again."

Doing what? The Cosmos answered back.

"Look, this is the sixth recorded adventure, and I have things to do. Which means we don't have for all that '*across space and time in the formless void sits a castle where blah blah blah*' crap we've done for all the other books. So we're gonna start with a sense of urgency, skip the prologue, and skip all that interstitial chapter nonsense."

The Cosmos smirked. *Do you really think you're capable of doing something new? Your stories aren't breaking any new ground, pal.*

"Never claimed to be original, just entertaining," I countered. "But seriously, we don't have time for the standard intro crap. Okay?"

Yet we have time for this pointless banter?

"Apparently, yes?" I sighed. "Now please, just go back to watching people like a perv."

The Cosmos shrugged. *Fine. But you may want to at least catch your audience up. Not everyone re-reads the previous adventures.*

Looking around what used to be Eris's old office, which was now mine—huh, or maybe it was really Randy's and Paige's now? Eh, didn't matter. Everyone else was busy with preparations except me. Maybe the Cosmos was right.

Okay kids, gather round. It's story time with Uncle Jackson.

Once upon a time, your beloved Shadow Master was once just a man. A great man, mind you. A great, *self-made* man.

Sure, I was born into affluence, befriended a djinn during my youth, and then later inherited a multi-million-dollar windfall when my parents died. But other than that, I was a total "pulled myself up by my bootstraps" kind of guy.

What? Why are you looking at me like that?

Oh, for the love of—you heard me say *dead parents*, right?

Yeesh… Do you give the other wealthy orphans this much crap?

Despite all his charisma and his charming quirks, Mr. Stark was responsible for thousands of dead men, women, and children. Both before *and after* becoming Iron Man.

Oh, and don't get me started on Batman. The Dark Knight has broken, maimed, and hospitalized countless crooks and henchmen over his career. And thanks to all the edgelords and deconstructionists who've penned his adventures, Gotham City only has two types of citizens—the mega-wealthy elite and the poorest, saddest, ugliest troglodytes under the sun.

Seriously. Based on the most recent movies, the average Gothamite elementary school is sadder than the homeless dogs in that Sarah McLachlan "Angel" commercial.

All this means that the city is overflowing with poor folks trying to make ends meet. Some, sadly, have no other option than a little crime. But after an unlucky encounter with a sociopath dressed as a flying rodent, their broken bodies are hauled to the clinic where they accrue medical bills they can't afford, thereby ensuring their return to crime.

Somehow these two get hailed as heroes and have major movie franchises, and I'm stuck doing indie books. It's villain discrimination, I tell ya. Anyway, back to the recap.

I eventually built my empire, then expanded outward. Using Sophia, I became a minor god by leasing a pocket dimension where I built a new empire, one based on villain advising. And man, business was good. I had countless adventures across the multiverse.

But like, in a cool way. Not like how everyone's currently abusing multiverses.

I did it before it was trendy.

Anyway, years go by, and I get double crossed and stuck in the generic fantasy world Caledon. It was a weird time in my life. My guard was down, family was out to get me, and I'd abandoned nearly all of my personal villain rules. But I met a gal, and we fell in love.

Well, at least I thought we were in love. Maybe it was just sexual attraction.

Anywho, she ended up pregnant. Yay? Which of course meant her hormones went crazy cakes. As such, I was somehow kicked out of my own dimension, from which followed my second recorded adventure. I fought comic book heroes and villains and gained my two loyal minions, and by the end, my daughter Evie was born.

We'll skip over the events of my third recorded adventure where I did nearly everything I could to save Evie in a classic sci-fi adventure. Apparently, *Villains Deception* is still a sore spot for some people.

No idea why.

Then things took a turn in my fourth adventure. Sophia, my oldest friend and nemesis, finally enacted her plan for revenge. She managed to kill me off. Obviously, it didn't stick, as I had a backup plan. I become a Titan… but it came with a cost.

A terrible one.

In the two years I was gone, everyone I'd held dear had moved on. But I came back, reunited the team, and wrecked shop. However, despite my villainous return, it turned out that Sophia too had a backup plan.

She was holding Evie hostage.

Upon my victory, Sophia and her cohort of conspirators fled from this very office through a portal, then dared me to follow.

Thanks to my Titan caseworker Frank, AKA the Malevolent Kismet Gambler, we'd learned that Evie was being held *inside* another Titan. One of the Great Infinite.

The Titan of Possibility.

All I knew was that she was alive and in school. Possibly some kind of villains' academy. Frank had opened a portal to Possibility; all we had to do was step through.

Which brings us to the here and now.

While the others busied themselves with last-minute tasks, I mentally prepared myself. Until Evie was safe, I'd remain unflappable. Laser focused. Unshakable. I'd be—

"Heya, TiT!"

"Sweet triple nipples on a Martian!" I squeaked… but in a totally masculine way. "Seriously, Frank? What the hell, man?"

Frank was in his generic paunchy, balding, and bespectacled middle-manager form. His bushy moustache wiggled as a bit of mischief gleamed in his eyes.

"It's time, Jackson," he said. "The portal will close soon. It's now or never."

CHAPTER 2

WHERE I CHAT ABOUT SENSATIONS, GAIN A BIT OF RESPECT, AND TALK A WALK

I looked at the portal. My mind spun with scenarios and contingencies, one fighting for dominance among them all.

"We go in, I get that. But any ideas on how we get back?"

"No idea," Frank admitted. "Sophia cooked something up. But I think it's contingent on you going in there."

"Oh, ya think?" I said, rolling my eyes.

"Lighten up, kid," Frank said, taking a half step back. "One of the best parts of being a Titan getting a feel for when something stupid is about to happen. When you've been around long enough, you start developing a sort of six millionth sense for these things."

I nodded in understanding.

Oh, I see that you don't.

Well, you know how you normies have five senses?

That was a test, and you failed.

Sorry, but if you still think that you only have five senses, then it's clear you've never picked up any scientific knowledge past the third grade. Yes, people have the base five that you know, but they also have senses like equilibrioception, proprioception, cociception, thermoception, and interoception.

Man, those will be fun when the audiobook comes out. Five bucks says Kafer can't get them right on the first try.

Anyway, in simpler terms, those mean balance, awareness of relative space, awareness of pain, awareness of relative temperatures, and awareness of one's inner state of being, respectively.

Some scientists postulate that humans have as many nine, twenty-one, or even fifty-plus senses. But that's a little pedantic as a bunch of them are just the brain sensing all the crap going on in your organs.

Gods have way more senses, as they have an awareness of everything going on in their particular worlds. But Titans? We grow new senses constantly just to compensate for all the shifts in reality.

And… *sigh*. Yes, we also have a sense to tell us when we're talking too much and not moving the plot.

Typically because we're scared of not knowing what comes next.

"So what you're saying," I began, pausing to light a black cigarette, "is that if I *don't* go in there, then Sophia and the rest are trapped?"

"That's my guess," Frank said. "Sophia's a tricky bitch, and she's playing some dangerous poker. She's all in, that's for sure. But she's clearly counting on you to take the bait."

"Bait? Evie's not bait. She's my daughter."

"Whom you barely know," Frank pressed. "She's what, seven years old?"

I glowered at my Titan mentor. Evie was—biologically—around seven. But during her time as a demigoddess of this realm, she'd used her powers to advance her age a time or two. By my fourth recorded adventure, and my mortal death, she'd appeared to be a little over fourteen. Which meant if time remained constant, then she'd be roughly sixteen-ish?

All those years, gone. Damn it.

"What's your point, Frank?" I asked, my voice taking on an edge.

"That she's *not* a Titan," he said coldly. "And you're not the god of this realm anymore, either. Humans are gone in the blink of an eye, as far as our kind's concerned."

"She's my daughter," I reiterated.

"You can make more," he said. When the look in my eye said that I did not care for that option, Frank threw his arms up in frustration. "By Kl'och'Tar's Transcended Taint, you can just grab another Evie from another reality if you want one so bad!"

"But that's not *my* daughter."

"Sure it is," Frank said. "You just have to see the relative simplicity of quantum entanglement."

"No. I can't do that."

"Oh, please don't tell me you're some kind of touchy-feely antihero with a hard-on for mortals."

"Like yours for Virginia?"

"Watch it, TiT," he cautioned.

I flicked my smoke away. "No, I haven't turned into a gods damned antihero. This is all about one thing and one thing only."

The corner of Frank's mouth turned slightly upwards. "Which is?"

"What's mine," I said. "Sophia and all the rest of those conspiring little pisswizards dared to fuck with what's mine. My daughter, my worlds, my life. And they are going to pay for it. So yeah, I'm going in there, and I'm going to beat them once and for all."

"Atta boy," Frank said.

"Is this a slow clap moment?" Randy asked. "It really feels like one to me."

I looked up to see my nephew leaning against his desk, hands waiting.

The dick.

He'd kept the beard from his time in the hollers of West Virginia but now wore a tailored navy blue suit that emphasized his blockier, more muscular frame. Paige stood at her desk in her own professional-looking attire. She smiled at me as she stood.

In fact, they were all standing.

Myst and Wraith Knight, who no longer wore their Comic Universe garb, stood together like the mixed-race power couple seen in cereal commercials. The ones from brands that acted like they cared about diversity in order to sell sugar-laced corn.

Next to them, Claudia's newer, hyper-futuristic chassis gleamed and twinkled in various neon colors, showing her approval.

It was Dutch, the tall, handsome, Tron-looking human-program hybrid, who shrugged. "I honestly don't find you that inspiring."

"That's why I haven't erased you yet," I said. "I appreciate your candor."

Lydia was the last to stand. My ex-wife wore black leggings with black knee-high boots and a dark green poncho-like off-the-shoulder number. No doubt hiding an obscene number of knives.

"Are we leaving now?" she asked.

"You don't have to go," I said, then turned to address the rest of the group. "I can do it on my own. You don't have to go. If things go bad, it's just me."

"That's my daughter as well," Lydia said. "You can't stop me."

I nodded, but I didn't totally believe her. Yeah, Evie was her child, but her stance on motherhood was well documented. No, I think this had just as much to do with the woman she'd fallen in love with, the succubus Mikayla, as it did about Evie.

But I didn't say any of that. Lydia had her own drama to deal with, and that wasn't my business anymore.

"Okay," I said. "But Myst, WK, you don't have to go."

"With respect, boss," Wraith Knight began, "fuck that."

"Wendell gods-damn Dench." I smiled. "Where you been hiding all this time?"

"Oh please, Jackson," Myst said, taking WK's huge hand in hers. "We've been there for her since she was born. We aren't leaving now."

I felt this strange, swelling sensation where my heart used to be.

Hmm… had to be indigestion or the Titan equivalent. I'd have to ask Frank about it once I got back.

With Evie.

"Randy, Paige, Claudia, and Dutch," I said, addressing them in turn, "you know your jobs."

"Keep the office running and the clients happy," Paige said.

"Maintain the highest levels of security in case this is a ploy by Eris and Sophia to attack your assets while you're not here to protect them," Claudia added.

"And?" I prodded.

"Curtail the spread of information about your absence as much as possible while also reminding everyone that your willingness to cripple those who fuck with your assets is infinite," Claudia clarified.

"Perfect," I said. "Dutch?"

"Get into every universe's system and steal every kernel of data that isn't nailed down," Dutch offered. "Which I was going to do anyway."

"Good, all of you," I said, then looked at Randy. "And you?"

My nephew let out a small chuckle. "Easiest job of the bunch."

"Oh yeah?"

"Yeah," he said, giving me a look of—*gasp*—respect. "I keep your seat warm. You bring my cousin home safely."

"I don't deserve you all," I said, addressing the group.

"Aw, Julie," Paige said with a wide, earnest smile.

"He means he deserves better than us, Mother."

I snickered.

"Goddamn it," she cursed. "I hate this family."

"Frank?" I said, the question not needing to be asked.

"Step through and think only of Evie. No matter what," he said, pointing at the swirling portal of every changing color. "You'll be entering tangible possibility, and you weren't exactly invited in. Every stray thought could lead you somewhere equally possible, so focus on Evie and your objective."

I nodded. "Okay folks. Let's go get our girl."

And with that, the four of us walked through the portal and into Possibility.

Naturally, I let the other three go first. No need to rush headfirst into something in case it was a trap or if they were liquified on the spot.

Seeing as they didn't explode into goo, I let myself pass through. I felt prepared for anything.

I was wrong.

CHAPTER 3

WHERE I EDUCATE YOU ON THE FINER POINTS OF PUNCHING DOWN, AIR OUT MY GUTS, AND COME TO A SUDDEN STOP

Have you ever had the entirety of your insides pulled out through your rectum?

No, for real. It isn't a set-up for a diarrhea joke, nor is it where I make a snide, backhanded comment at your expense to make myself feel better. "Punching down," I believe, is what some of the wimpy New-Age kids call it.

HA! Still pulled it off. Damn, I'm good.

But seriously, get thicker skin. Your modern fragility offends me. Especially since every person, group, or social class punches down. And before you argue, allow me to explain.

Stick with me because it's a bit of a walk.

The average human's ego is so huge and flexible that they simultaneously cast themselves as the hero and the victim in nearly every situation. But rarely as the villain. You know what I'm talking about. Gods above and below, you know *who* I'm talking about. Do any of these sounds familiar?

Look what you made me do!

I cheated because you pushed me away.

Oh officer, see what had happened was I was very stressed due to a mean comment written about me online and that put me in a place where I—I just can't even right now. So anyway, that busload of kids came out of nowhere! And, frankly, I don't think their daytime running lights were on. So clearly, it's **their** *fault.*

Okay, maybe that last one was a little hyperbolic, but these examples illustrate a simple point: "I was wrong" are the three hardest words for a person to say. They will come up with an infinite number of excuses while performing Olympic-level mental gymnastics to avoid saying "I was wrong."

What does this have to do with punching down? Well, I'm getting there.

You see, if a *person* can't be wrong, then a *group* feels fucking infallible.

Pop quiz. What happens when you take a bunch of like-minded people and bond them ethically, spiritually, politically, fiscally, or whatever? Right, you get tribalism. An oh-so-fun coalition of hero-victims with a group-think ideology that inevitably turns into "us vs. them."

Ergo ipso facto, this enlightened or "elevated" group loudly and frequently *punch down* from their righteous if rickety soap box, targeting another group whom they fear or hate.

And you know what? It's okay. It's your inalienable human right to mock others. Shit, I built a career on it. But tread carefully.

Those who choose to punch down from a place of hate are bigger villains than I am.

Yes, your pal Jackson's mocked countless people and countless groups. But I've never mocked a person for *what* they are, but rather *who* they are. Translation: If you're an asshole, I'm gonna call you out. Especially if I can do it in a darkly creative way and get paid.

But anyway…

The reason I ask you if you've ever had your guts, bones, organs, and blood pulled through your booty hole is because it just happened to me.

Oops.

Frank had warned us about various possibilities. It's just that, come on, we're walking into the literal unknown. "Crossing the threshold," as Joseph Campbell would say. And since there could be *anything* on the other side, I accidentally wondered, "What if there were an unseen fundamental force of the multiverse that turned someone inside out, butthole first?"

As it turns out, there is.

And it kinda tickles.

The four of us hurtled past everything and nothing, tumbling through the endless spiraling corridors of Possibility. I bore witness to the daydreams of the mundane and the mind-bending machinations of long-dead progenitor deities.

Basically, the opening credits of that one anime your weeb friends won't shut up about.

The only point of reference I had was a singular ball of golden light in the distance.

"What the shit?!" I heard from behind me.

I looked down and… yep, I was still inside out. A quick glance back and I saw that my guts, which trailed behind me like a gory kite tail, were slapping Wraith Knight in the face.

"So gross!" he spat, slapping at the gushy organs smacking against his open mouth.

"Hey, be careful!" I warned him. "I might need that."

"Then imagine the possibility of yourself right side in," Lydia hissed.

Unlike the others, my ex fell through the endless expanse like one of those wing suit enthusiasts you see in videos. The ones you secretly hope smack into the side of something large, hard, and unmoving. Like a mountain… or the ground.

Please, don't act like I'm the only one.

Taking her suggestion, I imagined myself in proper working order, body parts where they're meant to be, and suddenly I was.

Head forward, arms pinned to the side, and toes pointed, I mirrored Lydia and rocketed forward towards that distant point of light. Normally I'd applaud her diligence, but my keener Titan sense of perception picked up on a certain buxom succubus reflected in more than a few portals. It was clear Lydia's mind had wandered from Evie a time or two as well.

Eh, I couldn't blame her.

I noticed a portal or two that led to a life where Lydia and I were happy. Living the life I always thought we'd live.

As a Titan, I don't need to sleep, but the old human in me still enjoys the experience—just letting the stress of the day slip away as calming, blissful rest overwhelms you.

I've stopped doing it, though.

Despite my immeasurable power and growing levels of awareness, I kept reaching over to her side of the bed. And each time I found it empty. A little reminder that the god-slash-man who'd become a Titan now had far, far less.

Locking my melancholy away, I solidified my mind and focused on the one thing that mattered.

Evie.

As I did, the pinprick of golden light in the spiraling horizon grew bigger and bigger. I could sense it. Any moment now, we'd be with her. All I had to do was—

I plowed into the hard, unyielding ground at such an insane speed that my insides were once again on the outside.

Ow.

WHERE I CHAT WITH POSSIBILITY, SPOTLIGHT ROM-COM DECEIT, AND GET A TITLE DROP

Welcome, little cousin, I felt the entirety of the world around me say. *Be careful what you wish for.*

"I—ugh! I never said *I* wanted to be the guy in the wing suit!" I grumbled as I slowly picked myself up off the flat, cracked ground, stitching my body back together as I did.

That's true, Possibility resonated in my mind. *But since you also compared her to wing suit enthusiasts, then blathered on about how you hoped said enthusiasts would smack into something hard, I thought it might be possible you really meant yourself. As a way of self-punishment.*

"Don't head shrink me, please," I said, dusting myself off and making sure all the important bits were back where they belonged. "You took liberty with that one and you damn well know it."

Eh, fine, Possibility mentally shrugged. *But while you're here, you will abide by my rules.*

Before I agreed, I noticed that the other three were just dandy. They stood on the rocky ground without a scratch on them.

"Oh, come on, seriously? Are you just being a prick, or is this a 'haze the new Titan' thing?"

Possibility chuckled.

"Jackson," Lydia said. "Who are you talking to?"

"Possibility," I said, gesturing all around us.

"Are we in the right spot?" she asked, not caring about the conversation. "Where's Evie?"

I looked around at the alien sky of purples, magentas, and reds. There was no horizon line, no topography, and no discernible features other than the weird sky and the cracked barren ground. Gods above and below, we were a few fake robber rocks away from a bad *Star Trek* setting.

Well, that's not totally true. Directly above us, high in the sky, was a spiral of celestial bodies, like a cosmic vortex.

Huh, likely the portal we came in from.

You're right, Possibility said. *A change of scenery is in order.*

There was a vibration beneath us, followed by a deep rumble. I turned and flinched, jumping back as a mountain range, a whole gods damned mountain range, shot up from the ground. The sudden eruption of stone sent the four of us tumbling end-over-end down the ever-growing slope. I did my best to limit the damage to everyone, placing a higher priority on myself, obviously.

Once momentum and gravity stopped making us their bitch, I lay on my back and let out a small grunt.

"Again, *ow.*"

The four of us were now lying in a little patch of grass at the base of the mountain. We were just behind a rocky outcropping that curved around and blocked our view of the newly formed… world?

"Is everyone okay?" I asked, shaking off the experience.

"Do you remember that scene in *The Princess Bride?*" Myst croaked from the flat of her back. "Where Buttercup and Wesley tumbled down the slope? I feel a lot like that."

"I'll take your word for it," I said, getting to my feet.

"Take my word? Are you saying that you never saw *The Princess Bride?*"

"Nope," I said, stretching my neck and back.

"We watched it together," Lydia said, slowly getting her own feet under her. "Many times."

"Yeah… about that," I said. "I tended to play with my phone back when you'd have it on. I only half paid attention to certain parts."

She and Myst both stared at me.

"What?" I asked. "It's a chick flick. The kind of movie you watch because the person you're boning likes it. Duh. Back me up on this, WK."

"Sorry, boss, I like that movie," Wraith Knight said, offering a hand to Myst.

She took his arm, got to her feet, then began checking herself over for damage. But as soon as his paramour turned her head away, Wraith Knight gave me the slightest shake of his head, mouthing, "It sucks."

"I saw that!" Myst growled.

"But you said you loved it as much as I did," Lydia said.

I sighed.

"Like the billions of people before me and the billions who will follow… I've said, done, and tolerated any number of moronic things to get sex. I once watched the movie version of *Evita* in the theater because the girl I wanted to sleep with liked it. I should get a medal for that one alone."

"So, you lied to me?"

"Uh, *villain?*" I said, making a 'ta-da' gesture. "Besides, I don't think we want to have the 'who kept what from whom' talk, do we?"

"I never said I hated it!" Wraith Knight boomed, continuing his simultaneous argument. "It's just that I think the story of how Wesley became the Dread Pirate Roberts would've been a cooler movie. Princess Bride is cute and all, but—"

"*Cute?!*" Myst said. "I can't even with you right now."

"See?" I said to Lydia, pointing at the minions. "Sometimes it's better to live the lie."

She narrowed her eyes. "You'd rather me have lied to you and be miserable for the rest of my life?"

"Doesn't matter now, does it?"

I turned around, refusing to look her in the eye. I didn't want her to see me… *ugh*, vulnerable. Instead, I looked up at the colossal summit that had not been there a moment ago. Jagged golden-brown peaks jutted skyward like the teeth of an old god.

"Wait, that wasn't there a second ago, was it?"

"What, the mountain?" Wraith Knight.

"No, ass," Myst said, still not happy. "*That.*"

Nestled into the mountain's peaks, a huge and imposing castle made of gray stone with dark purple turrets manifested into reality. It loomed there with a sense of solemn antiquity. But more importantly, I sensed Evie. She was close.

"I think we're in the right spot," I said.

Oh, you are, Possibility said. *And if you want your daughter back, then you'll have to play the game.*

"Game?" I said aloud, then brought my finger to my lips, shushing the others before they spoke. "What game?"

A simple one, Possibility said. *Can you survive? I have watched you, little cousin, and I am forced to wonder, are you as good as you think you are? Sophia doesn't seem to think so. So much so that she made me a tempting offer.*

"Which was?"

She requested that I create a scenario to house and educate your child on the off chance that you came back from death. And should that happen, then she'd lure you here. And once the two of you were locked in, then only one of you would leave, Possibility explained. *I either keep a wish-granting djinn or a newly formed Titan.*

"I never agreed to that."

Nor do you have to, Possibility said.

Mother f—

"You this planned with her, didn't you?" I asked.

Yes, Possibility said bluntly. *Sophia's betting that your hubris and lingering compassion will be your undoing. So what will it be? Will you abandon these pesky ephemeral parasites, or will you stay and play the game?*

I relayed all this information out loud so that the others knew what was at stake. And damn me, not one of them asked to leave.

"You'd think I trained you better than this," I said, shaking my head at them. "Fine, we're in. But I want some conditions. Whatever happens between me and Sophia, my allies get to leave."

No, I don't think so, Possibility said, this time addressing the entire group.

The others looked stunned as the elder Titan spoke in their minds.

The blood leaking from their eyes was a dead giveaway.

Wimps.

They came here with you, just as Sophia's allies did, Possibility said. *Therefore, all of you are subject to the same rules. But I'm not a monster. Mostly. We will see where you place at the end of term.*

"Term? What do you mean, the end of term?"

Hurry along, little cousin. You don't want to be late for your first day. And remember, once you cross the line, there's no going back.

"What the hell are you talking about?!" I yelled at the sky, but got no response.

I felt my power… well, not leaving me so much as being suppressed. Reaching out, I knew I could tear through the barrier blocking my abilities.

Ah ah, Possibility popped back in, warning me. *Use your power on school grounds and I'll eject you and keep Sophia.*

That's not much of a punishment.

And Evie, Possibility added. *For all time.*

Fuck!

"Um, boss?" Wraith Knight said.

"What?!" I snapped, still reeling from Possibility's addendum. "What is so gods damned important?!"

"Jackson," Myst said in a calming tone. "You need to see this. It's really… weird."

"Define weird," I said, trying to get my temper under control. "I once counseled a nine-foot spider deity made of titties who spun breast-milk webs. And that was maybe—*maybe*—a three on my weird scale."

"Well not weird-weird," she said. "More of uh—oh just come over here!"

"Fine," I growled.

I joined the others to get a look at what was so weird. With the four of us peeking out from behind some rocks, I couldn't help but feel like a second-rate Scooby Gang or a first-rate pack of perverts. Regardless, I saw what had Myst so concerned. It wasn't weird exactly. If anything, it was oddly familiar. Mainly because I'd seen something very much like this back when I was consulting villains.

Past the outcropping was a huge, grassy field that'd been converted into a temporary parking lot, and it was full of vehicles like station wagons and SUVs. But there were also flying saucers, antique carriages, steampunk zeppelins, and the occasional dragon.

Little hooded creatures in black robes directed incoming traffic while also funneling a parade of humans, monsters, aliens, and the like carrying luggage towards the front gate of a lush estate. It became very clear very quickly that these beings were parents dropping off their children and luggage at the front of what looked like a walled-off estate and its incredibly ornate wrought-iron gate.

From our position, I could just make out a wide, flat reception area made from carved flagstone beyond the gate, and conical evergreen topiaries lining stone stairs that wound up the mountain, likely leading to the castle above.

After a pack of exceptionally large werewolves dropped off their pup and moved away, I saw a prominent monument sign made of black granite with golden filigree. The kind used for the most exclusive gated communities. Even from here, the chiseled words were easy to read.

Sablestone Academy
~ Aemuli Usque ad Victoriam

"Aemuli Usque ad Victoriam," I said, repeating the phrase aloud. "*Rivals until Victory.* All this… it's an academy for villains."

CHAPTER 5

WHERE LYDIA AND I HAVE A SPAT, YOUTHFUL BONERS ARE EXPLORED, AND I TAKE A STEP IN THE WRONG DIRECTION

"Well, that's not really much of a reveal," Lydia said with disappointment. "We already assumed it was something like this."

"I know. But that's not what has me worried," I muttered, my mind spinning.

"Worried?" Lydia said. "What do you mean, worried? We just go up there and get her."

"And stab anyone who gets in our way?" I snapped back.

"Obviously."

"Yeah, a bloodbath, that's helpful."

"What do you care?" she asked. "Aren't you beyond all mortal life or whatever?"

"Now?" I said. "You want to pick a fight *now*?"

"Will you two knock it off," Wraith Knight rumbled. "We get it, you're divorcees. But we have more important matters."

"I know," Lydia said, her eyes on mine. "I want to actually do something but he's acting all hesitant."

"It's not hesitance," I said, trying like all holy Hell to not lose my temper. "It's educated caution."

"It's being chickenshit."

Okay, now she'd done did it. The gloves were off.

"Clearly you and I are *not* good," I said, gesturing back and forth between us. "I had hoped that the one thing we'd agree on was Evie's safety. But you'd rather berate and undercut me than listen to my ideas."

"It's always *your* ideas," Lydia shot back. "All the gods damned time. It's always the Jackson Blackwell show with you."

"Well… yeah," I said, staring at her, hoping that she'd realize the stupidity of her comment.

She did not.

I sighed.

"What have you ever done that's worth paying attention to?"

The minions went silent. I could practically feel their collective mental "oh . . . snap," but I didn't care. This was bound to happen sooner or later, and we might as well rip that bandage off. If we had to stop pretending that we were friends so that we could focus on Evie, then so be it.

"I'm serious, what? What have you done?" I urged her, crossing my arms. "You're a nobody from nowhere whose only accomplishment was running a thieves guild… into the ground. Gods above and below, what have you accomplished *after* meeting me? Don't bother, because I'll give you the answer—it's nothing that wasn't backed by me and my power. Wait, that's not true. You did manage to get bamboozled by a big-titted demoness into forgetting your daughter even existed."

The slap across my face was sudden…but expected.

"I'm going to—"

"Don't," I said, rubbing my cheek. "Just—just don't. When we were a couple, I endured your constant death threats. They were cute aphrodisiacs. But now that we're divorced? They've somehow lost their luster. So how about you do us all a favor and holster the homicidal tough talk and listen for once?"

"You're a bitch," Lydia stated matter-of-factly. "A wormy little bitch who can't stand the fact that he's not as smart as he pretends to be. So stay here and make your little plans within plans. I'm going to get *my* daughter."

Lydia turned and moved like she was on a mission, parkouring over the rocky outcropping and making for the well-manicured lawn.

And that's when something Possibility had said came back to me. *Once you cross that line, there is no going back.*

"Ah, shit," I whispered.

"Boss?" Wraith Knight said. "What is it?"

"Oh Sophia, you *bitch*," I growled.

"Jackson?"

"Shut up and follow me!" I barked, and started running.

"What—what's going on?!" Myst huffed from right behind me.

"It's the worst of the worst, the lowest of the low!"

"You say that about literally… *everything*," Wraith Knight panted.

He may have had a point, but this time I was right.

"Y bloody A," I said.

"What?"

"This—all this," I panted. "It's the setup for a YA novel!"

I leaped and slid over the hood of hearse containing a family of vampires, then began weaving my way through the flustercluck of monsters and madmen gathered near the front gate. Blessedly, Lydia hadn't left a trail of stabbing victims in her wake.

"What do you mean, Jackson?" Myst asked when she caught up.

"Possibility… Sophia… end of term," I huffed in summation, loathing that I was forced to run. "It's a trap, one designed to make us live out a YA academy novel. Sophia knows how much I hate this trope, and I'll be gods damned if I'm going to do this for a full school year. There must be another way to find—"

"Evie," Wraith Knight declared.

"Exactly," I said.

"No, boss, Evie!" he said, pointing just past the gate.

And there she was. My one and only child. My Evie.

She looked… older now. I'd been right. She was sixteen—seventeen, maybe? A young woman, sure, but that was her. Taller than her mother, and maybe an inch or two shorter than me. Her wavy dirty blonde was cut to a uniform chin length. She had a slight tan to her skin that was inherited from my Persian mother. Her eyes were light green and full of intelligence. She was fit, I could tell that, despite the baggy black Sablestone Academy hoodie she wore. Evie was just past the gates, carrying a clipboard and addressing a group of six students.

Throwing my leg forward to stop myself, I swung my arms out wide, catching and slowing Wraith Knight and Myst.

"Wait," I hissed.

"Why?" Myst asked, but I ignored her, instead yelling at Lydia, who kept on running for our daughter.

"Lydia, stop!"

My ex-wife glanced over her shoulder, if only for a second, then ignored me—per usual—and kept on running towards the main gate.

"Boss?"

"Hold on," I ordered. "I need to see something first."

I watched Lydia run through the black iron gates of Sablestone Academy. And just as I suspected, her body changed.

Lydia was never tall to begin with, so she didn't shrink so much as de-age, reverting from a mid-thirties woman to the roughly sixteen-year-old version of herself. All the character lines smoothed, and her body became leaner and firmer. A noticeable vibrancy and youthful energy washed over her as her hair took on a vivacious luster.

"Crap," I muttered. "I was afraid of this."

Once she'd crossed the boundary line, Lydia became a teenager.

"Is—it that going to happen to us?" Myst asked.

"Yeah," I confirmed. "If what Possibility said is true, then once we cross that line, we're locked in. We will be bound to their rules within this… delusion. Last chance. Are you in or out?"

"We're in, Jackson," Myst affirmed. "Always."

"Let's go, boss," Wraith Knight said. "For Evie."

"For Evie," I agreed.

The three of us walked through the open gate and I felt the shift happen immediately. It was both pleasant and completely horrifying.

You relatively healthy young folks out there don't realize how many little aches and pains the body accrues over the decades. But when the pains are suddenly gone? It's heartbreaking. Both in relief and in realization of how much we carry.

Despite being a Titan, if in name only while inside Possibility, I felt my back straighten. My knees stopped aching. Decades of stress, anxiety, and worry all washed away.

And man oh man, lemme tell ya about my penis.

This might be bordering on the inappropriate, but I think it's fair to say that we've gotten to know one another over the course of these adventures. Personally, ideologically… sexually. What with you reading all about me, and me hacking your accounts to spy on you while browsing your files. Oh, and of course, all the cameras I have access to. FYI, that remote you're looking for is under the couch. It was accidentally kicked under there when your partner's… um, *friend* from yoga came over the other day.

Heh heh, don't worry, don't worry. They only did some yoga.

Some hot, *hot* yoga. The really bendy yoga that uses that one mantra… how does it go again? Ahh… "yes—yes, right there, right there… don't stop, *don't stop!*"

You're welcome and namaste. Now, back to my wang…

It felt… *woof*, beyond incredible. Being feisty in your middle years, whether that's as a human, god, or even a Titan, is good and all. Great in some ways. But none of that compares to being *young* and horny.

Which is basically saying the same thing.

Long dormant hormones erupted from my oily skin. The world was my oyster and damn me, I was gonna fuck that oyster. I felt like I could break cinder blocks with my erection, then pogo hop across campus on the damn thing.

For those unaware, a young man's genitals are a cruel compass constantly pointing them towards the worst possible decisions. I'm not forgiving nor am I making excuses for poor behavior, but every one of us who owns a dick has looked at that dick and said:

"Damn it, dick! Looks what you got me in to!"

To which the dick looks back, winks with his one good eye, and says:

"What did you expect? I'm a dick."

Overcharged libido aside, being young meant that I had countless ideas and thoughts while every opinion might as well be a universal fact. Within the deepest core of my soul lay the truest, most profound being to have ever existed, and everyone else was simply fucking fake.

Whoa… I needed to get a grip. I'd forgotten that being young was basically like being on constant cocaine.

I looked over at Wraith Knight, who now resembled an athletic, if nerdy, seventeen-year-old with glasses.

And wow, his afro was rocking.

Myst, however, looked… plain. Like, really plain. Not hot, not ugly, but far from the femme fatale I'd known for the last several years. She was a completely forgettable teenage white girl with dark brown hair and combination skin.

Ah, right. This was young *Doris*, the girl version of the woman she was before becoming Myst. Still, she had a quality about her. The kind of girl who'd hang with the guys and tell dirty jokes but was always overlooked as a woman.

"Looking, uh, good you two," I said to them, feeling like the big man on campus.

"You too, boss," Wraith Knight said, his normally booming voice now more of a deep tenor.

"How do you feel, Jackson?" Myst asked.

"You kidding me? I feel incredible," I said, gesturing at the young, fit, handsome teenage version of myself. "We're gonna own this school!"

And of course, that was when Possibility stepped in.

You know, for how I envisioned things, maybe we need to tweak this just a little.

I had no idea what this boomer of a Titan was saying. But before I could voice my expert opinion on all things big and small, I felt my body shift just a little more... in the wrong direction.

My body shrank down while my belly flopped out. The musculature I'd worked so very hard to gain in high school dwindled back to my doughy starting point, complete with pudgy boy tits. Gods above and below, even my clothes changed. My suit jacket and shirt remained basically the same, but my pants were now... shorts?

Oh, gods damnit. They were *short pants*. The ones popularized by boarding school kids, certain AC/DC guitarists, and... *sigh*. Child villains.

"Oh, fuck me," I said, my voice cracking. I looked up to the sky. "Really?!"

I think the villainous wunderkind is the right trope for you, Possibility said. *Welcome to Sablestone, young Master Jackson.*

CHAPTER 6

WHERE MY OUTIE BECOMES AN INNIE, I STRESS THAT READING IS FUNDAMENTAL, AND I SEE NEW OLD ENEMIES

I stood there in shock. All the vitality that I'd had only moments ago was now gone. My testosterone-driven desire to eat and hump was replaced with apathy, moodiness, and an overwhelming desire to go to my room.

"Hey, guys," I said in my new, squeakier voice while probing my round, puffy cheeks. "How old do I look?"

"What the hell, boss?" Wraith Knight said.

"Possibility," I growled as an explanation while running my hands over the horrible Beatles haircut my mom insisted on me having until I reached high school. "Seriously, what's your ballpark guess? How old do I look?"

"Eleven?" Myst said. "Maybe twelve?"

I dropped my hands in disgust. Out of morbid curiosity, I sucked in my gut, pulled my waistline out a bit, and snuck a peek down my pants.

Gods damnit. There wasn't much to tell ya about, folks.

I just shook my head at the pitiful bald patch of uncut pud down there. Memories of my awkward, late-blooming youth flooded back. Showers after gym class had been… unforgiving.

"Yeah," I sighed. "Definitely twelve."

"Hey, freshies!" Evie yelled out. "Quit looking at your dick and get over here."

"Are—are you talking to me?" I asked, my voice again cracking. I cleared my throat and tried again, overdoing it a bit more than intended. "*Are you talking to me?*"

"Yeah, you four idiots," Evie said. "Get in line with the others so we can get this orientation over with."

Villainous-looking students flooded by, giving our little group a wide berth. But each one gave us the side eye before hauling their luggage up the stone stairs towards the castle. There were a few cheers and wishes of good luck from the parents, but kids were kids. They were either lost in their thoughts, engaged in conversations with their friends, or outright ignored anyone above the age of thirty.

Lydia seemed oblivious to all this, stepping towards our daughter with her arms out. "Honey, it's me."

But Evie slapped Lydia's hands away with her clipboard, hooked her foot behind her ankle, and shoved hard.

Lydia stumbled back, hitting the dark gray flagstone with lung-busting *thud*. Her wide-eyed look was a mix of shock and heartbreak.

"Evie?"

"No touching, freshie," she said. "Not until the term officially begins."

"Baby," Lydia began. "It's me. It's Mom."

"Yeah, I know, and I don't care," Evie said, her words hitting Lydia harder than the ground. "Now get up and get in line."

"Evie," I said, trying to sound commanding yet calming, but this new voice of mine lacked my old gravitas. "We—*ahem*— we're here to take you home."

She lifted her glare from Lydia to me. "And I'm here to make sure you last-minute additions get the proper orientation, *Dad*. So, you, Mom, Auntie Myst, and Uncle Wraith stop standing around and *get in the gods damned line!*"

I glanced over my shoulder and watched the gates slam shut. Once they were in place, the world beyond melted away.

Once you cross that line, there's no going back.

Well, shit.

"Okay, come on," I told the minions with a shake of the head. "I think we can all see where this is going."

"A magical school," Wraith Knight said more giddily than a man should. "But for villains!"

I sighed. "You better not be excited about this."

"Can you blame him?" Myst said. "This is kind of the dream for a lot of nerds. A YA slice-of-life-meets-school setting?"

"Don't defend your man."

"I'm not," she said. "I'm just pointing out that there are countless books, manga, and anime that follow this formula. It's popular for a reason."

I rolled my eyes. "You do realize that back in the prime universe, classic literature and celebrated seminal novels are being replaced in public schools with generic YA novels?"

"Well, it's a sign of the times," Myst countered. "Many of those old books are out of touch with a modern audience. And at least the kids are reading."

"*At least they're reading*," I repeated in a mocking tone. "And of course the best way to get stronger is to lift sacks of marshmallows instead of cold iron plates, right?"

"That's not fair."

"Isn't it?" I asked. "To be physically fit, you limit intake of crap while pushing your body by engaging with activity that pushes your boundaries. The same principle applies to the mind. And while I love my own recorded adventures, they're literary junk food."

"This stance against the YA genre is what, ethics? Your version of 'won't somebody please think of the children?'," she scoffed. "It has nothing to do with your inability to market your adventures to a younger audience for easy money?"

"That and the strongly worded cease and desist letters from nearly every school board in America, north and south," I said. "For some reason, they don't want my brand of villainous— borderline nihilist—dogma masked as dark humor. Apparently constant sexual innuendo and poorly constructed, shallow narratives are not appropriate for any human, regardless of age. Their words, not mine. Alas."

"Hey! Don't make me tell you again, freshies," Evie barked. "Get over here *now!*"

"It may not be my place, boss," Wraith Knight said as the three of us walked over to join the others, "but Evie's become something of an asshole."

"Tell me about it," I muttered under my breath. "But she was basically kidnapped and abandoned here. So there's no telling her mental state. For now, play along and keep your ears open, okay?"

The minions nodded, and we joined the other kids. I stood next to Lydia and offered her a hand. She took it but said nothing. Part of me wanted to say something consoling.

And part of me wanted her to suffer.

I didn't know if that was me being a villain or just a spiteful ex-husband. And I really didn't care which.

"Nice legs, Jackson."

The speaker sounded all too familiar. I turned my head to the right and confirmed the identity of these other kids.

First was a teenage black girl with stylish hair, white designer clothes, and a condescending, know-it-all smirk.

An elfin teen with an overbite was next. He was dressed in fantasy garb and had an arrogance about him. But that's to be expected. Most people who own and wear fantasy garb are condescending buttholes.

Yes, Renn Fair enthusiasts, I'm talking about you. You suck and we all know it.

Next to him was a girl with similar clothes and a similar face, marking them as twins. But she had writhing serpents for hair and green scales coming in that looked like bad acne.

A pudgy white guy with glasses was next. And he couldn't look more like a propaganda poster for a comic store kid if he tried. A teen whose patchy beard looked like face pubes. Long greasy hair, greasier skin, and a man satchel slung over his shoulder.

The seven-foot muscled male demon with crimson skin and goat legs next to the dork was already showing signs of male pattern baldness and a beer belly.

The young demoness beside him was trying to pull off the goth look with her torn Hot Topic clothes and excessive makeup. And it might've worked, but sadly telescope-level prescription glasses made her eyes look five times larger than normal.

And last but certainly not least was a pinkish female djinn floating an inch or so off the ground. Her wispy blue flame hair was styled up in a rebellious punk look. She had four yellow cat eyes and needle-like teeth with braces.

Eris Pence, Valliar, Khasil, King Stanley, Y'olly, Mikayla, and Sophia.

"Nerd," King Stanley coughed, calling out my outfit.

"Shut up," Evie commanded, her voice carrying more than authority.

It held power.

"Sorry," King Stanley said, lowering his head.

Huh. An elder god and former holder of the position of the One shrank back from my daughter's command. Was this a power, a skill, or something to do with this place?

Or was it just her?

"Okay freshies, listen up," Evie began. "Officially you are enrolled this year at Sablestone Academy for Villains. Unofficially, you're pack of backstabbing assholes who are here for whatever reason, and I don't care."

"To bring you home," Lydia said.

"I… don't… care," she repeated. "Now, Sablestone is a three-year institution that teaches basic, intermediate, and advanced villainy. I am a third-year, and you are technically nothing. If you do not respect your upperclassmen, then respect will be taught to you."

Evie paused her little speech to stare at each of us before continuing. Her eyes lingered a heartbeat or two longer on me.

"To make it to the next year, you must accumulate the minimum number of points. Otherwise, you either repeat your year, if allowed, or you are cast into the Nothingness."

I kept my poker face like a professional. If I was going to beat Sophia and her little entourage, then I'd have to have more points than her at the end of the year.

"Now, as you did not bring luggage of any kind, this next part should be a lot easier. Follow me."

She turned and began walking up the stone steps that led to the castle high above. I looked at the minions, then at Lydia, and shrugged.

"I guess we follow her. Come on."

"What's going on, Jackson?" Lydia asked. "Why's she acting this way?"

"Maybe you should try just running ahead and see if that gets you some answers?"

Lydia clenched her jaw and gave me a dirty look. "Do you at least know what's going on here?"

"I thought it was obvious," I said as I began the climb. "We're going back to school."

WHERE I COMPARE GODS TO VLOGGERS, COMPARE FANTASY PEASANTS TO HILLBILLIES, AND GET STABBED

When I was a man, I liked to keep physically fit. And when I became a god, I kept the habit going. Seems odd, right? Aren't gods automatically buff? Well, not necessarily. The gods are like people in that they have similar emotions, desires, and vices. Which means that excessive sloth and gluttony—regardless of divinity—results in flapjack titties and a chunky butt.

Now, a god *can* cheat. We can melt the pounds off with an exertion of our will and a snap of our fingers, which we often do. I mean, if a mortal wants to carve a statue of us for worship, then we show up rocking a beach bod. But it's all fake. The deity equivalent of Photoshopped abs. Worse, it comes at a cost.

As we've already learned from previous books, a god's power is not infinite. They have a few options to keep a steady stream of power coming in. Acts of conquest and sabotage against other gods are my personal favorites. Being a villain, nothing's better than stealing another kid's lunch money. The standoffish, behind-the-scenes type of gods draw power from their world's harmony and balance. It isn't as good, but it does the trick. Fear also works. When a mortal fears a god? Man, that's like tongue fucking a wall socket. But… you know, in a good way.

But the tried-and-true method has always been the worship and adoration of mortals. So getting the power to stay lean means putting on theatrical displays for the masses. And when you step back and look at it, said actions are eerily close to those annoyingly vapid husks of vanity begging for your attention on the internet.

I'm referring, of course, to social media "gym-fluencers."

I feel gross even saying that word.

From the dude bro spouting sports pseudo-science to the mooseknuckle valkyrie and her porn pose routine, the internet is full of these... well, I won't call them "people" exactly. "Narcissist" is a word, but it gets tossed around so much it's practically lost its meaning. "Histrionic" might be a better fit, as that word denotes an overly emotional person with attention-seeking, theatrical behaviors.

Like the gods.

See what I did there? Pulled it right back to the main topic. I'm a pro.

Yes, dear readers, just like those tedious twats, the gods need to be *seen* "working out." Their actions and deeds are performances for followers and worshippers. It's all an act to feed a god-sized ego.

Now, as a Titan, I'm totally above this.

You know, except for publishing my recorded adventures to get your money, praise, and in some cases, ire. But other than that, it's totally different.

Now why am I talking about all this?

Because my young—and thoroughly devoid of muscle tone—body was about to collapse from climbing up all these gods damned stairs!

"I—I can't," I wheezed, collapsing onto the stone stairs. "I live here now."

My enemies, just as shitty in their kid forms, snickered and laughed as they walked by, around, and in a couple cases *over* me. A sudden pain just below the belt forced the air out of my lungs. I looked up to see Eris. Stuck-up bitch gave me the finger, then continued the climb.

Well... glad to see everyone else adjusting to this situation better than I was. Having sweated out my dignity several flights back, I threw an arm over my face and panted.

"*Get up*," Lydia hissed. "You're embarrassing us."

I lifted my arm a bit to give my ex-wife a squinting glare. A sixteen-year-old peasant from a fantasy world was basically the same as a deep holler Appalachian redneck from the real world. The kind of folk who could run for days with no need for shoes, work from sunup to sundown, and survive on bacon-slathered squirrel anus for nourishment.

Now, if any of that offends y'all south of the Mason-Dixon (as if you could read), then I highly suggest you'uns hire a better PR team. As it stands, we normal folks are obsessed with deep South culture… but not in a good way.

Potbellied blue bloods with "Colonel" in their name who talk like Foghorn Leghorn? Awesome. Videos from the Kentucky Derby where the snobby Botox wife in a big-ass white hat falls over the rail into horse apples after her ninth mint julep? Comedy gold.

But thanks to TV and movies, we see y'all as folksy folk who don't be needin' no fancy learnin' to get through the day. Nope, as far as the media is concerned, all y'all need is pig fat moonshine, some deep hills green magic, and a bit of banjo pickin'.

Oh, and of course, Oxy. Shitloads of Oxy.

Yeesh. Maybe I do punch down a little for the sake of comedy? Seriously, what kind of person mocks opioid addiction for a cheap laugh?

Heh heh, a villain.

"Seriously, *get up!*" Lydia hissed.

"In case you haven't noticed," I said, gesturing at my pathetic excuse for a body, "I'm clearly not built for this. The big secret is out: I was an indoor kid who bloomed late."

"Well suck it up. People will see your weakness and prey on it."

She wasn't wrong. And part of me already knew this. But there were multiple *me*s fighting for control.

There was a Titan me who was locked away and pissed about it. The me-me that sought to plot and manipulate every situation into a net benefit. And then there was the kid me, the one I was trapped in who hated physical exertion… but loved staring at bent-over Lydia's boobs.

Oh hey, quick aside. *Ahem…* I realize that being in kid bodies coupled with this series brand of "humor" might become a toxic cocktail. A disaster at worst and borderline cringy at best. But seeing as this is the sixth book in the *Shadow Master* series, I think we've come to trust one another. We're all adult enough to know that jokes, even sex jokes, are just jokes. Okay? I don't need the Facebook mommy mafia on my ass because I state the obvious: Teens are hormone-driven jerk-off machines.

But if you're one of those folks who just needs to grab a metaphorical pitchfork before organizing an online mob, might I suggest you turn your torches towards Netflix? They have a wide array of far more famous works who openly exploit awkward teenage sexcapades for profit and entertainment. *Sex Education* or *Big Mouth,* for example?

If you're still on the fence about being offended, let me posit this. Should moments like those pop up, think of them as the R-rated young adult sex comedies where all the actors are real-life adults who *pretend* to be teens. Movies like *Porkys, Fast Times*, the *American Pie* movies, *Not Another Teen Movie, Van Wilder, Easy A, The Girl Next Door, Superbad, Road Trip, Sex Trip, Eurotrip…* all the trips, really.

Huh. Wow. Turns out that we are really obsessed with young people fucking, aren't we?

Well, I guess that's better than the alternative. I mean, do you really wanna watch a raunchy comedy where some grandma goes on a road trip with her granny pals in a VW bus to Florida? Sooner or later, Gram-gram gonna be balls deep with some Viagra-enhanced, Vietnam-war-era wang. Now, I love the *Golden Girls* as much as anyone, but I never wanted to see Sophia getting raw dogged until her hip breaks.

Wait… do I?

Hmm, that might be comedy gold.

Regardless, I was ogling the crap out Lydia's cleavage. I mean, just look at 'em. Just poking out of her blouse. Yes, she was my ex and yes, this was completely inappropriate. But I had two solid defenses for my actions. One, I was twelve, and two… boobs.

She rolled her eyes and stood back up. "Seriously?"

"Don't tell me I'm the only one who is drowning in hormones here."

"Oh, you're not," Myst said, looking Wraith Knight up and down.

"I am not meat, woman!" WK said, then laughed. "No, I'm just kidding. I'm totally meat. Hey, do your shape shifting powers still work?"

"Why, you wanna fool around behind some bleachers?"

"Well, that too." Wraith Knight nodded, then held up his hand. It crackled with dark energy but remained a hand. "My shadow-shifting powers are on the fritz."

Myst thought about it for a second. Then her face rippled for half a second and stopped. "Yeah. Mine too."

"Hey!" Evie called from somewhere higher up. "Until the term starts, everyone is powerless. Now let's go!"

"Well, that answers that," Wraith Knight said with a shrug.

"Yeah, but how?" Myst asked. "What has the ability to nullify everything?"

"You people and your powers," Lydia said, drawing one of her many knives and beginning an intricate hand-flipping display. "You rely on them far too much. Good ol' natural skill is all a person needs to—"

The blade slipped from her hand.

The razor-sharp dagger tumbled end over end, falling no more than three feet before slicing deep into my bare inner left thigh. Funny thing about the inner thigh—the femoral artery runs right through there. And depending on how badly the femoral artery is cut, a person can slip into unconsciousness, and even die, within a few minutes.

Turns out that whatever was nullifying the minions' powers had also switched off Lydia's fantasy-world rogue dexterity.

Huh. She did have "powers" of a kind.

I thought that was a neat fact, right up to when my blood pressure dropped, my eyes went dark, and the blackest shadows I'd ever seen engulfed me.

Well, at least I didn't have to walk up those bloody stairs.

WHERE I FEAR BEING AN AFTER SCHOOL SPECIAL, FLEX MY GEN X, AND SEE A FAMILIAR FACE

I wasn't exactly sure what I was hearing… but I didn't like it.

Breaching the surface of unconsciousness, I became aware of a slurping sound, the scraping of metal on metal, and a dripping. I was on my back, lying atop some sort of table with a thin, vinyl-coated cushion. A skinny older man with white hair, pale white skin, and a sinister smile stood over me. His tapered fingers held a thin knife in one hand, and in the other, a comically large needle with an attached plastic tube.

Oh, and for some reason, a three-foot human-animal hybrid wearing a lab coat stood by the man's side, giggling.

Dear readers, I don't need to belabor the point that I came from wealth… but I'm going to. Stick with me, as this is germane to my situation. Because when I say I've woken up in some strange places, I mean it. For example, when you were working your fingers to the bone after high school to make ends meet, I was on a gap year, partying my tits off in Europe. And waking up hung over on a warm summer morning under an idyllic stone bridge while still inside a pair of sexually adventurous fraternal Swedish twins was hard.

Dare I say it was just as hard as working multiple jobs to provide for the baby you conceived on prom night. I mean, my head—and my ass—were killing me. I had no idea where my designer clothes were. And to make matters worse, my Drambuie-goggles had worn off.

Turns out that those twins had been—at best—a Swedish "6." Which was of course a Mumbai "4," a Columbian "3," a Manhattan "7," and an Idaho "14."

Now, does this make me better than you?

Yes, yes it does.

To this day I have no idea what the inside of Walmart looks like. Well, other than those hilarious Black Friday videos where you people literally trample one another for a cheap TV.

But the point is that rich or poor, waking up in strange places is hard for all of us. So I can sympathize with your woes.

"Oh," the creepy pale man said. "You're awake."

"Uh, yeah," I said, pushing myself up and away.

"There's no need to worry," the man said.

Yeah right. I'd seen enough "very special" episodes of 80s TV to know a perv when I saw one. I scrambled off the table and put some distance between us while checking for signs of molestation.

Short pants? On.

Fly? Up.

Sad excuse for a prepubescent man dangle? Still there, untouched, and safely locked within the cotton fortress that was my Darth Vader Underoos. But there was a throbbing pain in my left inner thigh.

I had a bloody bandage, and I felt the fresh stitches tugging against the flesh. Keeping the table between me and this weirdo, I scanned the room. One part mad scientist's lab, one part dungeon, and one part… school nurse's office?

Well, this was nightmare fuel.

"Who are you, where am I, and what in the name of the Never Realm is that thing?" I asked, pointing at the human-animal hybrid. "It looks like a redneck had a three-way with a warthog and the universe's one ugly otter."

"How dare you?!" he said, clearly offended for some reason. "Keith's sensitive about his appearance."

"Keith? You named it Keith?"

The mutant stopped giggling and looked—oh gods damn it, it looked sad.

"Keith a 'he,' not an 'it'," the mutant said.

"Shut up Keith," I said, keeping my eyes on the man who was still holding the scalpel and the needle with the hose. "What were you going to do with those?"

The man looked down as if he just realized he was still holding the instruments and chuckled.

"Oh, well now I just feel foolish," he said, then muttered, "seeing as you're awake."

"That didn't answer my question."

"Oh, well, yes." The man began waggling the scalpel. "After the headmistress brought you in after your accident, I stitched you up per her request. But you know how it is. A fresh, unconscious body just, *mmm…* lying there? It was too tempting. You understand, I'm sure."

"Uh huh," I said, rolling my hand in a 'get on with it' motion.

"So I thought, why not start with a simple vivisection?"

"Oh yeah, sure, simple stuff," I sighed. "And the tube?"

He shrugged. "Keith gets thirsty while I work."

I looked down and realized that the length of tubing ended in Keith's paw-like hands.

"So I was supposed to be his Slurpee?"

The man nodded. "More or less, yes. You must understand, the first day of school is hard on us, what with the no-death rule in effect."

"Oh, sure." I nodded in mock understanding. "Are you *fucking insane?!*"

The man actually jumped back a little. "My, aren't you rude? Maybe we should break the rule, just this once? What do you think, Keith?"

"Keith *is* thirsty," the mutant said, his piggy snout lifting upwards with his drooling smile.

If I had been any versions of my previous self—Titan, god, or even an adult—I would've had no trouble dealing with this guy and his pig-spunk abomination. But I was none of those versions. I was in a twelve-year-old's body and sadly lacked cosmic power, substantial body weight, and combat muscle memory. But as I alluded to before, I'd grown up watching classic TV and movies. I know I've said this in a previous recoded adventure, but I really, *really* need to foot-stomp this message: Things were better when we hurt children with fiction.

Allow me to clarify.

As a child of Boomers—and the grandchildren of WWII-era hard-asses—we had child predators in nearly every after school special. According to our mothers, psychos were out there putting razor blades in our Halloween candy. We were told, almost daily, to "suck it up," that "life is hard, then you die," and if we didn't, then our parents would "give us something to cry about."

Willy gods damned Wonka scared the bejeezus out of us with that "no way of knowing" boat ride rant. We watched Optimus Prime and Artax die. We saw Jed and Matt get mortally wounded in *Red Dawn*. And man… don't get me started on *The Outsiders*.

If you were an old-school Disney character, you weren't just an orphan; you got *to watch* your parents die. *Watership Down* scarred us for life, and Donald Bluth's animated masterpieces were brimming with death, fear, and isolation.

We knew for a fact that Ma Fratelli was going to maim Chunk's hand in a blender, then kill the rest of the Goonies. Every iteration of Biff Tannen tried to murder Marty McFly. If Wesley Crusher hadn't pulled a gun on Jack Bauer in *Stand By Me*, then those best friends would've been as dead as the body they'd sought to see.

And do I even need to mention original *Star Wars*?

I know there are some jackwagons out there think that "*Star Wars* is a franchise about space wizards for children" is some kind of hot take. And maybe it is? Let's see…

Space Nazi tyranny, check. Indigenous tribes attempting to murder a teenager. Well, that was their land. The charred, smoking husks of the only mother and father said teenager ever knew. Fun! Imprisonment and torture of a teenage girl. Lightsaber maiming. Actual murder (Han shot first and I'll fight anyone who says otherwise). Of course, the planetary genocide of billions was a hoot. Empire was chock full of betrayal and a little incest. Jedi had Hutt sex trafficking, carnivorous muppets, and a son forced to watch his father die.

Yup, *Star Wars* was for children. Children who grew up to be harder and tougher than these bubble-wrapped, helmet-wearing people with tissue-paper levels of resilience and dog therapy.

Apologies, dear reader. I tend to rant. Now, what did all that old man yelling at clouds have to do with my current situation?

Well, if you're from my generation, you already know the answer. But for you younger folks, lemme spell it out: If you wanna survive, you can't wait to be rescued.

Even if you're small and weak, you spaz the fuck out like the Tasmanian Devil.

When the doctor lunged for me, I screamed my head off in that shrill way that only kids can. I grabbed anything and everything I could to huck at his face. A lucky toss from a steel tray *clanged* off the bridge of the doc's nose. He cried out pain and dropped his scalpel. The slim piece of surgical steel *pinged* when it hit the stone tile, and I scrambled to snatch the precise cutting instrument.

Blade in hand, I rounded on Keith. The mutant hybrid squealed as he turned to run, but I jumped on his back and held the edge to his neck.

"Don't move!"

Keith said nothing and remained motionless, save for his trembling.

"Don't!" the doctor cried out. "Please! That's a very dangerous item!"

"Just stay where you're at or I start carving some bacon," I threatened.

Using Keith as "human" shield, I backed up towards the exit. I made it a whole four steps before a feminine chuckling came from somewhere within the dark recesses of the lab.

Tendrils of tangible shadow lashed out, gripping my wrist and prying my arm away from the creature's throat.

"I applaud the adaptability," the smoky female voice said. "But rules are rules. No one dies on the first day."

Before I could ask what in the bloody hell was going on, the dark tendrils launched me out the door and into the stone hallway. The door slammed shut, and I was left flat on my back with a forming headache and partially torn stitches.

Yay?

Sensing someone behind me, I turned and saw Evie standing there with her arms crossed.

"Hey, Dad."

CHAPTER 9

WHERE I DISCUSS PARENTING, FIND A ROCK, AND PREPARE TO DIE

I looked up at Evie, smiled, and offered my hand. "Wanna help your father out?"

She turned her back on me and walked down the corridor. "Come on, freshie, you're behind."

My bloody heart broke.

Pushing myself up on unsteady legs, I limped down the hall after her. I didn't really want to, but it's kind of what we must do as parents. Hold them close when they're small. Show them how to walk and how to do things on their own. Then we eventually watch them walk away from us.

And there, right there, is the dilemma. We can wait for them to come back to us, or we can follow after them. I'm not sure which one is the "right" way, if such a thing exists. I just know that I missed so much of my daughter's life that I wasn't going to throw any chance to be close to her away.

Even if she was acting like a right prick.

Bleeding stitches be damned, I did my best to keep up. The shadowy corridor was made of flat, angular, interlocking gray stone. Intermittent wall sconces gave off a yellowish-green light. No flames, just light. To say it was super creepy would be an understatement. But considering this was an academy for up-and-coming villains, I guess it was standard. And to be frank, after the encounter with Dr. Touchy Cut-Cut back there, I preferred the generic setting.

Even if we walked in silence for what seemed like forever.

It wasn't forever, mind you; it just felt that way. Parents out there can back me up on this one. When your child's ignoring you while you're desperately wishing to connect, the wasted time makes everything feel like a painful forever.

I'm sure it's the same for people without children. Plenty of people seek meaningful conversations and connections from friends and partners. But who gives a shit about you people? Odds are you're that person who refers to their pets as "fur babies."

No one likes that. Or you.

I would gladly—giddily, and without any sense of regret—sell any or all of you into forced labor if it meant I could better connect with Evie.

But what do you say to a child you haven't seen in two years?

Hi, how are you?

How's school been?

So… puberty's a bitch, huh?

No matter what came out of my mouth, it was going to be wrong. Another lesson you learn as a parent. But that isn't an excuse *not* to say anything. Like all good relationships, say anything to get the ball rolling, then lie and gaslight your way out of danger.

"Honey," I began, "I know you're probably mad at us, but we never forgot about you. Well, your mother did, but that technically wasn't her fault. Regardless, we came as soon as we could. We love you and—"

Evie turned around and punched me square in the mouth.

It was friggin' perfect.

Balanced stance, great weight distribution, and a blow that didn't overextend. My head snapped back, my knees went wobbly, and I collapsed. She loomed over me, maintaining a guard against a counter strike.

"Do not speak to me, freshie, until I allow you to."

Gotta give the kid credit—she knew what she was doing. And I'm not talking about her form. No, my kid sucker-punched a younger, smaller, and weaker target, then established the hierarchy of the dynamic.

She was the alpha and I was not.

Oh, another aside. This one for all the wolf nerds out there. Yes, we all know that alpha/beta thing was a mistake. But please—*please* shut up and stop correcting people. It's a thing now, deal with it. Every time you *"um actually,"* I literally pray for wolves to eat you. And in some cases when the nerd is exceptionally annoying, I make it happen.

Go on. Try me.

"As you wish," I said to my daughter.

When she turned, I got up, spat blood, and followed like a good parent should.

Believe it or not, this was progress.

Yeah, she belted me in the mouth, but it was the first real *emotional* response I'd gotten out of her. And if you ask any therapist worth a damn, anger is part of the healing process. So I followed my fuming daughter, keeping my distance and my lip sealed.

After a bit, the corridor opened into a circular stone room. I looked in, opting not to enter just yet. There were more of those flameless light sconces on the curved walls. Including the passage we'd come through, I counted five open arched entry points. Each one had a steel portcullis poised to drop to seal off the passage.

This room, whatever it was, reminded me of a central hub. Despite being bereft of adornment or grandeur, this location felt… holy?

No, that wasn't it.

This was *unholy*.

When Evie moved aside, I saw one of the room's three defining features. First, a broken, waist-high stone column that served as a plinth. It was old, ancient really, and covered with various carvings in a language even I didn't know. Second, sitting reverently atop the plinth was a simple black rock. At first glance the rock was nothing special, just a hunk of black volcanic glass that was maybe twice the size of a human fist. But that was only at first glance. The longer I looked at the rock, the more I sensed.

There was an old power in that stone.

You know how in those shitty kids' books they talk about love like it's some kind of powerful force that trumps all other magics?

A huge load of crap, I know. Not for nothing, but you bring your love to the fight and I'll bring a gun. We'll see who's left standing.

This rock was like that.

No, not love, dumbass. I mean a power unto itself.

Dark and malevolent, this thing bloody well *ate* love. It took what it wanted. Somehow, I knew it was a relic of anger and vengeance. I felt confusion and pride. Vindication and defiance. This thing was… well, villainous.

Something else tickled my near-dormant senses.

At the far end of the circular room, I saw a spot where the shadows seemed to pool on their own. No, not pooling. The light itself was slowly being eaten.

Well, that's not good.

Within that space of diminished light, I saw a sixth ingress. A closed door made of mixed metals and covered in obscure pictograms. Like the black stone, this door, or rather what lay beyond, craved more. It needed it. And this black stone was not only keeping what lay beyond at bay, but it was also somehow connected.

Evie looked at the door and then the rock, then back to me.

"As long as that stone rests here, you can only enter this room by choice. No person or power can force you to enter," she said, her tone flat. I went to step in, but she held up a finger. "If you willingly enter while the stone is here, then you leave all the power you possess behind."

I wasn't sure what was going to happen next, and it was oddly exciting. So I stepped into the room, and I felt this wave of power—or rather, anti-power—wash over me. I felt vulnerability in a way that I'd only ever felt once before.

When I was just a mortal.

Was that it? Was Evie going to kill me? Because in this room, I knew it was very much possible. And if anyone was going to truly kill Jackson Blackwell, I'd want it to be Evie.

So when my daughter rushed me, I didn't fight back.

I did, however, return her hug.

CHAPTER 10

WHERE I REUNITE WITH EVIE, RECALL ENGINEERING ACCIDENTS, AND LEARN THE STAKES

"Daddy," Evie said, her voice throaty as she no longer fought back the tears. "I missed you so much."

"Me too, little one, me too," I said, my voice quavering. "Love you."

"Love you too."

I held her for several long moments, never wanting to let go. I tried to pour everything I had into that hug. All my regrets for being away. All the hope I had for her future.

And, yes, I tried to pick her pockets.

Daughter or not, we're villains at heart, and my bitch-ass spawn had popped me in the mouth. Evie sensed the lift and broke the hug.

"Nice try, old man."

"It's this young, inexperienced body." I shrugged. "You gonna hit me again?"

"Tempting." Evie laughed, then shook her head. "But no."

"Thank you."

"I mean, I want to. I really do."

"What?"

"Dad," she said flatly. "Have you seen your yourself? I wanted to beat the nerd out of you the moment I saw you."

"You wouldn't be the first," I admitted, stepping back and looking my form over. "When this was me, way back when, well… let's just say that kids can be cruel."

"Oh yeah?" she said. "What did you do for revenge?"

"Me?" I said, placing a hand on my chest and feigning innocence. "Why would you ask me that?"

Instead of answering, she raised an eyebrow. You might ask if she got that from me, but no. Villains who do that particular move are cliché.

She got that shit from her mother.

"Well, of course I got my revenge," I said. "Childhood accidents happen all the time. Once those little snots were gone, the others fell in line."

"Wouldn't killing a bunch of kids leave a trail back to you?"

"Well, yeah," I said, then added, "if I'd *killed* them. But that amateur crap's the makings of a boring slasher movie. No, daughter, even young me wasn't that foolish."

"What did you do?"

"I waited until the field trip to the carnival."

"The carnival?" she repeated.

"Yeah," I nodded. "Since I went to a rich-ass private school, the board of trustees had rented that whole place out so that we didn't have to rub elbows with the common folk."

"Naturally," she agreed, then gestured for me to continue.

"So anyway, there used to be these rides back in the day that were all the rage. The Gravitron, the Starship, the Twister, and so on. Basically, a big cylinder that spins and the imposed centrifugal force pins the riders to the wall before the floor drops out. If I recall my facts correctly, it's like pulling 3 Gs, like astronaut training."

"Okay, I think I see where this is going," she said. "But aren't those things complex to operate?"

"You'd think that, wouldn't you?" I said. "Now, I'd done a ton of research on these things, the physics behind them, and so on. Based on my research, an amusement park mechanic required experience in engineering, pneumatics, gearboxes, conveyors, and hydraulics."

"But?"

"But to fuck one up, all you need is the basic understanding of what a limiter is and hundred bucks to bribe the underpaid carnie to take a smoke break."

Evie's eyes widened and I chuckled, recalling the memory.

"Heh heh, ahh, that thing just kept going faster and faster and it went on for way too long. By the time the folks figured out what was going on and pulled the master brake, it was too late."

"They were pulp?"

"Gods above and below, no. Weren't you listening to me before? Bodies create suspicion. *Accidents* happen."

"Okay, fine, continue," she conceded.

"Spinning for that long is bad because the human body really needs oxygenated blood to function. Long story short, my bullies became a pack of drooling kids with stroke faces who then grew into drooling adults… with stroke faces. Ugly burdens for their families to take care of indefinitely. Heh, good times."

"Still, that's a big risk."

I shrugged and gestured at myself. "I wasn't the only kid too short to ride a bunch of the rides. Plus, school uniforms. The poor carnie couldn't identify me even if he wanted to. Besides, he was between a rock and a hard place anyway. Admit he stepped away or admit he was at fault. It was a no-win situation. Therefore, it was ruled as a horrible accident due to negligence."

"I think you'll do just fine here, Dad," she said with a cruel smile.

"And where is *here?*" I asked, gesturing at the circular stone room. "You clearly wanted me in this room for a reason."

"Because this is both the safest, and most dangerous, spot in all of Sablestone."

"I don't follow."

"Because this is the one room in the castle where you can actually die. So if one wants to say something in private or—or to hug their father without being seen as weak by the other students, it's in here."

I felt a little lump in my throat.

But that stopped real fast.

"What do you mean, *actually die?*"

Evie gestured above us at the ceiling and this iris-like hatch. "Up there, above these catacombs, is where the real castle and all the classes and events take place. But you can't pack a campus with up-and-coming villains without mayhem going on. So there's an anti-death field in place. Oh, you can die, but you'll reconstitute back in your bed the following morning."

"Really?" I said. "How's that possible?"

She held up the back of her left hand. There, embedded in the flesh, was a flat black stone about the size of a quarter. I'd missed seeing it on her before, but looking at it now, I sensed a dark power. My eyes shifted to the similarly dark stone resting on the broken column.

"They're linked?" I asked. "That thing in your hand and the stone?"

"Mm," she nodded. "Killing is a heavy part of our grades. Those with the fewest deaths gets a big bump in class ranking."

"Murder is allowed?"

"*Allowed?*" Evie repeated with a small chuckle. "Dad, it's practically mandatory."

I wasn't keen on these lessons. Maybe I was too traditional in my way of thinking when it came to villainy.

"You know my stance on the subject," I said. "Killing must happen from time to time. But only weak villains and psychopaths rely on, or take pleasure in, the act."

Evie rolled her eyes. "I know, Dad. But since people come back thanks to being linked to the Sablestone, you get bonus points for the more creative and treacherous takedowns. Think of it like, golly, a school where you can let your hair down and live a little as a villain?"

She gestured at the black rock resting on the broken column. "Do you know what that is?"

"Thanks to not being an idiot and my uncanny skill at context clues, it's obviously *the* Sablestone."

"Yes," she confirmed. "And we're inside Possibility, right?"

"Yeah, so?"

"In this place, all things are possible," she said. "That rock right there, real or unreal, is the first murder weapon."

Whoa. I paused at that little revelation.

Throughout the cosmos of the infinite, there are only so many firsts of anything. Events so profound that the fundamental nature of a person or thing is forever changed. If this was the first murder weapon, then it was a relic of unfathomable power.

"Wait, that still doesn't make sense," I said. "The multiverse is too vast to comprehend let alone map out. How can this be the first murder weapon? Are we talking human murder? Alien murder? Metaphorical murder? Dare I even risk asking if this is biblical? Because I've always read Cain killed Abel with a donkey jaw."

Evie shook her head. "Again, we're inside Possibility. Maybe it's a sentient lump of anti-matter that exists across all time and space simultaneously and is the cause of all murder. Who knows? The point is, this is where the Sablestone rests, and according to the lore, the castle was built around it. Rumor has it that Headmaster Nyx uses it to remove our powers. But she can also summon it up to higher parts of the castle. If that happens, watch out. Wherever the Sablestone is, you can die… permanently."

"Nyx?" I said, repeating the name. "The Greek Titan of Night?"

"Yup," Evie confirmed. "After she saved you from bleeding out, she sent me to Dr. Moreau's infirmary to retrieve you and to finish your tour."

"Whoa, back up there. Doctor *Moreau*?" I said, not fully comprehending what she'd just said. "The *character*?"

Evie chuckled, then reached into her backpack, opened a hidden compartment, and pulled out a flask. She popped the top and necked back a swallow, then passed it to me.

"Mm, that's good. Yes, a lot of our instructors are famous villains that may or may not have existed outside of literature."

I eyed the flask. "You're underage, daughter."

She waggled the flask. "And technically, so are you, *Dad*."

Damn kid might as well have said "ya nerd" with how she stressed my name.

This wasn't exactly how I imagined having my first drink with my daughter, but life often doesn't turn out the way we planned. Well, for you, maybe. I always planned on achieving power. But I never once imagined getting power, then short pants and a bowl cut. I took the flask and tossed a shot back. It was whiskey, and pretty decent stuff too.

Well, the adult part of my brain thought so anyway. The twelve-year-old body I was in doubled over in a coughing fit.

"Th-thanks," I hacked. "But for real, gotta get you outta here. See, Sophia has you trapped here and—"

Evie pulled a well-read copy of *Villains Return* from her backpack. The spine had cracks and there were a lot of dog-eared pages.

That savage.

But that's when it hit me. "Ah, hell. Sophia made sure you had a copy, didn't she?"

Evie nodded. "All the books."

I recalled how Evie had taken Lydia to the ground just a few hours earlier and shook my head.

"You know everything that's going on with your mother and me, don't you?"

Again, Evie nodded. I went to speak, but she held up her hand.

"I know that being a parent has made you weak, from a villainy point of view."

"Honey—"

"It's okay, Dad, I understand. You love me, you always have. I love you too. But had you not met Mom and had me, you'd be… well, a douche. I think—I think that was part of Aunt Sophia's vengeance all along. She wanted you to become a little more human, despite being a god. It creates blind spots. Spots that a less emotionally attached version of you would've seen."

"Such as?"

Evie gave me that eyebrow again. "Look around, Dad. Where are we?"

"A school?"

"Right," she said. "A *three-year* school. This is my third year. As long as I have the points at the end of the year, I graduate and *leave*."

I almost laughed.

"Gods above and below. If we'd waited another year—"

"Then I'd be home," she finished. "Sophia dangled me like bait to get you here."

"Why?" I asked, then shook my head.

Damn me, I did have blind spots. The answer was obvious. In this place, near the Sablestone, even a Titan like me could die.

I took another sip of her whiskey.

Wincing, I inclined my chin at the closed door in the shadow. "What's in there?"

Evie's face darkened. "We just call it the Nothingness. I wasn't kidding about the school's consequences. Those who fail to meet the standard are sent in there. They don't come back."

"Well shit, that's not ominous at all," I sighed. "Okay, if I'm gonna beat Sophia then I'll need to know as much as possible. So hit me with it, kid. Tell me everything you've learned."

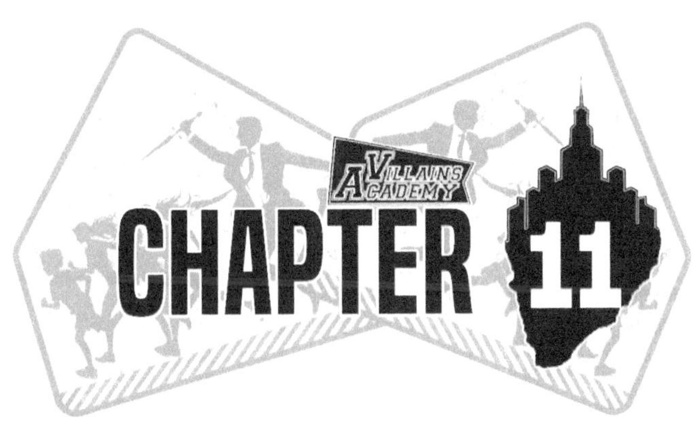

WHERE I TAKE A TRIP, REJOIN THE OTHERS, AND OGLE THE HEADMASTER

The Sablestone Academy amphitheater was truly awe-inspiring. Apparently, the campus's main castle wasn't built atop the mountain; it was sculpted *into* it. As such, the amphitheater was hewn on the back side, high atop the south-facing slope. With bench-style seating, the semi-circular design cascaded downward to a central dais-like stage. Past the central stage was nothing except empty air and a beautiful vista depicting the expansive mountain range beyond. The sun was setting, and the valley below was awash in tones of dark golds and deepening reds.

On the central stage, five thrones sat facing the audience. Elegant flags mounted behind the ornate chairs rippled in the wind. Thanks to Evie's debrief, I knew that the thrones and respective flags represented Sablestone's five villainous paths. Which was why the seating was currently roped off into six uneven sections—five for those students already assigned, and one for we incoming freshmen. In said section, I spotted the backs of familiar heads and made my way for my allies.

Engrossed in my search, I failed to notice the extended foot until it was too late. The dastardly juvenile prank caught my ankle and I tripped, falling hard onto the stone stairs.

"Sorry, Jackson," Eris said with a smirk.

Next to her in the auditorium style seating, Sophia winked two of her four cat eyes. "We totally didn't see ya there. Clumsy us."

"No problem," I said. Getting up and dusting myself off, I returned the false smile. "Accidents happen. Seven, apparently."

Eris, Sophia, Stanley, Valliar, Khasil, Y'olly, and Mikayla all sat along the back row of freshmen acting "cool." I'm sure you remember the shitty kids who sat at the back of the class or the bus. The ones who tried as little as possible to seem edgy.

Which made me… *gasp*. The nerd?

"You may go now," Sophia said with a "be gone" gesture, which elicited a chuckle from the others.

Time, you bastards, just give me time, I thought.

"Boss, where ya been?" Wraith Knight called out while waving me down.

"You okay, Jackson?" Myst asked from beside WK. "We were worried."

"All of you?" I asked, taking my seat and glancing past Myst.

Lydia sat there, her arms crossed over her chest and a look of… I wasn't sure what on her face. Anger? Confusion, maybe? Oh, gods above and below, was that guilt?

Was Lydia capable of guilt?

"Anything to say?" I asked.

My ex rolled her eyes and muttered something under her breath.

"Come again? What was that?"

"I'm sorry, okay?" she said, a little louder. "The knife just slipped."

"It's not your fault," I said, taking in our surroundings.

All three of them looked at me like I'd just taken my dick out and started doing the helicopter.

"What?"

"You're… *not* mad?" Myst asked.

"Why? Would it help?" I asked. "It was an accident and beyond her control."

"Are we sure this is him?" WK said, looking around. "Maybe a doppelganger? Do they have those here?"

I sighed. "How much of the tour did you get?"

"After that darkness swallowed you, Evie passed us off onto another student guide," Wraith Knight said. "We saw the campus towers, the sports fields, and the dining facility before being funneled here."

"They say that our dorms are in those towers," Myst added, "but we won't know which one is ours until after whatever this assembly is over."

"It's a sorting ceremony," I said, educating her.

"How do you know that?" Lydia asked.

"Three things," I said. "First, look around. Notice that that all the upperclassmen and people who look like they belong are sitting in different sections?"

"Yeah, I guess so?" Lydia said, looking around the amphitheater.

"It's because they've already been sorted into their respective villain paths," I explained. "YA likes to keep things simple and easily deduced, as they're stories written for dullards, and I don't mean actual young adults. Second, because this whole academy follows YA tropes, all newcomers will be divided up in ways that will shock and amaze so that they can learn lessons of love and friendship."

"But considering this is a villains academy, then they're lessons in betrayal and deceit?"

"Bingo," I said, shooting Myst a finger gun.

"Wait… sorted?" Wraith Knight said, practically vibrating in his seat. "You mean like—"

"Easy there, big guy, it's not exactly what you're hoping for," I told him. "There are five paths in this place, and each one has their own unique challenges."

"How do you know all this?" Lydia asked. "The last we saw you, you were bleeding out."

"Yeah, thanks for that, by the way."

"I thought you said you weren't mad."

"I never said I wasn't mad, I just said it was beyond your control," I clarified. "See, while you all got the mundane tour, I was with our daughter."

"You—you saw Evie?" Lydia asked, her voice hopeful. "Like, really spoke to her?"

I thought about rubbing her face in it, that I'd had time with our child. And while I was a villain, I wasn't a complete dick. So my human side won out.

But just barely.

"I did," I told her. "After I was nearly vivisected by Doctor *freaking* Moreau, Evie took me to a spot in the catacombs and laid it all out for me."

"How—how is she?"

"I think she's good," I told Lydia truthfully. "This place seems to be tailor made for her. She—she has an edge now, you know? She's intelligent and aware."

Lydia smiled while rubbing her thumb under her eye.

"Uh, boss? Did you say Doctor *Moreau*?" Wraith Knight asked.

"Yup," I said. "He's a professor and the school nurse."

"How?"

"Possibility?" Myst said, positing a guess.

"Man, Myst's on fire," I said. "Yeah, exactly that. While I'm getting sick of saying it, anything is possible while inside Possibility."

A werewolf girl with a side ponytail turned around in her seat and growled at us, "Will you all, like, shut up?"

"No kidding, right?" said a short, dorky cybernetic boy next to her. "They talk so much."

"Mind your own damn business," Lydia snapped, pulling a knife from her sheath.

"Try it, bitch," the wolf girl said, extending her claws.

"Oh, you're calling me a bitch?" Lydia sneered. "That's rich."

The wolf girl smiled. "I see what you did there. Nice."

Lydia sat back and sheathed her blade, a little smile on her face. She then turned to me. "Who's Dr. Moreau?"

"Who is—are you—what?!" Wraith Knight stammered in true dork fashion.

"Don't blow a geek gasket, WK," I said. "Lydia's not from any of our respective earths, so this kind of thing is foreign to her."

"Still," Wraith Knight said, adjusting his glasses with a huff.

"Dr. Moreau was the titular character from a famous **and very public domain book**, *The Island of Dr. Moreau*, by H. G. Wells," I relayed to her. "The story follows this guy, Edward, a shipwrecked survivor who ends up on this weird island."

"Dr. Moreau Island?" Lydia asked.

"No, it's not the name—just shut up," I told her. "In the story, Dr. Moreau was this crazy English scientist who liked to do live vivisection."

"Is there another kind of vivisection?"

"Again, shut up," I told her. "Anyway, the doc moved to this island, became a mad scientist, and created these weird human-animal hybrids. The book deals with pain, cruelty, moral responsibility, and human identity."

"Sounds interesting," she said.

"Oh, it is. And it's completely fucking *fictional*," I stressed. "Which is why I nearly shat myself when I met—and then escaped from—the guy before he and his little sidekick cut me up."

I pointed down at the main stage as five people came up from some subterranean stairwell and began taking their positions on stage.

"You see those folks down there? The ones taking their seats?"

"Yeah?" Lydia said. "A skinny old balding prick in an old-timey suit. A paler dork in an older, fancier suit. Some troll woman. A witchy bitch. And a lanky dork. So what?"

Wraith Knight squinted. "Wait, what? Are those—"

"Oh, my lord," Myst said, covering her mouth. "That—that can't be."

"Shush," I told the minions. "Lydia?"

"So, they're more of what?" Lydia said. "Fictional characters brought to life by the Titan of Possibility to teach at an academy for villains?"

"Huh," I said, taken aback by the astute inference. "Yeah, exactly that."

"So who are they?"

"Professor Moriarty, Dracula, Grendel's Mother, Baba Yaga, and Renfield," Wraith Knight whispered almost reverently.

"Life was so much easier before I met you," Lydia sighed.

Before another word was exchanged, the amphitheater went completely dark. It was as if the night itself had swallowed the sun and sky in one swift bite. There were, of course, the standard oohs, ahh, and obligatory fart sounds that always come with turning out the lights on an assembly of young people.

There was a movement within the shadows. An awareness. An intelligence.

Bit by bit, the darkness retreated, like smokey strands of black ribbon returning to the source. As the last vestiges of sunlight flooded back in, a beautiful female form stood at a lectern. She was tall, fit, and composed of night and starlight.

And she wasn't wearing anything.

Now before you flex those angry clicking fingers to refund this recorded adventure, let me be very clear. While she was not wearing clothes, she was not, I repeat *not*, naked in front of children.

Her mind-boggling long, voluminous hair, which was made of pure darkness, covered her. And I'm not talking in that sexy comic book way. I mean that the Titan of Night's hair enveloped her like a woman's formal business dress. No naughty bits on display, much to the chagrin of many. Myself included.

What? Look, we all had that one teacher growing up that… well, you know.

Gave you a tickle in your pickle?

Plumped your muffin?

Stirred an arousal in the trousers?

Fuck me, the Van Halen song "Hot for Teacher" wasn't written in a vacuum, people!

"Students of Sablestone Academy and honored professors," Headmaster Nyx began, her tone professional if a bit mischievous. "I welcome you all to another year of villainous education. The lessons taught within these hallowed halls are unlike any other that came before. Through our rigorous curriculum, we strive to make the word 'villain' mean something more than a mere antagonist. If you have not come prepared to give your all, to plot, connive, deceive, and most importantly, to learn, then the door is behind you. Anyone who stays will be pushed to, and beyond, their breaking point. We will, in essence, destroy you. Break you down. Find the core of you. And that's when the real work begins. Returning students know what this means. For you newcomers…well, it's time for the ceremony of discovery."

There was a rumbling, followed by a scraping sound. Headmaster Nyx turned away from the lectern and looked behind her. In the middle of dais, a circular hatch retracted, allowing a stone column to rise. The piece of black rock rested there, unmoving. Tangible power washed over the audience.

Death, real death, was in this room. And somehow, deep down, we all knew it.

"There are five villainous paths of education in this school," Nyx said. "The Mind Fire Calling, the Veil Walkers, the Forbidden Tome, They Who Hunger, and Those in Loyal Service. When I call your name, step forward and place your hand on the Sablestone. Let us all see who you really are."

WHERE I COROLLATE SCHOLASTIC TRIBES, PREDICT OUTCOMES, AND GET A POP QUIZ

"Ella Moontide," Headmaster Nyx called out. "Step forward."

The werewolf girl with the side ponytail stepped forward and placed her hand on the Sablestone. Like all the previous freshmen, her body locked in pain the moment she touched the dark rock. Purple-black waves of energy rolled over the lycanthrope as a connection formed between her and one of the five thrones.

"*They Who Hunger*," I said under my breath.

"You sure?" Myst said.

"Wanna put a bet on it?"

"Not against you," she said. "But what makes you so sure?"

I snickered. "Haven't seen the pattern?"

"Don't be an ass," Lydia said. "Spit it out or shut up."

"Touchy much?"

"You aren't the only one who no longer has to put up with the other's quirks."

"Eh, fair," I shrugged. "Okay, so five villain paths, right? The Mind Fire Calling, the Veil Walkers, the Forbidden Tome, They Who Hunger, and Those in Loyal Service."

"Right," Lydia agreed. "But we haven't seen any of the Mind Fire or the Loyal ones yet."

"And there's a reason for that," I said.

"Oh, get it," Wraith Knight said, and I gestured for him to continue. "While there's undoubtedly be some overlap, I'm guessing that the Veil Walkers seems like the path for otherworldly, supernatural types. Vamps, gods, demons, and the like. Corrupted types like dark witches and wizards, cursed ones, and dark fanatics would fit in the Forbidden Tome. They Who Hunger, like what our little werewolf friend there, is a path for the bestial and brutish folks, killer robots, and the like. With me so far?"

"Yeah, I see it. But like, man, isn't that racist or something?" Myst asked. "Or at least stereotyping?"

"Well… duh," I said with a shake of my head. "How else can you ensure the best training for kids?"

"Wait," Myst said "Are you arguing *for* school tracking? Despite it having been shown time and again to be stereotyping that has a negative impact on students' confidence?"

"Are you kidding me?" I laughed. "Of course I'm not for school tracking."

Myst sighed a bit. "Good."

"I mean, what control-level villain in their right mind wants a nation full of students who had individualized learning plans, are less prone to apathy, engage in healthy competition, and excel during creative instruction? No no, *I* want a one-size-fits-all model that not only spares a kid's feelings but also encourages them to bitch constantly about said feelings. I want a barely functional, middle-of-the-pack work force who will likely never achieve greatness in any capacity, thus allowing we elite few to run everything. Thank the gods above and below that no matter how many times that 'school tracking is bad' study is debunked, the feelings police cling to it like it's a gods damned life raft."

Myst just hung her head. "You really are a villain, aren't you?"

"*We* are villains," I said, correcting her. "But just to prove to you I'm not a monster, I'm gonna tear up WK's theory."

"What?" Wraith Knight said, sounding a little miffed.

"Look again at the kids who were picked for each path," I said. "It's not necessarily that they're vamps, wizards, cyborgs, or whatever. There are other defining factors at play."

Wraith Knight crossed his arms. "Like?"

"As near as I can tell, the Veil Walkers are this school's equivalent of those disgustingly annoying theater kids we knew back in high school. Which explains why Dracula sits on that path's throne. Gods, demons, and some monster types who thrive on spectacle."

Wraith Knight looked deflated. "But I was a theater kid."

"We know, Wendell, we know," I snickered. "Next to them are Baba Yaga's Forbidden Tome. Notice how they're pretty much villain versions of emo-goth kids? The ones who love tentacle porn and Cthulhu—which, I know, is redundant. As for They Who Hunger, I mean, come on. Dimwits, bullies, and jocks. It explains why Grendel's Mother is the head there."

I studied these versions of the classic villains. Dracula wore his classic opera tuxedo ensemble while Baba Yaga wore a witchy potato sack dress with all the dangling bone doodads and crystals you'd expect. Grendel's Mother was different. She was a handsome, if beefy, trollish gal wearing clothes best described as…well, there's no nice way to say it.

She looked like a lesbian gym coach.

Before you get all pissed at me for such an ignorant-slash-general statement, let me paint you a mental picture. Gray polyester short shorts that barely contained thick thighs while exposing thicker cankles. A dark purple, moisture-wicking polo shirt stretched across her muscular chest and a whistle dangling from her neck. The matching purple plastic sport visor showed off her hair, which was shaved up the sides and resembled a dude's faux-hawk from the mid-2000s.

Now, does that exonerate me?

Yeah, I thought so.

"They Who Hunger!" the dark, disembodied voice growled from the ether, announcing the werewolf girl's destination.

The furry girl gripped her hand in pain, a black flat rock now embedded in her flesh. The werewolf bowed her head, then walked over to stand by her respective section.

"Told ya," I shrugged. "It wasn't that she was a werewolf exactly. But rather that she was a total jock bully asshole."

"Fine," Myst conceded. "And the other two paths?"

"If I had to guess, then Professor Moriarty's Mind Fire Calling are the evil geniuses of the school. The rich-kid-meets-the-alpha-Chads of this place. As for Renfield's Those in Loyal Service? Well, I'm fairly sure they're the villain equivalent of the loser, stoner kids in high school. The ones who wore military surplus coats and ended up in Vo-Tech courses while everyone else took real classes."

Wraith Knight grumbled. "A lot of good, blue-collar people come from there and can earn six figures after getting their certifications."

"Wow, six whole figures?" I said, pouring on the false cheer. "Wow."

Wraith Knight narrowed his eyes. "At least they're not burdened by crippling student debt and their jobs won't be replaced by AI."

"Well, you got me there," I shrugged. "Thankfully, the world demonizes people with their name on their shirt. Still, you must admire the sheer sinister nature of higher education. I know people call me a villain, but predatory loan practices with unfixed interest rates that double or triple over the life of said loan? Allowing impressionable, dumbass kids to get degrees that have zero earning value post-graduation? And the coup de grace, reducing freshman-level admissions while raising tuition costs to create a sense of scarcity? *Mwa!* Chef's kiss."

"What are you driving at, Jackson?" Myst asked.

"I thought it was obvious," I said. "Those in Loyal Service are the support path. Familiars? Oh, come on, they're the bloody *henchmen*."

Myst and Wraith Knight went silent while Lydia snickered. "Well, we know which path you two are headed for."

"Not again," Myst sighed.

"Tell me about it," Wraith Knight added.

"Huh… why so few?" Lydia asked.

"*Hmm?*"

"Why haven't we seen any of the other students placed in those two paths?" Lydia clarified as she looked back at the amphitheater seating. "Both of those paths seem to have the lowest number of students."

"Makes sense," I said. "There really are very few evil geniuses. Plenty of smart folk, but a tiny percentage qualify as masterminds. As for the Renfields, clearly this is a school for the named henchmen, not the generic thug."

Lydia patted WK and Myst in turn. "Well, I for one think it's a noble path. We wouldn't have gotten as far as we had without either of you."

"Gee, thanks," Myst said.

Wraith Knight hung his head. "I wanna be with the vamp theater people."

"I know you do, big guy," I said, trying to console him.

"Mikayla of the Never Realm," Headmaster Nyx called out.

The crimson-skinned succubus with the Coke bottle glasses stepped towards the Sablestone but paused to look back.

Not at Sophia's clique, but at Lydia. My ex stared daggers back at her ex, who then glared at me for some bloody reason.

Gods damn it, I hate YA and its love triangle tropes.

Mikayla placed her hand on the stone, then locked up in pain while the dark energy washed over her. Normally, I'd have guessed the Veil Walkers. She had been a spy for me before being transformed into a succubus, so acting had been her jam. But there was a quirk about my former employee. She was the type to use powerful forces to get what she wanted. When the Sablestone announced "the Forbidden Tome," I nodded my approval.

"Good for you, Bethany," I said under my breath.

Valliar, Khasil, Y'olly, and King Stanley were next, with Headmaster Nyx calling out their true names in the respective tongues from their native planes. Which of course sounded like gobbledygook to everyone else but a few. And as predicted, the quartet fell into the more classic assignments and into the Veil Walkers.

They were all drama queens.

Looking back over my shoulder at the student dispersal, the nosepickers of Those That Hunger and the hissing bitches in the Veil Walkers seemed to make up the two largest paths.

Yeah, that made sense. Most sci-fi fantasy and horror villains were either a supernatural force or a slasher type.

The Forbidden Tome was smaller by comparison, and I think they were okay with that. Dark magics could bind gods and monsters, after all. Even within the *Star Wars* universe, a Sith lord was rare, and that rarity was reflected in the student body.

"Wraith Knight," the headmaster called out.

"At least they didn't call me Wendell," my former minion said before lumbering forward.

"No matter what happens, you're part of this family," Lydia said, not bothering to hide her amusement for the inevitable decision. In fact, it was rather sad.

The big muscular nerd's hand had barely touched the Sablestone before it loudly announced, "Those in Loyal Service!"

A ripple of "oohs," "ughs," and "ouches," went through the crowd. Renfield himself got up out of his throne and personally walked over. The scarecrow-thin man with glasses, frizzy red hair, and overalls shook WK's hand.

"Welcome aboard," the lanky professor said with a fawning giddiness. "We need strong minds and backs like yours."

Dracula rolled his eyes.

So did Wraith Knight.

When the former—and now again—minion looked back at me for support, I just gestured for him to take his place. With begrudging acceptance, he did. Standing off to the side by the rest of the misfit dorks.

Poor bastard.

"You're still a great villain!" Lydia called out.

"Myst," Nyx said.

"He needs company, dear," Lydia said. "Go on."

Myst took a deep breath, calming herself, and stepped forward. She placed her hand on the Sablestone, and I watched her body arch in pain. Oddly, though, there was a bit of a smile on her face.

"The Forbidden Tome," the Sablestone announced.

"How the shit did that happen?" Lydia asked, her mouth agape.

I could've told her that Myst was brimming with potential drive. That if WK and Myst had summoned a demon right there in a deal for power, he would've ended up a servant while she took the lead. But I didn't bother. Myst's wide eyes and placement explained all that.

Baba Yaga flashed a yellow-toothed smile and gestured for Myst to take a spot beside Mikayla. Myst rubbed at the new stone in the back of her hand while glancing back at me. I gave her an approving nod.

"Lydia Barrowbride," Nyx said, calling the next student.

"Watch this," Lydia said, stepping up on the stage.

I watched my ex walk up onto the stage with all the confidence in the world.

Poor girl.

A bit of movement from my peripheral pulled my attention away from the stage. Sophia and Eris moved up to stand next to me.

"What do you think, Jackson?" Sophia asked.

"I think it's obvious to everyone but her."

"Indeed," Eris added.

I shot the taller girl a nasty look. "Do you mind? The adults are talking."

Eris looked at Sophia for guidance. The djinn gave her a nod and Eris took a few steps back, leaving us with a semi-sense of privacy.

"I'm going to destroy you here," Sophia said under her breath.

"You will try," I replied.

We watched Lydia suffer for a few moments before speaking again.

"You know, this could be over," I told her. "You and me? All this? We could just let bygones be bygones."

"I must have my vengeance."

"You already got it," I told her. "You killed me."

"Well, it didn't bloody well stick, now did it?"

"You took everything I had."

"You took it back," she countered.

"Sophia," I began, projecting as much machismo as a twelve-year-old boy with nary a nut hair could, "you already played your hand against me and lost. If you press this, then I'll have to play mine. And I don't lose."

"Well then," she smirked, "I'll have to make sure I have a trump card or two up my sleeve."

Lydia staggered back, her eyes wide in shock, horror, and painful realization.

"Those in Loyal Service!" the Sablestone boomed.

"What?! No!" Lydia roared.

Renfield stood from his throne to shake her hand, but Lydia drew her knives. "Get the fuck back! I'm not some—some *sidekick!*"

Headmaster Nyx leveled her gaze her my ex-wife. "Take your place, Ms. Barrowbride."

"Kiss my ass!"

A tendril of inky night broke away from Nyx's outfit and slammed into Lydia, sending her skittering across the stage. She fell off, landing at Wraith Knight's feet.

The big man offered her a hand.

"You're still a great villain."

"Fuck you, Wendell," she said, slapping the hand away.

"Sophia Rose DeVrille," Nyx announced.

"See you around, Julian," Sophia said before floating up and placing a hand on the stone.

"Then there were two," Eris purred, taking Sophia's spot.

"Oh, you're still here. I'd forgotten."

"I think I'm going to enjoy this year," she said confidently.

"Whatever she promised you, it's a lie," I said. "I know you don't believe me, but it's true."

"As long as you suffer, I'm happy," Eris said.

"No, you won't be," I said. "Trust me, if anyone knows about gaining more but feeling less, it's me."

"The Twilight Veil!" the Sablestone announced.

Eris looked surprised. Undoubtedly my usurper expected Sophia to enter the mastermind path. But poor Eris was still too green when it came to these things. Djinn had incredible power, but their theatrical flair for screwing over wish makers made Sophia a shoe-in for the theater kids.

"When you're ready, find me and we'll talk," I told Eris, stepping forward even before the headmaster spoke.

"Ah, yes, Julian Jackson Blackwell," Nyx said.

I walked up, waved my hand over the stone, then immediately turned and walked away.

"The Mind Fire Calling," the stone announced with far less gusto than before.

I looked at Professor Moriarty and held out my hand. He was not amused and did not move from his seat.

I gave him a wink, then joined my "peers."

"How—how did you do that?" one of the earlier selectees asked. "That damn rock turned my whole being inside out, searching for what I truly was."

I looked up at the kid. He was tall and fit with long blonde hair and large blue eyes. I wasn't sure if it was his angular chin or lean frame, but I pegged him as one of those stock white guy anime villains.

It might have had something to do with his paramilitary gear.

Or that he was a living cartoon.

"I know what I am," I said, examining the stone in the back of my hand. "I don't need a magic rock to search my core."

Eris was last to go, but the headmaster called the name anyway. Before Eris put her hand on the rock, her eyes rested on me. The anime guy went to make a space for her next to us.

I stopped him.

"Really?"

"*Mm*," I grunted.

Eris suffered for a few seconds. But in the end, the answer was as predictable as the tide.

"Those in Loyal Service!" the stone boomed.

If a pin dropped, you'd hear it.

"No… no," she said, shaking her head and hand in disbelief. "I'm a mastermind, I—"

"There there," Renfield said, coming out of his seat to comfort her. "Villain support is an excellent path to success."

"This—this isn't right. I was promised—"

"*Shh*," Renfield said, guiding her off to her fellow henchmen.

Man, she looked crushed. I wish I'd snapped a picture.

Now a few of you out there in reader land might be saying, "I don't get it. Eris is so smart and capable." But let's be real, Eris was never going to be standing next to me. For all her bravado, Eris had always been an instrument of a more powerful mind. It's like I'd said to Sophia just a few moments ago, that it was bloody well obvious to everyone but *her* which path she'd be placed in.

But I hadn't been just talking about Lydia. And only Sophia and I had known it.

In the only canon that matters, Darth Vader was a henchman for the Emperor. A powerful, usefully named henchman, but ultimately a tool.

Still, one always has to be careful when dealing with henchmen. They're way more powerful than people realize.

The sun had finally dipped below the western mountain range, officially making it night and signifying the end of the first day.

"Freshmen attendees," Headmaster Nyx said, addressing the auditorium. "You have been sorted into paths and your links to the Sablestone have been established. And while official classes begin in the morning, I think a pop quiz is called for."

The entire audience began to murmur.

Headmaster Nyx gestured with her hand, and the Sablestone retreated into the ground with the sound of grinding stone. Once the iris in the stage closed, there was this weird feeling in the air, like a soap bubble popping.

"Your abilities have been returned and the immortality field is in place. The ten-minute murder brawl starts… now."

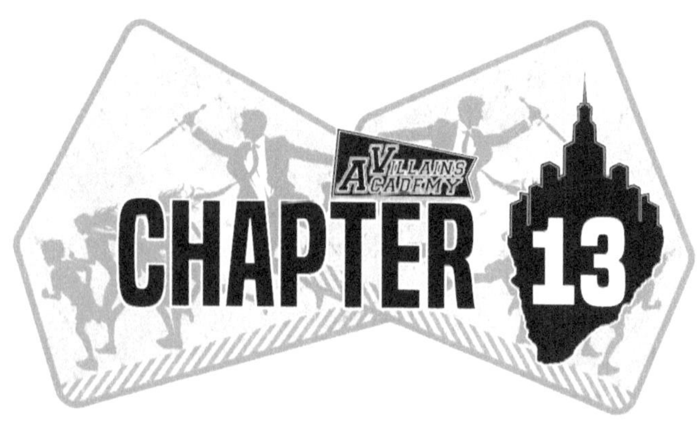

CHAPTER 13

WHERE I TRY HIDING IN PLAIN SIGHT, CRITIQUE MY PEERS, AND GET A GIRL TO NOTICE ME

The amphitheater was chaos. Bloody, destructive chaos. No sooner had the headmaster finished her sentence than the student body of Sablestone Academy turned on one another.

Well… that's to be expected. YA stories do so love it when kids kill one other.

The berserkers from They Who Hunger fanned out like a pack of predators, slashing, bashing, and zapping anyone who was not them. They were the jocks, after all, and this was clearly a physical test. Surprisingly, the sidekick crew from Those in Loyal Service seemed to hold their own.

Made sense, really.

It's like I'd said, henchman types weren't always dorks and hunchbacks. Darth Vader aside, Saruman was clearly Sauron's bitch boy. Countless Bond villains had super assassin sidekicks, most of whom had cool tricks like spinning death hats.

Too bad Eris had none of that.

She was still wearing that shocked look on her face when the werewolf girl Ella literally tore her in half.

Again, I wish I'd gotten a photo.

Wraith Knight, on the other hand, wasted no time in using his shadow shifting powers to wreck shop. Sure, he was younger and had far less bulk, but that meant fuck all when his fists became shadowy wrecking balls. Even Lydia seemed to be in her element, stabbing, jabbing, and slashing her way through a Black Lagoon-looking fish kid.

Mmm… sushi.

On the other side of the amphitheater, the artsy-fartsy theater kids from the Twilight Veil went after their natural nemesis, the Forbidden Tome. Aside from the obvious—magical types binding, imprisoning, and stealing power from the devilish and the divine—there seemed to be a deeper level of hate between them. It didn't take long to figure out.

Highlander rules, dear reader, Highlander rules. There can be only one…

Clique, that is, who gets to rock the trench coat look.

Vampires, demons, and minor deities took to the air to smite the emo wizards. But a few of the pleather and plaid upperclassmen threw up protective wards and shields. Those who hadn't moved fast enough became impromptu Slurpees for vamps and hungry demons.

The professors sat safely behind a dim protective dome of translucent night, provided by Headmaster Nyx. The bastards were taking notes and grading our performance.

Well, it was a school.

What was I doing during all this?

Well, dear reader, I was on all fours hiding behind a dead cyborg like the fat little kid I was. Or at least I tried to. Shortly after death, the corpses dissolved into nothing. Even weirder, they took whatever they'd had with them. So there were no extra guns, knives, or fireball wands lying around. But there were plenty of bloody puddles and piles of guts to slip in. Staying low while scrambling about, I did everything I could to avoid being noticed.

And where were my new mastermind classmates, you may ask?

It turns out that the Mind Fire Calling, totally bitchin' name aside, were in fact *not* the cool kids I assumed they were. Alas, I blame my confirmation bias.

Sad but true, such things happen to the best of us. We all have this tendency to see things the way we want them to be instead of how they really are. It's why people seek out data that reinforces their biases instead of challenging them. And who wouldn't? No one wants to actually think. They wanna feel smug so they can say, "See? I knew I was right, and the other side was wrong."

In relationships, confirmation bias frequently bites us in the ass as we tend to focus on the positive aspects of a perspective or current partner while ignoring the red flags. It's easy to let things slide when someone's a great listener, supportive, and humps like a rhino. But that doesn't mean we should overlook the fact that they might, I dunno, sleep fart, drop the occasional N-bomb, or are the kind of vegan who can't go out in public without bringing up that they are, in fact, a vegan.

Seriously, voluble vegans… I will eat you. You're grass fed, barbecue sauce goes on *any* meat, and there are a few countries where the practice is legal. You've been warned.

Now back to how my villainous confirmation bias blinded me.

When I'd inspected the Mind Fire Calling, I expected, therefore I saw, a young elite legion of Shadow Master clones. Turns out that I'd been… *ugh*. Wrong. They were, quite obviously now, the *dorks* of Sablestone.

Oh, dear reader, it was bad. Real bad.

Wiping away a strand of stray viscera, I saw them for who they were. Which was some of saddest, weirdest, and most depression-inducing pack of weenies I'd ever seen, and I've been to Authors & Dragons conventions.

Think of the beloved masterminds of sci-fi and fantasy. Lex Luthor, Palpatine, Dr. Frankenstein, The Borg Queen, Walter White, Annie Wilkes, and so on. Can you see them? Great.

Now imagine them during puberty.

Oh yeah.

Overbites and acne. Oily skin. Comically large facial features they were still growing into and clothes that hugged in all the wrong places. Remember the AV club back in high school? How about the academic decathlon team or the model UN kids? Yeah, those folks were prize-winning stallions compared to these fugly chuds. Worst of all, the students who comprised the Mind Fire Calling were mostly *powerless*.

Much like myself, it seemed.

Despite Headmaster Nyx "turning our powers back on," my Titan abilities were clearly not on the menu. And since I wasn't a god anymore, I didn't have those powers to fall back on either.

All I had was my intellect and the body composition of a kid who thought fruit snacks were a food group.

Huh. Maybe, just maybe, I belonged with these nerds. My late bloomer biology, haircut, and clothes were a testament to that idea.

They say that smart folks go on to rule the world. And in part, that's true. Those of us with intellect, and flexible moral fiber, corrupt your banks and politics. We control your medicines, your consumer habits, and your technology. We feed our greed so that you can barely feed your families. In that way, the geeks truly do inherit the world.

But high school ain't the world.

Sablestone Academy was more like a traditional school setting, where the jocks and hotties were the ruling kings and queens. And in a way, it made sense. It was only fair to give the muscle-brained and the vapidly attractive a time in the sun before life turned them into drug-addled, day-laboring rent-a-cops and strippers.

Day shift strippers. The ones who shuffle dance their tits n' tassels while you eat a mediocre steak buffet.

Apologies. Stress makes me ramble.

Amid the carnage, I noticed that one of my peers had what appeared to be telekinetic abilities. Their egg-shaped and veiny alien head was kind of a dead giveaway. But abilities like those required focus and concentration. And it's pretty damn hard to focus when a nearly seven-foot patchwork girl made of human remains from They Who Hunger is charging at you.

I'll give credit where it's due—the blue-gray skinned alien had chutzpah. At five foot nothing and ninety pounds soaking wet, he stood his ground, trusting in his powers.

Unfortunately, the flesh-golem girl had momentum. And while psychic abilities are cool, a couple hundred pounds of aggression was more than enough to break someone's concentration.

In the end, the only thing left identifiable from the little alien was a puddle of piss and a tattered Weird Al t-shirt.

And that was when the flesh golem girl covered in alien guts looked in my direction, and spotted me.

Well… shit.

CHAPTER 14

WHERE I DISCUSS MY BIOLOGY, CRAVE SOME PEZ, AND TAKE A DIVE

"Come here, you little dork!" the large girl growled.

"No!" I yelled back, scrambling away from her as fast as my scrawny legs could carry my pudgy torso.

It wasn't far.

Fun fact about the Shadow Master in his youth: I was built like a T-Rex.

No… it was not as cool as you'd think. For there's a curse that's plagued us Blackwell men for generations. We tend to suffer from skinny-fat-itis. That may sound like gibberish to some of you, but those who know, know.

When one is skinny fat, especially as a kid, it means you have, at least from the knees down, what some would call "chicken legs." While that's not the worst thing in the world, these poultry like appendages are matched by our noodle-like "spaghetti arms." Rounding out the food-themed analogies are our pot bellies and our pumpkin heads.

Are you seeing the mental picture yet?

Thanks to centuries of mushy, overcooked, nutrient-deficient English diets decaying our DNA, the Blackwell chaps, when left to our own slovenly devices, resemble the aforementioned T-Rex. Tiny arms with legs that stand out disproportionately to our bulbous trunks and heads. For this reason, along with family photos, I vowed to work out as much as possible to avoid ever looking like this again.

But fate, or rather the Titan of Possibility, is a cruel douche.

The Frankenstein girl didn't have to go very far before grabbing me, lifting me up, and driving me into the ground. The air burst from my lungs and I waited for the inevitable death blow... but it didn't come.

The brutish girl could have finished me off right then and there, but she didn't. Seems the stitchy bitch had a bit of a mean streak in her. Instead of caving in my skull, she rolled me over so that I could watch my impending doom.

Yay.

"I love crushing brainy types," the girl said.

"Gee," I wheezed. "And I didn't even buy you dinner first."

"What? You think you're smart or something?"

"Smarter... than you."

Yeah, great job, Jackson. Piss off the near-seven-foot monster on top of you.

But the girl chuckled. It was a nice laugh. Was it weird to notice this over the chaos of children destroying one another? Sure. But she was on top of me and there was nowhere to go. My would-be killer had one blue eye and one green eye, burned honey blonde hair, and high cheekbones. She'd clearly been assembled from of Caucasian, African, and Asian donors.

Well, that's not fair to assume. Maybe a mad scientist type had built her out of leftover buff cheerleader parts. Or perhaps two decent looking Frankensteins did the "monster mash."

It could happen.

Sure, I couldn't explain why there were surgical staples holding her face together and flexible sutures along her throat if she'd been biologically born. And truthfully, I didn't care. All I cared about was the angle at which she held her head, the positioning of her body atop mine, and the edge of the concealed scalpel in my hand.

The one I'd stolen from Dr. Moreau's office.

I lashed out with one deft slash of slim surgical steel. I'd meant to slice the stitches along the girl's throat, but the blade went far deeper than I intended.

Way deeper. The scalpel cut flesh, muscle, and cartilage with ease.

Holy shit, no wonder Moreau had said this thing was dangerous. Damn thing must have some kind of vorpal enchantment.

I followed up my attack with a palm-strike to her chin. Thankfully, the blade had done the lion's share of the work. My weak-ass punch was just enough to rock her head back and turn the very large girl into a teenage Pez dispenser. My joy turned to horror when the body released a pressurized eruption of half-coagulated blood. Thick spurts and chunky blobs of crimson ichor dripped down my face and chin.

Yuck.

I felt like the porn actor on the receiving end of the money shot.

You probably laughed at that mental image, didn't ya? Well, don't forget, I'm in the body of my twelve-year-old self.

Yeah, not so funny now, is it? Ya pervert.

The flesh golem girl collapsed on top of me, pinning me to the floor.

Okay, *that* might have been funny.

I tried like hell to roll her off, but this patchwork mountain of feminine muscle refused to budge. Gods above and below, why did I spend so much of my youth playing video games and plotting the demise of my peers? I knew that sooner or later this body would dissolve into nothingness like all the others. But until it did, I was in real danger of suffocation.

"Jackson!" I heard a deep voice call out.

The dead golem was pulled off me by a hulking bipedal brute with tentacles for arms. The hairy, musky thing looked like a mix between a gorilla and an octopus. One of the Gorillapus's thick tentacles reached out and pulled me to my feet. It didn't take me long to figure out who it was. Once you've been in a lover's embrace, you know the touch.

Especially when they have the ability to make tentacle suckers.

Don't judge me.

"Myst," I said, getting a confirming nod from the beast. "You okay?"

"Yeah," she rumbled, positioning her large body between us so that I wasn't an easy target. "What's the plan?"

With Myst giving me time, I put my brain into overdrive. Ten minutes was a long time for a real fight. When you're going all out, exhaustion sets in quickly. Another reason the jocks of the school had the advantage.

If everyone stayed put in this room, then there was no way this would go the distance, time wise. However, the amphitheater was oddly free of students. While the first wave of death had been swift and brutal, there should still have been way more kids there.

Ah, because this wasn't just a murder test. It was a survival and adaptation test.

Any fool could pull a trigger or wave a wand. Living to wreak havoc another day was Villainy 101. All we had to do was survive. So I ignored the bloody spectacle as a whole and looked for certain key figures.

King Stanley was shifting in and out of various knockoff superheroes and kicking much ass. Damn nerd was a one-god army.

Valliar and Khasil were working in tandem to fend off several wizarding types from trapping Y'olly in a demon circle. Mikayla was hiding near the edge of the scrum, unsure which side to join.

Sophia was still in her chair, cackling. Being a djinn, her wishing powers bent reality in such a way that every attack seemed to just miss her.

But they weren't who I was scanning for.

Ah, there she was.

Evie held a crude-looking sci-fi rifle in her hands and was laying down covering fire so that her fellow dorks could escape through a tunnel hidden in the wings of the amphitheater.

Gods above and below, she was impressive. I had no idea where she'd gotten the weapon, but she was a gods damn villainous vision in a hoodie and backpack. Evie saw me, saw the distance between us, and gave a small shake of her head. She was right, of course. I'd never cross the distance to that escape hatch.

But that didn't matter. This was a test, after all. And if I couldn't pass on my own merit, then I'd do what all great accomplished people do.

Cheat.

And to cheat properly, one needs to use the right person.

"Evie's up there, helping the rest of the Mind Fire escape," I pointed out. "But we'll never make it through the chaos."

"Then what are we going to do?"

"Survive," I told her. "If this goes for the full time, then it's a systematic slaughter. We need to get clear of all this and wait it out."

"But we don't know the layout of the campus," Myst said. "That tour was minimal at best."

"Oh, we know one place," I said. "But it's a real bitch to get to."

"Where is that—oh, oh no."

"Come on," I said, tugging on her tentacle. "Luckily, you can shape-shift, and I'm relatively small."

Together, we ran towards the dais and climbed up and over the shadowy dome protecting the professors. Moriarty sneered at me, while Nyx suppressed a smile.

"I'm still not great at flying," Myst said.

"Then glide like a motherfucker!" I snapped back, hopping into her arms.

Myst's form shifted, dropping the mass to turn into a winged, bird-like humanoid. She jumped off the dome, over the edge, and into the empty air, taking me with her.

That's the beauty of being a mastermind type. You don't need to have all the power.

But you damn sure keep those who do close at hand.

WHERE I FIND MYSELF IN A TIGHT FIT, ENDURE FEELINGS, AND GET PISSED AT MYST

"How long do you think we have left?" Myst asked. I'd been keeping a rough count, but when you factor in "holy shit, a pack of hormone-driven teens are trying to kill me," you tend to lose precision.

"Not sure. A minute or two at most," I said, conserving my air.

"Do you think there'll be an all-clear signal or something?"

"Your guess is as good as mine," I said, trying to relax my breathing. It was getting hotter and stuffier by the moment.

"Oh, Jackson, I'm sorry," Myst said. "Here, let me help."

Myst grunted slightly and a small tunnel of light opened, allowing cool, fresh air to flood into the steamy interior.

"Thank you," I said, taking in the deep, sweet musk of the tight space.

Me hiding inside Myst had become one of our go-to moves from when I was still counseling villains. From the super-cool adventures I never bothered recording.

What? Why are you staring at me like that? Believe it or not, I need a life away from you people. I need to do things that are not recorded and then sold back to you for profit.

What? Why are you still—oh, oh I get it.

You're hung up on the whole *me being inside Myst* thing. It's not what you think. Well, not this time anyway. Although we've obviously done *that* a few times. You never really know a woman until you've used your cosmic power to shrink down and go vajunking.

That's "vaginal spelunking" for the portmanteau deficient.

But that's not what was currently happening. No, Myst and I were hiding in plain sight by the Sablestone Academy's main gates. To the casual observer, nothing had changed. But a keen eye might've noticed that the black granite monument sign was slightly thicker in depth. Just enough so that a villainous "boy genius" could ball up and hide.

"There's no guarantee that the ten-minute duration was even real," I said. "We're dealing with villains here, so the rules might be complete fabrications. Can you see anything out there?"

"Lemme check again," Myst said.

The monument sign grew a pair of dark eyes and scanned the area. Far off, I heard a sound like muffled explosions.

"What's going on?"

"Nothing, we're safe," Myst said.

"Those sounds weren't nothing," I said.

"A trio of cyborgs had made their way down here, and for a moment I thought they'd spotted us with some kind of thermal scans or something."

"But?"

"But a pair of witches on flying brooms showed up and threw some fireballs," Myst clarified. "The cyborgs took off and the witches are pursuing. No one's around, we're fine."

"Good," I said, maintaining the mental count.

"Jackson?"

I sighed. "Yes?"

"Are we going to talk about the selection ceremony?"

"Which part?" I asked. "The part where you were placed in the Forbidden Tome, or why I *wasn't* put into the Twilight Veil with the rest of the higher beings?"

"Both, I guess."

"The Sablestone reads who you are, not what you do. I always knew you had potential, and so did the stone."

"But I don't have magic powers."

I sighed. "It's like you all don't even listen to me. It has nothing to do with powers or abilities, but who you are. You, dear Doris, are a person who will use any means at her disposal to achieve her goals."

"That's all villains."

"No, it isn't," I countered. "Brutes, slashers, and monstrosities rely on their strength, power, and natural fear. Otherworldly types have supernatural power. Masterminds and henchmen are intrinsically linked as both rely on one another, using their collective mind and wits. Only difference between the two comes down to charisma, hubris, and aspirations. But your group, no matter what they call it here, are the real danger."

"I'm waiting for the flattery to become an insult," she said.

"Good, because here it comes," I said. "Your group are the ones who are so angry at the world that when they get their hands on an evil book, a cosmic ring, or some mystical talisman, they don't play *just the tip* with villainy, no no. They go balls deep on the first pump."

"Is that what you think of me?"

"What was the first thing you did after signing a contract with me and getting power?"

"I—that's not fair."

"You turned into mist," I pressed. "You went up Harold's nose, down into his lungs, and blew him up from the inside out. But hey, no judgement from me. He was an abusive prick and got what he deserved. But it doesn't change the fact that once you had power for the first time in your life, you immediately lashed out at those who had wronged you."

Myst didn't speak for a few moments, and when she did, it was like she was holding back tears.

"So that's just it? We're sorted into our paths and that's it?"

"Gods above and below, no, you dolt!" I half-shouted, cursing myself for being too loud while hiding.

I took a breath and calmed myself.

"You, of all my former employees, have the wherewithal to see the forest for the trees. I swear, being back in a school setting is fucking with everyone's mind. Where you start is not where you end. Villains—fuck, *people*—can cross pollinate. Take me, for example. I'm a mental manipulator who became a god and later a Titan, yet I still see myself as the Shadow Master first and any cosmic power second. You started out as the equivalent of a fantasy world warlock, granted power by a patron. You want to become something else, then do it."

Myst went silent a few more moments, and I went back to counting down the remaining time.

"Jackson?"

Gods damn it. "*Yes?*"

"What happens after this?"

"We go back to our dorms and—"

"No," she said, cutting me off. "Should you beat Sophia, what happens after that?"

Sigh. I miss the glory days of heads-on-spikes leadership. Fewer questions from subordinates. Still, Myst had been loyal all these years. And frankly, I needed someone to talk to. After Sophia's betrayal and Lydia's and my… "it's complicated" status, I didn't have anyone to bounce ideas off, let alone talk to.

"Are you afraid I'm going to move on and forget you all ever existed?"

"I don't know, maybe?" she admitted. "When you hired us, it was as minions. But as we continued working together, we became something more. Cheesy, but we were a family. After you died, it—it wasn't the same."

"I'm gonna call bullshit," I said. "You said that you had a good life fighting demons and all that in the manga world."

"*Wendell* said that," she corrected. "For him it was good. And for him I kept my mouth shut. Yeah, we had good lives, in a way, but it wasn't the same life. We were *heroes,* for villains' sake. Working for a bloody church to fight demons. Demons that we sometimes knew thanks to Never Realm mixers and orgies."

"You're welcome for that," I said.

"But then you came back, came back for us," she said with a mix of joy and melancholy. "And while that's cool, I can't help but wonder."

"Wonder what?"

"Are you going to get bored with mundane mortals and seek higher forms of villainy, entertainment, or distraction?"

How dare she? How bloody dare she?! Are you hearing this crap?

Yup… heads on spikes would have solved this shit a long time ago.

Dear reader, riddle me this: What kind of person seeks confirmation that their time invested with another person has meaning and value? I'll tell ya who. A *weak* person.

Sorry kids, but who has the time, or the emotional capacity, to go around telling people what they mean to us? This new-school way of thinking only leads to more entanglements. If I tell someone how special they are to me, or what they mean to me, then they'll likely reciprocate their feelings. *Boom*, next thing I know I'm in cargo shorts at their house having a BBQ.

Or worse… helping them move.

Say it with me, folks: Suppress your feelings, share little, and drink heavily.

Sigh. I'm full of shit, aren't I?

Gods above and below, wasn't I in this place *because* I cared about Evie? And as my grandmother always said, "It's rude to lie to someone when you're inside them."

I never asked the old battle axe if she'd meant metaphorically or sexually. Mainly because I knew she'd tell me the truth. And as an eight-year-old, all I wanted to do was eat more Peanut Butter Cap'n Crunch and watch *GI Joe* reruns in peace.

"I'm not going to lie," I began. "So much has changed in such a short amount of time, and I have no idea how my Titan self will evolve. But this moment, this place, is about saving my daughter and beating Sophia. We're here together for at least the length of a school year. After that, we'll see. I wish I could give you more, but any promise is based on incomplete data."

"I—I understand," she said.

I think part of her broke right then. But before I could press further, there was a sound like a huge bell ringing, the clanging tone rolling across the campus in waves.

"Well done," Headmaster Nyx's voice boomed, coming from everywhere and nowhere. "Congratulations to the top killers and the survivors. Both aspects are vital to a proper villainous education. The world would have you believe that existence is simply a matter of kill or be killed. But as villains, we do not limit ourselves to the options presented. We make our own. All students will now report to their dormitories, where you will find your class schedules. Your first day of school begins tomorrow morning."

"Do you think it's real or a trick?" Myst asked.

I thought about it but ultimately went with my gut. "I think this is a place where the rules follow the classic lawful-evil archetype. So if we're told it's all clear, then it probably is. But still, let's keep an eye out. Just because the pop quiz is over, it doesn't mean students can't do as they please."

"Yeah, okay," Myst said, shifting back, releasing me from our makeshift camouflaged spot.

But I noticed that she hadn't retaken the form of plain teenage Doris, rather the hot-girl version of a teenage Myst. Interesting.

I peered out from behind the monument sign, not seeing any immediate danger.

"So, uh, where exactly are our dorms?" I asked. "I never got that part of the tour on account of me, you know, bleeding out."

Myst let out a little chuckle, and her eyes drifted upwards to the stone path and the various towers jutting off the side of the mountain.

"Go all the way up the stairs and you'll reach a large circular grassy courtyard area. You'll see the main castle building, but that's for classes. From the quad, you'll see branching paths to the five towers, one for each of the villain houses. Those are the dorms. The Mind Fire Calling's tower is the one with a banner depicting a key inside a spiderweb."

I nodded along at all this, but then stopped when something occurred to me.

"Why are you explaining it like you're giving me directions," I asked. "Aren't you going to help me up the stairs? You saw what happened last time. This body is not built for that kind of physical exertion."

My former minion leaned down slightly. "As my former mentor, employer, and lover often espoused, 'One does get stronger by going through the motions'."

Egad… my own words used against me. I didn't know if I was supposed to be proud or pissed.

Myst patted my ample belly. "See you up there, tiger."

She shifted into a long-legged alien gazelle thing and took up, bounding up the stone steps like they were nothing.

"Pissed. Definitely pissed," I grumbled.

I turned and slowly made my way up those gods damned stairs, thinking about heads on spikes.

CHAPTER 16

WHERE I UNDULATE, LEARN A SAD TRUTH, AND PONDER WEAPONIZING FELINE BUTTHOLES

"About time, freshie," Evie said when I walked into the Mind Fire Calling common room.

Well, "walked" may have been a liberal use of the word. I more or less *slithered* in.

Huh, even that might be too bold a word choice. "Slither" has a strong connotation, doesn't it? It evokes the idea of a powerful viper prowling through the grass, ready to strike and feed.

No, that was *not* how I made my ingress to the Mind Fire Calling common room. I'm not sure what verb to use for a slug's mode of locomotion, but whatever it is, *that's* how I entered the room.

"Now, freshie!" Evie boomed.

Schools are like prisons. Act weak and you will be seen as weak, therefore a target. There were other students watching, so I endured. Through force of will alone, I placed one aching, blistered foot in front of another.

The common room was, like everything on this campus, circular. Maybe because heroes thought in straight lines and angles while villains thought in curves? Eh, regardless, the place was large and ornate.

Aside from the main door I'd just come through, there were two more, one to the east and one to the west. Likely passages to the sleeping quarters above. The stone floor was covered in thick carpets. Tables and chairs were set up for kids to study or hang out, and medieval-like tapestries hung on the walls.

If you're one of those theater-of-the-mind dorks who needs a bit more to have a clearer mental picture, then picture this. Imagine a bohemian tea shop. You with me so far? The kind of place your hippie friends keep insisting you try. The places that have way too many plants and smell like lavender, body odor, and cat piss. Can you see it? Great. Now, add in a dash of that early nineteen-hundreds boarding school vibe. Dusty bookshelves, chess boards, and globes that are so out of date that they only identify white empires. Mix all that together, and you have the Mind Fire common room.

At the north side of the room, a series of dark brown leather couches and recliners had been arranged in front of a crackling fireplace. Evie stood by the fireplace's mantle, waiting. There was an open spot on the end of a couch, so I gave it all I had left. I crossed the space and plopped down hard. This was as far as I could go, and nothing within this entire known or unknown multiverse could make me move.

"Hello 'zer," a guy to my left said with a vaguely eastern European accent.

He was a lanky sprat with a dirty mustache and slicked back hair, and thanks to his uniform and coat, he all but screamed sci-fi fascist.

"You look terrible," said, appraising me. "I love it. So what is your ethnicity, exactly?"

Well, fuck you, known or unknown multiverse. I went to get up, but Evie put her hand up.

"Stay put, freshie."

I capitulated and remained in my spot. Oh, trust me, dear reader—I wanted to argue. But I was too short, too young, and too out of shape to argue. My chubby inner thighs had rubbed together so badly that chafing had become heat blisters and my stitches were seeping.

I know, gross.

Again, remember, I'm technically twelve. Stop picturing my inner thighs, weirdo.

The space fascist kid chuckled at my obvious pain, but Evie just glared at him.

"What? Who died and put you in charge?"

"Everyone who's ever stood in my way," Evie said, leaning over and putting her hands on her knees so that she was eye level with the young man. "What's your name, freshie?"

"Dieter."

"Get this through your head right now, *Dieter*. You're not in your world anymore, you're in mine. And here, you're nothing. You've earned nothing, you have nothing, and I have the pull to make sure it stays that way. Wanna try me, go ahead and find out if I'm bluffing."

I smiled. I love that kid.

"That goes for you too, *Jackson*."

Pain in the ass kid. Always was and always will be. And did you hear her use my first name? Brats. All modern kids are brats.

Evie stood back up and addressed the room at large.

"Before any rumors start, yes, that is my dad," she said, pointing at me. "Don't ask me how he's here or why he's so young, I don't care. And no, I will not treat him any differently than how I treat any of you. Understood?"

There was a grumbling chorus of agreement. Clearly my daughter was not someone you wanted to mess with.

"Like, who cares about him?" I heard a feminine voice ask. I turned, looking for the voice's owner, but didn't see the source. That is, until I looked up.

There, hanging from the chandelier, was a gods damned talking koala. It had some kind of mechanical apparatus wired into its head, obviously augmenting the thing's intellect. It was a monstrosity of science.

I wanted to hug it so badly.

"How were our standings after the pop quiz?" the koala asked.

"I'm getting to that, Emily," Evie sighed, "but we might as well get into it."

Evie turned slightly towards the large oil painting above the fireplace. It was a simple, elegant design that depicted a flame-wreathed key within a spiderweb, the symbol for the Mind Fire Calling. She waved her hand and the image rippled, shifting to a swirling black background with series of names and numbers illuminated in various glowing text. It didn't take a villainous genius to figure out what it meant.

"What are we looking at?" Dieter asked.

"It's the student rankings," I said, pulling a throw pillow out from behind my back and positioning it cross my arms and hide my kid gut.

"How do you know?"

"Because I'm not stupid," I said, inclining my chin. "Each column represents one of the five villain paths, the students are listed by their standing within their respective path, and their associated number is their overall school rank. If their name is in red, then they died. If it's in gold, they lived."

Dieter looked at the board, then nodded. "Of course."

I rolled my eyes.

"Jackson's right," Evie said, pointing to the board. "And, per usual, we suck."

I gave the board another look, burning as much of the info into my mind as possible. It was true that Mind Fire Calling was behind in total points. Worse, I wasn't sure how they could ever hope to catch up. Near as I could tell, there were approximately four hundred students at Sablestone. No need to bother remembering their names. Most villains, like people, never became exceptional, let alone noteworthy.

Still, it was a numbers game. They Who Hunger and the Veil Walkers both had about a hundred and twenty students each. The Forbidden Tome had around eighty, while the villain sidekicks in Those in Loyal Service sat about fifty kids. But the Mind Fire Calling? Thirty students.

Huh. There weren't even close to thirty kids in the room. A quick head count and I tallied only thirteen.

Oh, that's right. Evie had told me that if you die, you come back the next morning. Still, if there were more of these battles where the various paths took each other on, then no wonder they—shit, *we*—suck. We just didn't have the numbers or the raw power to compete.

"We did okay," Evie continued, "all things considered. Some of you remembered our training and used my hidden tunnels. A couple of new faces managed to survive. But more than a few of you failed to heed the school's most sacred rule."

"Which is?" Dieter asked.

"Always be prepared," I said aloud and in unison with Evie.

My daughter gave an appreciative look, then nodded. "Exactly. Always, always, *always* be ready for something to go down. Several of you thought you could fight one on one with the others. But that's not what masterminds do, is it, Mentalax?"

The room was once again filled with murmurs as the students searched for the name's owner.

"Don't bother looking," Evie instructed them. "Our dear alien friend met his end when he tried to take on Beatrice."

The room let out a collective "ouch."

"I assume Beatrice was that flesh golem girl?" I asked.

"What do you mean *was*?" Emily asked.

"I killed her," I looked up and told the hyper-intelligent koala. "Bullshit."

Even her cursing was adorable.

"Believe what you want," I told the furry ball of chlamydia. "But look at the scoreboard. Unless there's another Beatrice in They Who Hunger, her name's in red while mine's in gold."

Again, all eyes swung up to the names on the board. Evie was at the top, naturally, because she'd killed a few kids, survived, and engineered an escape.

I was second. Huh… that was interesting.

"I saw it happen," Evie said, backing my story and breaking my thoughts. "He slit her neck stitches open and punched her head off."

I produced the scalpel, gave it a little waggle while looking at Emily, then put it back inside my jacket's inner pocket.

"Huh," the koala girl said with a nod of her head. "Cool."

"So how do we raise our ranks?" Dieter asked.

"Good question. For you new people, listen up. The moment you received your path, you also received your mark," Evie said, holding up her hand to show the embedded stone. "This creates a link with the Sablestone. Every time you come up with a scheme, pull off an assassination, or engage in something nefarious, it'll know and assign the appropriate number of points based on your level of success or failure. The more in-depth, the better your points. It can also serve as a communication device, linking you to any student."

"How do we know what kind of schemes or plans earn the most points?" Dieter asked.

"In each of your rooms, you will find a student guidebook," Evie said. "I highly recommend you read it and know the rules."

I was half listening to her explain what I thought should be obvious to everyone. But my mind was on the glaring question.

"It seems like you—damn it, *we*—don't have the numbers or the raw power to compete with any other path head on."

"We don't," Evie said, confirming my suspicion. "Almost no one in this path has some kind of superpower or ability beyond our minds."

"How's that fair?" Dieter asked

We both looked at him as if he should already know the answer.

"Ah," he said, realizing his mistake. "It isn't."

"Are all these tests physical?" I asked.

"More or less," Evie said, confirming the worst. "As we're taught in class, it's a villain's job to one day confront a hero. And while there are many ways of going about it, sooner or later things come down to a physical altercation. While we earn points in our respective schooling and path assessments, Sablestone likes to reinforce physical confrontation. Which is why slaughterball is our school sport."

I had no idea what that was, but I'd figure it out later. I had more pressing questions.

"Do we ever have a chance to do what masterminds do? Plan, prepare, and execute?"

"Too few," Evie said with a sad shake of her head.

It's true that showdowns between heroes and villains often happen. Many stories across many worlds are predicated on this eventuality. But typically, they're told from the hero's point of view, in cases where the hero wins. And this seemed counter to what this academy stood for. Why train potential losers?

A good villain—a good mastermind—only confronts the hero when they have a backup plan or four, a nuke on standby, and no fewer than seven kittens waiting to be injected with a highly contagious strain of ass cancer for leverage.

Man, they better be teaching classes on that.

"What about—"

Evie cut me off. "No more questions for tonight. Second and third years, you know your business. You freshies, though, I'd get some sleep if I were you. Hell Week starts tomorrow."

WHERE I TELL YOU A CORPORATE SECRET, HIGHLIGHT YOUR INNER CANINE, AND THROW MY WEIGHT AROUND

My assigned room was located at the furthest end of the eastside living area.

Man… it was a crap hole.

Look, I get that a lot of people look back fondly on their time away at college. The parties, the academic triumphs, the lifelong friends… who inexplicably abandon you by the time you're twenty-seven.

But that wistful nostalgia normally does *not* extend to the small, cramped rooms. No amount of Pier 1 decorative crap or Target-brand brushed-nickel goods can make residing in an off-white cinderblock rectangle better.

As loath as I was to spend time in a space like this, the villain in me had to respect the higher purpose it served. The mental conditioning alone was nefarious and clever.

Oh, my apologies. I'm referring to an insider secret that's not meant for the public. But… screw it. I like you. Lean in because this is important.

The reason K through 12 school and college dorm rooms have remained functionally and architecturally stagnant has nothing to do with budgetary constraints or building permits.

It's for socialization… but not in the way you think. It's how we, the powerful, create compliant little workers and consumers. By packing you common people into cramped, miserable spaces before you can even wipe your butt properly or tie your shoes, we're engineering your behavior.

Each classroom, dorm room, or board room is filled to the brim with strangers who don't necessarily share your beliefs or values. Hell, they barely acknowledge personal space or safety boundaries. Which is, of course, intended and another nudge in our desired direction.

You don't believe me, do you?

Lemme ask you something. Why do folks take their pups to doggy day care? *Hmm?* Or the park? To socialize, right? The best way to get a dumb animal to not bark, make a fuss, or attack other people is to get them to sniff butts and move on. Those who can't function in a pack are taken away and put in isolation before being put down. Those that obey get treats.

Any of this sounding familiar yet?

When you go to work, is it by chance a location where you're forced to work with people you don't know, fully understand, and sometimes downright hate? Maybe you can smell the seafood they reheated for lunch. If you attack them, or lose your temper, you lose your job. But if you comply with the human resources department's standards for behavior and do your job, you get a treat. Er, paid.

Dear reader, happy workers become happy consumers. Happy consumers take out loans for homes that are way bigger than those psychologically damaging classrooms, schools, or the twelve-by-nineteen, two-hundred-and-twenty-eight-square-foot pressure cookers called dorm rooms. They then spend even more money to decorate said homes. Often in ways that are downright garish. And that's okay. You earned it, right? From all your hard work.

You chose this life… right?

And the bad dogs who don't conform and consume properly? Well, we have tiny rooms with bars set aside for them.

Ah, your social conformity was programmed into you the moment you painted your first hand turkey in kindergarten. Now, is this revisionist history? Am I cherry picking points to strengthen my argument?

Shut up, wage-slave, and get back to your labor!

This educational message was brought to you by Big Villain Incorporated.

So yeah, back to my room in Sablestone Academy.

It was, as expected, little more than a gray stone rectangle. There was an arched window on the wall opposite the door. That was nice. But the bars on the window gave me pause. Had there been an issue with students jumping out… or being thrown out?

Dark wooden wardrobes beset the window on both sides. Two side-by-side desks lined the wall to my left. Both desks had this world's version of rolling office chairs. One of the desks, the one closest to the door, was covered in debris and assorted candy wrappers. Whomever I was rooming with had a bit of sweet tooth, it seemed.

To my right was a set of bunk beds. Both the top and bottom were empty, but the top one had clearly been claimed by a male occupant. It was the little clues that I keyed in on.

Clues like messed-up blankets, the general smell of onion in the air, a crusty sock sticking out from under the pillow, and the array of Boris Vallejo, semi-nude fantasy people posters on the wall.

I know a lot of current-year nerds like to sound ultra-modern when they talk-slash-complain about impracticality of bikini armor on females in fantasy. And while that's totally fair, those summer child nerds don't know their history. As impractical as steel-clad D-cups were, they had a hundred percent more blocking potential than Conan's or the Beastmaster's exposed nipples.

I sat down at what I assumed to be my desk and looked at the two objects sitting there. A class schedule and the Sablestone Academy Guidebook. Ignoring the schedule for the moment, I picked up the guidebook, opening it to the first page. Like I'd said to Myst, I still thought of myself as the Shadow Master. And the only way to beat, bend, or break the rules was to know them.

Sadly for me, I didn't even get one sentence in before something small but heavy landed on the back of my neck, driving my face down into the desk. I turned my head as best I could, trying to avoid breaking my nose. But the sudden impact drove my cheek into the table, causing my jaw to blossom in pain.

"Ah, gods damn it!" I half yelled, half slurred, unable to properly move my mouth.

"Get out!" a shrill voice squealed from behind me.

The declaration was followed by a flurry of rabid—if a bit clumsy—hammer punches against the back of my skull.

"Not your room!"

"Get off me!" I yelled back at my attacker, twisting in my seat while throwing awkward back elbows.

Well, I tried to.

As we've already seen, this untrained body had the reaction capacity of a chubby spastic tween. Instead of devastating blows meant to dislodge, disorient, and destroy my attacker, my defensive efforts were akin to a chicken flapping a pudgy wing. The sudden shift in weight caused my chair, and thus the pair of us, to topple over into a heap of embarrassingly bad youthful aggression.

"Get the frick off me!" I yelled, my eyes half closed because I hadn't learned how to keep them open in a fight yet.

"Keith's room!" the voice yelled back. "No one's allowed in Keith's room!"

Wait, *Keith?*

Oh, fuck me.

CHAPTER 18

WHERE I AM PRETTY SURE I WAS RACIALLY PROFILED, MAKE A NEW FRIEND, AND APPRECIATE AN OLD NURSERY RHYME IN A NEW WAY

There Keith stood in all his porcine glory. An animal-human hybrid with a tuft of curly brown hair atop his pointed head, pinkish wrinkled skin, and little tusks.

Landing a lucky, shoving kick, I pushed the swine-like mutant off me. I reached into my coat's inner pocket and pulled out the scalpel before the cross-eyed piglet-boy could get back on his feet. Keith spotted the weapon and instantly froze. A second later, I smelled the pungent aroma of pig piss.

"You?!" Keith said, trembling.

"Yeah, me."

A second or two passed and neither of us spoke. Keith did, however, finish urinating. With a small shudder and look of slight satisfaction on his face, Keith backed up, his little hoof hands held in surrender.

"Take what want, but go, please."

"What are you talking about?"

"You steal from Keith like everyone else, right?"

"What? No, I'm not robbing you, I'm—wait," I said, looking the creature up and down. "Are you saying this because I'm brown? Well, light brown?"

"No!" Keith said, his little eyes getting wider. He snuffled a few times, searching for his words. "Well—no, no Keith not. But people come here to steal Keith's stuff."

"No, I'm not here to rob you," I said with a shake of my head. I put my weapon away. "I'm your new roommate."

"But... Keith don't have roommate," Keith said with a shake of his head, causing the curly tuft of hair to wobble. "Keith never have in all years Keith been here."

"Well—wait, all the years? How long have you been in this school?" I asked, looking past his diminutive frame and pig-parts. But it was impossible to guess his age.

"Mm... Keith born in castle."

"And how long ago was that?"

"Keith is thirty-four."

"And you... go to school here?" I asked. "Like, school-school."

"Yeah, Keith take classes."

"And you haven't graduated yet?"

"No? Why?"

I didn't want to say the obvious. Not to spare Keith's feelings, mind you. But it's been brough to my attention that there are certain words, ones that were freely used in a bygone era to describe a person's mental capacity, limitations, and number of chromosomes, that are no longer socially acceptable. And as long as I want to keep taking your money, I find it best to stick to said social conventions and *not* speak them aloud.

Even though I was thinking the fuck out of it.

"No reason," I said. "Well, it's just that I was informed that this was a three-year institution... for kids."

"That's just suggestion," Keith said. "Father say that everyone matures at own rate. Keith eventually get enough points to graduate."

"Sure, of course," I said, going along with this while pondering what in the Never Realm it meant.

If I had to guess, when Sablestone was created inside Possibility, it was done in such a way that the school came with an existing backstory. It didn't pop into existence on day one, but rather came in with a history. But that then begs the question, were the students and staff real? Or were they window dressing?

I looked around the room again, taking note of the posters on the wall and the candy wrappers on Keith's desk. Keith clearly had a hookup.

Interesting.

I was about to hop up onto his bed and check behind the posters for some Shawshank tunnels, but the little pig boy caught me by my jacket and pulled me back down.

"Stay off Keith's bed!"

"Okay, okay, settle down there, Babe," I said, holding my hands up in momentary surrender. "But you know some secrets about this campus, don't you?"

Keith looked around, unsure how to answer. "Keith isn't supposed snoop, but Keith gets bored."

"Of course. I don't blame you. Repeating the same classes over and over, I'd get bored too. I bet there's a lot of cool stuff out there, just waiting to be seen," I said, trying to empathize with the kid.

Or at least, I was trying like hell to come across like I was.

Before you give me any crap, remember that a key ability in villainy is the subtle art of emotional manipulation. Good villains make it look seamless and natural. Like we're in that moment with you, connecting with our would-be targets on a fundamental level. And if all goes to plan, an alliance is formed with the target being none the wiser.

But you have to be careful in how you phrase it. Bad villains, and by proxy bad writers, say shit like, "We're not so different, you and I."

"Lemme guess," I said, keeping the flow going. "Keith found secret rooms with stuff that ended up in the castle by accident?"

The piglet smiled.

"Well done, young man. Very well done."

"Yes, Keith is smart," he said, his little curly tail practically vibrating.

Oh, this was going to be easy.

"Yes, I can see that," I told him. "And guess what? No one is going to steal your stuff again. I'm your roommate now and I won't allow it."

It was Keith's turn to look me over. Clearly, he wasn't convinced that this mountain of pudge was any more offensively effective than he was. I patted the jacket pocket where I kept the scalpel.

"Don't worry, my new friend. I may not look like much, but I know how to take care of my friends."

"Are—are we friends?" Keith asked, just as predicted.

"Do you want to be?" I asked, carefully laying the emotional trap. "If you have enough friends, then I don't mean to intrude. And while I truly do apologize for my earlier actions, know I would never do that to a friend."

Keith took a moment to think this over, but ultimately nodded.

"Yes," he said, coming to a decision. "We can be friends."

"Excellent," I said, extending my hand. "My name is Jackson. Jackson Blackwell."

"Keith is Keith," the pig boy said, taking my hand in his.

"And it is excellent to meet you, officially and politely this time," I said with a smile, shaking that gross, *gross* hand. "So, is there anything I should know for my first day of school?"

Keith laughed, letting go of the handshake. "No, school on first day is easy. Keith do it many times."

"Fair enough," I said. "Thank you."

"You is welcome," Keith said. "And Keith promise to not suck you off when you asleep."

I paused on that one.

"I—uh, I'm gonna hazard a guess that you mean that you will *not attempt* to drink my blood, as when we first met," I said.

"Yes!"

"Great," I said, shooting him a pair of finger guns. "But whaddya say we work on rephrasing that?"

"Okay!" he said, mimicking the gesture back at me. "But Keith is tired now. Jackson should sleep too."

"I will in a moment," I told him. "I want to go over my class schedule first."

"Hurry up, then turn off lights," Keith said then hopped up onto his bed and got cozy under his blankets. I was going to mention that he was still wearing piss-soaked clothes, but I let it go.

Working on Keith would take time. So for now, baby steps.

Sitting back down at my desk, I looked at my schedule and my heart immediately sank. Every day, Monday through Friday, first thing in the morning… was freshman gym.

Oh, it gets better. It was a gym class conducted by Grendel's Mother, the head of They Who Hunger. Great, just great. Let's just start our day with bullies and exercise. Twelve-year-old me wanted to collapse into a puddle of flub and ooze under the bed.

But if this is what it took to beat Sophia and get Evie home, then so be it.

The rest of the schedule was designed so that each day consisted of three classes, a morning class followed by breakfast, a second class, lunch, and then the third class with dinner following. Evenings, it seemed, we were free to do as we saw fit. That wasn't so bad. The courses seemed standard enough:

- Anatomy & Biology for Death and Dismemberment, with Dr. Moreau;
- Villainous Architecture & Lair Construction, with Captain Nemo;
- Dark Mystique for Beginners, with Dracula;
- Neophyte Skills & Powers, with Baba Yaga;
- Basic Resource Management, with Professor Renfield;
- Crew Management and Child Labor Practices, with Captain Hook; and so on.

But it was the last class on Friday that was the most intriguing. A course that had me as giddy as Keith.

Introduction to Villainy, with Professor Moriarty.

My dear readers, there's something you need to know about your old pal Jackson. Professor Moriarty has always been my idol. I mean, come on, he's an icon for a reason. A criminal mastermind who used his intelligence and resources not only to go up against Sherlock Holmes, but also to provide criminals with winning strategies and protections from the law, all in exchange for a fee or a cut of profit.

Sound familiar?

My entire villain model had been based on this guy. And sure, he didn't seem pleased when I joined the Mind Fire Calling, but I'd dazzle him in class. If I'm anything, it's charming as fuck.

But I'd first need to get some sleep.

Unlike Keith, I took the time to remove my clothes and put them in the wardrobe, whereupon I found a variety of clothes in my size, including school uniforms, athletic wear, and pajamas. Once properly dressed, I turned out the lights and got into bed.

"Goodnight, friend."

"Goodnight, Keith," I said.

I lay there, letting the events of the day wash away while allowing a well-deserved sleep claim me. But before I drifted away, I was unfortunately privy to an unwanted sound.

No, it was not snoring. These dulcet tones were far worse.

I was the lone appreciator of a mid-thirties pig boy masturbating. It appeared that—roommate or not—Keith had a nightly ritual and he'd be gods damned if my presence was going to change that. After several minutes of sausage slapping, Keith reached a *Deliverance*-like crescendo. A high-pitched squeal of ecstasy followed a thump, and he was out cold.

It seemed the little piggy finally went to market.

Today might have been rocky at best, but tomorrow would be a good day.

I was going to own this school.

HELL WEEK: DAY 1 - WHERE I AM THE EXAMPLE, CHAT WITH A YOUNG BAT MAN, AND AM MOCKED FOR MY SWIMWEAR

"You're late, Blackwell!" Grendel's Mother screamed when I reached the field on that warm Monday morning.

"I know… ma'am," I huffed as I limp-slash-jogged up to the other freshman students standing in line.

My still sore and now bleeding inner thighs were on display because Possibility thought it would be a hoot to transform my sweatpants into sweat shorts. The really pervy kind made popular in the seventies.

Please, don't Google this unless you want to see your parents' hairy junk on full display. Or maybe you do? Freud was right about a few things.

"Coach Mother."

"Excuse me?"

"*Coach Mother*," she repeated. "You will always refer to me as Coach Mother, or simply Coach. Do you understand."

"Yes, Coach… *Mother?*"

"And why are you late, Blackwell?"

I tried not to sigh.

Dear reader, this technique is used by shitty teachers, shittier parents, and all drill instructors since the beginning of time. Find the smallest fault, blow it out of proportion, make the subject squirm, repeat. But I'd recently been through Titan basic training.

And once you've been through it, you know the trick of defeating it. Speak with authority and without excuse.

Problem was, my excuses were just that, excuses.

I could try explaining that my roommate not only masturbated before bed, but also suffered from night terrors. Constant waking to a pig-boy screaming due to vivisection PTSD did not make for restful slumber. Additionally, I'd never received the actual campus tour. Despite having the academy guidebook, its crude map was cryptic at best. And asking for directions from my fellow academics resulted in me being chased and nearly killed.

Twice.

But instead of saying all that, I simply bowed my head in apologies and said, "I'm sorry, Coach. It will not happen again."

"I don't believe you, Mr. Blackwell," Coach said. "And true villains do not apologize. Five deathmerits on your record."

There was this sound, like a funeral toll, that rang out five times from the stone in my hand. Damn it.

According to the guidebook, each student could gain or lose deathmerits. Which, as the name implies, is a demerit system. Once you reached one hundred deathmerits, it counted as a kill and you died. It wasn't so bad, considering you'd come back the next morning. But for one, you'd miss out on all your daily classes, and more importantly, the school's point system heavily weighed the least number of deaths. Ergo, this was not something I wanted.

"Timeliness," Coach Mother continued, "is the key to all successful villains. No matter if it is a bank heist, burning an orphanage, or sacking a peasant village, timing is everything. And to be on time, you need to be *capable* of being on time. My job is making sure you are physically capable. I had planned on making your first day memorable by introducing you freshmen to our school's beloved sport, slaughterball. But instead, I think it will be memorable in another way. Thanks to Mr. Blackwell, you will spend the remainder of gym running the mountain stairs."

Every eye swung my way.

I thought about trying to explain that because this was "Hell Week," Coach Mother likely did it to every freshman class. But I held my tongue. People who allowed emotion to overrule logic were morons, and right now I was surrounded by them.

Besides, it wouldn't be that bad. Many of these people had abilities, and a simple run would be no problem for—

"Oh, and no powers!" Coach Mother announced.

The eyes that were on me had grown a wee bit madder. Coach Mother pulled a whistle out from between her leathery ogre boobs. She blew it twice.

"Now run without powers!"

Our legs began to move on their own, bereft of abilities and compelled by whatever magic was in that whistle. We all began jogging off the field, towards the awaiting stairs. And although our bodies were forced into motion, nothing stopped my fellow freshmen from making sure I had an extra memorable day.

"What the crap, Jackson?!" Lydia said, slapping her tray down and taking a seat to my left.

The colossal subterranean cavern deep inside the mountain serving as the cafeteria was a loud and kinetic mess. Kids rushed in from all over to wolf down meals or socialize before their next class. The air smelled of stale, stagnant water, mass-produced breakfast foods, and teenagers in various states of cleanliness. Apparently, only the freshmen had gym first thing in morning, which was then followed by mandatory showers. But the rest of the student body, despite being villains, were exactly like every other teenager.

They were BO-generating machines.

"It wasn't my fault," I said, trying to eat my oddly wet scrambled eggs in peace.

"Then whose was it?" she demanded.

"Just—just let me eat, please."

"You gonna eat your apple?" she asked.

"Take it," I said. "They make me gassy anyway."

"I've seen you eat apples before."

"Not human me," I said. "Besides, I hurt so bad that even bringing food to my mouth, let alone chewing an apple, is an exercise in pain management."

Which was all true. But I needed nourishment, so I pushed through one bite of eggs at a time. That was until one of the other freshmen, a tall, bat-like Nosferatu-looking dork from the

Twilight Veil with glasses, came up to my table and slapped the fork out of my hand. I watched the utensil, and my protein, land on the cavern floor.

"I was eating that," I said, too tired to get up.

"You were," the bat boy stressed, then pressed his fists down on the table next to me. A pair of zombies from They Who Hunger flanked him. "Who do you think you are, screwing us all over like that?"

"A villain?" I said, looking up at him. "Crazy, I know, what with being in a school for villains."

"So, you admit it?"

"Listen, whatever your name is—"

"Prince Burresh of the Arcavian Clan," he said.

"No way I'm gonna remember all that," I said, picking up my eggs with my fingers and eating a bite. "I'm just gonna call ya Burt. See Burt, it wasn't my plan to be late. But it happened. We ran. You all chased me and knocked me down the stairs many, many times. I'm in pain. It's done. Get over it."

"Maybe I'm not over it?" Burt said, bearing his fangs. "How about I kill you now?"

"*Hmm*," I said, considering his question while I picked up another couple mouthfuls of food. Ultimately, I shook my head in the negative. "Nah, I'm good."

"What?"

"Had you said something cool like, 'I'll be seeing you soon,' maybe I'd be scared. But you didn't. If you wanna go over there, practice some new lines for ten minutes or so, we can try again."

The bat boy, no longer amused by our back-and-forth, reached back with a clawed hand to tear out my throat. But his wrist was snatched by a muscular young black man with glasses and huge hair. Burt spun around to find a waiting Wraith Knight.

My former minion, despite holding two stacked breakfast trays in one hand, easily restrained the skinny vampire who was now searching for backup. It was only then that Burt realized that his sidekicks were both in a headlock thanks to Myst in her gorillapus form.

It was good to have friends.

"Walk away before I take away your ability to walk," Wraith Knight told the vampire boy.

"See, *that's* the kind of line you should have delivered," I told Burt, finishing my eggs before moving on to my bacon.

Pro tip, take one or two bites of bacon at the start of breakfast. Then save the rest for the end. No matter how good or bad the rest of the food is, you want to end every meal with a positive memory.

Burt sneered at Wraith Knight. "Like you could hurt me, *henchman*."

"The Arcavian Clan of Horriech are a bestial type of vampire, shunned by the more human-passing and the Sanguine Nobility," Wraith Knight rattled off as if reading from a monster manual. Still holding the boy's arm, WK leaned in, "While not as susceptible to things like running water, the Arcavian Clan is incredibly weak to silver and fire. I hear that Baba Yaga's class is labs-based. It would be a shame if a lowly henchman were to *accidentally* misplace some silver thread or start a fire."

"This isn't over," the vampire spat.

"Yes it is," Wraith Knight said, letting the boy's wrist go. "Now get the fuck out of here before I actually get mad."

Myst let the zombies go, and the trio scampered off to lick their wounds. WK set his and Myst's breakfast down, and the pair took a seat across from me and Lydia at the bench-style table. I noticed more than a few sets of eyes watching us, including Sophia and her cronies.

She mimed tipping a hat.

I gave her the finger.

"What happened to your uniform?" Myst asked.

I let out a small sigh. The school uniform had been a simple black blazer and pants combo with grey pinstripes. But the moment I put mine on after gym, the pants shrank, turning back into a pair of schoolboy short pants.

"It seems that Possibility refused to allow me even a shred of dignity."

"I don't care about the pants, boss," Wraith Knight said before digging into his food. "We have to have a talk about your attitude."

"Me?"

"Mm," he grunted while chewing. "You, the you of right now, is gonna get yourself killed, a lot, if you don't knock it off."

"That's what I was trying to tell him," Lydia added over a buttered English muffin.

"And where were you during all that?" I asked.

"Right here doing nothing," my ex-wife said. "I wanted you to get cut. You made us all suffer in gym."

"It wasn't his fault," Myst said, eating her bowl of cottage cheese and fruit. "Coach Mother was going to make us do that no matter what."

"You're defending him?" Lydia asked, spitting crumbs.

Myst shrugged. "Just stating the truth."

"Friggin' Mild Fire Bawling," Lydia mumbled over another mouthful of carbs.

"What?" I asked.

Wraith Knight looked to Lydia, who shook her head.

"Out with it."

"It's what their path calls yours," Myst informed me while Lydia let out an exasperated sigh.

"You told her?"

Wraith Knight hung his head. "She's my girlfriend."

"What's all this now?" I asked.

"Your house is basically Vizzini," Wraith Knight said.

"Who?" I asked.

"Wallace Shawn's character from *The Princess Bride*," Wraith Knight said. "Physically the weakest but think they're the most important."

"Aw, babe," Myst said.

"I'm trying to be better."

"And," Lydia added, "the path that complains the loudest then shifts blame when things go tits up."

"Where the crap are you hearing this?"

"Our upperclassmen told us all about it in our common room last night," Wraith Knight said.

"And we talked about it some more in our room."

"*Our* room?" I asked, looking between them. "You two are roommates?"

"Well, obviously. You think I'm gonna room with some rando… or Eris?" Lydia said, glancing over at the sad-looking girl sitting at Sophia's table, then shuddering. "No thank you. I know Wendell and we're just fine."

"You didn't tell me that," Myst said, eyeing her boyfriend.

"I didn't want you to think there was anything going on," Wraith Knight said a little sheepishly.

"And you thought *not* telling me would help?"

"How's Eris?" I asked, ignoring the brewing lovers' quarrel. "Gym wasn't the best time for me to get a read on her. I'm assuming you two had some interaction with her last night?"

"Dunno," Wraith Knight said. "She died during the pop quiz, then reappeared in her room this morning. She didn't say much to anyone."

"Can you blame her?" Lydia said. "She didn't exactly take her path selection well."

We all stared at her.

"What? Okay, I may have overreacted a bit."

"You told the headmaster, publicly, to kiss your ass," Wraith Knight said.

"*After* pulling a knife on Professor Renfield," Myst added. "You know, *the head* of your path?"

"I said I *may have overreacted!*" Lydia hissed. "But… after talking to some of the upperclassmen, I'm seeing the benefit to this path."

"Really?" I asked, not believing her. "That doesn't sound like you."

"Like you've ever known what I think or want," she sniped.

Ah, exes. Nothing but quality, supportive conversation.

Wraith Knight jumped in, breaking the awkward tension. "The other students in our path helped us realize that in most cases, hench—eh, villain support personnel—are like nurses to doctors, the ones with the real power doing most of the work."

I blinked a few times.

"You uh—you really believe that?" I asked. "Because if you need lifesaving surgery, who you gonna call?"

"Come on, boss," Wraith Knight said. "The Three Storms in *Big Trouble in Little China* outshined Lo Pan. Bellatrix Lestrange was way cooler than Voldemort. What about Gogo in *Kill Bill*, Jaws in James Bond, or Darth Maul? They were all the scene stealers."

"And they all died," I added, pointing out the obvious.

"I… well, shit."

I saw what WK was getting at, and for his sake I nodded along. "I know what ya mean, big guy. But my question was, how is Eris dealing? I'm sure in her mind she thought she was a player, only to realize she's Sophia's pawn to get at me."

"Well, she isn't looking great," Lydia said, shifting her eyes slightly away from the table.

I hazarded my own glance over at their table. Eris looked tired, but so were most of the freshmen. It was the spark in her eye, or rather its absence, that I noted.

I looked for Evie and spotted her at a far table, laughing with students from all the paths. Each student seemed to be a powerhouse in their respective fields, including that big golem girl, Beatrice.

Lydia leaned over, rising just a little in her seat to catch a glance.

"I should go talk to her."

"Bad idea," Wraith Knight said.

"No one asked you, Wendell," Lydia hissed.

"Everyone calm down," I said. "We have our next class in a few minutes."

"Which brings me back to my original point," Wraith Knight said. "You need to lay low and not call more attention to yourself. I won't be there every time to bail you out of trouble."

"What do you think I'm trying to do?" I asked.

"Wait, was there another time?" Myst asked. "You didn't mention anything else."

The big nerd looked a touch flustered. "It uh, it was just before breakfast."

"Gym?"

"After that," Wraith Knight said.

"There isn't a class between—oh," Myst said.

"What?" Lydia asked.

"The showers," I said. "WK is talking about the showers after gym."

Lydia blinked in confusion. "What happened?"

Wraith Knight looked to me for permission. I just shrugged. It would be talked about sooner or later. Might as well rip that bandage off.

"Go ahead."

"Jackson, he—uh, he kinda wore a swimsuit in the showers."

The girls looked at me, and I gestured to below the table.

"I'm a gods damned underdeveloped twelve-year-old," I said. "Do the math."

They laughed at me throughout the rest of breakfast and all the way to our next class.

Remember just a few moments ago when I said it was good to have friends? Never mind. Friends suck.

CHAPTER 20

HELL WEEK: DAY 1 - WHERE I FEAR CHICKEN LEGS, TALK AROUND BOOBS, AND ALMOST MAKE A DEAL WITH A DEVIL

"Welcome to Neophyte Skills and Powers," Baba Yaga called down from her house's front porch.

For those who know the legends, yes, her house was indeed a rustic, two-story cabin that sat atop a pair of colossal ambulatory chicken legs. The freshman class had followed instructions and gathered in the forested glen nestled in a valley along the eastern slope of the mountain. We'd been wondering exactly what this class was when the hut showed up.

The white-haired, wart-nosed old witch smiled down on us, revealing a mouthful of iron teeth. She extended a jaundiced, leathery arm and pointed deeper into the woods.

"Today is a simple assessment. To teach you how to better use your abilities, I need to know how you react in high-pressure situations. So run, my little chicks, run!"

Before we could ask a question, the chicken hut began to move. It took one earth-rumbling step towards us all, and the crone of Slavic folklore cackled with glee.

Ahh… crap. More running.

All the freshmen, myself included, scattered. I looked for my allies but found that they'd all gone their separate ways, doing everything they could just to stay alive. I thought about calling them on my hand rock, but not knowing the layout of the land meant any directions given were pointless. And with Baba Yaga in motion, I couldn't take the time to orient myself. So I picked a direction at random and ran as fast as I could.

Which of course was not very fast at all. Damn shame too because the chicken hut seemed to be hunting the chubby, slower kids first. To my right, an overweight hunchback goblin girl with a wooden leg loped along beside me.

In fact, she might've actually been passing me.

Oh, fuck me. Behold, the once great and feared Shadow Master, barely keeping pace with a one-legged fat kid. But what's the adage when being chased in the woods by a bear?

You don't have to be faster than the bear, just faster than the person beside you.

"Sorry not sorry!" I said, then kicked her peg leg out from under her.

With a string of guttural curses, the goblin girl tumbled tits over teakettle. She tried to scream "you suck!" but all heard was "Yoush—" before Baba Yaga's hut's right foot crushed her with a squishy pop.

Ugh. My uniform was ruined.

We've all seen *Jurassic Park*. If righty just pulped Dildo Baggins there, then that left foot, and yours truly, were next. Pivoting as skillfully as a plump kid could, I kinda dove but mostly jelly rolled to the side, narrowly avoiding my fate.

"Not bad, Mr. Blackwell," Baba Yaga called out. The house paused its rampage so that the professor could have a brief conversation. "Good instincts, but what's your big brain going to do against my bigger house?"

"How—how about when I get out of… here, oh dear lord, I give you your—your own planet to… dominate?" I loudly panted, clearly offering the professor a bribe while trying to get my wind back. "Or maybe a… team-up? You, my old client Frau Kinderfresse, and a couple of other crones? The market's ripe for a witchy *Golden Girls* knockoff."

"So nothing but run your mouth then?" Baba Yaga sighed. "Too bad, I expected better."

"Better than what?" I asked. "I can't use my powers here. All I have is my mind and this useless body."

"And what's stopping you from learning new skills or powers? *Hmm*?" she asked. "A villain who's a one-trick pony is future glue."

Damn… that was a good line. I was totally stealing it.

"Well, maybe you'll do better tomorrow," she said, conjuring a magical fireball in her hand.

"Oh, bloody hell," I said.

Just as the old witch wound up her pitching arm to hurl flaming death at my face, I caught a shadow of movement coming in fast.

"Jackson, hands up!"

I didn't even hesitate. When presented with a choice of either facing a fiery ball of death or trusting a mysterious plot contrivance, you choose the contrivance. I threw my arms up and I felt strong hands clamp down on my wrists and haul me skyward, just as the fireball hit the ground.

The roaring flames crackled and burned beneath me, adding a few new blisters to my already damaged legs. But at least I was alive and flying through the air.

Well… kinda.

I was, at best, twelve feet or so off the ground, and that number drastically shifted based on my savior's skill and wind current.

"For the love all that's unholy, how much do you weigh?!" my rescuer grunted.

Looking up to see who'd saved me did no good because of her… uhh, *hmm*.

What's the best way to describe a teenage girl's big breasticles without being a perv?

Fuck it, it's impossible. Sorry folks. We're gonna have to forgo narrative mystery on this one and just be blunt.

Mikalya the succubus—who like me was a legal adult trapped in the body of her teenage self—had flown in on her demon wings to save me. And the reason I couldn't see shit was because her anything-but-aerodynamic endowments were not only blocking my view, but the damn things were basically sitting on my forehead.

See why I had to spell it out? No way you could get away with imagery like this in a real YA book.

"Seriously," she grunted, "did you eat bacon-fried mayonnaise for breakfast?"

"There's no reason to be shitty!" I yelled back, trying to see anything but boobs. "Believe it or not, guys can also be sensitive about their weight!"

"I don't—*argh*—care about your feelings, I care about weight-to-thrust ratios!"

The demoness with the thick glasses awkwardly swooped, banked, and steered us through the woods. But it was clear she was getting tired.

"Ah fuck it, good enough."

"What do you mean good e—"

Mikayla let go and I fell, hitting a tree branch stomach-first. The impact knocked the wind, a few tears, and a fart out of me. But my descent wasn't over. No. I flipped over backwards, all flailing limbs with zero cool, and crashed down into what had to be the world's hardest bush. I wish that'd been a sex joke. Alas, it was not. It was a painful, prickly reality.

I lay there panting, groaning, and assessing the damage when Mikalya banked around and landed gracefully next to me. She folded her wings around herself like a cloak and didn't even act like she heard the obvious sounds of stomping and screaming kids.

To be fair, the sounds were further away, and we seemed to be safe. Mikayla offered me a hand up. I was fairly sure I had a pinecone stuck halfway up my ass, so I took the offered assistance.

"Thank you," I said as she used her far superior demonic strength to pull me free.

"You're welcome," she said once I was on my feet. "So, you're probably wondering why I helped you."

"No, that part's—*ahh*, damn it— easy," I said, pulling thorns and splinters out of my bloody wounds.

"Oh?"

"Lydia," I said. "You want me to help smooth things over with Lydia, right?"

"Well, yes," she admitted.

"Figures. Well, saving me from Baba Yaga was the perfect opportunity to grease the wheels, as it were. That being said, your new friends gonna be cool with you saving me?"

"They all scattered. Other than Baba Yaga, no one's seen us together."

"Okay, you have my attention," I said. "What's going on? Why haven't you talked to Lydia yourself?"

"You don't think I've tried?" Mikayla said. "She won't even acknowledge me."

"Well, what did you expect?" I asked. "Big hugs, sloppy kisses, and scissoring?"

The succubus rolled her eyes. "Could you be more of an ignorant douche?"

"Yes," I said flatly. "You seduced my wife, banged her brains out while I was mere feet away just to piss me off, and let's not forget the whole 'you made her forget she had a child' thing!"

"First, fuck you," Mikalya said, her hands on her hips. "Don't do the whole 'you wronged me' crap to justify being a prick. You killed me in Caledon just to further your own motivations. And dying in a fantasy world meant my soul went to the Never Realm. I came back as a succubus because my only other option was eternal torment. Second, yes, I was sent to find her. However, *she* came onto *me*, not the other way around. But what you may not have known is that Y'olly had sub-leased my contract to Valliar and Khasil. *They* compelled me to make Lydia forget about Evie. I literally had no choice."

"And the other part?" I asked. "The whole Richter Scale sex thing?"

"Please, you've partied in the Never Realm. You know how we get down."

I nodded; she wasn't wrong. In fact, she wasn't wrong about any of it.

Looking back on my life, things had been easier when I was an island unto myself. The moment I added friends and family is when things got complicated. I sighed in frustration, then centered myself.

"Mikayla, or Bethany, if you prefer—"

"*Mikayla*," the teenage succubus said, stressing the name. She tapped the side of her head between her curled horns and raven black hair. "Bethany Madison Jacobs is in here, deep down, but that's not who, or what, I am anymore."

"And I'm not the same Jackson who hired that quirky girl with thrift-store clothes and face tats all those years ago. I'm still a villain, mind you, but an evolved one."

"What are you getting at?" Mikayla asked.

Ugh. The truth really was a villain's nemesis.

"I wronged you, Beth—Mikayla, I know I did. I killed you back in Caledon because I had to, as you said, further my own motivations. You were a victim of my narcissism. If you want, when this is all over, I'll do what I can to get your old life back."

"Are you kidding?" she asked, gesturing to herself. "Even the gawky teen demon version of me is hot AF. No way I'm going back."

She was right. Even in glasses and a school uniform, she was stupidly attractive. Huh. Maybe more so?

Yeah, let's not go down this path.

I looked Mikayla in the eyes. "Do you love her?"

"Whoa, let's not bring out the L-word."

"Answer the gods damned question."

"I—yes, I think I do?" she admitted. "What we had was real. Or, well, real enough with a demon. She was an assignment, but I cared for her. It's cliché, but it's the truth. But every time I try and tell her, she—"

"Walks away or pulls out the knives?" I asked. When she gave me an odd look, I chuckled. "I was married to her."

Was.

If she and I couldn't be together, did I want her to be happy? Oh, dear gods above and below, was I growing as a person? Did I want my ex to actually be happy without me? What kind of New Age, "let the past go" crap was this?!

Nobody wants their ex to be happy. That's why Facebook really exists, isn't it? To keep tabs on your past relationships and see how miserable, or hopefully fat, they became? Man, the joy you get from seeing a forlorn love balloon up like a carbo-blimp? *Mwa!*

Oh, don't judge me. People say they don't wish bad things for their exes, but they don't mean it. People are two-faced walking crap factories, and I think I speak for the majority of us when I say that we want our exes to be jaded, poor, and sexually dissatisfied.

However, there really was no future for Lydia and me. Not anymore. And I didn't hate her. I wasn't sure if Mikayla was right for her, but even I wasn't blind to the reality that they were a better fit.

Insert another scissoring joke here.

"Then what're you offering?" I asked. "Let's say I talk to her, what's the quid pro quo?"

"I—I don't know," Mikayla said, deflating a bit. "I have no idea what Sophia's play is. And as far as she and the others are concerned, I'm a support player at best. But since this is a YA setting, connections have to be made as close to the first day as possible. You know that. So, I'm asking for your help."

She wasn't wrong.

Fiction, especially YA fiction, loves it when kids meet in a school-like setting on the first day and become soulmates. But I refused to do anything for free.

"I could always use a spy again," I said. "One inside Sophia's gang."

It was clear she wanted to say something but couldn't. There was sweat on her brow as she fought something. She was on the brink of her mental reserves.

"You're still under a compulsion, aren't you?" I asked. "Even here, you can't work openly work against Sophia and her gang, can you? Not while Y'olly holds your contract."

Without another word, Mikalya took to the sky, flying away.

"When you have something to offer, you'll know where to find me!" I called after her, a smile on my face.

The smile faded when I felt the tremors once more. Baba Yaga and her gods damned hut were on the way.

Running. Why did it always come down to running?

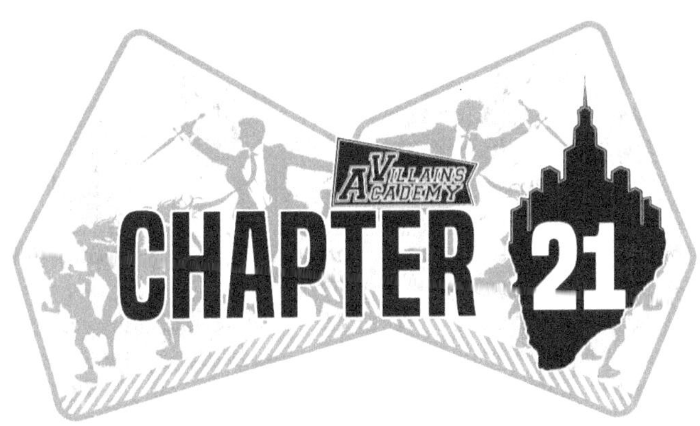

CHAPTER 21

HELL WEEK: DAY 2 - WHERE I RECEIVE A WARNING, SPEAK THE TRUTH, AND FEEL ANALLY VIOLATED

By the time Monday had come to an end, I was sitting on the couch in the Mind Fire Calling's common room, unmoving. Evie popped in, looked at me, and laughed.

"Hell week, huh?"

"I'm never running again," I announced, knowing it would be a lie.

She looked around to make sure we were alone, then plopped down next to me and slapped me hard on the thigh.

"You're out of the will," I flatly told her.

"If I want anything from your old empire, I'll just take it," she said with a smile. "So how was the day?"

I groaned, as even recalling data was an exercise in pain. "After gym, Baba Yaga chased us through the woods on her hut just to see what we could do. After a mediocre lunch, we had Basic Potent Potions, with Dr. Jekyll."

"Oh yeah," Evie mused. "I remember those. So how many freshmen are left?"

"Very few," I said, gesturing around the common room that was bereft of first-year students.

"Well, rest up, Dad. Tomorrow is gonna be worse."

Worse? How was it going to be worse?

It *was* worse. So much worse.

How many of you out there have ever made a New Year's resolution to get in shape? Maybe you've never worked out or were on a prolonged absence. Regardless, it isn't the day you work out that sucks… it's the day after.

Everything, and I mean everything, hurt. I'm not just talking about my ligaments, muscles, and cartilage. I mean every gods damned part of my being from tits to toes ached on a subatomic level. Which of course meant that the walking canker sore of a classic literary villain had us running the mountain stairs.

Again.

"Running's good for you," Coach Mother bellowed from the stairs' midpoint, her cruel eyes ever watching.

Each footstep sent vibrations of anguish across my already wrecked body. And while I was not alone in my misery, I couldn't help but notice that many of my peers seemed to be… fine?

Better than fine, really. The uppity fucks seemed to be rejuvenated. But before I could ponder it further, Coach Mother was again extolling the virtues of this barbaric form of exercise.

"Aside from the endorphins," Coach Mother boomed, "running increases bone strength, promotes weight loss, and tightens your core."

"And it causes stress fractures, shin splints, and a condescending sense of superiority," I muttered under my breath.

There was a sharp, piercing whistle burst followed by Coach Mother's booming voice. "Stop!"

Under the compulsion of her magic whistle, the entire freshman class ceased running all at once. Yeah, this wasn't good.

"Something you wanna say, Blackwell?"

"No, Coach," I said, snapping off the response just as I had in Titan basic training.

"Uh huh," she said, before putting the whistle to her lips and giving it a short blow. "Tell me what you really think."

"Running is dumbest exercise for the dumbest people," I said, compelled by the magic of her bloody whistle. "Countless other high intensity interval training methods produce superior results to running. Because running's been the primary means for the poor and stupid to get from point A to point B for centuries, the idiotic practice lives on in soccer and running is the only way third world countries can compete in the Olympics. The good thing about running is the number of annoyingly vocal white people it breaks, cripples, and kills annually."

"I see," Coach Mother said. "Anything else?"

I didn't want to say what was on my mind. But thanks to her damn whistle, my lips moved on their own.

"The reason is painfully clear why those in They Who Hunger are required to run. Most of them will end up as stock horror movie rejects who chase sex-crazed teens or stalk mortals, so they need cardio. You can't be a winded werewolf and look cool. But the real reason you demand that they run to get good grades in your class is because anything beyond one foot in front of the other is too much mental effort."

Coach Mother stared at me, a grin on her face. "Y'ollgorath!"

"Here, Coach!" Y'olly said, stepping out of the crowd.

"You knew Jackson from before, correct?"

"Yes, Coach?"

"Hurt him for the rest of the gym. But don't kill him," she cautioned the demon. "Death is a release from the pain here at Sablestone Academy, and I want this smart-mouthed little shit to suffer. The rest of you, double-time it back to the practice field for some of Jackson's high-intensity interval training."

"Yes, Coach!" the class said in unison, each one glaring at me.

The whistle blew and everyone did as instructed. I tried to run, but made it a total of two steps before I felt a huge hand on the back of my neck. Y'olly picked my chubby butt up and tossed me *down* the stairs.

Fun fact: Tumbling several flights over rough stone won't kill you. But it will hurt like unholy hell. By the time I reached the next landing I was bruised, bloody, and all but broken. And that was when Y'olly landed on top of me with what I could only describe as an atomic elbow.

"What—*ah*, gods damn it!" I cursed.

I wasn't going to cry, I wasn't going to cry, I wasn't going to cry—

I cried.

"What—what happened between us, man?" I managed to say between gasping, snotty sobs.

"Short version? You stopped having fun," the big demon said with a shrug. "We tore it up back in the day. But once your recorded adventures started coming out and you became a family man, you lost your cool factor. You got old, hoss, plain and simple. All your villainy was suddenly about creating subversive methods of order and control. You forgot the fun factor. Blowing shit up or burning shit down is cool."

Well, he wasn't wrong. I had grown up. At least a bit.

Young villains, just like any other young person really, are prone to acts of spectacle. Shock and awe levels of villainy. I'm talking about garish outfits, giant letter-shaped fortresses, the desire to carve your name into the moon for all to see.

But let's be real—that kind of villainy is bluster and peacocking. Dominating everything and everyone seems like a lofty goal, but it's shortsighted. If you think it through, once you have control of or have killed off all opposition… then what? Who's gonna run the bloody city, kingdom, or galaxy? Seriously, what does the average villain even know about sanitation, infrastructure, or economic development? That's why power, real power, comes from subversive levels of control.

Trust me on this, folks. If you think a world leader or political cabinet has power, then you're completely missing the billionaire or megacorp conglomerate pulling their strings. The ones who enjoy the fruits of their—and especially *your*—labor so that they can live in luxury.

To grow, either as villain or as a person, you have to cast off the patterns of your youth. Sure, enjoy the occasional explosion or sophomoric romp like my recorded adventures. But those are the exceptions, not the rule. There's a reason only the very young—or the very stupid—still have a *Scarface* poster hanging on their wall. For only they, again, the very young and/or stupid, believe that idolizing aggressive ambition that leads to downfall is in any way cool.

But my old pal Y'olly, a nigh-immortal being, would forever be stuck as that stereotypical college douche who refuses to grow up. The kind of person who still uses the nickname they had when they were twenty, prefaces each sentence with the word "bro," and thinks that 90s-era Jim Carrey or Adam Sandler movies are the pinnacle of comedy.

"So—so that's it then?" I said, wincing as I tried to get up. "We're done?"

"Yeah, pretty much," he said, dropping another elbow into the small of my back.

I was worried that the beating might cause me to piss myself. But good news: I was pretty sure my kidneys were dangerously close to failure.

"What—what about the others?" I choked out. "They... *nngh*, hate me that much too?"

"Dunno," Y'olly said, picking up my leg and putting me in an ankle lock.

I screamed while the big demon applied just enough pressure to make the hold hurt beyond belief, but not to keep me from passing out from the pain.

"You've fucked with the Caledon gods for so long that seeing you suffer is a vacation for them, even if Valliar's paladin heart isn't in it. As for King Stanley, my gut tells me that he's like any other nerd. As soon as they feel intellectually challenged, they lash out. You were a minor god who saved him and his whole universe from Randy's plot. And now you're the Titan that owns his universe? No way that's sitting well with the old guy. And do I even need to count the ways you messed things up with Sophia? Face it, Jacky-boy. Your Shadow Master days are behind you."

"If the gods don't abdicate, their worlds could die," I said, trying anything to get out of this.

"And?" he said, keeping the pressure on. "The less they know the better. And when Sophia beats you, you'll cease to exist in any way, shape, or form. Which just means that the next Titan will take over."

"Will they be as much fun?"

I felt the pressure lessen just a hair and I squirmed, slipping my foot free from my shoe in the way that only a bullied chubby kid could. Bereft of one sneaker, I tried to get my feet under me to run away, but Y'olly was faster. The demon held me tight by the back of my gym shorts.

Oh... please no.

"Y'olly, look, you don't need to—ah, fuck me running!"

Yes, dear reader, it had happened. Y'ollgorath, Exalted One from the Eighth Plane of the Never Realm, had given me a wedgie.

I hung there a foot off the ground while what felt like a mile of cheap cotton violated the sanctity of my pre-teen butthole.

"You—you sure you weren't—ah shit, weren't supposed to go into They Who Hunger?" I grunted. "You're a great bully."

"You're not wrong," he said, letting go and dropping me like garbage. "The Sablestone was this close to putting me in there. But in the end, I love the showmanship of being a demon. Spotlight isn't just my middle name. It's where I belong after all."

A bell rang out, signifying the end of gym, and thus, the end of the demon's compulsion. Still, the brute gave me one more kick in the ribs before jogging off.

I lay there, unmoving.

Save for the smile creeping across my face.

Sometimes you have to take a beating to get exactly what you need.

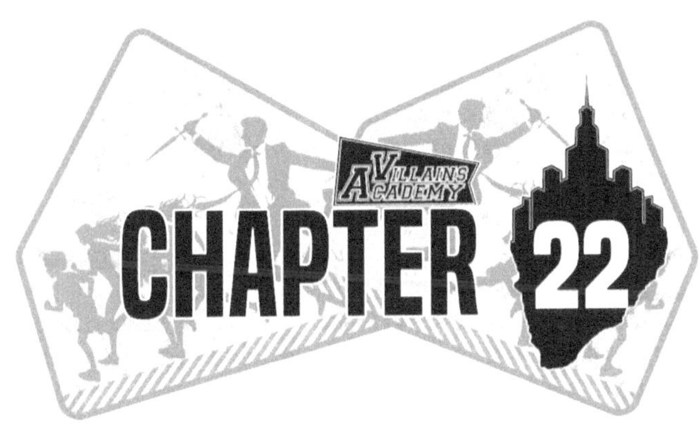

HELL WEEK: DAY 2 - WHERE I THROW SHADE AT A CULT CLASSIC, SOW THE SEEDS OF DOUBT, AND AM GIFTED WITH ARTWORK

"No no *no!* This is all wrong!" Professor Dracula loudly complained in his thick Transylvanian accent.

At least, I think it was Transylvanian.

Near as I could tell, he could have just been copying the Count from Sesame Street. But considering how bad I felt, I was happy just to sit in the open-air amphitheater and not move.

"I don't know what you want, Professor," Valliar said from center of the stage.

"But of course you don't."

Throwing back his cloak with a flourish, Dracula stood, transformed into a bat, and flew the whole fifteen feet or so from his front seat to the stage. He reformed with a puff of smoke into his classic pale-skinned, widow-peaked self. The iconic vampire thrust one hand forward, pointing his forefinger and pinky at the elvish-looking teenage god.

"Dark Mystique for Beginners is a course designed to instruct villains on being the master of the room," Dracula said to the old god in a young god's body. "To bask in the glory of the audience's collective awe, you must give them something awe-inspiring. And an introduction followed by the maniacal laugh is crucial."

Sigh. See what I mean about theater people?

By now I'm sure a few of you fans out there are about to call bullshit on your ol' pal Jackson. Especially with me having mentioned my acting and improv classes multiple times throughout these adventures. But please, stay your hand. I took those classes to be a better liar. Full stop. What I am *not* is an attention-seeking narcissist who—

Okay, yeah, I just heard myself. Apologies.

While I may have a touch of those aforementioned quirks, I'm not a tool who reminds everyone about their theater experience every chance they get. The booming-voiced, pseudo-cultured thespian twat who creams their jeans the moment anyone mentions *Sweeney Todd* or *Rocky Horror.*

Especially *Rocky Horror.* Gods above and below, that thing just... sucks.

Save your gasps, nerds. I've heard it all before, and I don't give a shit.

Yes, Tim Curry's an icon, and it was a cult classic about sexual liberation. But I'm here to tell you that play-slash-flick is way more cringy than you remember. Gonna be blunt: If you condemn "Baby It's Cold Outside" as a problematic song instead of seeing a playful dance between the sexes, then you must accept the fact that Dr. Frank-N-Furter used his power, position, and ideals to sexually force himself onto both Brad and Janet.

Probably Rocky too, the more I think about it. Wasn't he like, a day old? Man, and we thought *Weird Science* and *Revenge of the Nerds* were all kinds of wrong.

Anyway, what was I saying?

Oh yeah, theater kids suck.

"I want you to try it again," Professor Dracula told Valliar. "But this time, imagine a sea of cowering peasants."

"Okay, I'll give it a shot," Valliar said.

The godling centered himself, cleared his throat, and took a step forward.

"Mu hah, ha ha ha... *ha?* I am your god, Valliar, kneel and... tremble?"

Dracula hung his head. "It is like you don't even care about instilling fear into the hearts of your supplicants."

"Well, I—"

"Just sit down," Dracula said, shaking his head. "You, Khasil, come up and try. See if you can do better than your brother."

The snake-haired teen got out of her chair and climbed onstage, exchanging a glance with her twin that looked both sympathetic and competitive.

Siblings. Always a weird dynamic.

Valliar took a seat in the amphitheater, far away from other students. Dracula had insisted that we space ourselves out so that we would focus on the stage and not on our friends. Which of course meant that every student was having private conversations thanks to the Sablestone conduits in the back of our hands.

Or as the kids called them, "rocky-talkies."

I tapped mine and in a low voice spoke. "Valliar."

The god looked down at his hand before turning to search the theater. He spotted me far in the back, then shook his head.

The amphitheater seemed to dim just a bit, and the temperature dropped several degrees. An earsplitting crash of thunder boomed throughout the room while a cloud of greenish-black smoke burst outwards from the stage. Purple lightning crackled and danced within the roiling darkness, silhouetting the shadowy form of writhing serpents.

"Lower your heads and cower, mortals, for the Queen of Cold and Darkness has come," Khasil's icy voice slithered on the wind. "Worship me or die! Mu ha hah haaa!"

"Bravo!" Dracula applauded.

"Seems like your sister is better suited to villainy than you are," I whispered into my rocky-talky.

"Leave me alone," Valliar whispered back.

"What're you even doing here?" I pressed. "We both know this isn't a place for you."

"Even gods of light allow atrocities to happen to keep a balance."

"*Balance*?" I snorted. "You think all the people of Caledon, to include your beloved elves, dying is balance?"

Valliar whipped his head around, narrowing his eyes. He lifted the rock to his mouth.

"That will never happen."

"It will if you don't abdicate your position," I informed him.

"You're lying."

"Normally, sure," I admitted. "But this time it's true. Without an appointed god in position, it will crumble. And if Sophia somehow beats me, what happens? Which Titan will come along next? Would they even want a dead universe? Don't answer me now, just think about it. But while you do, consider this: Sophia knew the whole time what would happen when she formed her little cabal."

"Bullshit," Vallair cursed.

"Y'olly knew," I countered. "Talk to him if you like. Why did she leave you and the other gods out of this equation? You already saw what happened to Eris. You think Sophia has your interests at heart?"

"And you do?"

"No, not really," I said. "But I care about what's mine. I own your world and I'm content with letting you run it. Better the devil—or Titan—you know, Val."

He thought on that for a few moments before speaking.

"How long until Caledon dies?"

"I'm not sure," I admitted. "I have caretakers in place, staving off the implosion. Maybe it'll last until the end of the school year, maybe not. But I promise you this—

Sophia does not care."

I ended the conversation after that. Best to let the god think on it. Villainy is just as much about waiting as it is about action.

"Blackwell!" Dracula called out. "Your turn."

I was way in the back, the stage was a long way away, and I was in a lot of pain.

"Move it!"

Ah, crap.

By the end of the second school day, and following a lackluster dinner, I was done. Mentally and most definitely physically done. First Year Anatomy & Biology for Dismemberment with Dr. Moreau had been a little boring for those of us who'd already been in the field. Still, thanks to Keith trying to… *ahem*, suck off an involuntary vivisection volunteer, I'd managed to steal some pharmaceutical-grade painkillers and accelerated healing meds during the distraction. So it wasn't a total waste of time.

Limping slightly from Y'olly's beating, I crossed the quad in silence, doing as much as possible to not draw attention. It's already been said, but I'll say it again: Schools are like prisons. Act weak and you will be seen as a target.

Head down, I made like I was ignoring the other students, all the while keeping an eye on the clusters of kids on the quad. The Mind Fire Calling tower was just ahead, and while I loathed the idea of stairs, the sweet siren song of my bed was calling. Even Keith's wank-a-thon wouldn't keep me from the sleep I so desperately needed.

But as I walked, I noticed that the nearby students were all looking away, as if the sky or the ground were suddenly very interesting.

Ah, crap.

I stopped and turned, expecting to see Y'olly or one of Sophia's crew following me. What I saw, ever so briefly, was a very large fist on a collision course with my very punchable face.

"Fuck!" I yelled, my cries drowned out by the audible crack of my nose breaking.

I fell without dignity onto my back, my book bag lost in the fall. Looking up, I saw a familiar figure looming over me. A patchwork girl with mismatched eyes.

"Hey there, freshie."

"Beatice, wasn't it?" I said, recalling the seven-foot golem girl's name.

"Yeah," she said, cracking her knuckles.

"And I'm assuming this visit has something to with our little scrap during the pop quiz on the first day?"

"More or less," she said, working her neck from side to side. "A freshman djinn girl told me what you said today about my path. You got something else you wanna say about Those Who Hunger before I break your neck?"

"No, not really," I admitted, sensing my impending doom.

Huh, maybe Wraith Knight was onto something? My attitude was not in fact winning over the student body. I pondered that thought for the rest of the waking day.

All seven seconds of it.

By the time I came to, it was full dark. My backpack was still there, but my pants and shoes were missing, and someone, or multiple someones, had taken the time to draw cartoon dicks all over my exposed skin.

The word was out; I was now a target. Yay.

CHAPTER 23

HELL WEEK: DAY 3 - WHERE I DISMISS ACADEMIC BESTIALITY, ENJOY A FEW TRUTHS, AND MAKE A PROMISE

"Seriously?" Myst said. "Right out in the open?"

"Mm," I grunted.

"It's been getting worse," Wraith Knight added. "After gym this morning, a few of the students jumped him in the showers before I could get there."

"Are you okay?" she asked.

I just glared at her from beneath my two black eyes, swollen split lips, and half dislocated jaw.

"Sorry, Jackson."

"I wish I'd been there," Lydia said.

"To help?" Myst asked.

Lydia stifled a snort. "No, so I could've watched."

I ignored my ex-wife's jibe and refocused on the class. Entry Level Manipulation & Social Engineering, with Professors Lady MacBeth and the Cheshire Cat, wasn't particularly engaging for me. I just didn't want to give Lydia the satisfaction of seeing me in pain.

Well, in more pain than usual.

"Eye contact is critical," Lady MacBeth said, continuing the lecture while walking the aisles between students. "You want to look your target in the eye for roughly sixty to seventy percent of the time. A bad liar maintains direct eye contact to appear truthful. Knowing when to look away is equally vital to selling your deceit."

"Agreed," said the Cheshire Cat from Lady MacBeth's shoulder, bunting at the Scottish woman's chin from time to time. "And as always, a winning smile, with a hint of mischief, can and will disarm most people. Even if they sense deception, the air of mystery you give off will keep them engaged."

"So, they're screwing, right?" Lydia whispered. "It's not just me?"

"Maybe," Myst said. "I don't know if they're screwing, exactly—"

"I hope not," Wraith Knight cut in. "Have you ever seen a cat penis? They're barbed. Plus, I think there's a size ratio thing we gotta consider. I know they say it's not the size of the boat, but the motion of the ocean. But you don't go to war in a canoe."

"Body language is also key when it comes to social engineering," Lady MacBeth droned on. "Careful observation of your target will provide you with subtle context clues."

"Indeed," the Cheshire Cat said, hopping down to twine about her legs. "How your target sits, points their feet, holds their posture will all give you insight into their subconscious thoughts and feelings."

"It may not necessarily be intercourse, but you're right, it's definitely something," Myst continued.

"Plenty of folks have voyeur-based kinks that are very satisfying," Lydia offered.

"What do they get out of it?" I asked.

"If I had to guess," Wraith Knight said squinting, "she… um, *pleasures herself* while he watches and licks his own butthole—"

"What the—*no!*" I hissed. "Not that, you moron. I'm talking about *them!*"

Inclining my chin slightly, I gestured towards the other side of the classroom, where Sophia and her crew sat.

"What about them?" Myst asked.

"What do they get out of coming here?" I said, rephrasing the question. "You all love me—"

"Not anymore," Lydia cut in, her words stabbing deeper than her knife.

"Fine," I spat, still not looking at her. "You all at least love Evie and came here to save her. But if we don't beat her group, we're stuck here. And I'm getting the feeling that their team doesn't realize they're in the same boat."

"Why do you say that?" Myst asked.

"Valliar," I said. "He didn't know about his and Khasil's world dying without abdication. Which makes me think Khasil and King Stanley didn't know either. Say what you will, but they love their worlds. And it's not like any of them to put that at risk, even on the chance of beating me and locking me away inside Possibility."

"That's not exactly true," Lydia said.

"Look, if you're just going to argue, would you—"

"You, we, aren't going to be locked away," she said, cutting me off. "Evie said during orientation that those without enough points to move on to the next year either repeat a year or are cast into the Nothingness, whatever that is. And they also heard the same thing."

That... was an excellent point. One I was kicking myself for forgetting. Gods damn this kid body and kid brain.

"When did you become so detail oriented?"

Lydia didn't answer. It was Wraith Knight who spoke up.

"In our path, or at least in our common room, we're taught that every great villain, especially ones who see themselves as academics, often forget the little things, and it's up to the hench—the *assistants* to remember."

"If for no other reason than to use information to destroy our potential bosses," Lydia added.

"And does Eris also receive these private lessons?" I asked, eyeing the girl.

"Sure?" Wraith Knight said. "We get a nightly lecture. Well, those who aren't dead do."

I filed that information away while circling back to Lydia's point. "Why would they be willing to bet their existence on beating me?"

"Have you met you?" Lydia said.

Eh, she had a point.

"And that is why the truth can be so much worse than a lie," the Cheshire Cat said. "When properly applied, a truth can make your target question their sanity."

"Wait, what the hell have the professors been talking about?" Lydia asked our little cluster. "I have no idea."

"Truth is a weapon," I replied. "Keep up."

"We're now going to practice," Lady MacBeth announced. She went to the front of the room and pulled out two unused chairs, placing them across from one another.

"When we call your names," the Cheshire Cat said as he hopped onto the desk and put on a pair of reading glasses, "we would like each of you to come forward, sit across from one another, and tell your partner a truth that will devastate them."

For the remainder of the class, pairs of students were called forward, sat across from one another, and told painful truths to the other. Or at least they tried to. The bulk were little more than mean-spirited observations based on a person's outward appearance or a backhanded compliment. A few of my favorites were "It must be great being a zombie, nobody expects you to be smart," "Wow, you're so well spoken for a Drow Elf," and my favorite, "The freshman fifteen looks good on you."

When my name was called, I sucked it up, hid my pain, and went to the front of the room. But when I heard my exercise partner, I smiled.

"King Stanley," Lady MacBeth said.

The pudgy god of nerds stood, finger-combed his long, greasy hair to one side of his face, adjusted his glasses, and walked to the front. We both sat down, facing one another.

"Hey there Stanley," I said, leaning forward on my elbows.

"Jackson," King Stanley replied with a smirking nod. "It's nice to know that even after you grow up, your legs stay the same size."

"I'm sorry, it's hard for me to take you seriously," I chuckled, crossing my chicken legs. "You look like an incel who's not allowed within five hundred yards of a school."

"Not your best work," the elder god said, shaking his head before letting out a small sigh. "But half-cooked is what we've come to expect from you."

"Says the has-been deity who chases trends instead of getting ahead of them," I scoffed. "But news flash, old timer: Sophia fucked you all over. Without the gods being in their universe, your worlds are going to die. It's just a matter of time. Unless, of course, you formally abdicate to a half-cooked Titan like me."

That one hit the old bastard; I could tell. He glanced back at Sophia, who remained stone-faced. King Stanley was pissed. Leaning forward, the elder god looked me directly in the eyes.

I smirked. "Go on, old boy. Give me your best—"

"About six months before Sophia killed you, Lydia and I had a conversation about her seeking asylum in my universe."

"… What?"

"Silence, Stanley," Sophia hissed.

King Stanley ignored her, his eyes sparkling with cruel delight.

"She was going to leave you," he continued. "She was going to take Evie and run away to one of my fantasy realm micro universes. I told her to wait a bit. To give you another chance. But I only said that so we could put the finishing touches on the plan to tear you down."

I thought about the blade in my inner pocket. About the distance between us and how I wanted to slice his throat. Then I thought about his ability to transform into any number of super-powered people, and how insignificant my weapon was.

I looked over at Lydia. Her lips were pursed. She knew better than to say anything right then.

"I believe King Stanley is the winner in this exercise," Lady MacBeth said. "Well done. Next time we will go over—"

"If you keep fucking with me," I began calmly as the fire in my heart turned cold, "then I promise you, whether or not I beat Sophia, I will kill you. And one way or another, I will take control of your world for my own, if only to piss on your creation."

Lady MacBeth looked to the cat and nodded. "Well done, Mr. Blackwell."

"Very well done," the Cheshire Cat added.

The class was quiet when I returned to my chair. The only sound was my hard-soled shoes clacking on the tile floor, punctuating my little victory with each step.

I felt kinda badass… right up until the Cheshire Cat knocked Lady MacBeth's coffee mug off the desk for no particular reason, causing the class to laugh.

Cats.

CHAPTER 24

HELL WEEK: DAY 4 – WHERE I TALK WITHOUT TALKING, SEARCH MY FEELINGS, AND REFUSE TO ESCAPE

"Jackson," Lydia called out. "Wait up."

Another downside to being this out of shape was that there never seemed to be an end to the pain. Coach Mother had taken my comment about high-intensity interval training to heart. The old troll had devised a rather brutal training regimen for gym this morning. Lemme tell ya, dear reader, you haven't lived until you've experienced simultaneous muscle failure and projectile vomiting while doing pushups.

As such, I didn't have the energy or willpower to hobble away from my ex-wife. So I turned to face her.

"What?"

"You've been avoiding me ever since yesterday," she said, stating the obvious.

"No shit."

She somehow managed to keep from rolling her eyes. Clearly, she was prepared for my level of enthusiastic engagement on this subject.

"Well, I thought that after some cooling off time you'd talk to me. I'd hoped to see you at breakfast, but you weren't there."

"I laid unmoving in a puddle of my own puke for the last bit of gym," I explained. "Kinda killed my appetite."

"Jackson, talk to me, please."

"No," I said, my hand coming up.

For what, I didn't know. A shove? A punch in the face? Maybe just the finger or a good old-fashioned choke? In the end, I did none of those things.

"Leave me the fuck alone," I told her without any emotion or passion. "I don't want to talk to you, be near you, or have anything to do with you. As far as I'm concerned, you don't exist."

I braced for the stabbing. That I was ready for.

Not the tears.

Lydia brought her books to her chest and stormed off, sniffling as she fought to maintain her self-control.

Shit, had it always been that easy to get rid of her?

Maybe you think I was too harsh, but as far as I was concerned, it was time for scorched earth. The thought of her leaving me had been bad enough. But taking my daughter away from me? Why? I may be an asshole, but I'm a good father.

… Aren't I?

Ever since King Stanley dropped that truth bomb, my mind had been a mess. I couldn't even escape it when I slept. My dream last night consisted of me living in a shitty one-bedroom dimension where I was old, bald, and fat. I sat in my recliner wearing a stained tank top eating a "goulash" made from ground beef, Manwich, and canned peas out of a square knockoff Tupperware container. My one-eyed, diabetic cat was waiting for me to die, presumably to eat me before finding a better owner. Instead of TV, I was cyber-stalking Lydia and Evie's social media on my phone, looking at the better life they had without me.

Look folks, I'm gonna be real with you. I've read a few of your comments about my recent recorded adventures not being as fun. Several of you don't like the fact that I have feelings. You want me to go back to the happy-go-lucky joke, fuck, kill, repeat kind of villain. To this I say:

What series have you been reading?

Lemme break it down for the slower readers at the back of the truncated yellow school transportation vehicle.

The rules I told you about in the beginning of my adventures were an allegory for youth, you idiots. When you're young, you get to make all the bold proclamations you want. But once you've gained a few miles on your soul, you realize that libertine self-service has a shelf life. All vices lose their luster, and our precious rules for life, even my villain's rules, are the very chains limiting growth. Breaking my self-imposed compacts opened new doors and allowed me to expand my business, my power, my social circle, my soul, and most importantly, my family.

Now, I'm not saying everyone needs to go out and have kids or anything. In fact, most of you *shouldn't* breed. I've seen your social media profile pics and... *woof*, keep that shit out of the gene pool. But doing something more than feeding a narcissistic existence is essential for survival.

This is all a fancy way of saying I grew up a bit.

Sure, dick jokes and action-packed sex romps are great. But when that's all you have, then that's all you are. And in time, what you truly will be is alone.

Just like me.

Frank had said it best. That I failed upwards. I laughed it off before, but the truth was staring me in the face. In my quest to be the best, to crush my enemies and feed my narcissism, I pushed those closest to me away. And worse still, I became a Titan, the loneliest of all cosmic beings, save perhaps for the One.

Maybe Lydia had seen the writing on the wall. She may not have predicted my Titan ascension, but perhaps she saw me backsliding to my old way. If so, then she did what any good parent would: make plans to give their kid the best life possible.

Which meant I *was* the asshole.

Great.

Well, after this next class with Professor Renfield, we had a free period. Maybe I'd talk to her then? I wasn't going to dump all my crap and admit I was maybe, possibly, in the wrong. I was still a villain, after all.

Hmm... maybe I could come up with a way to settle things but still make her feel bad.

"Come in, come in! Welcome to Basic Resource Management," Professor Renfield said giddily, welcoming the freshmen into the odd room.

I say "odd" because the gigantic rectangular room was, like the cafeteria, deep within the mountain and made of a rusty red and blackened stone. And it was full of… junk?

When I say junk, I really mean junk. I saw things like antique clocks with alien numbers, an old grand piano that easily had two hundred keys, a stuffed three-eyed chihuahua, and a glowing, hot pink set of fantasy world armor.

There was no rhyme or reason for the stuff on display, and everything smelled of soot and old coins. It was as if a dragon had plundered multiversal storage units and thrift stores for their treasure hoard.

Something in all this tickled the back of my mind, telling me that I'd seen this all before. While I couldn't put my thumb on it, everything felt nefarious… yet profoundly stupid.

I wasn't the only one perplexed, as all the freshmen looked over the random crap with confusion. The only person who seemed happy was Professor Renfield. The thin man with the round, wire-rim glasses and overalls seemed to be bubbling over with excitement as he ushered the last of the class into the room.

"Welcome, class. Today's lesson is a simple one that I think you'll enjoy," he said, then pointed to my side. "No spoilers, Keith."

"Keith no say nothing."

This caused the class to murmur. This was Hell Week and thus far, no one was enjoying anything. Well, except maybe Keith. The little pig-kid seemed content to eat the crayons he'd found. Eh, I couldn't blame him. An orange crayon always looked tasty.

"Are we going to be here for long?" Ella Moontide asked, flipping her hair from one side to the other. "Free period is next and some of us have more important things to do."

Professor Renfield didn't react in the slightest. If anything, his smile got wider.

"Well, that depends on you all, really," he said with a shrug. "This class can be over early, if you like."

This caused another round of mumbles and whispers among the students.

"How early?" Ella asked.

Professor Renfield considered the question as he walked among the students. He picked up an object or two as if looking for something special before finally settling on what looked like a Fabergé egg. The professor suddenly whipped the priceless object as hard as he could.

Give the skinny man the credit he's due—the scrawny bloke had a helluva arm. All eyes turned and watched the piece of jeweled art spiral the length of the cavernous room before shattering against the far wall.

But before anyone could ask why he did that, the singular thick door we'd just come through slammed shut, locking us in. This was followed by the sound of incredibly large locks sliding into place. Through the door, we saw Professor Renfield looking back in from a rectangular viewing window.

There was a click, like an intercom coming on.

"We in the villain support career are constantly tasked with the impossible," Professor Renfield said over the intercom. "From simple things, like hauling dead bodies away undetected by authorities, to more complex things, like providing maintenance for the inner workings of advanced machinery. The arch henchman-style villain is, after all, a jack of all trades. And while some of you in other paths may scoff at this notion, it's my duty to instill the sense of ingenuity and creativity my kind uses on a regular basis."

There was another click, and that's when we heard the ticking.

Above us, red warning lights began to flash. And it was with that little bit of illumination that I had the sudden realization of what was going on.

First, the walls weren't rusty-black stone. They'd been blackened by scorch marks and reddened by caramelized, aerated blood.

A lot of scorch marks and a lot of blood.

"To answer your question, Ms. Moontide, one minute," Professor Renfield said over the intercom. "You have one minute to find and disarm the bomb hidden somewhere in this room. I don't know about you, but I just love escape rooms."

Gods… damn it. Escape rooms. *That* had been the thing my hindbrain tried to warn me about.

I could go on a rant about how escape rooms are a hobby for the barely-above-average intelligent who want to seem smart. I could go on and on about how unlocking locks using puzzles lying around and fucking about with magnets is basically just live Dungeons and Dragons that you pay for. But I won't.

We only had thirty seconds left.

With how everyone scrambled about, the message was clear. Sometimes you're in a no-win situation, and you always need to be ready for anything. Something Evie had tried to warn me about in the common room the first night, but I hadn't understood until now.

No, with how things had been going with me recently, I didn't bother. Maybe they'd find and disarm the bomb in the fifteen seconds left, but I had my doubts.

So I just sat down next to Keith. He offered me a yellow crayon and I took a bite. It wasn't lemon like I'd hoped. But as the Stones taught us in verse, we don't always get what we want.

Boom.

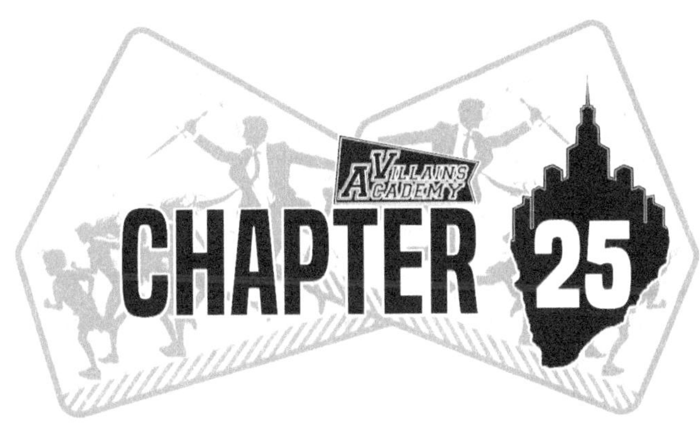

CHAPTER 25

HELL WEEK: DAY 5 - WHERE I LEARN TO LOVE THE BOMB, PONDER THE MERITS OF SELF HARM, AND DECIDE ON BREAKFAST

I woke up groggy, but I felt *incredible*.

Every ache, pain, and drop of misery that had been forced upon my young body was suddenly gone. Not gonna lie, dear reader—I may have shed a tear or two from the pleasure I felt due to the complete and sudden absence of pain. I believe it was Epicurus who said, "Pleasure is the first good. It is the beginning of every choice and every aversion. It is the absence of pain in the body and of troubles in the soul."

Poetic crap aside, my young flub was no longer on fire, and that's all that mattered.

Swinging my legs out of the bed, I felt a little unsteady. I wasn't in pain, but I felt terribly tired. A glance at the desk clock told me it was five fifty-seven in the morning.

Ugh, no wonder I was tired. But why did I still have the yellow crayon? For that matter, why did I still taste the waxy coloring stick? And bloody hell, why was I still in my school uniform?

"Morning, friend," Keith said from the bunk above me.

I stood on fresh legs and looked up at the pig boy, thankful he wasn't a morning masturbator.

"Morning, Keith," I said. "Why're you awake?"

"Keith awake because this when everyone who gets dead wakes," he said.

"Come again?"

The little piglet let out a squeak of laughter. "You not so smart, is you?"

I sighed. "I've been told that a time or two."

Keith nodded. "When youse die in school, youse always wake up how you died and at same time. Five fifty-seven."

"The clothes I understand. But that's an oddly specific time," I said. "Is there a mystical meaning behind that? Some deeper occult lore?"

Keith shrugged. "Keith think because it not enough time to get back to sleep. It's worst time to wake up."

He was not wrong. A few minutes before six was the magic, soul-crushing number. Not enough time to really get back to sleep for students or people with normal jobs who have to get up and get ready.

"I applaud the villainy," I said, appreciating the little touches. "But why do I feel so… good?"

Again, Keith snort-squealed. "Because you is healed."

From the mouth of babes. Or Babe-adjacent, as it were.

As soon as Keith said the words, things began to make more sense. Despite me having severed them, Beatrice's reformed stitches had looked thicker and stronger. And then there was what Coach Mother said when she'd instructed Y'olly to beat the snot out of me.

Death is a release from the pain here at Sablestone Academy.

I twisted my torso and stretched my arms. I felt… *gasp*, something akin to muscle growth? I wasn't ripped in any sense of the word, but I could almost see the tips of my toes past my slightly shrinking belly.

"So, you're saying that every time we die," I began, thinking it through, "our wounds, all of them, are healed? This includes the micro muscle tears from exercise?"

"*Hmm*," Keith hummed, considering the question. "Maybe? Keith just knows that when Keith die, he not feel bad. Daddy-doctor say that dying is a sword with two eggs."

"A double-edged sword?" I offered.

"Same thing," Keith said. "You die and feel good. But most times dying comes from student so you lose points. Hell Week is always one guaranteed dead day. Daddy-doctor say it there to hurt as much as it help."

Was it sad that I could understand what Keith was saying?

First, removing all the pain was nice, but it also meant you got to experience all the fresh pain over again. Secondly, if all it took was dying to heal back up, then it would be an easy thing to do in a school full of future killers. But each time you died by the hands or machinations of another, they got points while you lost points.

But what if you took matters into your own hands, as it were?

Once more I looked at the bars on the windows. Something told me that I was not the first person to have thought of this idea. No doubt the school wouldn't allow such a loophole to exist.

Or would they?

Would the desire to win at all costs, a trait found in most villains—and most heroes, come to think of it—even allow them to consider such a thing? Say what you will about heroes, but they're the kind to make the self-sacrifice play. They wouldn't do it for personal gain. Villains, on the other hand, tend to see self-deletion as anathema. If they were gone, then how could they bask in the accolades of their deeds?

Well, with the exception of taking their enemy with them. That kind of mutually assured destruction, like Moriarty had in *The Final Problem* when he and Holmes fell from the Reichenbach Falls—

Oh, my sweet hairless bean bag… it's Friday.

Being free of pain, my kid brain had once again asserted itself. My rational mind dropped the rule-bending suicide concept as it was suddenly flooded with gooey, hormone-driven gleeful anticipation.

"Introduction to Villainy with Professor gods damned Moriarty," I said aloud. "Hey, Keith?"

"*Hmm?*"

"Moriarty," I repeated. "What's he like?"

Keith took a moment to answer. A dark cloud settled over his little mutant face.

"You have to get used to being punished for when not smart," Keith continued. "Moriarty does not like when not smart."

"I think I'll manage," I said. "But thanks for the advice."

"Is welcome."

I looked back at my bed longingly, but the lil' porker had been right, this was the worst time to wake up. Besides, I had a thought. I went to my desk to jot down a letter but noticed something out of place. Or rather something *in place* that shouldn't be.

"Keith?"

"What now?"

"Where did this clearly evil book come from?" I asked, gesturing at the worn, leather-bound tome sitting on my desk. "It wasn't there yesterday."

"Yes it was," Keith said. "Demon girl with big, um… *glasses*, give to Keith to give to you. Her say that you is getting beaten up a lot and that you need magic. Keith tell big glasses that you has knife. Her say that words are stronger than knife. Keith think she's stupid, but Keith bring you book anyways. Then we exploded before you see book."

"Did anyone see this interaction?"

"No one ever pays attention to Keith."

Aw. That almost made me sad.

Almost.

Hmm… assuming that Mikalya was the demoness in question, then was this her way to fulfill the quid pro quo? Being a former god, I was no stranger to magic. And even in this reduced human form, the mindset was there to wield such powers. Plus, I'd always found it to be piss-poor villainy if a potential mastermind didn't have multiple tricks in their arsenal. And having once wielded goldy magic, it'd be foolish to not always have a metaphorical "loaded gun" on me.

Still, that was a creepy-as-fuck-looking book.

"Keith, could you do me a quick favor?"

"What?"

"I need to jot down a quick letter to your doctor-daddy," I said, grabbing a pen and some stationery. "While I do that, would you be so kind as to open that book for me?"

"What if titty trapped?"

"Booby trapped?" I suggested.

"Keith like Keith's way better," he said. "You just want Keith to blow up if is trap."

"Fine," I admitted, realizing he was smarter than his vocabulary suggested. "I do. I really want to go to Professor Moriarty's class today, so I can't afford to get dead. Did you plan on going to class today?"

"No," Keith admitted. "All fun stuff is over. Keith hate gym. First class after breakfast is boring class."

"Fair," I said, finishing the note. "But I have a proposal for your doctor-daddy. One that will make all three of us happy."

"How happy?"

"He would get to do what he loves while you will get to—gods above and below—

suck me off."

"Keith listening."

"You open the book," I said, setting the letter on his desk. "Regardless of whether you blow up or not, you can take that letter to Dr. Moreau with my proposal."

Keith looked at me, the letter, then the book.

"Deal."

I took a step back as Keith opened the mystery book.

As predicted, he immediately burst into flames. The little pig boy barely squealed before the boobytrap flash fried him in seconds. The magical flames died down as quickly as they'd appeared, leaving the rest of the room untouched. Stepping over the smoldering husk of roommate, I examined the book, which was an entry-level spell grimoire from the Forbidden Tome's library. Turning the aged, yellow parchment, I found a note tucked between the pages.

I hope this got you. I owe you, after all. But knowing you, I only got your roommate. Regardless, consider this a step towards our agreement.

It wasn't signed, but I didn't need it to be. I knew exactly who it was from and why it was here. Yes, this would do nicely.

It was going to be a good day, I could feel it.

Looking back, I noted that Keith's husk had disappeared, having vanished into nothingness. But based on the scent left behind, I was gonna have a huge plate of bacon for breakfast.

CHAPTER 26

HELL WEEK: DAY 5 - WHERE I PONDER MY IDOL'S PENIS, REVEL IN SOME SCHADENFREUDE, AND GET CALLED OUT

While gym had been grueling as usual today, I was in a much better place physically than I had been before. As for the first class of the day, Keith had been right. Crew Management and Child Labor Practices, with Captain Hook, had been incredibly boring. While he tried like hell to come across as menacing and dastardly while expounding on organizing henchmen, I couldn't take the cripple seriously.

For villain's sake, he lost to kids.

Before you call me out, I know I praised *The Goonies* back in chapter eight. However, that example highlighted the benefits of fear-based storytelling for children, not the impracticality of legendary villains losing to sprats who still have their baby teeth.

But that was behind me. This was the class I'd been waiting for all week.

The lecture hall was packed with freshmen. Moving down the aisle, I searched for familiar faces and an empty space. Eris was at the front of the class at the lowest level of the room. I couldn't see her face completely, but from what I gathered, something in her was still broken.

Good.

Khasil, Valliar, King Stanley, and Y'olly were a clustered quartet in the back of the hall pretending not to care. Mikayla sat in the row ahead of Y'olly, looking miffed. She caught my eye, then looked over at Lydia and back to me, her eyes asking the unspoken question.

I nodded.

A small, barely perceptible smile crept onto the demon girl's face.

There was a loud bang behind me. I turned to see the lecture hall doors slamming shut, and a tall, lean, balding man in a Victorian suit strode in.

Professor James Moriarty.

Sir Arthur Conan Doyle had described my idol as "reptilian" and "ascetic-looking." In person, he appeared to be gaunt weirdo who abstained from everything that made life worth living, i.e., good food, great drugs, and the right kind of bad sex.

Seeing my hero up close, I felt conflicted. I wanted to see… well, *me* reflected back. A mastermind with a smirk. What I saw was a dude who seemed above giving his crank a wank. I've had, and broken, many rules over the years. But one was ironclad: Never trust a person who doesn't masturbate.

"Take your seat, Blackwell," Professor Moriarty said, passing me and heading towards the front of the lecture hall. "Now."

Bloody hell. I plopped down in the first open spot I found and realized who it was I was seated next to.

"Hello, Jackson," Sophia said, her voice low.

Ah shit.

"Sophia," I said, acknowledging her.

She glanced down at my ever-present short pants. "Nice legs."

"Nice braces."

Her smile faded and she closed her mouth.

Little inside baseball for y'all, Sophia's always been sensitive about her teeth. Djinn culture is not unlike the Philippines when it comes to dentistry. Just nasty.

What?

Oh, don't get pissy with me for saying that. If anything, get mad at the Philippines College of Dentistry who found that nearly ninety percent of citizens suffer from tooth decay and that nearly one hundred percent of children between three and five years old have cavities.

Google it if you don't believe me.

"Ms. DeVrille and Mr. Blackwell," Professor Moriarty said, his back to us as he wrote on the blackboard. "You will be done your conversation by the time I am done writing."

"Yes, Professor," Sophia and I said in unison.

"What is a villain?" Professor Moriarty asked, reading aloud the question on the board. "This is not a question with a simple answer. One might as well ask 'What is life?' Let us see what your fledgling minds think."

Professor Moriarty pointed at a bucktoothed, inbred-looking cannibal kid.

"You. What's your answer? What is a villain?"

"Um, a bad guy?" the hillbilly said with a slight southern drawl. Moriarty glared at the kid, who stammered a bit before trying again. "The uh—a person who's like, wicked? Like, who does criminal… things?"

"You are no doubt a part of They Who Hunger," Moriarty said, more as a statement than a question.

"Um, yeah?"

"Then consider it a blessing your path values muscles over the mind. Ten deathmerits on your record," Moriarty said, the dark tone echoing through the room. He snapped his fingers and pointed at my lunchtime pal, Burt. "You. What is a villain?"

Burt stood up with a flourish, having affixed a cloak to his uniform. He bowed his bald head slightly.

"Esteemed Professor, I am Prince Burresh of the Arcavian Clan. And I believe that—"

"Did I ask you your name?"

"No?" Burt said, looking up from his bow.

"Correct, I did not," Moriarty said. "The reason I did not ask is because no one within the Veil Walkers has ever earned my attention or my respect. Which in turn means I never bother to know their names."

Moriarty took the time to eyeball each and every vampire, god, demon, and eldritch being in the freshman class.

"I am sure Professor Dracula will find you all an asset to his instruction, while I find the majority of you to be absurdly disappointing," Moriarty declared with no fear whatsoever. "Abstract powers born into privilege, nothing more. Yet for some reason, you feel entitled to the name of villainy. In all my years of teaching, there has been one and only one student born with power that I respect. And you, vampire boy, are not him. Alas, I am here to instruct you not to cater to your egos. If anything, I openly cheer for the heroes who ultimately triumph in killing your kind."

"I've been saying the same thing for how long now?" I whispered to Sophia under my breath.

Burt, the uppity little snot, sighed. "May I sit back down now?"

Moriarty looked as if he were considering the question. But upon closer look, it appeared he was tallying the number of Veil Walkers in the class. Eventually he shrugged and simply said, "One hundred deathmerits."

There was no flash of fire. No great demise. Prince Burresh of the Arcavian Clan simply fell over dead. Moments later, his body and clothes dissolved into nothingness. The room went quiet, and Moriarty smiled a cold, cruel smile.

"I believe I have your attention now," Professor Moriarty said to the class at large, but with directed emphasis at the gods. "Always remember this quote attributed to Ludvig van Beethoven: 'What you are, you are by accident of birth; what I am, I am by myself. There are and will be a thousand princes; there is only one Beethoven.' So, does anyone else want to try? What is a villain?"

A steampunk-looking girl at the front of the lecture room tentatively raised her hand. Despite wearing a school uniform, she was loaded down with all manner of useless cogs and sprockets. But I assume you already knew that.

I did say "steampunk," after all.

"Yes, you," Professor Moriarty said, inclining his chin at the girl.

"Is this a case where nothing we say will be correct, and you're just—forgive me, Professor—berating us, because this is Freshman Hell Week?"

Moriarty's smile grew. "What's your name and path?"

"Maureen Sparx," the girl said, "and I am a proud member of Those in Loyal Service."

"I see."

Professor Moriarty strode across the small lecture space to the front row and swiftly slapped the top hat off her head. The affixed goggles shattered on impact with the marble floor.

"No one likes the little shit who tries to guess the ending to a story."

From beside the steampunk girl, a new voice spoke up. One that did not wait to be called upon.

"Villains are perceived criminals or scoundrels whose evil actions, or motives, are in direct opposition to a hero."

Professor Moriarty looked the girl over. "What's your name?"

"Eris Pence," the girl said.

"And what in the name of all that is villainous, Eris Pence, made you think that I sought a textbook definition?"

"Because I—"

"Why have a yearlong course at all?" Moriarty said aloud, cutting her off.

Gods above and below, I loved this guy.

"Why even hint at the desire to seek deeper meaning?" he asked, continuing his speech. "I'm sorry, class, in all my years of infamy I've been mistaken. Eris Pence, henchman in training, solved it for me. Bloody cretin."

The professor sighed and walked back to the front of the hall and pointed at the question again.

"What is a villain? I ask this because there is no real answer. At least, none that any of you could understand, let alone express. At least not yet. Introduction to Villainy is my favorite subject to teach because I get to look upon a new crop of students and tell each and every one of you that none of you are worthy of being a villain."

There was shocked silence as the air was practically sucked out of the room. Each prospective villain sitting there felt as if they'd just been hit below the belt.

Well, maybe them. I knew better.

This was obviously a tactic the professor used to break down students and then build them back up. I myself had used a similar method when I would conduct my consultations. As such, I knew that—

"All of you," Professor Moriarty said, his gaze fixed on me alone. "Especially you, Mr. Blackwell."

I was, for once, at a loss for words.

Sophia, it turned out, was not.

"I don't know about you," Sophia whispered from my side, "but I'm loving this class."

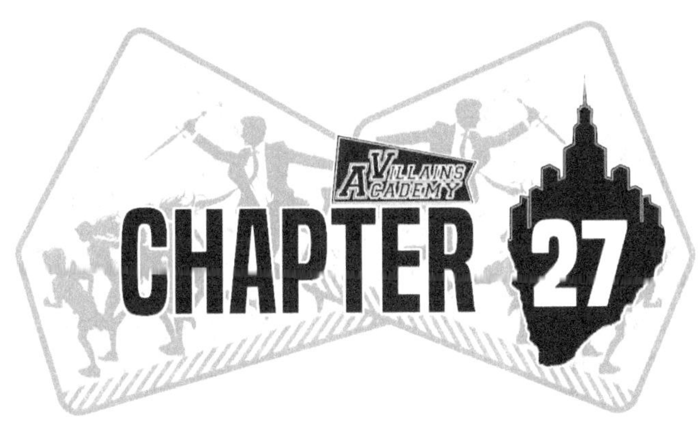

"Ex-excuse me?" I finally managed to say once the shock passed.

"I did not stutter, Mr. Blackwell," Professor Moriarty said. "I said that none here are worthy of the name villain. You above all others personify my proclamation."

"Hah!" Sophia said, barking out a snorting laugh that definitely caught Moriarty's attention.

"Something to add, Ms. DeVrille?"

"No, Professor," she said. "I just couldn't concur more when it comes to Jackson."

"Your opinion is as welcome as your presence," Moriarty said.

"Sir?"

"While the djinn are amazing little chaos goblins, your kind has no ability for advanced levels of thinking. Twisting wishes is, at best, a party trick. Power is useless lest you have a mind to wield, which is why beings like you need a guiding hand. The one thing Blackwell here did semi-correctly."

"With respect, Professor," I said, trying to keep my temper in check. "I'm here to take the class like everyone else. Just because the look of hope didn't die in my eyes like the rest of these nobodies does not mean I am not a villain. If anything, I already am a villain. A well-established one that's basically just auditing this year's curriculum. So respectfully, sir, maybe we should just continue the lesson?"

"We are continuing the lesson," Professor Moriarty said. "This introductory session is designed to delineate true villains from pretenders such as yourself."

My jaw clenched at that one.

Audible "oohs" were heard throughout the freshman class. The loudest, of course, were from Sophia and her cronies.

"*Pretenders?*" I said, repeating the insult.

"You see, students," Professor Moriarty said, stepping back and addressing the class as a whole, "the worlds in which you will go are full of people like Mr. Blackwell here. People who believe themselves to be villains. What they happen to be is nothing more than petty criminals, ne'er-do-wells, and bad actors doing bad things. Adult children drunk on their perverse power fantasies. Which is why, of course, I chose to begin this class with the theme for the year. What is a villain?"

"Me," I said, repeating myself with something of a snarl. "*I am a villain.*"

Yeesh… these tween hormones were really making it hard to separate emotion and logic. My feelings were clearly facts, and the world needed to see that… or else.

Gods above and below, kids suck.

"Fine," Professor Moriarty said with a sick smile. "I will indulge this fantasy of yours for the moment. Please, Mr. Blackwell, come down here and explain to the class what makes you a villain."

Moriarty didn't wait for me; he simply stepped aside and gestured for me to take the floor while he took a seat behind his simple desk. Ah, the ol' "If you think you're so smart, you teach the class" gambit. Typically, the loudmouthed kid backed down when faced with the limelight. Or, because chaos was a cruel fucker, said kid would suddenly pop a boner or start their period.

But let's be real, the limelight was where I belonged.

The upside of being in *this* body, any boner I may or may not have wouldn't be noticed. So I stood up, walked down the stairs, and turned toward the sea of faces.

And I nearly crapped my pants.

All that shit I just said about being in the limelight? Yeah, that was adult me talking. Kid me had yet to experience such moments. In my youth I'd been as awkward and introverted as any other kid. I mean sure, plotting—and sometimes enacting—

the demise of one's peers might come off as the telltale sign of the cocksure… and the psychotic. However, all that's done from the shadows. A place where it's easy to hide and orchestrate. But standing up in front of others for a speech? I was one sphincter spasm away from shitting myself.

First-time public speaking is a lot like youthful sex. If you didn't want to blurt out everything onto your audience in less than a minute, then you needed to practice. Rehearsing your speech over and over was the orator's equivalent of furious, dry-rub masturbation.

Ya gotta get desensitized somehow.

Oh, quick side note: If you go that latter route, then tread carefully. Crotch callus isn't as sexy as it sounds.

My adult mind told my kid body to stuff a cork in the butt and play along. Kid body listened… for now.

"I am a villain," I half announced, half squeaked, inwardly cursing my prepubescent voice for choosing that exact moment to crack.

Naturally, my "peers" chose this moment of weakness to giggle, snicker, or make fart noises. I glanced back at Moriarty, who did not react in any way. He was giving me enough rope to hang myself. The message was clear: I was there to flounder, wither, and most importantly, obey.

Well, fuck that and fuck him.

"I am a villain," I repeated, putting as much big-boy bass in my voice as I could, "because I *choose* to be. That's the secret, really. That's the big reveal Professor Moriarty's going to spend a school year belaboring, dancing around, and teasing out of you. All things come down to choice. Choose to do good or choose to do evil? These are petty thoughts for small minds. No, my juvenile classmates, the choice has always been about power and whether or not you choose to take that power."

Ooh, yeah. That felt good.

The real me was still in there, waiting to come out. And from the wide-eyed, pursed-lipped look on Moriarty's face, I'd either come close to nailing his lesson plan with a few simple words, or he'd just gotten his dick caught in a zipper. Since a guy like him used button flys, I was betting on the former. Now that I was feeling a bit of the old Shadow Master mojo, I decided to flaunt it.

"For those of you who don't know, I've been a villain for over twenty years. I ran a rather successful business counseling villains. No doubt a few of your parents were my former clients. I've orchestrated the rise and fall of businesses, empires, and worlds. I've accumulated vast wealth, defeated countless enemies, and not to brag, transcended humanity several times over."

"Then what're you doing here?" a cyborg fella asked.

"I'm here on a technicality," I explained, then shot a finger gun at Sophia. "One which I am sure will be resolved in my favor."

Most of the class wore unbelieving, smug expressions. It wasn't their fault. The young simply lacked the context and humility that came with age. But my enemies knew better. They gave me wary looks. Only Sophia seemed unfazed. If anything, she looked pleased.

That was never good.

"What makes you think you know more than the professor?" the steampunk girl asked.

"Maureen, right?"

I picked up her begoggled top hat, dusted it off, and handed the damaged headwear back to her.

"I never said I knew more than he did. I just know the difference between classroom and practical education. And between you and me, Maureen, you, and all of those In Loyal Service have a better chance of lasting success than the rest of these fools."

This caused the majority of the class to turn on me.

"A henchman?" someone called out.

"You're a fool!" called another.

"Shut… UP!" I said as loud as I could, wresting control back from these mongrels. "If you don't believe me, go crack a book, watch a movie, or just wait to grow up and see that I'm right, *as usual*. Brutes, gods, demons, mages, and all that crap exist to be defeated by plucky underdogs. Many of these heroes have, at most, five kills and two bed partners under their belts. But the arch henchmen? They sit at the right hand of the masterminds, learning. And when our time in the shadows ends, it is they who pick up the mantle."

This time, I made sure to catch Eris's eyes. This speech was really for her benefit, after all.

"The rest of you," I said, continuing my thought, "better hope you're popular enough to be brought back for a sequel or a gritty reboot. Which brings me nicely to the next part of what makes a great villain. Popularity. There's an adage that says a great villain sees themselves as the hero in their own story. And that is one hundred percent... *wrong*."

No one spoke. Their mouths hung agape at such blasphemy. Yet a few were waiting to see what I'd say next.

That's right, baby birds. Mama Jackson's gonna vomit up all the villainous nutrition straight into your hungry mouths.

"That expression is woefully one-sided and exceptionally limited. After all, it's predicated on the story being *the hero's* story. Ms. Pence was right that classically, villains stand in direct opposition to the hero's motivations. And in that paradigm, a quote-unquote 'great' villain does see themselves as the hero. However, that means the villain is likewise defined by the hero they oppose. Dunno about you, but *I* define me, not some do-gooder schmuck. But what if we break that paradigm?"

I used this moment to turn and go to the blackboard, writing out my own question. Finishing, I set the chalk down and stepped back so the class could see.

"Why bother with heroes?" I said, reading the question aloud. "That's what Professor Moriarty was building toward in his transparent attempt to tear me down. In all my recorded adventures, I've never had a 'side-of-right' enemy. No Peter Pan, no Van Helsing, and damn sure no Sherlock Holmes coming for me. My opponents have always been other villains gunning to take my spot. Why? Because my recorded adventures, farfetched and fucking foolish they may be, are based on my world, that being the prime universe."

I looked over at Moriarty, winked, then faced the class.

"In the *real* world, there are no heroes, not really. Sure, we commonly say the crap like teachers, firefighters, soldiers, and medical professionals are the real heroes. But that's because every leader or icon is either corrupt or will fail given enough time. In fact, we kinda revel in it. Nothing my world likes more than to prop someone up, hold them high for a few shining moments, then laugh as they fall. Those who attempt to be virtuous we mock, dismiss, and occasionally crucify before we go back and watch TV. It's a villain-eat-villain world where I come from, and I'm hungry.

"So what is a villain? I'll tell you. It's the person who isn't afraid of greatness. A person unburdened by moral constraints who stands up and either creates or takes the power necessary to achieve their goals. And some of us are so gods damned good at what we do, people cheer us."

"I believe we've heard enough from you," Professor Moriarty said.

But I wasn't done. I started a slow clap.

"Fellow students, let's give it up for Professor James Moriarty, the Napoleon of Crime."

"You're done, Blackwell."

"Do you know why he's called that?" I said, ignoring him. "Because that's what Scotland Yard called *Adam Worth*, the Victorian Era criminal back in the prime universe. The *real* person Jimmy here is based on. The one who wasn't hunted by a fictional crime-fighting superhero detective."

"*Enough!*" Professor Moriarty screeched, the veneer of tranquil control gone. "Get out of my classroom."

"Gladly," I said, making my way for the door.

They say never meet your heroes. Always seemed foolish to me, but I got it now. The reality and the idea almost never line up. But since he was such a dick, I paused at the door and turned back.

"One last thing," I said to the class. "There's another adage to keep in mind. Those who can't, *teach*."

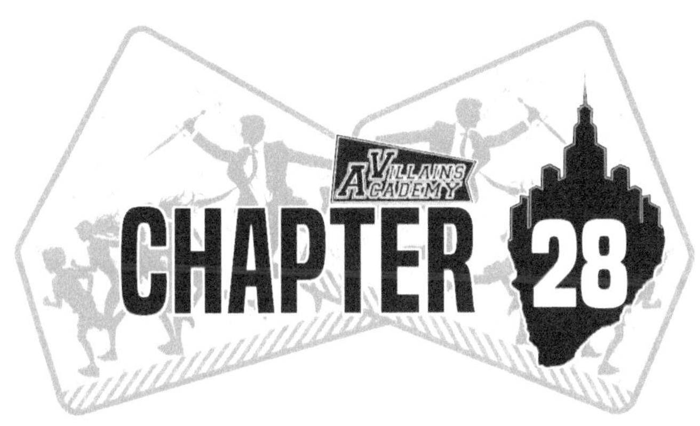

CHAPTER 28

WHERE I GO TO THE PRINCIPAL'S OFFICE, LEARN A BIT ABOUT THE BEGINNING, AND AM GIVEN HOMEWORK

"Well, that took less time than I thought," Headmaster Nyx said from across her desk. "Take a seat, Jackson."

I didn't see a reason not to comply. With a slight shrug, I sat down into a chair and took in the grandeur of her office. As swirling vortexes of shadow and night go, this was classy. It reminded me of my old pocket dimension, minus the occasional howls from beyond the veil, obviously. And while the scent of Tartarus hung heavy in the air, the office décor was a tasteful ancient Greek pastiche.

"You were what, expecting me to get kicked out of class?"

The being composed of night and starlight considered the question.

"Eventually, yes," she said. "You are who you are."

"Fair," I said. "But why did he kick me out and send me here instead of killing me with a hundred Deathmerits?"

"Because I ordered it."

"Really?" I said with a suspicious grin. "Or perhaps, each professor has a limited number of kills per day? Just enough to evoke fear, but not too much so as to sway overall points per path?"

"Let's not be coy with one another, Jackson," Headmaster Nyx said, skillfully avoiding my supposition. "I assumed you would either walk out, or be kicked out, of a class. So let's consider this a reprieve. A gift from one Titan to another that allows us time to talk."

"About child murders?" I mused.

Headmaster Nyx rolled her dark eyes. "It's not precisely murder, seeing as they come back the next morning at five fifty-seven AM."

"Yeah, why is that?" I asked.

Nyx let out a small chuckle. "Research showed it to be the most annoying time."

"Huh, so Keith was right."

"He has been around for a long time."

"Do I have to worry about him?" I asked.

"Pardon me?"

"Look, every villain out there has been fooled a time or two by the mastermind pretending to be an idiot thing."

"No, that was only you," she said. "In your first recorded adventure, I believe."

"Well, that's not totally—"

"And second adventure as well?"

I glared at her.

"No, Keith is not another Randy in disguise," she assured me. "Keith is… Keith."

"So how in the name of the Never Realm did he end up in the Mind Fire Calling?"

Nyx just gave me a knowing look.

"Ah, I see Dr. Moreau massaged the system," I proposed. "Eh? We have the same thing back in the Prime universe. Entire crops of affluent parents who think that having money means that their kids are gifted. Ergo, they demand that their spawn be placed in advanced-level courses when in reality, said kids are barely a step above eating glue."

"Precisely," she concurred. "Now, if you'd like to stretch your legs a bit, feel free."

"I'm not following," I admitted.

The outline of a person amid the starlight shape gestured towards me. "Feel free to be you again. Unless you enjoy that form?"

"Ah," I said, but paused before doing anything. "Possibility said that if I used my abilities at all, I'd forfeit and he'd keep Evie."

"*On campus*," Nyx clarified. "I believe the deal was using your powers on campus. This office is my sanctuary. A private, secluded nook away from prying eyes, to include Possibility's, that's technically not on campus."

I thought this might be a trick. But even with my powers behind Possibility's block, my senses were still there. And I felt the vibration of this room. It was like my old pocket dimension. A place that was not part of the fabric of reality. Reaching inwards to the dormant, partitioned portion of my Titan self, I found the power waiting. Still, it wasn't worth the risk. Nyx smiled.

"I swear to you, from one Titan to another, my father's decree does not extend to my domain."

"Wait… father?" I asked. "Forgive me for Greek-splaining, but *Chaos* is your father."

"He was," she agreed. "But you know him as Possibility."

"Well, now's as good a time as any for an exposition dump," I said, then took back control and became the adult version of myself.

My clothes, however, did not change.

"Oh, gods damn it," I grunted in pain as adult me overfilled the child-sized school uniform, causing it to tear at the seams.

Famous American motivational writer William Arthur Ward once said, "To make mistakes is human; to stumble is commonplace; to be able to laugh at yourself is maturity."

But Mr. Ward never suffered the painful humility of rapid-onset testicular torsion.

Headmaster Nyx winced. "Apologies. I should have warned you."

"Yeah, would've been nice," I said, passing a hand over my body and replacing the uniform for a tailored, open-collar suit. Summoning a black cigarette with silver tips, I took a deep pull.

Oh gods… yes.

"So, you were saying? About Chaos becoming Possibility?"

"In a moment," she said. "First, what have you discovered about what this place is?"

"A bad attempt at a YA novel?"

"Jackson," Nyx sighed.

"It's a prison," I said, blowing out a plume of smoke. "Or at least a refuge for wayward beings."

"A bit of both," Nyx said. She leaned back in her chair and steepled her fingers. "What do you know about me?"

"That according to lore, you're the personification of night, daughter of the first Titan, Chaos. That you're the sister-wife to Erebus, the aspect of darkness."

"Correct," she said. "And as night and darkness always comes before the dawn, I am mother to Light, Day, Death, and many more."

"I see," I said, acknowledging her agency. "So, you uh, banged your brother?"

"Well, it just sounds gross when you say it like that," she said, deflating a bit.

"Greeks, I swear," I mused. "But something tells me you're not here by choice."

"I am not," Nyx said. "I am a prisoner here. I continue to exist within this construct because I, and this school, have purpose. But when that purpose ends, so do we. Do you understand?"

"Evie," I said. "This place was designed to hold her. And should she graduate, then the purpose for this construct ends. Then what? Possibility absorbs everything like the Sarlacc Pit."

"A crude but somewhat accurate analogy," Nyx said. "Should you lose against Sophia, then you will join me and the endless worlds contained within my father."

"What if Evie doesn't graduate?" I asked.

"What do you mean?" she said with false naivety. "She's one of the most gifted students we've ever had. Even Moriarty loves her."

"Don't act stupid and don't make me spell it out."

"Say what you mean or say nothing at all."

Gods damn her.

"Fine. There's a bloody rock in this castle that allows for true death. Don't act like the thought never occurred to you."

"There is," Nyx nodded. "But I don't know what would happen. While this academy was created as a place to hold your daughter, her death—her real death—

may be a loophole. Or it would just end the construct sooner. But would you—could you—do it?"

"No," I said without hesitation. "I'm many things, but not a monster. I'd rather be swallowed whole if it means my child survives. And that's what Sophia is counting on."

"Indeed," she agreed.

"So, the whole 'cast into Nothingness' thing, that's really part of the deal."

"It is," Nyx confirmed.

"Ugh, great," I groaned. "How is that even possible? How can nothingness exist inside the Titan of Possibility?"

"This is what brings the conversation back to my father's… transformation," Nyx said, leaning back in her chair. "There are so many creation stories across so many mythoi. But most agree that there was nothingness before there was something. In my telling of the mythos, Chaos was that nothingness."

"It's my understanding that from that mindless, roiling void eventually came Titans like Gaia and Tartarus."

"Yes," Nyx agreed. "But how? What most don't know is that before them, from nothing, came a singular idea for *something*. That nugget of an idea became a very real thing. A simple, solid concept. What if. This powerful thought 'killed' the Nothingness. Or at least defeated it long enough so that more… well, just more, could emerge."

"The Sablestone," I said, puzzling it out. "The first murder weapon. An idea given form that quote-unquote killed Chaos, who then transitioned into Possibility."

"Exactly," she said.

"Lemme guess, this isn't exactly in the curriculum?"

"Heh, no," she said with a smile. "There's no reason for instructing the students about this concept, as they'd never truly understand. Just we Titans have the capacity to understand how an idea can kill."

"Lemme guess, it takes a Titan to guide the stone," I said. "That's how you nullify the students' powers, right?"

She smirked at me, then opted to continue the conversation.

"However, the original concept, the power of the emptiness, the Nothingness, remains."

"Locked within Possibility," I said.

"Yes," she nodded.

"But how's one rock supposed to keep it locked up?"

"It doesn't," she said. "It keeps a weaker version of Nothing subdued. And the One ensures the Nothingness remains weak."

"Wait… the One?"

Nyx nodded. "In addition to maintaining the balance of power between Titans, gods, mortals, celestials, infernals, and djinn, the One's primary charge is ensuring that the fundamental power capable of returning the known and unknown multiverse to that natural state of nothing remains locked away."

"There are endless worlds within Possibility," I said, recalling Nyx's words while thinking it through. "Lemme guess, the One gives them over for feeding to the Nothingness."

"It's our great cycle," Nyx said. "Titans create the realms. Gods populate and run them. But when they've run their course, they're food for the Nothingness."

"They never covered this in Titan basic training," I said, pondering this unsettling thought for a few moments while smoking my cigarette.

Part of me always wondered how the multiverse could truly be infinite. Turns out, it wasn't. Some realms, worlds, and states of being were discreetly dealt with like a cancelled TV show or a city's homeless population.

"You don't want to stay behind, do you?" I asked, stating the obvious.

Nyx leveled those starlight eyes at me like I was an idiot. "I would prefer to not remain… inside my father."

"Yeah, figured as much," I said, leaning back in the chair and lighting another cigarette. "So, just so I'm clear, I not only need to beat Sophia, but you want me to figure out a way to get you and the rest of the school free from Possibility's control?"

"Mostly me," Nyx said with a smile in true villain fashion.

"Well, I'm not above a little cheating," I told her. "Perhaps a thumb on the scale, as it were?"

"I wish I could help you more than I have," Nyx said. "Despite the nefarious nature of the school, there are rules in place that even I cannot break. I've done as much as I can."

"Worth a shot," I said. "Thanks for the heads-up about dying and healing. That was you, right? Having Coach Mother say what she said?"

"I have no idea what you're talking about." Nyx smiled. "But I will caution you on that front."

"How so?"

"You're not the first to discover that particular loophole," she said. "And those who abuse it often pay the price."

"Meaning?"

"Meaning this is a school for villains," Nyx said, sounding more than a little agitated to spell it out. "There are always eyes watching. Patterns become predictable."

"Mm," I grunted. "Sabotage from peers."

Nyx nodded. "One student used to frequent a particularly remote lookout point on the south side of the mountain to kill himself at night."

"Until?" I asked.

"Until his peers caught wind and positioned safety wires. Instead of plummeting to his death, every bone was broken to include his neck. He lay there, paralyzed. Dying of dehydration and exposure is not a pleasant experience. Needless to say, he was never the same. And that is just one example."

"Noted," I said, tucking that away. "Be that as it may, Sophia really has me over a barrel on this one. There has to be something we—I—can do. Even an entity like Possibility has an order to it, rules I can exploit."

"You are right in that there are rules that govern this place. Like the one that prevents relations with students, despite their both being consenting Titans."

"Right... wait, what?!"

"I would read your student guidebook cover to cover," Nyx suggested, ignoring my outburst. "Now, go."

With that, I was ejected from her office. I was once again a twelve-year-old standing in the hallway.

Well, inuendo aside, my assignment was clear.

Read the fucking rule book so that I could do what I do best.

CHAPTER 29

WHERE I COMPARE FOOD TO SEXUAL FRUSTRATION, TAKE A COMPLEX CRAP ON "STRONG WOMEN," AND ADMIT THAT A DICK IS A DICK

The subterranean cafeteria cavern was busy with kids coming and going. The last class of the week was over, and now it was essentially free time. And while most people were celebrating the end of Hell Week, I was sitting alone at a table rolling around the same question, over and over, in my head.

What did she mean, "Read your student guidebook?"

I had read it. So what was I missing?

I'd been pondering this while dining on my expertly prepared dinner. And by "expertly prepared," I mean of course that it was lumpy mashed potatoes and Salisbury steak slathered in bland gravy. Not only did my Friday night dinner deny me nourishment, but it also was an act of culinary villainy. With each bite, my brain was anticipating the gravy's oniony zest, the seasoned meat with a hint of Worcestershire and mustard, and the potatoes' blend of butter, garlic, salt, sour cream, and cheese.

But it never came. Like a sneeze that starts and then goes away, the mediocre meal denied me my dopamine hit.

Foodie blue balls. Diabolical.

I looked about, and eyes were on me. It seemed that after my little blow-up in Professor Moriarty's class, the school rumor mill had started. Amazing, really, the speed with which people, especially kids, could spread bullshit. More amazing was their willingness to accept gossip and rumor as fact.

Eh, I shouldn't be surprised. Most people get their news from social media anyway, glossing over headlines fed to them by an algorithm. Because taking the time to learn is hard.

Out of all the rumors I'd heard so far, two had been established as the most likely. The first: I was a plant by the school to narc on the kids illegally summoning demons from the Never Realm to do their homework.

The other rumor, likely started by either Lydia or Sophia, was that I was just a whiny little bitch.

Needless to say, people had been giving me a wide berth. Even my so-called friends. Over at a table, Those in Loyal Service kids were tinkering with all kinds of weird-looking gadgets and tech. Lydia was there, no doubt advising them to add more knives and stabby things. Wraith Knight was with her, keeping watch. Eris was at the end of the table. She seemed to be even more distant than before.

It would soon be time to confront her. But not yet.

Myst was with the rest of the emo kids in the Forbidden Tome. While old Doris never would have been part of such a clique, "Myst" fit in just fine. Even her name was perfect for that gaggle of goths. Mikayla the nearsighted succubus sat a few seats down. But instead of engaging with the rest of her fellow witches and warlocks, her eyes were boring holes into Lydia.

Poor girl.

As if she sensed it, Mikayla looked up and caught me watching her. She shot me a questioning glare that said, "Have you talked to Lydia yet?!"

I'm bloody well working on it, I tried to say with my eyes.

Based on how she bared her fangs, apparently my eyes had told the succubus to "calm her tits."

Well, my eyes were right. Talking to Lydia after our latest revelation wasn't going to be easy. And I wasn't even sure I wanted to. Still, a deal's a deal.

I shook my head and tried to refocus, cursing my youthful ADHD. All this gods damned YA drama had made scouring this bloody guidebook for clues practically impossible. Flipping the pages, I scanned the same sections again and again, having yet to come up with an answer.

The Sablestone Guidebook was, if anything, just a normal student manual, like the ones I'd had in private school. There was a general code of conduct for all villain students, policies, regulations, student organizations, and the like. The standout was the complex series of rules, tables, and regulations describing the point values assigned for villainy and how to achieve notoriety.

For example, killing another student outright in plain sight gained you one point. Doing it in private with no witnesses was worth two. Sabotaging another's plans in a way that did not lead back to you, or not until the right time to reveal, was worth a base-level five points with bonus points per machination level. And so on.

But what I wasn't seeing was a smoking gun to defeat Sophia nor a way to remove her inner circle.

And that, dear reader, was really chafing my nips.

I was so lost in thought that I failed to see the shadow of death coming for me until it was too late. By which I mean a very large patchwork girl on a direct course for my table.

"Crap," I sighed as Beatrice made a beeline for me.

Gods above and below, I really, really hated dealing with all the so-called "strong women" when I was galivanting across the multiverse. And the YA versions were so much worse. Okay, Jackson, you got this. They're all the same.

Call me a misogynist if you want—many have. Yet I remain uncanceled. Because when it comes to this archetype in our fiction, there's a truth we all know but refuse to admit.

Oh, you don't know? Lean in so I can tell you. Ready?

Psst. There's no such thing as a "strong female character." *Ta-da!*

Ooh, I can literally feel the heat coming from a few of you right now. Good.

The term "strong female character," at least what the modern world thinks of when the term is used, is in fact a carefully crafted, produced, and marketed selling point, created by corporate assholes… like me.

We manufactured this fiction the same way we created pink razors for women. Take what already exists, give it a superficial paint job, then blast out the marketing message: "Feminine folks need this!" We were so good at our jobs that an entire generation of storytellers adopted our simulacra as a fact. Wanna know the best part? To create the SFC, we just took a toxic male character and slapped on some tits.

Heh, you still don't believe me.

Let's see: an aggressive, hard-nosed type who's quick to anger, vengeful, dangerous, and often self-righteous. They see the people and the system as a challenge to their status and are willing to hurt others even though they're considered the "hero." Oh, and of course, they're rather snide to the opposing gender. After that, all we had to add to sell the audience on the character being female was a line or two about anxiety and self-doubt while drinking wine.

Oh, I forgot about the pet. Cats tend to work the best.

And just so you know they're strong, the SFC will *tell you* how strong they are as often as they can. Little speeches about how much they've had to endure, or how many people who've tried to hold them down. How they've had to fight every day for… whatever. Look, we skip those people's social media posts in the real world for a reason. Long story short, CrossFitters, cultists, and born-again vegans have nothing on the insecure SFC when it comes to announcing their "strength."

So, on behalf of the corporate producers, publishers, and writing staff, thank you. Thank you for accepting this overused cliché. The alternative, the outdated "damsel in distress" trope, had become harder to sell. We tried the "adorkable confident-not-confident girl" for a while. And while it worked for ninety percent of all animated female-led projects over the last twenty years, you people rejected the live-action. You labeled her the "manic pixie dream girl" and then abandoned her. So sad.

FYI, she's dead now. Someone left the door open and she got lost chasing rainbows and died of exposure. Hope you're proud of yourselves.

Complex characters, dear readers, like real complex people, are the ones worth caring about. Yeah, they can kick ass, but they continue to learn and grow while overcoming their dark past or darker present. Complex is breath of fresh air compared to the "strong female character" or the "man of action" types plaguing our fiction and comment sections.

Best of all, complex doesn't have a gender. Hero or villain, complexity is what creates a connection with the audience and is vastly more interesting than some schmuck who's "strong."

So when I say, "so-called strong women," I mean it to be just as condescending and dismissive as it sounds. Because I've known far too many people who emulate all the wrong connotations of strength.

I mean, have you met my ex-wife?

Seriously, go back through my recorded adventures and you'll see what I'm talking about. Due to her experiences in life—real or perceived—Lydia sees everything as a challenge to her person. As such, she's always willing to stab first and talk second.

That, dear reader, is an asshole. And I'm the idiot who fell for her—and the many versions of her—throughout my life. What can I say? Hyper-competitive, aggressive assholes are always, and I mean always, tigers in the bedroom.

And you bloody well know it. It's the only reason society hasn't killed them off yet.

But for comparison, look at the other women in my life. Evie is complex. Myst is complex. Gods above and below, Eris and Sophia are complex. Lydia's just a dick.

Try as you might, one cannot maintain a long-term, healthy relationship with a dick. I know, I own one. And it has always gotten me into trouble.

By the time I'd finished my little internal rant, Beatrice had arrived to ruin my day and likely to knock out my teeth.

"Hey there, freshie," the flesh golem said, taking a seat opposite me. "I think it's time we have another little chat."

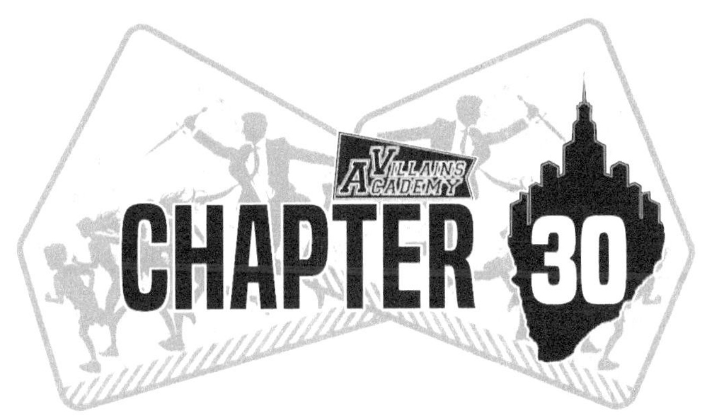

CHAPTER 30

WHERE I CONFRONT MY BULLY, MY MISOGYNY BITES ME BACK, AND I YEARN TO BLOW A ROBOT

Beatrice leaned her elbows on the table. Resting her chin on her fists, the muscular golem flexed her thick arms to the point where the black school uniform jacket nearly ripped at the seams. She stared directly at me in a way that was thirty percent flirty and seventy percent menacing.

My scalpel was inside my uniform jacket's inner pocket, but she'd see me go for it and stop me. Dumb as she might look, I doubt she'd fall for the same trick twice. Worse, WK and Myst were too far away to help. Even if they rushed over, something told me that Beatrice was ready for them.

So I stuck with the "strong female" gameplan.

"Back on the first day I did what I had to in the moment, and I don't apologize," I said, looking directly into her mismatched eyes. "You're looking better than ever and your stitches have come back rather nicely if I may say so. But if you take a step closer, I'll make you bleed."

Don't move, don't panic, don't do anything to show fear. Confidence is key. Compliment in a roundabout way, add a threat, and appear to be engaged. Then, let them make the next move on their terms. If done right, and in a way where they feel they have the position of higher power in the dynamic, then they often extend the tiniest level of connection. But that's all it takes. Once you're in, you just play to their ego while being occasionally dickish.

Yeah… it works.

"You're not afraid of me, are you?" Beatrice finally said.

"Do you want me to be?" I asked.

"You don't talk like the other kids in your path."

"Because I'm not like them. No one's like me," I said. "Look, Beatrice, you have size, power, and…heh, *strength*. I don't. So, I gotta be ruthless. If you wanna kill me, then go for it. But this will become a war of escalation."

The Frankenstein's monster girl smiled.

Just like I knew she would.

"You're okay for a nerd."

"And you're pretty damn cool for a brute," I said with a well-crafted smile. "Actually, you're more than that."

"You kissing my ass?"

"Little bit," I mused. "But I've barely been in this school a week and even I know that people fear you. When you graduate, I think you'll have a long and menacing career as a villain."

She eyed me up and down, appraising me and my words.

"I heard a rumor—"

I sighed. "No, I'm not a spy for the school, nor a whiny bitch."

"No, not those," she said waving a stitched-together hand. "I heard that you're, like, some kind of villain advisor or something, who's trapped in this school?"

I looked at her, searching for some kind of deception. But either she was an amazing actress, or she was being completely earnest. Normally I trust… well, no one. But my Shadow Master senses were tingling, and I smelled a potential client.

"Yeah, I was," I eventually said. "I was a minor god who advised villains across the multiverse for years."

"Was? What happened?"

"I became a Titan," told her, ending that line of questioning. "Why do you ask?"

"Because I also heard you stood up to Morifarty."

I tried not to laugh at such a base and crude juvenile joke.

I failed.

"Mori-*farty*?" I asked, chuckling.

"Yeah," she said. "That's what we all call him. He's the kind of guy who's in love with the smell of his own farts. An arrogant, condescending ass who thinks he's smarter and better than everyone else. And he loves to hear himself talk."

"Oh, yeah, I really hate those types," I said, ignoring the irony.

"He goes on and on in his lectures about how great he was and how we'd never make it in the real world of villainy."

"Like he'd know," I laughed. "I've been doing it for decades and he's a fictional char—he's been out of the game for a while. Theory is fine for a foundation. But application and experience trumps anything you learn in the classroom."

"That so?"

"That's a Shadow Master guarantee."

"Who's that?"

"Don't worry about it," I said. "But you're asking me all this because you want something, right?"

"Yeah," Beatrice said, standing up. "I want you to give me and a few of my friends some lessons on real-world villainy."

"Why?"

"Because if don't pass his class in third year, I don't graduate."

"I see," I said.

Back in the real world, many American high schools had different requirements for graduation. Three years of math, two of science, and so on. But in far too many, four years of English was the norm. Which meant your senior year English teachers were essentially king and queen makers. To get out of that zoo, you had to get through them. And many of those teachers not only knew it, but also relished their sliver of power.

"Okay, what's in it for me?"

"You teach us, and I'll make sure no one fucks with you directly."

"What about indirectly?"

"We're all on our own when it comes to that, freshie."

"Fair point," I conceded. "Okay, you have a deal."

"Cool," Beatrice said, looking me over. "But protection or not, I still have a reputation to consider."

"What are you talking abou—"

Beatrice hauled back and clocked me in the face so hard that I'm pretty sure she broke my soul.

I flew off the seat and over the table behind me and landed in a bloody, toothless heap.

"This one's my bitch," Beatrice announced to the room at large. "Fuck with him, you fuck with me."

There was a murmur among the kids as understanding settled over them. I tried to get up but failed. Apparently not fucking with me also meant not helping me in any way.

Once the blinding pain became manageable, I got to my wobbly feet. Needless to say, I'd lost my appetite, and dinner was officially over. I went back to my table, gathered my few things, and began the slow, vomit-inducing trudge back to the relative safety of my room.

But as I did, an idea formed. I didn't know if this was the brain damage talking or a flash of personal growth, but seeing as I'd just gotten my ass handed to me by a strong woman, it made me think of another strong woman I'd been avoiding.

It was time I buried the hatchet with Lydia.

Now… where could I find a hatchet?

After getting lost due to having a very bad concussion, I eventually made my way across the quad and found the bench closest to the tower for Those in Loyal Service. I plopped down, bleeding from my mouth, and did my best to not pass out. For what felt like the thousandth time, I really wished I was back in the headmaster's private sanctum, where I'd had my powers.

And where I could summon cigarettes.

Gods above and below, I missed smoking. One of these kids had to smoke, right? It was a school for villains, after all. Where were the smokers? I'd even settle for a vape.

Normally I equate vaping with hipster chumps who suck on their little robot wieners and breathe in blueberry mango chai bullshit. But after a week like I had, I'd gladly—and repeatedly—suck a robot cock for a steady hit of nicotine.

"Boss?" I heard Wraith Knight say.

I blinked away the mental image of cradling a robot's disco ball testicles and turned to see Wraith Knight and Lydia walking towards me. I went to stand up, then promptly fell back down. My body was happy where it was. So I turned to them and smiled.

Lydia abruptly stopped and brought her hand to mouth palm out, as if to slap the sight of me away. "Oh, fuck me, you're ugly."

"Hurtful," I said through the gap in my broken teeth. "Thith ithin't pleathant for me either."

"Can't you, like, do something about it?" Wraith Knight asked.

"Like what?" I slurred. "I don't have my powerth."

"Please, Jackson, let me kill you," Lydia offered. "At least you'll come back healed."

I narrowed my eyes. "You'd like that, wouldn't you?"

"Yes, I really would," she said honestly.

I felt a great number of comments bubble up… but I pushed them back down. I wasn't here to start a fight. I was here to settle them.

Two, specifically.

"Can we take a walk?" I asked. "Justh you and me?"

Lydia eyes me with suspicion. "Why?"

"Becauthe we need to talk," I said, realizing that with my prepubescent voice and toothy lisp, I sounded like a bad Mike Tyson impression. "And I don't know about you, but a whole thcool year is too long to thtay pithed off at one another."

Lydia considered my words. Clearly, she too was having her own internal debate about whether to have this very real conversation.

That was the thing with hate.

It's so bloody hard to let go.

"Fine," she eventually said. "We can take a walk and talk."

"Thank you."

"Want me to come along?" Wraith Knight asked.

"Yeth, I really want you to tag along for Lydia'th and I's heart to heart."

"We'll be fine, Wendell," Lydia said.

"Okay, be safe."

I rolled my eyes and tried again to stand. My legs were a little less rubbery, but I still felt like hammered crap. Yet this was a conversation I needed to have, and I refused to be held back by a thing like pain. So I forced my body into motion.

I made it a whole three steps before I puked.

"Oh, for the love of—how about we just sit on the bench and talk?" Lydia offered.

"No," I said, spitting up chunks of half-digested mashed potatoes while sucking the Salisbury steak bits from my tooth gaps. "I got thith."

"Is this male pride or you just being stubborn?"

"Both?"

"Fine," she sighed. "Lead the way."

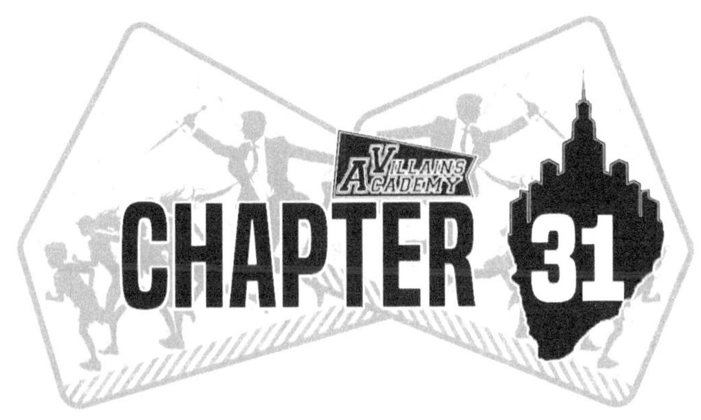

CHAPTER 31

WHERE I LOVE HATE, ACTUALLY LISTEN TO LYDIA, AND GIVE MY EX THE PUSH SHE DESERVES

According to a lot of mental health professionals, some people, often those with low self-esteem, are prone to hold onto grudges as a form of self-protection. Now, I'm not sure I believe that, at least not exactly. I think we need hate, because without that ball of acidic lead in our bellies, we feel empty.

Love and hope are like cotton candy dreams compared to the very real and present sensation of hate. We know it's poison. But it's a real feeling that anchors us. And there I was, prepared to ask Lydia to set her hate aside.

Provided I could bring myself to say it.

I was the one who wanted to have this conversation, so clearly, I would need to be the one to break the silence. I just wasn't sure of what to say. Weird, I know, considering how much I tend to talk. But as we walked south to the far end of campus, finding the remote scenic overlooks, I eventually found my courage.

"What happened too uth?" I asked when we reached a nice private spot.

"Oh, for the love of—just put your finger over your teeth or something, please?"

I sat down on the lip of the mountainside and let my feet dangle, gesturing for Lydia to do the same. When she took a seat to my right, I did as requested and covered the gap with my fingers.

"What happened to us?" I repeated, taking my time to enunciate. "Or were you hoping to come up with an answer in the few seconds it took me to ask again?"

Lydia looked upwards at the ever-darkening night sky.

"I don't know, Jackson. I really don't."

"Yes, you do," I said. "But you don't want to hurt my feelings. It's okay. Just say whatever you want to say."

"I was in my late twenties when we met," she said. "Eight years later and I'm still younger than you were when we got together."

"Your point?"

"That I still have so much to do, to see, and to become," she said. "You were already established as the Shadow Master. And I was—"

"A nobody?" I offered.

"Still discovering who I was, ass," she said, finishing her thought. "I went from a thieves' guild to a multiverse. But before I had time to comprehend anything, I was married with a child. I—I hadn't really lived yet."

"Was I holding you back from all that?" I asked.

"I—I don't know how to answer that," she said honestly.

"We were a team. A partnership."

"Yeah. But it was always *your* team," she said, stressing the word. "I said it before—

we weren't equals. And maybe we never will be. It's no wonder I ended up in the sidekick path. Even deep down, I don't see myself as worthy of lead villain status."

"I never cared about that," I said. "It didn't matter to me."

"Of course not," she said. "You held all the power."

Ouch.

"Over time," she continued, "I realized I was just… unhappy. I wanted to be more than your wife or your assassin."

"So you became Morry's assassin instead?"

"Don't be a prick," she sighed. "You were gone, and I was stuck in Caledon. So yeah, I carved out something for myself. I used Morry's power and influence to get on my feet, but the work was mine. It—it wasn't the same with us."

"No, I suppose you're right," I admitted, hating the truth in her words. "We—we were a round peg in an oval hole. Close, but not the right fit."

"Obvious sex joke aside, yes," she said. "We were what we needed at the time."

"At the time," I said, repeating her words. "But that time's over."

"I'll always love you, Jackson," she said. "You know that, right?"

"I know."

"And Evie," she added.

"She still not talking to you?"

Lydia looked over at me with her patented glare.

"Sorry," I said, not expounding on the topic.

"Why's it easier for you two?" Lydia eventually asked.

I started to say something nice, but then changed course. The time for being delicate was over.

"You said some hurtful things in that last book," I told her. "That's hard to process for an adult, let alone a kid."

"I know," Lydia said. "But even before that. She preferred your company to mine."

"I can't answer that," I lied.

Child psychologists claim any number of reasons for parent preference. Things like routine, time spent together, genetics, independence, and so on. In some cases like Lydia and I, it was simple: The kid leans towards the one they don't fight with. And in this case, that was me.

Personally, I was okay with it. I loved being the cool one.

Plus, and this is kinda shitty to say, Lydia had already admitted that she wasn't ready to be a mom. It's not her fault, not really. Some parents aren't ready to be parents. They're not ready to put others before themselves. But the hard truth is that kids sense it.

Evie damn sure did.

"I think," I said, treading carefully, "that when you do talk to Evie, you do it from a place of her needs, not yours. As parents, we have to—"

"Don't do that," Lydia said, wiping her eyes. "Don't give me advice."

"Well fuck me for trying to help," I sighed.

"Stop trying to fix all my problems."

"Gods above and below, woman, I'm not trying to—never mind. Fine. Whatever," I sighed, bracing myself for the next big question. "I get, now, how unhappy you were. But did you really think that taking Evie away from me to hide in King Stanley's world was going to work? You had to know I'd come for her. I may have been a short-sighted husband, but I'm a good dad."

It was her turn to sigh. "I wasn't going to do that."

"Bullshit," I countered. "The professor knew Stanley wasn't lying."

"I—damn it. Look, Jackson, have you ever known me not to be straight up with you?"

"No?"

"Right," she said. "Immediately coming out of Mikayla's mind mojo, I told you to fuck her up and that we weren't together anymore, right?"

"Your point?"

"My point is that for an assassin, you'll know when I stab you because I always like to look at my targets when I move in for the kill."

"Okay, that's fair," I admitted. "So what actually happened?"

"King Stanley had come by the office a few times, sniffing around whenever you were out. I thought it was odd since he'd never been a client. I didn't trust him, so I made the offer. I spun him a story I knew he'd swallow because it was a half-truth, like you'd taught me. I told him I was upset, unhappy, and wanted to leave. I added that there was no way I could ever return to Caledon because the gods there hated you for being you, and me for being an escapee. He told me to give it time."

"I see," I said, my mind turning this new information over.

And damn me if it didn't fill in a few missing gaps that I had hoped weren't there.

"Why didn't you tell me?"

"What? That a former contentious ally had come by the office? What was there to tell? I wanted something concrete before I brought the issue to you."

"Yet," I said.

"What?" she asked, confused.

"A little bit ago, you had said that you didn't see yourself as being worthy of lead villain status. And I'm saying 'yet.' You have good instincts. And knowing what we know now, he was likely looking into things as part of the Eris-Sophia coup. He may look like a friendly old man, but King Stanley is an elder god, former holder of the One position, and is hands down the most dangerous person on Sophia's team. This is a long way of saying you did the right thing and I believe you."

"Thank you."

"There's one last thing to talk to about."

"What?"

"Mikayla," I said, holding up my hand before she went ballistic. "I—gods above and below, I can't believe I'm saying this—you need to give her another chance."

"That bitch took away my memories and love of my daughter!"

"Because Khasil and Valliar compelled her," I said. "Y'olly had leased her contract to them, so she was literally forced to do all that crap."

"Why are you defending her?"

"Because—aw fuck it," I growled, which was hard to do with my fingers in my mouth. But it was time to show some gods damned maturity. "Because while you and I were not meant to be, you and she were."

"How?"

I sighed. "Both of you were independent women who I screwed over and used for my own gain. You're both intelligent people who have a desire to grow. Both are quick to stab, and because I had a front-row seat, sexually compatible. I'm man enough to known when I'm punching outside of my weight class."

"You were always… good."

"I was good with help from god powers and vibrators," I clarified without any sense of ego. "And with all honesty, I don't regret anything about our time together. I'll always love you too. But as you said, that time is over. And as much as I am loath to admit it, I want you to be happy. Even if that's not with me."

We sat in silence for a bit, allowing the emotional weight of our words to settle. When Lydia next spoke, she sounded scared.

"We're going to get out of this, right?"

"I've been outmaneuvered by an older, more powerful enemy," I admitted. "Sophia's holding all the cards."

"Looks like you need to be the gods damn Shadow Master again."

And in a way, it was nice. Encouraging, even. Her way of extending the smallest of olive branches.

I took my hand out of my mouth and hugged her. She hugged me back. And in many ways, or rather in the ways that meant the most, it was a hug goodbye.

An ending of who we used to be to one another.

We broke the hug and looked at one another with the new eyes of "just friends."

And that's when I shoved her ass off the mountainside.

"*Asshooooooole…*"

Next time I talked to Nyx, I'd have to thank her for telling me about these secluded spots.

Trust me, dear reader. If you ever have the chance to shove your ex off the side of a mountain, do it. Not only is it cathartic as fuck, but it really puts a stamp on the end of the relationship.

Now did I mean any of that shit I just spewed?

I dunno, probably.

I think I made it clear earlier in this tale about how people don't really want their exes to be happy without them. However, if this is what it took to push Lydia into Mikayla's arms while also flipping the succubus to my side, thus gaining another source of intel from Sophia's camp, then it was worth it.

I could just make out Lydia's impact splatter far below. Man, she was gonna be pissed when she came back tomorrow morning.

Huh. I wonder how many points I got from luring my ex-wife in for a heart-to-heart and then killing her without being seen. Minimum ten points, right? Maybe more because of the guise of legitimate feelings?

Eh, I'd find out tomorrow.

Well, it looks like those safety wires Nyx mentioned were gone. Good, because I wanted my teeth back.

With a sense of poetic justice, I heaved myself off the edge of the plateau.

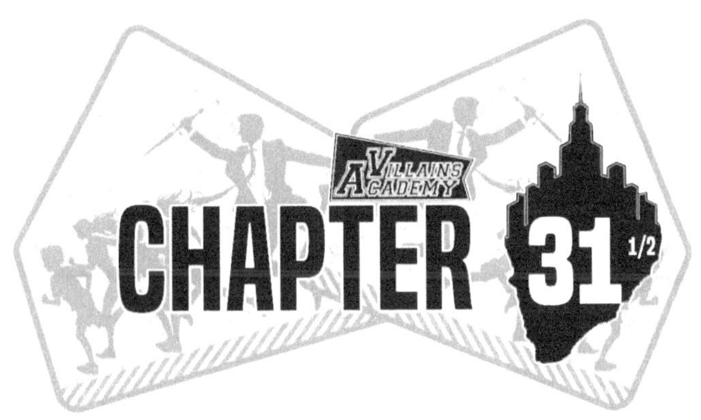

WHERE I WALK THROUGH MY YEAR AND LEAP FORWARD

When I was human, or even a minor god, I'd start my workday as usual in early January, get into a flow, and before I realized it, *BAM*, it was almost Christmas. There I was, wondering where the Hell did my year go?

I had to piece my missing year together from the brief, flickering memories associated with seasonal activities. Standard, multiversal events like the Valentine's Day Orgy, the Easter Sunday Zombie Walk for Criminal Charity, and the Juneteenth Hunt a Honky Hoedown & Hootenanny.

American Independence Day was naturally celebrated while on holiday in the UK. I love the Fourth so much that I ship a Humvee over to jolly ol' England, paint it red, white, and blue, and then drive it on the right side of the road. Trust me, dear reader, you haven't lived until you've crushed tea-drinking Union Jack-offs under six thousand pounds of American steel.

That's two thousand, seven hundred and twenty-one kilos for you metric users. Or, to take a step further for the sake of this joke, four hundred and twenty-eight and a half stone.

Let's see. Summers were spent chumming coastal waters for hungry sharks and gators to thin the gene pool.

Now now, no need to thank me; we all know beach people are the worst. Their smell alone is enough to warrant the effort. But worse than the pungent reek of seawater, BO, and suntan lotion is their insistence that sitting like well-oiled slugs atop the grittiest shit possible under the fiery radiation machine we call the sun is somehow "fun."

Hear me, beach people: You deserve a violent end. This is the one time I'm cheering for cancer.

But soon, the weather shifted and autumn was coming. Which for me meant producing new hydroponic strands of mega-calorie pumpkins specifically for white lady lattes. Drink up, gals. You totally deserve the fall taste of cinnamon, nutmeg, ginger, and cloves wrapped in nearly four hundred calories and fifty grams of sugar. And since I owned stock in multiple boots and leggings companies, thickening cankles and fatter asses meant higher profits for me.

Thanksgiving was a pretty standard affair in the Blackwell home. We visited alternate history realms where I negotiated deals for Native American colonizers to buy European land for the cheap.

Food's pretty much the same.

All this blathering about losing a year is meant to highlight the fact that time just slips by.

Psst, in case you're too dense to get the hint, we're time jumping a bit. If you want true slice-of-life, long-form genre fiction, then go read a Drew Hayes novel.

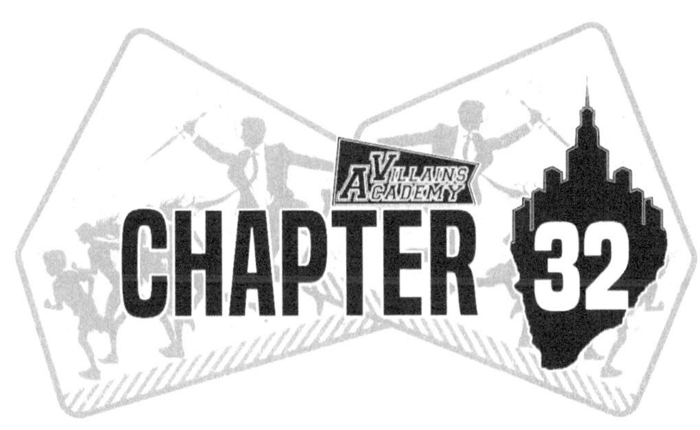

CHAPTER 32

WHERE I COMMENT ON RODENT MUNITIONS, CATCH YOU UP, AND PREP FOR BATTLE

"And that, class," Professor Renfield said, putting the finishing touches on the blackboard diagram, "is how you can turn a dead squirrel into an improvised bomb. Now, are there any questions?"

"Professor?" I said, raising my hand.

"Yes, Blackwell?"

"Have you considered a live squirrel?" I asked, checking my notes.

"Oh sure, many times," Professor Renfield said with a dismissive wave, then pointed back to the very detailed chalk diagram. "But they're not only harder to procure, but there's no guarantee that the bomb will go off in your desired spot. Death throes and adrenaline can turn those fuzzy fuckers into Olympic sprinters."

"You misunderstand, sir," I said, getting out of my chair and walking up to the board. "May I?"

"By all means," the professor said, handing me the chalk.

I worked in silence for a few moments, outlining my thoughts and appreciating the relative peace in which I worked. As promised, giving Beatrice and a few of her jock friends private villain tutoring had rewarded me with her prison-like protection.

Rumors dried up and direct attacks against me, even from my enemies, had gone to nearly nonexistent. Plus, I received a surprising side benefit for my extracurricular activities.

Since I had to return to Moriarty's class to take my metaphorical lumps, I was prepared for some kind of retaliation. And while the old bastard ranted, raved, and used me as the butt of his lectures, oddly, it never went past that. Yeah, he assigned me extra homework, but it wasn't anything I couldn't handle.

After a couple of weeks, Moriarty eventually called me into his office for a private meeting. Turns out, *Coach Mother* had put in a good word for me. Since I'd agreed to help her bottom-barrel bastards get better grades, the ogress had gone to bat for me with Moriarty. He admitted that he'd been watching me and was impressed. He claimed that it reminded him… of him.

Whatever. I'm pretty sure Coach Mother threatened to kick the shit out of him if he didn't ease up. But here's a free villain tip: If a windbag wants to help you, let them. Just know when to bail before you're guilty by association.

As for Coach Mother, sure, the freshman class still had to work to the point of puking, but water breaks were more frequent. As for the rest of school? Well, Professor Renfield's class was still my favorite. Considering the amount of time I'd spent in various worlds, often with limited power, I was already rather adept in this subject. Which meant I was at the top of class.

Yes, dear reader, I'd found my groove.

"Any day now, fatty!"

Sigh. Groove with exceptions.

I didn't bother looking back. I knew King Stanley's voice.

"Settle down, nerd boy," Ella Moontide, the werewolf girl with the one-sided ponytail, told the comic book god. "Unless you want his girlfriend to break your face."

"I'm not afraid of her," King Stanley said.

"And you're not afraid of dessert either," Lydia said, getting a chuckle from the class.

"Everyone settle down," Professor Renfield said, then added, "but please hurry up, Mr. Blackwell."

"Yes sir," I said, finishing my diagram. I took a step back, appreciating my work, then addressed the professor and the class. "The professor's concept of a dead squirrel being turned into an improvised biological weapon made me think of the time when I was advising some villains in a zombie universe."

The professor went to say something, but I held up my hand.

"Apologies for not being clearer," I said. "It was one of those deconstructionist worlds. The kind whose ruling gods act like pretentious authors. The kind of twits who think 'what if mankind were the real villain' is somehow artistically creative. Anyway, I was hired to counsel the human warlord who needed a way to get rid of the zombie menace. It was clear that the warlord had two things in abundance, old world explosive resources, and orphans. So peanut butter… meet jelly. By stuffing orphans full of explosives, we could lure hordes of zombies into selected locations."

"I see," Professor Renfield said, looking at my design and following the logic. "The orphans, who were obviously making noises of pain due to having had their arms and legs hacked off, attracted the zombies for a free snack."

"Obviously," I concurred.

"And by wiring the bomb to the respective orphan's heart, you effectively turned them in a dead man's trigger, thus ensuring maximum payload delivery."

"Yes sir," I said. "I figured that same method could be applied to your design. "Chop off a squirrel's legs to prevent the scramble factor, and thanks to bleeding out and rodent screams, you now have a time-delayed weapon. Using your initial premise of anthrax or whatever toxin you have on hand, the explosive compound you outlined will deliver both an explosive blast as well as contagion over a vast area."

Professor Renfield nodded while jotting down notes. "This is good work, Mr. Blackwell. The lesson was on extreme-situation survival, so again the live squirrel acquisition may be an issue. But I will gladly adapt this and add it to my advanced lessons on guerilla tactics."

"By all means, Professor."

"*By all means, Professor,*" Eris said, mocking my prepubescent voice.

"Ms. Pence," Professor Renfield said, glaring at my pseudo-nemesis. "While I'm all for maniacal mayhem and skillful bravado, I will not tolerate outbursts of unjustified belittling."

"Sir?" Eris said. "King Stanley made a fat joke."

"And? Mr. Blackwell is chubby," the professor said before looking over at me. "Apologies for stating the obvious."

"None taken," I said, patting my belly.

"And like Mr. Blackwell, Mr. Stanley has an enlarged midsection despite six weeks of Coach Mother's training. These are all factual statements, and facts cannot be argued."

"All I did was make a joke," she said, waving a hand.

"No, you're undermining a better student," the professor said. "Facts, in my class, above all else. If you cannot handle facts, then I suggest you grow a thicker skin."

"He's not better than me—"

"He has an A in this course so far and you barely have a C," Professor Renfield said.

"Okay, whatever," she said, trying to dismiss the issue. "But, like, he has more experience in this, so that's not—"

"If you say, 'that's not fair,' then I will remind you of the school you are currently enrolled in," the professor said, cutting her off.

Moving to the center of the room, Professor Renfield addressed her directly.

"I read your file, Ms. Pence, and despite your intellect and prior education, you show no aptitude for original thought. You've done nothing but copy Mr. Blackwell. Yet somehow, you deem yourself competent enough to critique the efforts of others. Now, are those enough facts for now, or would you like me to continue?"

"No, I'm good, Professor," she said, barely maintaining her composure.

Professor Renfield's snarl melted back into his easier, happy-go-lucky persona.

"Excellent! Now seeing as there's a qualifying game this evening, I don't see any reason against an early dismissal. Class is dismissed. Have a nice study period, and I'll see you all at the match. Good luck to all competitors."

Everyone gathered their belongings and began filing out. I hefted my backpack, but Professor Renfield cleared his throat.

"Mr. Blackwell, a word?"

"Yes, Professor."

Wraith Knight shot me a look, but I waved him off with a nod. My former henchman looked between us, then nodded himself. After the last of the class had left, Renfield shut the door.

"So, Blackwell, you've really stepped up in a short amount of time, haven't you?"

"Yes, Professor."

"I've heard that you've been studying magic?"

"I've picked up a few spells and cantrips."

"Pish," he said. "I heard you were invited to join Baba Yaga's private study group?"

"I have," I admitted. "I'd be a failed mastermind if I didn't take advantage of everything the school offered."

"That's a late-night group."

"Yes, Professor. The witching hours."

"So you're burning the candle at both ends then?"

"I am," I admitted. "But I'm learning a lot."

"Anything useful?"

"Some," I shrugged. "A lot of basic spells for offense and defense. But I've been really getting good at transmutation."

"Oh?"

I picked up a piece of chalk and a pencil from his desk and looked to him for permission. When the professor nodded, I set the chalk down and placed my right hand on the chalk and my left on the pencil. I gave a slight muttering of powerful arcane words, then removed my hands. The pencil was now a copy of the chalk. I looked up at the taller man with a smile of satisfaction.

"Um… neat?" he said, clearly not impressed with my simple trick.

"Eh, it's a work in progress," I told him. "The spell is simple, changing similar size objects. Problem is when you come across something enchanted. You have to have another, equally enchanted item of the same size and rough mass. The copies are decent, but will crumble after five or so uses. Still, I think this idea has potential."

"Well, just make sure you rest," Professor Renfield said. "I've seen too many students do exactly what you've been doing, and they never make it."

"I know how to manage my time, sir."

"Good, good," the professor said. "And your *other* extracurricular activities?"

And there it was. Renfield was not so discreetly asking if I'd figured out a way to stop Possibility from shutting this whole experiment down and trapping him and the staff inside. But since he didn't have Nyx's little pocket dimension space, then anything we said aloud would be known to our Titan host.

"I'm doing what I can," I said. "This project is a little harder than most. But I'll crack it. Don't worry, sir."

"Maybe you should get more rest then," Renfield said. "And a salad wouldn't kill you?"

I smiled and patted my belly. "Maybe you're right."

"No offense intended, son, but like King Stanley, you're not showing much improvement physically. Eight weeks of Coach Mother's regimen should have melted more of that off. Your face is thinner, and I like the new haircut, but… come on."

"I'll take it under advisement, Professor," I said, then paused. "While I have your ear, sir, I do have an odd question for you."

"Oh?"

"I'm sure this has been asked before, so my apologies for almost certainly repeating it."

"Out with it."

"How many points does a student get for killing a professor?"

Renfield didn't say anything. But his body shifted in such a way that I knew he was preparing any number of contingency plans.

"Not you, sir. Never you. You're one of the few I like."

"That's not helping your cause," Renfield said. "This is a villain school."

"Heh, fair enough," I said. "I was just honestly curious. Each of you have your own connection to the Sablestone, so I assume you get revived should death occur. Maybe you all kill each other? But is it even possible for a student to kill a staff member?"

"All things are possible," he said. "And the points, should such a thing ever occur, which it has not, would be… considerable."

"Thank you," I said, packing up my stuff. "Now, is there anything else you need, sir?"

"Actually, there is one thing, for me, personally."

"Sir?"

"Kick the shit out of them tonight," Professor Renfield said.

What he asked was no small feat. Sablestone Academy's sport of slaughterball was, as the name implied, lethal. Tonight's matchup between Moriarty's Mind Fire Calling and Dracula's the Veil Walkers was projected to be a one-sided game at best.

And I was not on the winning side.

But considering Renfield's tenuous relationship with his former master, it was no wonder he wanted me to win.

"Is this germane to the conversation we just had?"

"Heh, no," he laughed. "But I would greatly love to see my former mas—Professor Dracula… put out, if you catch my meaning."

"I'll do what I can, sir. But if you were to offer me any insight or advice?"

Renfield chuckled. "Would that I could. All I can say is that when battling gods and otherworldly powers, it's a good thing your team has you on their side."

"Thank you, sir."

"You're welcome. Best of luck, Blackwell."

WHERE I KEEP RUNNING INTO Y'OLLY, EXPLAIN THE GAME, AND RALLY THE TEAM

"And stay down, ya little bitch!" Y'olly roared.

Once again, the much larger demon slammed into me. I was launched several feet before landing in a heap. Gasping, I rolled over and tried to recall the last time I'd been hit that hard.

Oh yeah, like thirty seconds ago, when the last player hit me.

And twenty seconds before that… and almost a minute before that.

You get the picture.

From the flat of my back, I had to squint due to the field's nighttime floodlights. Despite the chest protector's padding, I felt all three hundred plus pounds of a teenage Y'ollgorath adding more than a little insult to injury. Demon bastard had stomped a cloven hoof onto my chest.

"Really… Y'olly?" I wheezed, digging my nails into his ankle. "I helped you get a couple of promotions!"

"Yeah, you did," he said, laughing at my pathetic attempt to dislodge his foot. Despite the small trickle of blood, he pressed down harder. "I've already been informed by my superiors that beating a Titan is gonna get me a spot in the ninth and final circle of the Never Realm."

"And if I beat you?"

Y'olly increased the pressure on my chest. "Then they wouldn't be happy with me, now would they? But that's never gonna happen."

A sharp whistle disrupted our "conversation."

"Oh, bro, look, we scored again," Y'olly said, looking at the far end of the field before glancing back down at my prostrated form. "Man, is there anyone on our team that hasn't laid you out?"

"No… don't think so," I said, coughing up equal parts phlegm and blood. "Seems that without Beatrice, everyone's taking out their frustrations on me."

"Heh heh, yeah," he chuckled. "She's a powerhouse, that's for sure. But I'm an eighth-circle demon. Except for Sophia and Stanley, no student's more powerful than me."

"You ever think Sophia's just using you?"

"Everyone uses everyone," Y'olly said.

Captain Hook, the game referee, blew a three-burst whistle, signaling the end of the half. Y'olly looked down at me once more and smiled.

"See ya in the second half, bud."

"Look—looking forward… to it," I managed to say before my former friend tore his hoof out of my feeble grip.

Y'olly trotted off to his sideline, leaving me there in my misery.

While the Veil Walkers were celebrating their first-half success, I took in the totality of my team. And it was not good.

Lemme put it to you this way: The Mind Fire Calling had the combined athletic prowess of an eighteen-year-old diabetic cat. Sitting there on our sidelines, they reminded me of those paintings depicting wounded Revolutionary War soldiers. But, you know, in cheap high school-level lacrosse pads and jerseys instead of colonial pantaloons. Still, if there was a dude playing a death march on a fife, it would complete the picture.

Good. Exactly what I wanted.

I think.

With a massive amount of grit, I pushed myself up from the grass and found my footing. I was wobbly, yes, but I could move. Limping, I made for my team's sidelines.

A slaughterball field was roughly the same size and length as a standard soccer pitch. But instead of being flat and free of obstructions, a slaughterball game zone was littered with all manner of boulders, overturned cars, and other random obstacles. These were meant to simulate a "real world" battlefield terrain.

At either end of the field was a circular scoring zone with a twenty-foot-tall elevated platform. A spiral ramp led to the top, where each team's scoring bucket rested. The game used a singular oblong ball, like a rugby ball, called a Screele.

The goal of the game was simple. A maximum of eleven people per team met at midfield and fought in a scrum for possession of the Screele. They then moved the ball any way they could, fighting off the other team, to deposit the ball into the other team's scoring bucket. Doing so earned one point. After that, the buckets would magically return the Screele to midfield, and the whole process would start over. Repeat for two thirty-minute halves.

But what about powers? you ask.

Well, if you have powers, use 'em. Lightning bolts, fireballs, or animal transformations? All legal. You brought a flaming battle axe? Swing away. Dirty tactics? Yes please. Hell, if you somehow managed to stuff a Soviet era tank up your butt and then crapped out said tank onto the field with the intent of driving it down the throats of your opponents, then happy hunting, comrade.

Teams could sub in new players on the fly, provided the relieved player either left the field for the sideline of their own volition… or were dead. Unconscious, frozen, paralyzed, et cetera, did not matter. Which often meant teammate-on-teammate mercy killings were totally a thing.

And yeah, that's it. That's the end of the rules.

In slaughterball, there were no turnovers, no penalties, and no fouls. Typically, each path showed up in its respective entirety and cycled people in and out due to the whole "teammates dying" thing.

Dr. Moreau was obviously present, either patching kids up or putting them down. More times than not, it was the latter. And considering that the Mind Fire Calling had about thirty students total, most of which lacked superhuman powers or abilities, the good doctor spent the majority of his time on our side.

"Jackson!" Evie yelled out.

I was pretty sure I saw three of her, so I aimed for the one in the middle and approached.

"Yes?"

"You good?"

I just stared at my daughter-slash-player coach. "Do I look good?"

"You look like hammered shit," she said, handing me a disposable cup filled with an orange liquid.

I gladly accepted the cup and knocked back the drink in two gulps. It wasn't bad for generic Gatorade. But it wasn't the flavor that the team appreciated; it was the fact that I'd spiked it with a shitload of the painkillers and accelerated healing meds I'd filched from Moreau's class back during Hell Week.

"All part of the plan," I said, tossing the cup away.

"There's a plan?" Emily said. "You sure?"

The cybernetically augmented koala stood on the bench and pointed at the scoreboard, which read thirty-seven to three.

"Okay, we're at a bit of a deficit," I admitted, looking down at her. "But trust me. We're giving the other team a false sense of security."

"You're full of shit," she said, crossing her furry little arms.

Gods above and below, I still wanted to hug her. Even angry, she was too cute for this world. But she wasn't wrong about the embarrassing score. Evie had scored two of those points herself. Armed with automatic weapons, vials of holy water, and a shitload of pluck, my pride and joy had put us on the scoreboard. It had cost her several broken fingers, a pint of blood, and a whole host of bruises, but she'd shown us all what could be done.

The last point was a complete accident.

Or at least, it looked like an accident.

Under my instruction, Keith had hung back by our scoring bucket. He'd always said that people didn't notice him, and he was right. Just as the team dunked the ball in our end zone, Keith jumped out and followed the ball into the bucket. Both he and the Screele reappeared at midfield. Then the little dude just took off running, more out of fear than strategy.

You ever tried grabbing a piglet who doesn't wanna be grabbed, let alone a sweaty, squealing pig boy? Let's just say that they both can haul ass when necessary.

"Yes, I have a plan," I told the team. "But none of you are going to like it."

They all started grumbling and vocalizing how it might be best for me to go off and fornicate with myself. I could see it in their bloodshot, weary eyes that it was going to take a helluva lot of convincing, emphasis on "hell."

I looked up into the stands, spotting Lydia. She was sitting with Mikayla under a blanket, sharing a hot chocolate. It was sweet. My ex caught me looking and gave me the finger. But I could tell she was smiling when she did it.

But it wasn't her that I was trying to communicate with.

Mikayla looked over the field, looked back at me, and gave the slightest of nods.

Good. If I pulled this off, then I had a new ally.

"All of you, shut up," Evie told our remaining players. "I don't like to lose at anything. So unless any of you have a plan, then shut up and listen. Jackson?"

"First, I have one question," I said as if this had been rehearsed between Evie and me.

Which it had.

"Do you wanna win?" I asked the team.

While everyone looked confused, it was Emily who answered. "Yes?"

"What about the rest of you?!" I said, raising my voice so all my teammates could hear me. "Do you wanna win?!"

"Yes!" several of the Mind Fire Calling called back.

"Then let me fucking hear ya, do you want to fucking win?!"

"Yes!" my team roared.

"Then bring it in," I said, forming a huddle on the sidelines.

It wasn't that difficult, considering half the team was dead.

"Okay nerds," I began, "I have a foolproof plan to steal victory out from under these cloak-wearing see you next Tuesdays. And all I need are two things to make it happen."

"I'm guessing number one is keeping you alive?" Evie said.

"You got it."

"Then I really hope that Mentalax's telekinetic powers are not the second," Evie said, breaking the huddle and pointing over to the benches. "Because I'm pretty sure he's dead... again."

I looked over to see Dr. Moreau checking the alien's pulse. But considering that his bulbous head was split neatly down the middle, I found myself agreeing with Evie's medical assessment.

Well, shit.

"Okay, new plan," I said.

"Is this one still a guaranteed victory?" Emily asked.

"Um, sure. Well… about sixty-five percent guaranteed," I said, ignoring the groans from the team. "But I'm gonna need a few more things."

"What?" Evie asked.

I smiled and checked the halftime clock. It was gonna be close. I looked back to where Dr. Moreau was treating the dead alien with the young pig boy by his side.

"Keith! Get over here, buddy!" I yelled. "You're gonna help us win the game!"

"Keith is?" he asked.

I smiled. "Yes, Keith is. Can you steal a bunch of your dad's scalpels?"

"You got it, friend!"

CHAPTER 34

WHERE I STUMBLE OUT OF THE GATE, TAUNT A DEMON WITH MY BUTTHOLE, AND MAKE A SACRIFICE PLAY

"This is not going to end well for you," Sophia said to me from across the midfield line.

"The game, or your little trap?" I replied, keeping an eye on the ref.

"Both," she said, oozing confidence.

The larger and more physically fit players positioned themselves at midfield, awaiting the start of the second half. Being smaller, I was on the wings of the impending scrum, which was fine with me. Our team had little in the way of physical specimens, and it showed. While the Veil Walkers didn't have the same amount of raw beef as Those Who Hunger, they damn sure weren't couch potatoes.

Still, I had faith in my plan. Which meant not allowing Sophia to get into my head.

"Things are going to get so much worse for you," she said, continuing the trash talk.

"We'll see," I said, just as the ref blew the whistle. I charged forward—

And fell flat on my face.

A quick glance down, and I saw that my cleats' shoelaces had been tied together.

"See ya!" Sophia said with an exaggerated wink, then charged off.

I couldn't be mad. Using her probability powers to tie my shoes together without me noticing? Bloody perfection on an effective, time-honored classic villain trick. Rolling over, I quickly untied my cleats.

With no surprise to anyone, the Veil Walkers had gained possession of the Screele. Sophia floated down the field with the rest of her team, providing as much luck as possible. Not that they really needed it. The Veil Walkers were running over players or just tossing them into the field obstructions.

I winced when that Dieter kid was sent crashing spine-first into the burned-out husk of a replica of a Word War Two bunker. The outer brick wall collapsed inward, burying the steampunk fascist under several hundred pounds of irony.

It was perfectly legal under the game's lack of rules. Yet I felt it was a little uncalled for when Y'olly took a moment to teabag the dying Dieter. But that's the game. And in a way, a perfect example of life. Smart people can plan all day. But people with no fear of reprisal or consequences do as they please.

And the Veil Walkers were brimming with power.

As a former god, a long-buried part of me sensed it, that connection. A vast wellspring of energy transcending space and time tethered to each person in that villainous path, imbuing the respective recipients with power. Divine, unholy, or in between, it didn't matter. For each member of the Veil Walkers tapped into something that made them otherworldly.

Bloody perfect.

Dieter was just the first to die. Over the next ten minutes, play after play, I watched as my teammates were crushed, bludgeoned, smote, or just plain ol' killed. Just to add insult to injury, the Veil Walkers made sure to let their freshmen get some extra field time.

One of our players, Janna Hatchet, was the daughter of a notorious smuggler in her pirate fantasy world. She had dreams of organizing all the privateer forces into a unified fleet to control the seas. But she ended up being burned alive by Valliar's holy light.

King in Waiting Vistaar Corona the Fourth, the next in line to inherit the throne of some lazily written space opera universe, was exsanguinated by my dear friend Khasil. The serpent-haired bitch made sure she locked eyes with me while she drank poor Vistaar dry.

Even King Stanley got in on it. Having transformed into some generic superhero douche with laser eyes, ol' Stanley melted Jason Lancaster Dagget, a bio-mech engineering genius from my team. I can't say as I regretted that guy's death, as JLD was a Jigsaw-type serial killer mastermind. The kind of villain that makes murder podcast-addicted women horny.

Seriously, people, if your wife or girlfriend loves those kinds of shows and podcasts, just walk the fuck away and thank me later.

Unless you're into choke kink.

And even then, she's likely thinking of ways of framing you for her murder.

Teammate after teammate was wiped out, and our reserves had nearly run dry. When that anime kid, Astigaath, had come onto the field to fill a missing spot, Sophia herself did the deed. To his credit, the living cartoon had done his damnedest to play defense. But although Astigaath had a keen mind and an athletic body, Sophia was a djinn, and spiteful one at that. The djinn dug her claws into Astigaath's back and literally pulled him apart, spilling ink on the field and dropping the halves like snotty used tissues.

With laughs and high fives, Sophia and her little team of suck-ups, save for Y'olly, jogged off the field, subbing in four new fresh players.

Things had gotten dire.

With eight dead teammates, we had only four players left alive. There were ten minutes left in the game, and the score was now forty-six to three.

It was now or never.

"Positions!" I yelled, then sprinted back to our scoring zone.

Evie and Emily took to the wings of the field, near the sidelines. When the Screele appeared in the midfield, Y'olly grabbed the ball and took off directly down the middle. Now, his aggressive move might have been because he really wanted to score. Or perhaps it had something to do with me having slipped the elastic waist of my shorts down, bending over, and taunting the demon with my brown eye.

Who knows for sure?

I did know that staring inverted through my own legs made the timing of my next move difficult.

Difficult, but not impossible.

"Y'ollgorath, stop!" Sophia called from the sidelines, sensing something was up.

But the big dumb demon ignored her and charged right for my rectum. Just when Y'olly got into the correct position, I yelled out, "Keith!"

You see, dear reader, I did say that there were four of us left. Me, Evie, Emily, and… heh heh, Keith. My dear roommate who was very good at not being noticed.

The little mutant jumped out from cover and into Y'olly's path, tripping the giant demon and causing a fumble.

Pants now up, I dashed forward and recovered the Screele. But instead of charging up the field to face an entire team, I instead turned and ran back to *my team's* scoring bucket. Sprinting up the ramp, I reached the top of the platform and jumped into the scoring bucket with the Screele.

Thanks to my earlier tests, I rematerialized at midfield with the ball. Sure, I'd given the Veil Walkers another point, but that didn't matter. Their whole team was on my team's side of the field.

Phase one complete. Now for phase two.

Keith shot me a wink, then took out one of his father's scalpels, and without hesitation, the little pig slit his own throat. His blood flowed and his eyes went glassy, but the little bastard had a smile on his face. I tossed Evie the ball, reached under my jersey for a second, then slammed my hands down, digging my fingers into the field at the midpoint line.

You see, Professor Renfield had only scratched the surface when he mentioned just how much time I'd spent learning magic over the last couple of months. Fun fact: A lot of taboo arcana is about stealing power from otherworldly forces. It's what the Forbidden Tome's model is based on and why their course curriculum details how to create binding circles.

Like the book I'd gotten from Mikayla.

The Veil Walkers had an abundance of raw power. So naturally, that made them blind to the machinations of mere mortals. What can I say? Tropes are tropes. They had had so much fun killing my teammates, no one seemed to notice exactly *where* on the field my teammates died.

Check that… where they had *willingly died.*

After all, my teammates had said they'd do anything to win the game. Which brings me to my ol' pal Y'olly.

The demon had bragged about how much power he had. And as you may recall from the last chapter, I'd made a point of really struggling under his hoof… while drawing blood from his ankle.

Folks, it's no secret that you can do a lot of things with blood, magically speaking. A fast mixture of concealed ingredients, hands on the ground, and a few bullshit words in faux Latin later, a nine-pointed star flared into being, connecting the spots where each of my teammates had *sacrificed* their lives. Charged by the blood of a powerful demon, the barrier held firm, keeping them not only trapped on my team's side of field but also frozen in place.

The spell was slapdash at best and would only last for… ten minutes or so?

"This is the bullshit!" Dracula called out from his sideline to Captain Hook.

"Maybe," Hook said. "But it's legal. If you want subs, then you know the rules."

"But they are frozen in place!" Dracula countered, rolling his *r*'s. "They can't leave the field!"

"Yeah, cool, isn't it?" I said, daring to taunt the professor. "Shame someone thought ahead on how to abuse the few rules this game has."

"This is not over, Blackwell!" Dracula said, flashing me his fangs before dramatically whipping his cloak around so that only his yellow eyes were showing.

Sigh. Have I ever mentioned how much I hate theater people?

With the remaining time left on the clock, Evie, Emily, and I took turns sprinting down the enemy field, dunking the Screele into the Veil Walkers' scoring bucket only for it to reappear at the midline for the next person to take off and repeat the process.

Without anyone stopping us, the game was now one of endurance. But seeing as we had a chance for our first win ever, we were not going to quit.

When the whistle blew, signaling the end of the game, we were sweaty, tired, and out of breath.

Captain Hook announced the final score.

"Veil Walkers, forty-seven. The Mind Fire Calling, sixty-nine. Winners, the Mind Fire Calling!"

The crowd erupted, leaping to their feet and cheering. Professor Dracula changed into a bat and flew away while Professor Renfield clapped so hard he nearly broke his hands.

Do I even need to tell you how good it feels to be publicly praised for being a master villain?

"Yeesh, Dad, did we need to run the score up to such a juvenile number?" Evie laughed.

I shrugged an insincere apology. We'd won the game, but more than that, I had just earned a metric fuckton of school points by having my own teammates willingly kill themselves for my nefarious scheme. I looked to our sidelines and saw Professor Moriarty. He mimed tipping a cap, and I returned it with a respectful nod.

But I had one last move.

With a few seconds left on my spell, I ran back to the midline and put my hands back into the earth, feeling the waves of the binding spell.

"Y'ollgorath Ig'paan'ah VanDammed, Exalted One from the Eighth plane of the Never Realm, by the nine points and the nine circles of the Never Realm, you are held helpless," I began. "With your true name freely given and your blood deceptively stolen, I banish you, back to from whence you came!"

"Fuck *youuuuuuuu…*" the demon cursed as he faded out of existence.

I then looked to Sophia on the sideline and mouthed, "One down."

WHERE I KEEP MY SECRETS, HIGHLIGHT DEMON DISSATISFACTION, AND BRING PEOPLE TOGETHER

Resting her back against the plinth holding the Sablestone, Evie pulled her flask out of her backpack, popped the top, and took a sip.

"Oh, I needed that," she said, then passed it to me.

"Mm, thanks," I said, taking my own gulp of the fiery whiskey before passing it back. "Do we need to talk about your 'needing at drink' at your age?"

Evie shrugged. "Maybe? But considering I'm the daughter of the Shadow Master and an assassin, living in an academy with teenagers training to be villains, it's either the occasional drink or a lot of teenage sex to keep my sanity."

"Question retracted."

"You sure?" she said. "Because I've found that when I'm doing it, I—"

"Blah blah blah, not listening," I said, making a fatherly show of putting my fingers in my ears.

She in turn made a show of finger puppets doing all manner of lewd things. I turned away, acting upset.

I wasn't, of course.

Considering the home she'd grown up in, we'd had "the talk" long ago.

"Don't worry, my girlfriend and I know how to be safe."

"Girlfriend, huh?"

"Well, the girl I'm seeing, but… yeah." She smiled. "But don't ask who. We're very private. If the school knew, then people would—"

"Use it against you," I said, filling the blank.

"Yeah," she said. "We're together but… you know. Keeping it loose."

I nodded, but didn't push. This was her opening up, and I wasn't going to jeopardize that with a dad question. Instead, I grunted and stood up, ditching my mesh jersey.

Pulling my t-shirt up and over my head, I dropped the sweaty ball of cotton to reveal a foam pregnancy belly strapped to my torso.

"Okay, seriously, how'd you pull that off?"

"*Hmm?*" I said, undoing the low-profile buckles and letting the molded foam drop to the ground. The little hidden bottles and various spell components rattled and jangled in their straps and housings.

The cool air felt nice on my now flatter, and much trimmer, stomach. I stretched a few times, working out the sore muscles. I was so looking forward to dying tonight.

"What can I say, Keith's a miracle worker," I said. "With all the random crap that ends up in this place, there's nothing the little guy can't find or steal."

"That's not what I'm talking about."

"Oh, you mean the secret about my disappearing chub?"

"That's a way of saying it."

I shot my daughter my classic smirk. "I found a cheat code."

"Oh?" she said. "What kind?"

I always loved the parlor scenes in murder mysteries. The part when the mastermind character gets to brag. It's like heroin for me. But… sometimes you had to keep things to yourself. It's like Ben Franklin said. *Three men can keep a secret as long as two of them are dead.*

And we need to respect this man. Especially considering that Benny was a brilliant polymath who claimed founding father status while avoiding the presidency *and* was frequently balls deep in an ocean of Parisian whores.

Game respects game.

No, there was no upside to confiding my secret to Evie. That I'd worked out a way to safely die and heal up without losing points. And since we woke up at 5:57 every morning post death, rested if groggy, I could stay up all night studying magic or whatever else I needed.

"Sorry, kiddo. Some things are best kept close to the vest," I said.

"Fine. Keep your secrets, old man," she said. "It's more fun to learn them anyway. But that fat suit isn't going to fool the other students for long."

"I know," I told her. "But as long as most folk still see me as the chubby kid, they'll underestimate me. Plus, I need a place to stash my spell-crafting components. And this works perfectly."

"So, about Y'olly."

"What about him?"

"Come on, Dad. Removing a student against Possibility's will?"

"Rules, little one. Rules," I said. "You have your student guidebook in your backpack?"

"Yeah, why?"

"Turn to the section on student withdrawal."

Evie flipped through the pages until she reached the section. "Okay, now what?"

"What are the terms for early withdrawal or disenrollment?"

Evie scanned the page. "Dissatisfaction with the school, financial constraints, relocation or change in family circumstances, and health or personal issues."

"Exactly."

"I'm not sure I follow," she said.

"Look, kid, this whole farkakteh school and setting is iffy at best," I said. "But Y'olly *is* a demon from the Never Realm, and as such, he answers to powers higher than him. He admitted that he was betting his next promotion on being integral in the defeat of a Titan—namely, me. To put it bluntly, the big red bastard put all his chips on Sophia."

"Okay, but that doesn't explain how—"

"Patience, youngling, I'm getting there," I said. "The Never Realm technically touches all planes of being, presumably even here. So when I cast that spell using willing sacrifices, Y'olly's blood, and his true name, I established a connection to the Never Realm. I took my own gamble, betting that his superiors were so pissed that he was trapped like a common demon that they'd have a withdrawal letter drafted. A letter outlining their dissatisfaction with the school for letting something like this happen, their intent to relocate Y'olly, and that he would definitely have future health problems."

"Okay, you banished him. But aside from taking away one of Sophia's minions, what else did it do?"

"I essentially canceled all his contracts."

"Ahh," Evie said, seeing a bit more. "Which means that Mikayla is no longer his possession and she's now a free agent."

"Score one more for me."

Evie once again gave me that appraising look. "How'd you know his true name?"

I chuckled. "Child, please. Back when we were business partners, I already knew his first and last name, which was confirmed during the sorting ceremony because I speak demon. The key came when the smug fuck told me his middle name was 'Spotlight.' So for the spell, I just translated it back into demon."

Evie gave me my own slow clap. "Well done, Dad."

"Trust me, kiddo. Knowing the right moment to strike is less impressive than creating the right moment. Speaking of, I think it's time."

"Time for what?" Evie asked.

"You out there?" I asked, raising my voice.

Lydia entered the Sablestone room, her head down. She wasn't wearing her blade holsters, likely having left them out in the hallway. This didn't mean she wasn't carrying any number of concealed weapons on her. Still, with how she fumbled with her hands, it was clear she didn't know what to do without the reassuring steel.

"Hey, baby," Lydia said to Evie, her normal bravado gone.

"Mom," Evie said, using the word like a slur while shooting me the dirtiest of looks.

Gods above and below, the emotional tension between them was so thick I was practically choking on it. Watching these two stare one another down made me happy that I was an orphan.

Yeah, I said it.

But none of that mattered right now. The rift between my ex-wife and daughter needed to be addressed. Gods help me.

"You two have been ignoring one another since we got here, and I think it's time we cut the shit and deal with this, as a family,"

I said, gesturing among the three of us. "I hit Sophia hard today, which means she's gonna hit back even harder. And I need to know that we three are united."

Both turned and looked at me. It was not pretty.

"Really, Dad?" Evie said. "You bring Mom in to talk but somehow make it about yourself?"

"See?" Lydia said. "This is the shit I've been saying all along. Everything's about him."

Well... that didn't take long. It's like they didn't hear me say the words "we," "family," and "united."

Yeesh. Dem bitches be cray cray. But if they were agreeing on something, I should bloody well run with it.

"Yeah, it *is* about me, and it's high time you two put aside your petty bullshit and realize that."

I swear the air visibly grew colder.

"Okay, I'm sensing that I may have overstepped a bit."

"*Ya think?*" they said in unison.

"But to put things in perspective, this is a trap for me," I said. "And you two being mad at one another is a tale as old as time."

"I'm not mad," they both said, again in unison.

They looked at one another, both standing there with arms crossed and their hips canted the exact same way. Neither knew what to do, so they turned on me.

But I was prepared.

"Evie, babe, you said before that Sophia had made sure you had the last recorded adventure, right?"

"Yeah, I got it and read it. Not your best work," she said. "Kinda full of mushy stuff and self-improvement bullshit."

"Yeah yeah, get in line with the rest of the critics," I said. "We were parodying those journey of self-discovery books and Gibson got carried away. Point is, you read it, right?"

"Yeah, I read it," she said, giving Lydia the side eye before reaching into her backpack and pulling out the book.

She flipped to an earmarked page and read aloud.

"*Ahem... This may come as a surprise, Jackson, but I never got to make that choice. You knocked me up the first night we screwed. It wasn't something I planned on, or honestly, wanted. Even our relationship was rushed because of the baby. Sure, she grew up fast and I didn't have to deal with the shittier parts of rearing a child. But it was never something I wanted. So now she's off doing whatever? Good. I wish her well.*"

Lydia threw her arms up. "I was literally under Mikayla's spell."

"Uh huh," Evie said.

"Let me see that fucking thing," Lydia said, snatching the book. She flipped to a later page. "Ah, here. See? I told Jackson to kill Mikayla because she'd robbed me of my memory and love for you."

The cruel smile that spread across Evie's lips meant that Lydia had played right into her hands.

"Then why're you two dating again?"

"I—well, we—"

"Save it," Evie said. "It's clear what's important to you."

"Oh, blow it out your ass," I told my daughter.

"Excuse me?"

"No, I won't," I said, squaring up on my child. "Get this through your head, kid. We're not your friends, we're your parents."

"I—"

"Shush," I said, miming a hand puppet closing its mouth. "Friends come and go, but the relationship you have with your parents lasts the rest of your life and long after we're gone. We can be friendly, loving, laughing and all that. But our role, good or bad, is to guide you and teach you. In that dynamic, we all learn things. First up, parents are people too. And people make mistakes."

"I'm a mistake then?"

"Yes," I said, but continued before she interrupted. "A wonderful, beautiful, smart, mistake. Neither of us planned on conceiving a child that night. We were just two consenting, horny adults going to pound town."

"Jackson, maybe this isn't how we want to—"

"You shush too," I said, showing Lydia the same hand puppet. "This is for your benefit as well. Evie, I'm sorry your mom and I split up, I really am. But the math just wasn't in our favor."

"Math?" Evie said.

"Mm," I nodded. "Over fifty percent of marriages end in divorce."

"I know that."

"But did you know that when polled, nearly seventy-five percent of the remaining fifty percent admitted that they only stayed together for the sake of kids or fear of losing out on money? That means only approximately thirteen percent of couples are happily in love."

"That's… bleak," Evie said.

"Yeah, but you do it anyway because love is worth it. Your mom and I took our shot, and it didn't work out. And now, she's dating Mikalya because she's in love with her. Love makes us do stupid, crazy things. Like, oh let's just say, throwing ourselves inside an elder Titan, knowing it's a trap, to get our child back. And while I was being cautious, your mom was busting in, ovaries out, ready to kick down doors and stab faces to make sure you were okay. Do you get it yet?"

Evie looked at her mom. "Really?"

"Yeah," Lydia said. "Your father was acting like a little bitch."

Oy vey.

"I—I messed up a lot," Lydia said, taking Evie's hands. "I can't fix the past, but I want us to have a better future. All I'm asking is that you give me another chance. Please."

"And if you could do it quickly so that we can discuss the Sophia strategy—"

Again, both of them glared at me.

"Fine, fine, it's not like we have pressing issues," I said. "How about this, I'll leave you two alone and I'll see you at breakfast?"

They didn't answer me. Mother and daughter held one another, forging a new bond over the broken bits of their past.

It was truly beautiful.

And it made getting between them awkward.

"Sorry, you're standing over my—yeah, right there, my shirt and jersey, and—oh please move, your foot's on my fat suit. I need to—gods damn it, *move!*"

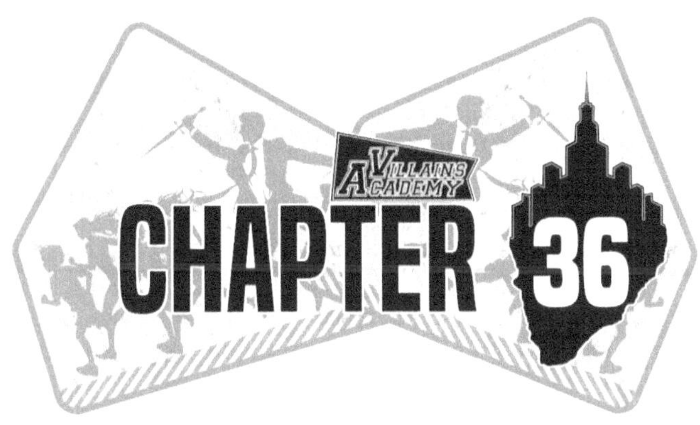

CHAPTER 36

WHERE I BEGRUDGINGLY GIVE VAMPIRES RESPECT, COMMISERATE WITH AN ADVISOR, AND OFFER EMPLOYMENT

It was later than I expected when I came up to the quad. That was the problem with the bowels of the main castle—no sense of time. Despite the late hour, there was a dull roar across the campus of students being young.

I missed that.

Don't get me wrong—I'm not the "eat dinner at four, asleep by eight" kind of old, but I was older. In mind and soul if not in current body. And aside from Evie, there were few young people here I could tolerate.

Isolation, dear reader, is the price of experience.

The more you do, see, and experience, the more intolerant one becomes when dealing with the young. It's not their fault. They just don't know yet that nearly every thought, feeling, or idea that crosses their limited minds has already been thought, felt, or conceived of a million times over by more refined minds.

It's the reason vampire stories still exist.

I'm not really a fan of vampire lit, and I've never hid that. Aside from all the obvious jokes, normally at the expense of those tiresome fanatics who go ga-ga for vampire literature, there's nothing there for me. Excluding those authors who put a twist on the old formula, the core is the same. Some old, dusty-ass vampire bemoaning the modern era while cursing their continued existence.

We get it, Lucien—because it's always a pretentious name like "Lucien"—you're a dark poet, and the modern world is soulless compared to fourteen ninety-whatever-the-fuck. We've heard it all before.

But as I get older, Lucien starts to make sense. Stupid character name aside, the point is that with experience comes the inability to relate to others, excluding those with similar experiences. Over time, the more one does, the fewer there are who can understand you. And for someone like me, there are almost none.

Almost.

There are a few of us out there who know what it's like to be screwed over by cosmic-powered entities, and even fewer who know what it is to be the Shadow Master.

"Evening," I said to the lone dark-skinned girl sitting on the bench near the Mind Fire Calling's tower.

Eris turned around, her eyes betraying nothing. I'll give her poker face credit; she could have just been sitting there or planning my assassination. The only thing working against the girl on the bench was that I was expecting this moment. Not necessarily tonight, mind you. Just this eventuality. Which was why I sat down next to her, fearing nothing.

"Aren't you going to ask me what I'm doing here?" she said as I leaned back against the bench.

"No," I said, crossing my legs. "I know why you're here."

She rolled her eyes. "Of course you'd say that."

"Well, to be fair, I've been at this a bit longer than you," I told her. "And there are really only two reasons that you're here. Either to kill me or to get my advice."

"I could be here as part of a plot to get into your confidence."

"Are you?"

She sniffed and shook her head. "No."

"Which brings us back to murder or advice," I said. "If it's the former, I'm gonna be mad. Not about dying, mind you. Having had the shit kicked out of me during the game, I wouldn't mind the rest. But seeing as most of my path is dead, at least for tonight, I was looking forward to the whole tower being quiet."

"I'm not here to kill you," she said.

"Then what advice are you looking for?" I said, following the logical conclusion.

She just stared at me.

I stared back.

"Come on," I said, coaxing it out of her. "You did the advisor thing while I was gone. You can't help a client if they're unclear about their wants. Sophia screwed you over, so let's talk about it."

She didn't say anything at first. She didn't suck on her teeth or look around while she considered my words. She just kept her eyes trained on mine, blinking at normal intervals.

Like I said, great poker face.

But the face is only one part of body language. Lady MacBeth and the Cheshire Cat covered this already. Hands, feet, and posture are giveaways if you know what to look for. But for the Shadow Master, the real key is the nipples.

Yup, I said it.

You can't control 'em no matter how hard you try, which is why the nip-nips are nature's lie detectors. You bedfellow says they're into you and what's going down? Lefty and righty will confirm or deny that shit real quick. And for villains, planning, conniving, or talking smack about adversaries—or co-conspirators—is basically foreplay for us. And the chest before me said I needed to know.

She really wanted to screw someone over.

"How am I supposed to deal with being used by her?" Eris finally said, breaking down. "I thought we were partners, and now I'm stuck here in bloody *henchman training?*"

I didn't laugh... much. A chuckle at most.

"Screw this," she said, moving to stand up, but I put my hand on her arm.

"No, stay," I said. "I'm laughing because I had a similar reaction when Sophia screwed me over. It's not your fault. It's the mark of a good villain, actually."

"How?"

"It's like being successful at anything back in the Prime Universe," I told her. "You haven't 'made it' until you've been sued by several people. In villain terms, you're not a real villain until someone has made a play for you. So, congrats."

"And the henchman part?"

"Well, that one's kinda on you," I said. "The Sablestone reads who you are at the time. And if you look back on it now, Sophia used you to get at me."

"But I planned your downfall."

I rolled my eyes at that. To her it meant something. For me it was a Tuesday. Plus, she didn't. Brighter, more devious minds were at work. She just thought she came up with the plan. But now wasn't the time to burst her bubble or provoke her.

"Look," I said, easing the conversation to where I wanted it to go, "I wasn't blowing smoke up everyone's ass during Moriarty's Hell Week class. Plenty of henchmen go on to bigger things. But you have to fight for it. Which is why you're here now and why I didn't come to you before now."

"Excuse me?"

"Really?" I scoffed. "Come on, Eris. If I'd approached you after your path placement, what would you have thought?"

"That you were making some kind of play," she said. "A false ally, at least. Or more likely, that you were angling to have an insider within Sophia's group."

"Exactly," I said. "So why, then, did I wait for you to come to me?"

"Because…" she started, then sighed. "Because a client who comes to you is seeking your help, not the other way around."

"Two for two," I nodded. "Coming to me before a show of strength would've been foolish. But seeing as I publicly banished a demon tonight, I've proven my mettle. So again, what advice are you looking for?"

She didn't answer.

"Eris," I said, turning slightly towards her, "why do you hate me? And don't say because of your uncle. We both know Courtney wasn't a good man. He worked for me, after all, and we both know what he was paid to do."

"I—I don't know that I do hate you," she admitted. "I don't like you, that much is clear. But you were this… symbol, maybe? A thing for me to aim all my ire and frustration towards."

"Oh, I get that," I said. "Turns out that I can be terribly frustrating, damn near infuriating sometimes. But here's the deal, kid: You above all the others on Sophia's squad have walked a few miles in my shoes. You too went from mortal to minor god to villain advisor, if only for a while. Regardless, you know the job's not all it's cracked up to be."

"Clients whine *so much*," Eris said, pinching the bridge of her nose. "Like, all the time."

"Yeah," I said. "And it never gets easier."

"Then why did you do the job?"

"Honestly?"

"Do you know how to be honest?"

It was my turn to glare. "I did the job because, in my heart, I'm a gods damned villain. I relish the fact that I'm better than everyone I go up against. Call it narcissism, power trip, ego, I don't give a shit. Nothing tickles my taint more than knowing I'm going to win."

"You really think you're going to beat Sophia, don't you?"

"It's what I do. And, if I may be so bold, it's why you're here. You wanna defect."

"I—"

"Don't," I told her. "Just listen for now. This may not be the advice you were looking for, but it's what I think you need to hear."

I took a breath, then looked across the nighttime campus. It was quite lovely.

"I am going to beat Sophia. Me, my team, and my daughter are leaving this place. But there's a little caveat that I've been rolling around my head these last couple months. Possibility never said that the teams were locked in. And why should they be? Sport teams acquire new players all the time. So why can't we?"

"You want me to join your team?"

"Well, I never did get my answer."

"Answer?"

"I offered you a job," I said with a hint of amusement. "*Villains Return* chapter thirty-eight for the continuity nerds out there."

"I did answer you," she said. "Before we left to come here."

"Bah," I said, waving a dismissive hand. "You had to say that to save face in front of the rest."

"After everything we've done to one another, you'd actually offer me a place by your side?"

I shrugged. "Why not? I gave a position to Randy, and that little shit tried to take me out twice."

"I don't understand what you're getting at—"

"Loyalty," I said, cutting her off. "I reward loyalty and punish betrayal. I frequently give positions to those who tried to cross me. That's ambition, and I respect that. But disloyalty? No, never. Courtney and Steve died because they were disloyal. And soon, we're going to add Sophia to that list."

"Your sister betrayed you," she said. "And you killed Mikayla when she was Bethany, acting as Lady Aliana. She didn't betray you."

"Paige is an idiot—or rather, she was. But she's family, so like Randy, she got a pass. Mikayla… well, when she was Bethany, she tried to back out of our contract. Plus, I was more of a dick then. Point is, you have an opportunity."

I stood and took a couple steps towards my path's tower. I paused for just a moment.

"Midterms are right around the corner and winter break is fast approaching," I said. "I expect an answer, one way or the other, by the break. In the meantime, if you want help with your grades, you're more than welcome to join my private study groups. Pass that along to the rest of your crew if you like. Bye, Eris."

"She's planning something," Eris called out as I walked.

"She's always planning something," I replied over my shoulder.

"This is something big," she said. "She hasn't told us what, but it's supposed to shake you to your core."

I smirked. "I wouldn't have it any other way."

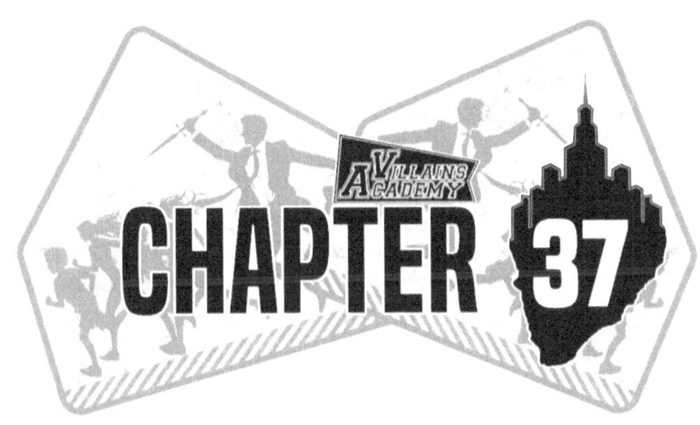

WHERE I PAINT WITH A BROAD BRUSH, ENJOY TEACHING, AND CONSIDER A DANCE PARTNER

Wraith Knight looked at me like I'd just stuck a finger in his butt. Not that I would… again. Apparently, harassing your employees is considered taboo these days.

Who knew?

"You did what?!" he said, his question nearly drowned out by the roaring crowd.

"Offered Eris a job," I repeated, watching the players take the slaughterball field.

This week's matchup was an interesting one. Tonight, the Forbidden Tome took on They Who Hunger. And while I wanted to put my money on Myst and Mikalya's spell-slinging path, there was something to be said about brute force. Spells and magic were amazing tools when properly used. But you ask any seasoned adventuring party, and they'll tell you that spell casting works best when hiding behind a wall of meat shields.

But They Who Hunger *were* the meat shields. Man, this was going to be brutal.

"Why did you wait a week to say anything?" Wraith Knight asked.

"Reasons," I said, watching the opening scrum.

Again, this game was highly physical, so naturally the bullish brutes from They Who Hunger got immediate possession of the Screele.

"What reasons?"

"The kind that don't concern you."

"Boss?"

"Look, WK," I began, "I have a feeling some bad things are coming our way very soon. Planting the bug in Eris's ear about switching sides now was done for a very specific reason. Me not telling you right away is my way of giving you all time to be young and have fun. Okay?"

"Okay, boss. I trust you."

The entire crowd *ooh*ed when Beatrice plowed through some goth-looking kid holding a wand.

I realize that doesn't describe much of anything for you fine readers. But to be fair, do you know how boring it would be to describe the same thing over and over? Aside from the few unique-looking ones like Mikayla, the rest of the Forbidden Tome looked exactly like what you think when I say "emo," "goth," "kid holding a wand." For the sake of this diatribe, just imagine a propaganda poster for a San Fran-Portland-Seattle pop culture vlogger-meets-video game journalist in a wizarding cloak, okay? For flavor, give 'em dyed hair with some part shaved, then slap on some chonky glasses and a septum bull nose ring.

You know, because they're "so unique."

Yes, yes, it's reductive. Compartmentalizing people into groups so we can hate, mock, and dismiss is easy. It's how we exist. Nobody has time to see another person as a person, let alone as a person with thoughts, fears, hopes, and dreams. So slap a label on a group, put them in a mental box, and then set that box outside for recycling. And on behalf of the ever-growing oligarchy, we thank you all for being so close-minded.

Now, back to the game.

Screele in hand, Beatrice stomped her way down the field in true brutish fashion. But there was a moment just before she reached the Forbidden Tome's scoring tower that I saw something special.

Lateral thinking.

Being a Frankenstein's monster-like flesh golem, Beatrice was little more than an electrified juggernaut of dead flesh. So smash, bash, repeat had been all the tools in her limited bag of tricks.

Had been.

In my tutoring sessions, I'd been trying like hell to counsel these fledgling villains on lateral thinking and creative solutions. It was, after all, the only way to keep your enemies guessing. Once someone knew your predictable patterns, you were doomed. Plus, if you wanted to stand out from the crowd, you needed a few flashy tricks. Those little differences were what elevated the run-of-the-mill villain to a superstar.

On the field, a pair of defenders popped out from literal nowhere, likely invisibility spells, and were now preparing to unleash something nasty upon my quasi student. And it was with a swelling of pride that I watched Beatrice extend her personal electrical field to magnetize the husks of two burned-out cars.

Those twinklefingers had a whole two seconds to register surprise before the oppositely charged hunks of scrap metal came flying in. The spray of viscera and black eyeliner was the icing on the cake for me.

Without losing a step, Beatrice parkoured over the newly formed obstacle, ran up the ramp, and dropped the Screele into the scoring bucket. From atop the opposition's platform, my towering bodyguard looked up into the stands, caught my eye, and gave me a thumbs-up. I gave her a well-earned nod of respect.

Huh. Maybe there was something to all this teaching stuff.

I had to admit, while watching Beatrice charge back up the field for the next possession, I felt a sense of parental satisfaction. She had properly applied a lesson, which resulted in direct and immediate success. It was noble. It was just. It was—

Oh, look. Mikayla had the Screele and flew over the entire team to simply dunk the ball.

Well, that was less impressive. Effective, but hardly an example of lateral thinking.

"Woo!" Lydia screamed from the sideline barricade, lifting her shirt to flash her tits.

Well, I guess everyone has their own way of seeing things.

And of showing appreciation.

"Something going on there, boss?"

"No, that ship has sailed," I told him with one last look at Lydia's boobs. "We'll always love one another, in our own way. But we're working on a friendship. It'll take time."

"No, I mean you and Beatrice," he said, clarifying his question. "Seems like you two have gotten pretty cozy, if you know what I mean."

"Excuse me?" I said, turning to look at the big nerd. On instinct, my hand went to the magical scalpel in my pocket. "Wanna say that again?"

Wraith Knight's hands went up in a defensive gesture. "Easy there, boss. Just saying it looks like there's something between the two of you and I was asking."

"She's a teenage girl, dipshit," I told him. "And no matter what I look like, I'm still an adult."

"Technically a child Titan," he muttered.

When I began to pull the surgical instrument free, Wraith Knight shifted away.

"It's not me, boss," he said. "The whole school is saying it. I thought you knew."

Sigh. Leave it to kids to assume that two people spending time together are boinking.

Huh… maybe it wasn't just kids. A lot of adults do that as well. Apologies, dear reader. Allow me to edit the above statement to read, "Leave it to *fucking morons* to assume two people spending a little time together are boinking."

Psst, just in case it's not clear, yes, I'm talking about people who "ship" any combination of characters. You people are the reason that creativity dies daily. Keep your horniness out of other people's work.

Once again, the crowd cheered as the Forbidden Tome scored, making the game two to one. Once again, Myst had shifted into gorillapus and distracted everyone so that Mikayla could fly in another point.

Beatrice looked pissed. My bodyguard-slash-mentee looked up at me for advice. Wraith Knight caught that and smirked.

"We're not an item," I growled.

I subtly gestured running, then made a widening circle with my hands, hoping she'd get the hint.

"It's an exchange of services," I said. "She provides protection while I provide education."

"But like, do you need protection now?" he asked. "Everyone in the school knows you've been dabbling in magic and that you're not an easy target."

"You never know what you need until you need it," I told him. "Best to be prepared."

"What you need is a date to the dance."

"Dance? What dance?"

"Boss," Wraith Knight said in a scolding tone. "You had to have seen the flyers on campus. The end of semester Winter Dance is coming up."

"Oh, that," I said. "Yes, I've seen those. But I didn't plan on going."

"Why?"

"Aside from being a waste of time," I began, "dances are a contradiction in behavior. On one hand, they are allowing hormone-driven sex machines to grind their bodies against one another. On the other hand, we teach kids to keep their distance and not give into those impulses. It's like teaching a puppy to stay and go at the same time."

An explosive pulse of crackling blue electricity lit up the field and brought a smile to my face. Beatrice had properly interpreted my guidance.

As previously stated, she was a walking bag of meat and voltage. And her charge built up with kinetic motion, like the generator in a hybrid vehicle. After a good hard sprint and a quick release of power, both Myst and Mikayla were spasming on the ground.

"I'll cut your tits off, you electrified bitch!"

Lydia. Always classy.

"What's the real reason?" he asked, showing a surprising amount of insight.

"If Sophia were to make a big, public move against me," I began, "when and where would it be?"

Wraith Knight nodded in understanding. "I get it. But, like, wouldn't she account for you *not* showing up?"

I grunted, saying nothing while They Who Hunger scored a couple of times in quick succession, bringing the score to three to two.

"I'll think about it," I said.

"Did—did you ever go to school dances when you were a kid?"

"A few," I said with a half-truth. "Mostly later during my junior and senior years of high school."

"After you… um, bloomed?"

"What's your point, WK?"

"That you should ask Beatrice to the dance," he said, then held up a hand to stop the rant he knew I was about to lay on him. "I'm going with Myst. Lydia is going with Mikayla."

"So?"

"Think about it, boss. How many people have ever asked *Beatrice* to a dance? She's a giant golem. Villain or not, maybe you should do something nice?"

I looked back down the field at her, then gave a slight shrug. If for no other reason, my being the shortest and her being one of the tallest would make for a great photo.

"Fine," I said. "I'll think about it. But why do you care so much?"

"Most of us are only young once," he said. "And by the time we're older, we realize how much time and potential we wasted while we were young. But here? We get a do-over. And if for no other reason than to nurture the soul, we should take these opportunities."

Huh. As Wraith Knight, my former minion was a head-cracking bastard. I guess the man underneath was smarter and wiser than I gave him credit for.

"Plus, I'm totally shipping you two. It's adorable."

Never mind. He's a fucking moron.

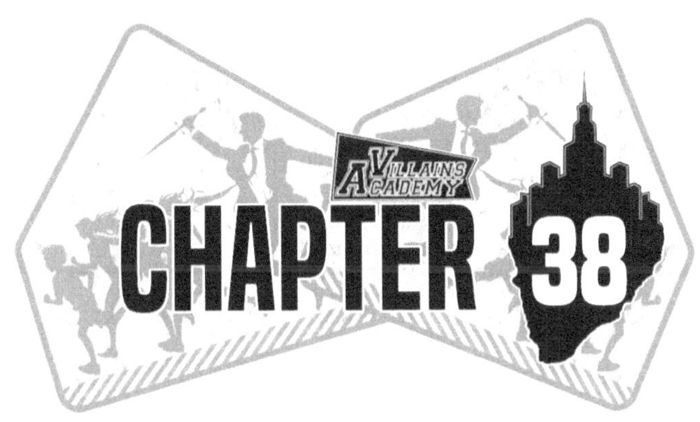

WHERE I DRAW A CROWD, COP A FEEL, AND GET A NEW TOY

As predicted, They Who Hunger destroyed The Forbidden Tome. And the score… *woof*. It wasn't close. Despite the Forbidden Tome's strong opening, it did not end well for them.

I know I mock them, but the core skill of slashers has always been adaptation and resilience. And while both Mikayla and Myst did everything they could to help their team, in the end, there was just too much brute force to mitigate.

But their journey wasn't over. No one's was yet, not really. There were plenty more games in the season. And besides the spectacle, this was the social event of the week, which kinda perplexed me. We were a villain academy, not some redneck town in the ass end of Texas watching high school football.

I mean, sure, the bulk of YA thrives on the spectacle of child endangerment, killing, or bloodbaths. But after you've seen your thousandth teenage axe-to-the-face, you kinda wanna see what else is on Netflix, right?

And that's when it clicked.

Way back on the first day, I'd asked Evie if there were opportunities for us, the mastermind-style villain, to plan and execute events. Her answer had been "too few." But slaughterball was where all the students showed up to watch and study their potential opposition.

Now why am I telling you all this?

Because I'm stalling, of course.

While my mind has been jabbering on about this bloody game, my legs have been moving me inexorably towards one of the greatest fears a young person can have.

Asking someone out on a date.

Look, folks. Your old pal Jackson has gone out on a lot of dates in his time, ranging from dinner and a movie to sport hunting unicorns. I've become adept in asking someone out. But while the adult me had no problem with the act, kid me was freaking out.

If I pulled this off, then I could kill two birds with one metaphorical stone.

When I reached the field, Beatrice was talking with a few of her teammates and Coach Mother, going over game highlights and strategies. But when they noticed me, they all stopped talking and stared at me.

Yup… my butt puckered.

"Blackwell," Coach Mother said.

"Coach," I replied, nodding with respect.

"What do you want?"

Dear reader, there are times when I wish my adventures would transcend the literary world into television. Live action or animation, I'm not picky. Seriously, if you know anyone in the biz, tell them I'm a dirty whore and I'm willing to sell out.

But the reason I say this is because *describing* to you how my guts were churning and my knees were nearly knocking is not enough. You really need to *see* the panic on a kid's face when they're trying to ask someone out.

"I, um," I began, my voice breaking slightly. "If it's not too much, um, trouble, I'd like to uh, talk to Beatrice."

"Then talk."

"Um, what?"

Blink and you'd miss it, but Coach Mother's lip twitched, ever so slightly, into a smile before vanishing. The old ogress had my number, and she was enjoying this.

"You want to talk to her, then talk."

Fuck shit ass titties… damn it!

"Sure."

I turned slightly to look up at the far taller Beatrice. She was still flanked by two of her female friends, a mutant insectoid fly monster covered in coarse body hair but with a pink bow atop her head and a nightmare-fuel cyborg girl with tech plating skin grafts and wires who looked like she'd been swallowed by a machine and then spat out.

Even in villainy, the moderately attractive gal will gather lesser-looking attendants to be "besties," thus making herself the hottest of the group.

A few of you nerds reading this know what I'm talking about. Those that don't… sorry?

"Ladies, congrats on the win," I began. "Um, Bea, I was—"

"*Bea?*" the fly girl said. "You two have pet names?"

"I—"

"Who are you, again?" the cyborg gal asked. "Do you go to this school?

Beatrice sighed. "Remember, I told you about the kid who runs my tutoring class?"

I blinked at that one. *Kid?*

"Oh, right," the cyborg girl said. "He's that little smart man-child, right?"

I sighed. "Yes, that's me."

"Then what are you doing here then?" the fly girl asked while her micro appendages smoothed down stray bristles. "Shouldn't you be with the rest of the nerds?"

"I want—um, I wanted to ask Beatrice a question."

It was then that I realized fly girl and cyborg were now to my left and right while Coach Mother was behind me. I was boxed in, my palms were sweaty, and I kinda felt like I had to pee, poop, puke, and run all at the same time. On instinct, my fingers began tracing arcane symbols.

"Um, a question in private?" I said, hoping that they'd stop fucking with me.

Yeah, I knew that was stupid the moment I said it.

"What do you want to ask?" Beatrice said, finally throwing me a lifeline.

Here it was, the moment of truth. Okay, kid brain, you got this.

"I—I wanted to, well, you know there's a dance coming up and all. And I was—"

"Oh my god!" the fly girl said. "He's asking her out on a date!"

"How embarrassing for you!" said the cyborg, adding to the dog pile.

The two of them laughed for what seemed like an eternity. My blood pressure spiked and my heart thumped in my chest. I felt so vulnerable and exposed that I'd rather explode than take another breath.

So I did.

"Enough!" I roared.

Raising my hands, I released the spell I'd been conjuring. It'd been a simple cantrip of compressed air, little more than a hard shove. Both the fly girl and cyborg were forced several steps back.

I didn't dare try anything with Coach Mother. I'm brave, not suicidal.

The two girls giggled but kept their distance. I put my hands in my coat pockets and tried to salvage what little was left of my dignity.

"Bea, you're cool, but your friends are dicks. I just wanted to know if you had a date to the dance. If you don't, I'd love for us to go together."

"You're cool too," she said. "But you're not really my type. I'm kinda… eh, it doesn't matter."

"I'm not looking for romance," I said with a shake of my head. "Just a buddy to fuck shit up with while having a few laughs. So, you wanna go?"

The patchwork girl with the mismatched eyes smiled and gave me a playful punch to the chest.

"Sure, why not?"

A playful punch, by the way, is relative. From someone like Beatrice, it was more like being tagged by a half-swung sledgehammer.

I staggered back, my right hand coming out of my coat and looking for purchase to keep from falling over.

And I found it in the oddest, and possibly the most inappropriate, way.

What I felt in my right hand was not totally *unpleasant*. Thick, somewhat spherical, but sturdy. Like a slightly deflated medicine ball. But not a modern one. No, this felt like the kind you saw in old-timey gyms from the turn of the century.

Huh. There were two of them?

Oh… right. Coach Mother was still behind me, wasn't she?

I looked back at the very large mythical monstress. She did not seem pleased that I was groping her breasts. I mean, it wasn't a treat for me, either. It felt like I was squeezing a couple of old catchers' mitts.

Unsure of what to do, I kinda just patted the space between them twice and left my hand over her cleavage.

"Um, my bad? So, uh… how've you been?"

"Blackwell," Coach Mother said, licking her bottom tusks, "how would you like to die?"

I removed my hand, put them both in my pockets, lowered my head, and said, "Swiftly?"

"Find me tomorrow when you wake up," Beatrice said. "We'll make plans. And uh, thanks for asking me out. Most people don't."

I dunno if it was what Beatrice had said, or that I was tutoring her and her friends, but Coach Mother granted my wish. The thunderous blow that came down killed me instantly.

When I woke up at five fifty-seven the next morning, I smiled.

Now, why was I smiling? Could it be that I managed to procure a date for the Winter Dance? Sure, that was nice. And yeah, I did manage to make a misfit girl feel good about herself. But the real reason I was grinning like a fool was because of what was still in my hands.

Sigh. No, it wasn't my dick.

Mindful readers will surely have noticed a little quirk concerning the death and resurrection process. When I died the first time from Professor Renfield's no-win-situation bomb class, I woke up the next morning in the same clothes with the yellow crayon still in my hand and the taste in my mouth.

Again, not a euphemism for a dick.

Remember when I told Professor Renfield I was working on transmutation? I mentioned you couldn't transmute an enchanted item unless you had another enchanted item of roughly the same mass?

Well, let's just say that asking out Beatrice was, as I said, one of the two birds I wanted to kill. Sometimes in life, you have to fondle a calloused, weather-beaten, and wizened tit to get the job done. And if the opportunity doesn't present itself naturally, then you must orchestrate one and take that tit by the horn.

Wait, did her tits have horns? Eh, doesn't matter.

I opened my left hand to reveal a whistle. More precisely, a copy of Coach Mother's whistle. A magic whistle that could command others to do your will.

Sure, I had to give up the vorpal scalpel to do it. But I did tell Keith to steal a few of his daddy-doctor's blades during our slaughterball game. And being a good friend, Keith delivered.

I had a drawer full of the fucking things.

Yes, dear reader, let's just say I had plans for this little gadget. As I told the professor, copies would break down after a few uses.

But a few uses were all I needed.

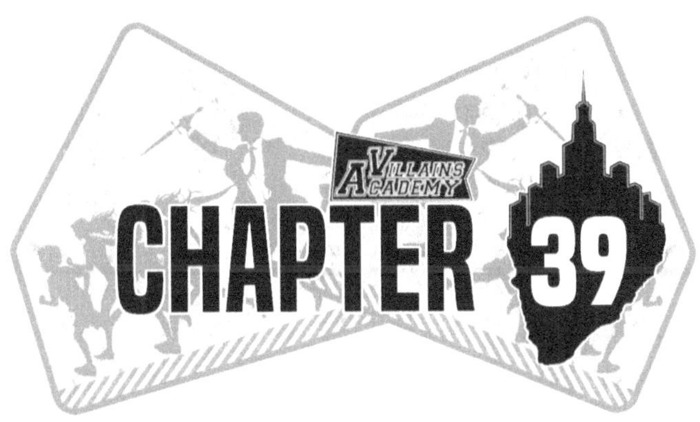

WHERE I WELCOME NEW STUDENTS, EXPOSE WRITING SECRETS, AND GET A WARNING

"There are certain truisms when it comes to the genre fiction that makes up the multiverse," I told my private study group. "Understanding them is how I built my business and how you should approach your future careers in villainy."

"I thought this crap was supposed to teach us how to be better villains?" said Beatrice's friend, Melina the fly girl.

Beside Melina was Annie, the cyborg gal. "Yeah, like, what does this have to do with getting better at killing heroes?"

"Shut up and pay attention," Beatrice said, scolding her friends.

It wasn't their fault, not really. Like Beatrice, and all the other kids that had joined the now-swollen study group, they didn't know much of anything of value beyond the limits of this academic institution. Maybe they'd gleaned a lesson or two from their parents. But come on, how many kids between thirteen and twenty listen to their parents?

"By knowing the genre and hero tropes," I continued, explaining the point to the two newcomers, "we can predict patterns of behavior to subvert inevitable outcomes."

Melina and Annie exchanged looks with one another. "Huh?"

There was a collective groan from the gathered students.

The initial study group had been nothing more than Beatrice and a couple of her brutish classmates. Over the months, a bunch of second- and third-years across the paths had joined. Freshmen mostly stayed away because, like all really young people, they resist any idea that isn't theirs. My crew didn't attend often because… how did they put it?

They'd "heard enough of my pontificating bullshit"?

I wasn't surprised when Eris joined after our little chat. The real shock had been when bloody Khasil had come the following week.

Yeah, I know, right?

When the Caledon goddess showed up, I obviously thought it was a plot by Sophia. Sure, she claimed it was to learn, but I can smell a plant sent to learn my secrets. But the more I thought about it, the less I cared.

Clearly, I've never been shy about doling out my thoughts on villainy. For me, things like this seemed obvious and came easily. But for people from various worlds, to include the gods that govern them, holistic thinking was beyond them. Well, normally beyond them. With a little help from me, even the densest stone becomes a bit more porous. As such, I tolerated her presence.

"He's trying to say that if you know what kind of hero you're going up against, you'll know how to kick their ass," Khasil hissed.

"That's… accurate," I admitted, giving the goddess a nod of respect.

Tolerating her does not mean that I like her. But credit where it's due, Khasil had a savant-like skill when it came to villainy. Sadly, it was her innate impulsivity and poor decisions that kept her from greatness. To put it another way, Khasil was the girl you knew in high school who aced the SATs but dropped out due to teenage pregnancy.

"I get that and all," said a guy with a flaming skull for a head. "But is there a way to spot and end a potential enemy before they even rise in station?"

"Ah, a good question," I said. "Think of the universes like the books and stories from where they draw influence. Metaphorically, knowing the motivations of the hand that holds the pen will allow you to see the reasoning behind the prose, thus allowing you to identify the potential protagonists sooner."

"Such as?" Skull Head probed, scribbling notes.

"*Hmm*, let's see," I said, pondering a few examples. "Horny dork writers create harem lit because they want to bone down all the hotties from high school who never gave them the time of day. While the authors may have lost genetic lottery, their heroes will be rolling with a gaggle of gorgeous gals like he's a seventies pimp. As for the classic snarky action heroes, they're often written by pseudointellectual twats who got their black belts from a strip mall McDojo. The key there is to look for the person, usually a guy, who thinks he's the funniest fucker in the room while also desperately trying to be the "tough guy." Remember the rule of thumb: Jawlines and comedy don't mix. Very few hot people are actually funny. People just tell them that because they're hot. So, if you see anyone who looks like a CW lead with an impeccable sense of humor, that's the protagonist and you kill them on sight."

Beatrice raised her hand. "What about the ones you talked a bit about before? The Mary Sue and the Gary Stu types?"

"Gods above and below," I sighed. "Well, we may as well talk about them because many of you are likely to end up in some form of YA genre fiction. So, let's talk about these monumental wastes of ink and prose. The first thing to remember is that these heroes will very frequently be coded as autistic."

This caused a collective wince from the audience. Villains or not, some subjects are touchy.

"Bloody relax," I told the class. "I never said these character types *were* autistic, just they come off as being written as functionally autistic. The thing you should be mad about is that coding a character as autistic, and not outright saying it to your audience, helps no one. We should normalize such things, even in our fiction."

This caused the crowd of surprisingly PC villains to calm down.

"As I was saying, to spot these heroes you'll look for the characters who hyper fixate on goals and tasks while either disregarding or not understanding social cues. Additionally, because of main character syndrome, they often don't understand the constant amorous advances or heaps of glowing adoration from every other primary and secondary character. First up is the ever-classic stunning-slash-brave 'plain girl' version of the Mary Sue. She'll have innate skills and talents that no person her age should have in addition to a few personality quirks. While the following soliloquy does not encapsulate every permutation, you'll get the gist."

I cleared my throat, clasped my hands over my heart, struck a dramatic pose, and because I'm a dick, affected a mocking falsetto. *Ahem…*

"Oh, what am I ever to do? I have this super important mission, but all these people I meet keep telling me I'm so smart, funny, beautiful, creative, and different from everyone else. Can't they see I don't understand why I'm getting all this attention? That I don't see things the way normal people do? This is so uncomfortable for me, but… somehow, I'll find the strength to carry on, for my mission is all that matters."

I finished my speech with a thumbs down and a fart noise.

"It's no secret that these characters are written by the cerebral dorks who always wanted to be recognized for their intellect and their… 'inner glory,' or some such shit," I said with a shake of my head. "But I'll bet a thousand bucks these same people desperately wanted to be lusted after like Becky McBig-Tits back in high school. Regardless, any flaws these heroines have will be minimal at most and exist solely to discredit Mary Sue rumors. To deal with them, I recommend learning where they sleep at night and firebombing the entire block."

"And the Gary Stus?" Beatrice pressed.

"Same as the feminine version," I said with a dismissive wave. "Products of insecure writers who ape the *Reacher* model of wish fulfillment. Protagonists who often personify the summit of testosterone mountain. So look for the giant, handsome, ripped guy who's smarter than Sherlock, stronger than a Kodiak bear, and as impervious to pain as a bath-salt-smoking hobo. Bonus points if Gary Stu is equally clueless about blatant sexual advances from others as Mary is. But I can't stress this enough, either by fault or design, women will have to beat this guy over the head with their vaginas for him to notice. But since he's a Gary Stu, when the trip to pound town does happen, he'll be so endowed that he could use his cock as a shillelagh."

This elicited a chuckle from everyone. Villain or not, saying "cock" in front of high school kids will always get a laugh. Probably a police charge and a few lawsuits as well, so I don't recommend doing that back in the real world.

"Okay, I think we're good for today," I said, checking out the clock. "Since next weekend is the dance and the end of the semester, I doubt any of you will want another session until after winter break. Good luck this week on your midterms."

There was a chuckle from a few of the second- and third-year students.

I looked about, then caught Beatrice's eye. "What's going on?"

"Heh, nothing."

"It's about midterms, isn't it?"

"Yeah, but nothing I can tell you," Beatrice said, flashing me the black stone in the back of her hand. "Compulsion magics won't allow us to tell freshies about their test."

"Damn it," I grumbled. "I was afraid of that. Is there anything you can say?"

"Three things, actually," she said while gathering up her things. "First, you better not be late to the dance on Friday. Second, each year has a different style of midterm and final, so there's no use in looking for information."

"And third?"

She smiled. "Watch your back."

CHAPTER 40

WHERE I POKE FUN AT FONTS, LEARN MY PLACE, AND BECOME A CONTRACT KILLER

"Quickly now, take your seats," Headmaster Nyx instructed the freshman class as we filed into the amphitheater. "We've much to cover."

"There's no upperclassmen here," Myst said, looking about.

"Mm," Wraith Knight grunted. "You think this is about our midterms?"

"Has to be," Lydia said as we marched down the aisle. "After that message? No way it's anything else."

The message in question that Monday morning had been a short but demanding missive delivered to each freshman's rocky-talky: Get up, get dressed, and report to the amphitheater prior to the morning gym session.

"It is," I told them, inclining my chin towards the stage. "Look."

Coach Mother, Dracula, Renfield, Baba Yaga, and Moriarty came in from offstage and took a seat in their corresponding thrones. When the last of the students had been seated, the woman composed of night and starlight spoke.

"Freshman class of Sablestone Academy, your midterm evaluations are upon you," Headmaster Nyx announced. "Before we begin, I'd like to take a moment to spotlight a few of your peers. The following students are your class's current top ten."

The entire morning sky above the open-air amphitheater darkened, as if the night itself rejected the dawn and sought to reclaim control. Gleaming starlight swirled amid the darkness until it began to form words.

Or more aptly, names.

Nigh-unreadable names. Has there ever been a school presentation where someone design-deficient jackwagon didn't used some gaudy-ass font because they thought it looked "spiffy"?

What was that, Trajan? Yeesh. And why in the name of the Never Realm did Nyx choose black letters on a dark background?

All educators are ironically PowerPoint deficient.

Critiques aside, I was pleased to see some familiar names as tenth through sixth place were revealed.

"Number ten is Lydia Barrowbride from Those in Loyal Service at one thousand, one hundred and twenty total points," Headmaster Nyx said, reading the results aloud. "Number nine, also from Those in Loyal Service, is Wraith Knight, with one thousand, one hundred and ninety total points."

Professor Renfield positively beamed with pride. I had no idea how often any of the kids from the henchman path made it into the top ten, let alone two of them. Regardless, good work was good work. I looked over at WK and Lydia and gave them both a thumbs-up.

Numbers eight and seven weren't anyone I was friendly with. Eight was that werewolf girl Ella Moontide from They Who Hunger and seven was that prick vampire kid from the Twilight Veil, Prince Burresh of the Arcavian Clan. Six, though…

"Mikayla of the Forbidden Tome," Headmaster Nyx announced, "who has one thousand, three hundred and eighty total points."

I'll be damned. Well, I guess that was to be assumed. Working against Y'olly and the others, in addition to whatever else she'd been up to, had netted her a decent number of points. But while Mikayla had some good numbers, the difference between the bottom five and the top five became very apparent, very quickly, as the next position was revealed.

"Myst of the Forbidden Tome," Headmaster Nyx said, announcing the fifth slot, "with two thousand, seven hundred and sixty points."

It was Baba Yaga's turn to clap for her students. The old Slavic crone looked quite pleased.

I think. It was hard to tell, what with the lazy eye and all.

"Holy crap," Wraith Knight said, looking over at his girlfriend. "How'd you do that?"

Myst just gave a slight shrug. "A place like this and powers like mine? I've been able to do a lot of fun things."

"Well said," I told my former minion. "Never admit to more than absolutely necessary."

"Just like you taught me," she smiled.

"At number four, with three thousand, one hundred and fifty points is King Stanley of the Veil Walkers."

Whew. That was another jump in points, and Dracula applauded the placement. I spotted the greasy-haired youth sitting a few rows away. As if he sensed me, the pimply-faced fuck turned to look at me, a smug expression on his stupid face. I had my theories about how he'd done so well without being on my radar.

"Anyone else feel like we're getting some unwelcome attention?" Lydia asked as she looked around the amphitheater.

She was right. A lot of the freshmen were shooting dirty— borderline deadly—

looks at me, my circle of friends, and my enemies.

"Eh, screw 'em," I said. "They had their chance to join my study group. Besides, aside from a couple of one-offs, we're dominating the top ten for a reason."

"Experience," Wraith Knight offered.

"Bingo," I said, shooting the former minion a finger gun. "We have time in the field, experience, and—"

"Number three from the Mind Fire Calling, with five thousand two hundred points, is... Keith Moreau."

What the fuck?!

My roommate stood up and shook his piggy mitts to the sky. "Keith is Keith!"

"How in the Never Realm did that just happen?" Lydia asked.

I closed my mouth, which had been hanging open, and thought about it. Up on the stage, Moriarty looked more embarrassed than proud. Like he'd seen this before. And that's when it clicked.

"Experience," I half snorted, repeating Wraith Knight's earlier assessment.

"Bullshit," Lydia countered. "There's no way that that little freak has—"

"Cumulative," I said, cutting her off. "Nyx said as much at the beginning of the assembly. An accumulation of points and grades. Keith's been here for like twenty years. Those are his *total* points."

"Oh," she said, deflating. "Then isn't that a little sad?"

"Maybe? But just look at how happy he is."

Keith continued to do his snorting happy dance until Headmaster Nyx cleared her throat. "Keith?"

"Keith is sorry," he said, taking his seat.

"Now, for the first time in Sablestone Academy history, we have a tie," Headmaster Nyx said.

A murmur rippled through the freshman class. My friends all looked at me, but I didn't return their gaze. I had eyes for only one person in the room.

A certain smirking djinn.

"As such, there is no definitive second or first place," the Headmaster continued. "With a total of seven thousand, six hundred and sixty points, each, we have Sophia Rose DeVrille of the Twilight Veil and Jackson Blackwell of the Mind Fire Calling."

Moriarty gave a polite nod, his way of showing his pleasure at having a top placement. Dracula, though, stood and took a bow, as three of his students were in the top ten, more than any of the other paths.

"A freaking tie?" Myst said, looking over at me. "How's that possible?"

"How indeed," I said, lightly gesturing around me. "It's almost like we're inside the Titan of Possibility and playing out a contrived YA school plot."

"Yeah, I guess that's fair," she said. "Still, a tie between you two seems farfetched, even for YA."

"Not really," I said. "There's a certain plausibility. I've been doing well in classes, and all my extracurricular activities have added up. Not to mention, I might have a few schemes and plans that are still ongoing. Which damn sure means that Sophia's doing the same. Gods above and below, just being here is her doing. If anything, the real shocker is that I'm tied with her."

Myst nodded along, then looked at me. "Can you beat her?"

I just smiled.

"Look to these ten students," Headmaster Nyx said. "For they are not just your superiors, but they are also your targets next semester."

My friends looked at me for insight, but I just shrugged. I had no idea what she was going on about. Nyx waved her hand and the dark sky retreated, allowing the dawning sun to have hold of the sky once more.

"After the winter break, when the new semester starts, the rules change," Headmaster Nyx said with a wicked grin. "After defeating a student, you will gain a portion of their points. That number will be based on how clever, inventive, cruel, brutal, or devious you are. And it is with that concept in mind that we circle back to your midterm exams."

Again, the freshman class began to whisper and talk among themselves.

I just kept my eyes on Sophia. And my former personal assistant gave me the courtesy of returning the glare. That was how it was with the best of friends and greatest of enemies. Mutual respect.

"The exam is simple, yet complex, and will last the duration of the school week, ending at midnight on Friday," Headmaster Nyx explained, raising a hand to silence the muttering freshman class. "Yes, that means the game will be live during the first part of the Winter Dance. When the test begins, you'll receive the name of another *freshman*—

I stress this because the upperclassmen have their own exams and are not part of your exam. The person whose name you receive is your target. Eliminate your target, take their target's name, and move on. But remember, while you are hunting, someone out there is hunting *you*."

The Assassin Game? Really?

For those not familiar, the Assassin Game, or sometimes called Killer, Hunter, or Assassin Killer, is a game that's been played across college campuses for decades. Normally using NERF weapons, water guns, and the like, students do exactly as Nyx outlined. You get a name, find that person, "kill" them, and take their target's name. But someone out there has your name. The concept was designed to create tension and paranoia while teaching creativity and quick, reactive thinking.

And it was bloody perfect for a school like Sablestone.

That said, I'm guessing we weren't using foam weapons.

"At the start of the evaluation, each of you is worth ten points. The longer you last, and the more people you eliminate, the more points you accrue, thus making you worth more for the person hunting you. You will not lose your points upon elimination, but you cannot gain any more. Once you are out, you are out. That said, you can only be eliminated by a freshman still taking the exam."

Several hands went up to ask questions, but Nyx didn't bother calling on anyone.

"I know all your questions," she told the assembly. "Yes, classes are still going on as usual and you are expected, but not required, to attend. You are considered 'safe' in the classroom, *while classes are in session*, but that is it. Where you rest your head at night is your business. Maybe you trust your dormmates, maybe you don't. There is only one way to find out. Scorched earth techniques, like explosives, are allowed. But there is a caveat. If you eliminate someone who is not your target, then you are immediately disqualified, so be smart. Once you are disqualified, any attempts to target students still engaged with the exam will result in overall point penalties and your immediate death."

Despite Headmaster Nyx answering all the pertinent questions, a few hands remained up for clarification. Again, she did not call on them and pressed ahead.

"Yes, I have been obtuse by using the word 'eliminate' in reference to your targets," she said. "Killing is an option, of course. But if you can subdue your target for a total of twelve consecutive hours, that counts as an elimination. Yes, you may eliminate the person targeting you, but it will not stop others from coming. Whoever had that person's name will receive yours via their connection to the Sablestone."

Almost all the hands were down now and the room was buzzing with energy and anticipation. You could see these kids practically salivating at the idea of hunting their peers. But Nyx wasn't done.

"As for your last two obvious questions, the evaluation begins the moment you have your target names in hand. And as for your targets, well… you picked them already. They are in an envelope under your seat. Good luck, and happy hunting."

CHAPTER 41

WHERE I COMPARE MURDER TO MARSHMALLOWS, PAY THE PENALTY FOR THINKING BIG PICTURE, AND GET SCHOOLED

The amphitheater was filled with the sound of ripping paper as a hundred-plus students tore into their envelopes like it was Christmas morning. I, on the other hand, grabbed my friends and took off running.

"What're you doing?!" Lydia hissed. "We need to—"

"Shut up!" I growled back, pulling her and the others along while scanning for the spot. "Where is it, where is it?!"

"Where is what? Oh, holy shit!" Wraith Knight yelled.

The freshman class had, as predicted, turned the amphitheater into a killing field. Kids being kids is a universal thing, regardless of wealth or moral alignment. When given the chance to run free, they always do.

I'm sure you've heard of the marshmallow test. The experimenter puts a marshmallow in front of a kid and tells them that they can eat it now, but if they wait like fifteen minutes, they can have two. It's supposed to test delayed gratification while also somehow studying socioeconomic class hierarchy bullshit. Long story short, something like sixty-seven percent of kids can't wait fifteen minutes.

The same was true here. These kids wanted points and blood, and they wanted them now.

But since I'm not a damned child, no matter what my penis said, I knew the value of one, waiting, and two, knowing when to freaking run.

"Damn it, where is it?" I said, pushing against the stone hewn into the mountainside.

"What are you looking for?" Lydia asked.

"During the pop quiz murder brawl when we first got here," I said, pushing at rocks, "Evie used a secret tunnel to get her and the other Mind Fire Calling upperclassmen out of danger. I know it's here; I just don't know where exactly."

"And she never told you where it was?"

"Well, I forgot to ask," I admitted.

"Move," she said, shoving me aside.

My ex-wife studied the rocks for less than three seconds before shaking her head. "There's nothing here."

"How can you be sure?"

"Rogue stuff," she said. "If it was there, I'd have found it."

"We have to move, people!" Wraith Knight said, warning us about the growing danger.

"Fuck it, this way," I said, running out the entrance and into the castle proper.

With everyone on my heels, I took the stairwell down into the bowels of the castle. There was one place where we could be "safe" and talk things out. We just needed to get there first.

My little crew followed along in relative silence, only occasionally grumbling and shoving as children are wont to do in stressful situations. Eventually, we found ourselves in the catacombs beneath the main castle.

"Follow me," I told the rest, and led them down the hall.

After a few more minutes of silent walking, we reached an archway that led into a familiar circular room.

"If you haven't been in here before," I began, "then you must willingly enter. Crossing this threshold means you leave all your power behind you—"

"We know," Lydia said, stepping in. "We've all been here before."

Huh. Okay. With no reason to explain any further, I stepped into the room that held the Sablestone. Only Myst was a touch hesitant to enter.

"Problem?" I asked.

"I don't like letting go," she said.

"None of us do, Doris," I said, stressing her real name while also letting her know that I understood the source of her hesitation.

Myst let out a breath and passed the threshold. As she stepped in, the teen image of Myst reverted to the plain, borderline frumpy teenage Doris.

"I hate this."

"I know. But we'll only be here a short amount of time," I promised. "First off, is everyone okay?"

"Yeah, I think so," Wraith Knight said.

"So, are we going to look at our targets?" Myst asked, then flinched when Wraith Knight glared at her. "What?"

"What if it says *me?*" Wraith Knight asked.

Myst shrugged. "I kill you, then see you the next morning for breakfast?"

"Seriously?"

"Both of you shut up," Lydia said. "It's clear that Jackson has a point in what he's doing, so we should hear him out before doing anything else."

All of us stopped in our tracks and stared at her.

"What?" Lydia asked.

I turned around several times, looking my body over.

"What are you doing?"

"Looking for holes," I told my ex. "Because there's no damn way I didn't get stabbed in the back after a line like that."

Lydia sighed, rolling her eyes. "Whatever, ass. You're the mastermind. WK and I are support. Myst is… whatever she is."

"I'm the magical one."

"Are you?" she asked. "I haven't seen you do any tricks."

"Do you want to see me pull a rabbit out of your ass?"

"Everyone just shut up," I said. "Okay, before you look at your assassination target, I want to—"

There was a rip as Lydia tore into her envelope. I sighed.

"Was all that hype just so you could get a head start?"

"Don't judge me."

"Whatever," I said. "I was going to say that no matter who's on it, even if it's one of us, do nothing."

"Why?" Lydia asked.

"Well, for one, we're in the room where death is permanent," I said. "Second, and I hate that I have to remind you all of this, but we're in a bloody *team competition* with Sophia and her crew! Whichever team has the most points gets to leave, and the losers stay. With that in mind, it behooves us to work together. If we're all in the final four, then—"

"Are we?" Lydia asked, cutting me off.

I looked at her confused. "Are we what?"

"A team," she clarified.

"Why wouldn't we be?"

"Because—shit, boss," Wraith Knight said, exchanging a glance with Lydia and Myst. "That's not exactly what Possibility said, now was it?"

"What are you—"

"We've all been talking about it."

"About what?"

"Possibility said that because we came here with you, like Sophia's crew, we're subject to the same rules. That's it," Wraith Knight said. "That could mean that while you and she are in competition, we're in a competition of our own against her crew."

"Or against everyone," Myst added.

"I—"

Shit… they might be right.

I'd been so caught up with thinking I knew what was going on. But because of kid brain, I may have misread a vital piece of fine print.

"It's what we're taught in our path," Wraith Knight said. "That while the masterminds think holistically, with big broad strokes, it's the henchman's job to do the linear thinking so we can iron out the details."

"We don't know for sure," I said, shaking my head. "It still makes the most sense for us to stick together and—"

"I'm not sure it does," Myst said. "I'm sorry, Jackson, but Wendell's right. We've been talking about this. Even before Nyx's little reveal about next semester and the point system, we realized that it might come down to us against them, everyone, or… you."

I looked at the three of them. My love was a nut-hair away from becoming hate.

"Be very careful with your next words."

"We came for Evie," Lydia said. "But she's going to graduate anyway, right?"

"That is what Nyx believes," I said, giving them nothing more.

"Then our survival comes down to points," Lydia said. "You have a chance of getting out of here as a Titan. We don't."

"We have to do everything we can to survive, boss," Wraith Knight added.

"It's what—shit, Jackson, it's what a good villain does," Myst finished. "It isn't personal, it's business."

"Take your cliches and shove them up your collective ass."

"Boss, please," Wraith Knight pleaded. "You have to see it from our perspective."

"Which is?"

"We're in the top ten, all of us," Myst said. "But Eris, Khasil, and Valliar aren't."

"Which means?"

"Which means we're winning," Lydia said. "And we want to stay that way. So either you accept it and we maintain a professional cordiality, or—"

"Or fucking what?!"

"Or we all walk out of this room on opposite sides," Lydia said.

"Go ahead," I told them. "It's clear we already are."

There was a very still but very loud silence between the four of us. Lydia, ever pragmatic, opened her envelope and looked at the name.

"Heh, cool. See you all later."

She departed, saying nothing more. Wraith Knight looked to Myst, who nodded. He repeated the process by tearing open his envelope and reading his assignment.

He let out a sigh of relief.

"It's not you, boss," he said, then looked to Myst. "Or you."

"Get the fuck out," I told him.

The big guy hung his head and left in one of the other tunnels, away from Lydia. That just left Myst and me.

"Something you wanna add?" I asked her.

"Couple things," she said. "First, if we're wrong and it is a team thing, we're still going to do everything we can to get points. Second, if you keep teaching your villain course, you might be arming your enemies with more ammunition. Just something to consider. Whatever you do, just remember, it's not an official class. You're not safe. And, if I may be blunt?"

"Just spit it out."

"Helping others is kind of a hero move," she said. "Spin it however you want, but you know I'm right. It's a good thing we're in a school, because it looks like you've forgotten a lot of what you taught us."

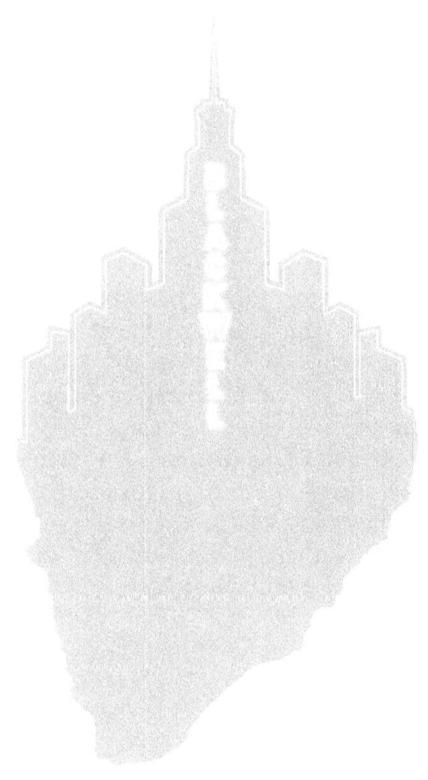

WHERE I AM CLEARLY NOT OVER IT, EMBODY ARCHIMEDES, AND BRUISE MY BACKSIDE

"I can't believe them, I really can't. After everything I've done for them, taught them, and put up with, they just walk away? I mean, sure, I may—*may* have been wrong about the whole 'team' thing. But we don't know that for sure. And to be fair, all I was proposing was that we work together to coordinate our kills. If we did it smartly, we could've engineered the whole midterm so that we were the last four, thus maximizing the most points for each of us. But nooo, they had to go out on their own. Let's be clear—none of them are ready to fly solo. I mean, yeah, sure, they did okay by themselves when I was gone for those two years. But that's just it, they only did okay. WK and Myst were sucking King Stanley's nuts acting like gods damned anti-heroes in that anime world. Lydia? *Yeesh.* For all her talk about independence, she was working for Morry. Plus, she had an anachronistic AI robot helping her, so that's not really being on her own. And let's not forget the whole being fooled and fondled by a busty sex demon. *Hmm…* foolondled? Fonfoolded? Which one do you guys like better?"

My bound prisoners didn't answer me. They just continued hanging by their respective length of rope over the cliff face with wide, panicked eyes.

Sigh… they were useless.

"Fuck it, doesn't matter," I said, continuing my rant. "The point is it's been three days and I'm still pissed. That little pack of second-tier twats should be kissing my ass. If I reach out and grab my Titan powers, I'd trap Evie here. Maybe them, who knows for sure? So I haven't. But do they care or thank me for my sacrifice? Of course not. Because they're selfish. Take it from me, kids—never let your underlings have agency. The moment you do, they'll start thinking they're equals. Which they clearly are not."

I rechecked the simple machine for stability. It wasn't my best work, but considering the time my captives had left, it'd do. A solid wooden beam served as the contraption's mounting arm and a roundish boulder acted as the fulcrum. At the far end of the device, I'd mounted a T-shaped cross beam where the load, meaning my captives, dangled over the edge of the cliffside by a length of connected rope. In a way, they looked like marionettes, which I guess they kinda were.

Essentially, I'd constructed a seesaw murder machine. Fitting, since we were kids. Because of the boulder's position and thanks to physics, I had just enough weight to sit on my end, the effort end, to keep them aloft.

For now.

To my left was Devlin Ketritch, the half-demon, fire-wielding psychopath freshman from They Who Hunger, and the latest uppity prick who'd gotten my name for the midterm assassin game. To be fair, even as a teen, Devlin had a good villain look. Reddish hair with black streaks, a sharp angular jaw, and eyes that were vertical slits. But like all people who wielded fire-based powers, and most young men, he was all flash.

Yes, pun intended.

To my right was *my* target, none other than good ol' Prince Burresh. Both the snotty vampire boy and the demon half-breed looked legitimately perplexed as to how they ended up in this situation. And I don't blame them. They were just out of their league.

You ever see one of those videos where a young punk steps up to an old man? The kid talks shit, but before you know it, the old bastard has knocked the punk out. Reason being that the old guy has both experience and that freakish old man strength. Now, I didn't have the old man strength in this body, but that's not what this metaphor is about. What I did have over those two punks was buttloads of villainous experience.

Ergo, it wasn't all that hard to make them do all the work for me.

The right combination of patience, simple illusion spells, and a well-laid trap had Devlin and Burt throwing hands. The chloroform rag for the half human boy and silver-threaded rope for the vampling did the rest.

No one better tell Wraith Knight that I was actually listening to him, okay?

"Sorry for venting, fellas," I told my captives. "I know it's not fair for the older generation to complain to the younger folk, what with you all looking up to us and all that."

"You will die drowning in your own blood!" Prince Burresh hissed after biting through the soft cloth gag.

Devlin cranked up the heat, his body pouring out flames to burn away his gag. "I'll burn you to cinders! You'll die screaming!"

"I know, I know, I hear ya," I said, shaking my head. "We're your heroes, I get it. But trust me, boys, as you get older things don't get easier. Life brings new challenges almost daily and surprises that you can't even fathom. Sorry if it seems like I'm talking down to you."

I stretched my legs a little, raising my end up and dipping the two prisoners further down over the mountainside.

"Sometimes life becomes so overwhelming that we gotta talk before we explode, you know. Ironic, really," I chuckled. "Back in my day we were taught to keep it all bottled up. Fast forward a couple generations and now everyone's a blabbermouth when it comes to their feelings, ailments, needs, and phobias. With everyone and their moms on Facebook bending over backwards to make things quote 'better for the next generation,' we've legions of adults complaining like kids. When I was growing up, a man was—no, wait, that's sexist. A *person* wasn't defined by their limitations, but rather by their goals, aspirations, accomplishments, work ethic, and those they called friends. Any limitation was the cherry on top so that you could say, 'See that, motherfucker?! I did that in spite of my limitations!' Now we display and exchange our limitations like trading cards. Alas, we've grown soft."

Devlin and Burresh looked at one another, confused.

"This test really is bringing out the worst in me. I get the point of it, I truly do. Hyper-levels of frustrating paranoia are good for potential villains. If you can't cope, then get out of the game. But it's really making me feel like I made a mistake in letting people into my life. Maybe Y'olly was right. Maybe I was better when I was on my own."

Even as I said it, I knew I was full of shit. Because one good thing had come from all my growth.

Evie.

"Sorry, that's the moment of weakness talking. Happens to all of us. Don't worry, you'll get there. Anyway, this brings us to your predicaments."

I bounced up and down on the seesaw a few more times. If the constant bobbing didn't freak them out, then the distinct sound of cracking wood did.

"You two little shits had the misfortune of having me as your target and as your hunter, respectively. Not only do I have decades more experience, I clearly have a lot of steam to blow off, hence this contraption. You, Devlin, are so bloody arrogant you thought you'd just burn a path of destruction right to me."

"Fat lotta good it did me," he said with a hint of humility. "I couldn't even find you until today."

"Yeah, I know," I told him. "I haven't been to class because I don't need to be. My grades are high enough that they won't suffer. And each day I survive, I earn more points. So I sit back and let you idiots kill each other off. When I do surface and go after my target, like you, Burt, the more points I get."

"Prince Burresh," the vampire said in a snotty tone, correcting me.

"Really, Burt? You wanna do that shit now? Freaking kids, I swear," I sighed. "Now here's the deal. You're both going to die today. Sorry, but that's how it goes. But hey, it's not real death, it's just the end of your exam."

"You think I'm afraid to fall?" Burt asked. "Even bound in silver-laced rope, I'll survive the fall and I'll—"

"*Shh*, the adult is talking," I said, cutting him off. "I know you'll survive the fall. Which is why you'll be dead before you hit the ground. Devlin, on the other hand… well, he'll just enjoy the drop."

Again, they looked at one another, confused.

I sighed.

"He makes fire. You're susceptible to fire. Silver is an excellent conductor of heat. And thankfully one of us, meaning me, was smart enough to presoak your ropes in oil just in case. So when Devlin burned away his gag, he already lit the metaphorical, and in this case literal, fuse. Now we're just waiting for nature to take its course."

I pointed to a spot at the edge of the seesaw above them, a point they couldn't see due to their respective vantages. Devlin's flames had trickled up, traveled the six-ish feet of crossbeam, and was now coming down Burt's rope. The vampire could only watch as the flames came inexorably towards him.

"I'll find you! I'll tear your—Ahh!!"

I felt the backblast of heat as Burt erupted into flames.

"Yeah, I mighta gone a little heavy with the oil for your side, Burt," I admitted. "But I figured what the heck, right?"

Poor Devlin could only watch as the vampire he was connected to, and their shared rope, burned away. Not that flames mattered to him. He was immune to such things.

The many thousand-foot drop on the other hand? Eh, not so much.

In seconds, there simply wasn't enough rope, or Burt for that matter, to hold Devlin up. The demon boy plummeted to his death, trailed by the flaming husk of Burt.

My end of the seesaw hit the ground rather hard, bruising my assbone. So it was a fair tradeoff.

As these boys—these children—fell, screaming with fear and pain, I was overcome with a deep sense of self-doubt. I, the adult, had just sent two kids, the next generation of villainy, to their deaths. Like all the others that had come for me this week. And my troubled mind had only one question.

Would this count as my kill?

Or would this, like, be a penalty against Devlin for killing a target that wasn't his?

Eh, screw it. That was for the Sablestone to figure out. I got the points and they got dead. Hear me, young one: Don't fuck with your elders. For we are wiser and meaner, and we don't give a shit.

That being said, I was tired. It was time for my nap.

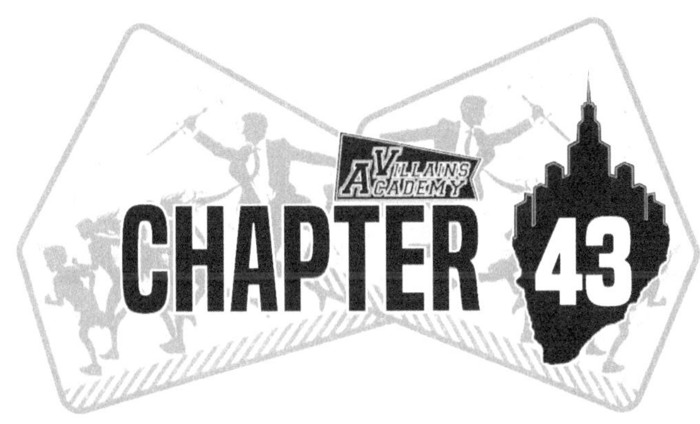

WHERE I BOND WITH EVIE, ADMIT MY GREATEST FEAR, AND ANTICIPATE ABUSING LYDIA

"Solitude, it seems, brings out the worst in me," I said, recounting to my daughter what I'd done to those boys. I took a sip from her flask.

"Are the midterms getting to you that badly?" Evie asked, then accepted the flask as I passed it back to her.

"Heh, no," I sniffed. I leaned back, resting my head against the Sablestone pillar. "The paranoia and all that is nothing compared to doing the job for real. No, sweet child of mine, with Lydia and the rest flying solo, I am forced to live with the person I often hate most."

"Who?"

"Myself," I answered.

Evie turned her head to look past me with that one eyebrow up.

I swear the kid did that just to annoy me.

"Seriously?" she said.

"What?"

"You hate yourself?"

"Even the most devout narcissists sometimes hate themselves," I said without directly answering her question. "And it makes sense if you give it a bit of thought. Insecurity, low self-esteem, and the drive for an idealized level of perfection are the unspoken tenets of many villains. It's why so many of us have this hole in our being that needs to be filled with vice, riches, or

257

power. And we're so damned angry, we rely on malice, cruelty, and blood."

"Are you trying to have an after-school special moment with me?"

"Do I need to?" I asked, glancing at her hand.

Evie caught my eye and put the flask back in her bag.

"I'm fine."

"I'm opening up here, kid," I said, dropping all pretension. "And I want you to do the same."

"I—fine," she said. "Do you know what happens between semesters? After the Winter Dance and at the end of the school year?"

"I assume a winter and summer break?"

"Yeah," she said. "Most of the kids go home. I didn't have a home to go back to."

Ahh, hell. "Evie, I—"

"You died and everyone was gone. Mom was in Caledon with Morry, Aunt Sophia went to her cosmic trailer park, and Uncle Wraith and Aunt Myst were back in the comic universe. So I got to stay here. And lemme tell ya, the kids who stay behind are the worst ones."

"I'm so, so sorry."

"I know you are, which is why I don't hate you," she said. "I know I wasn't abandoned; I knew you'd be back. But I still felt thrown away."

"Evie—"

"It's okay, Dad. I'm opening up, like you asked."

I nodded, then allowed myself to open up a bit more as well.

"Do you know what my biggest fear is?" I asked.

"Finding out you're not as funny as you think you are?"

"Heh, please," I snickered. "I know I'm hilarious and I have an audiobook trophy to prove I'm funny."

"In twenty-nineteen, maybe," she muttered. "And Kafer was the funny one."

"Being alone, smartass," I said, cutting through the bullshit. "From the moment we're born, we seek others for food, safety, and belonging. And if our biological family won't provide that sense of acceptance and peace, we find it in other places. Sometimes in healthy spaces that promote positivity, sometimes in groups with more nefarious and destructive ways. Gods above and below, why the crap do you think so many of these gods-awful YA settings are about kids seeking a sense of belonging? Being placed into houses, camps, or whatever feeds our innate need to find our tribe."

"I thought YA existed was so publishers could repackage murder porn and romance and then sell it back to women between the ages of thirty and fifty?"

"Well, that is true," I nodded in agreement. "They are, in fact, the biggest demographic for the genre. That aside, these stories are cautionary tales for those who don't find that acceptance. I mean, what happens when a person feels more alone than ever before?"

Neither of us said anything. We already knew the answer.

"In my case, I became the ultimate villain. Because no matter what, no matter how hard I searched the multiverse, I never felt like I had a tribe. That was until..."

"Until you met Mom?"

I flicked her ear.

"Ow!"

"No, dingus," I said, scolding her. "Until I had *you*."

"Me?"

"No parent, at least none of the good ones, wants a copy of themselves. They want a better version. A child who surpasses them. One day, you will. And while I can't wait, I want to be there for your journey."

Evie sniffed, then rubbed at her eyes. It was dusty down here, after all.

"There is one thing and one thing only that can stave off the madness that afflicts the majority of people, and perhaps especially, we villains."

"Family," Evie said.

"Family," I repeated. "Blood family or found family, it doesn't matter. So if you've found people that make you feel like you belong, then hold onto it. I screwed up with mine. My search for power was too successful. It alienated me from everyone I held dear. And damn me, it took me away from you."

"Is that what you're trying to tell me?" she asked. "That you're going to one day move on? And that I should smell the roses while I may?"

"More or less, I guess?" I said. "I knew that family would be the downfall of me. I knew that being alone was the safest thing. But I also knew that a life in isolation was pointless. No matter how rich, powerful, or successful, it is lonely at the top. So, I allowed family in. And for a time, it was glorious."

"Why do I feel a but coming on?"

"Because you're smart," I said. "But… there's something you won't understand until you're older, so please don't think I'm talking down to you. The old adage 'You can never return home' is painfully accurate. The family you make, the groups you form, the moments you are living in are not static. Despite how crystallized in time they appear in our minds, they will shift and change. And when you try going back to that moment, that 'home,' it won't be the same. It's like trying on clothes from your youth. You know them, have fond or painful memories, but you've outgrown them."

"They'll exist as a memory," Evie said. "And while you can revisit a memory, you cannot live in one?"

"Precisely," I said, awed by such wisdom at a young age. "It's why middle-aged men buy stupid cars, dress young, have affairs, or join over-forty sport leagues. Transparently vain attempts to recapture their youth."

"Fair enough," she nodded. "What about a woman's midlife crisis?"

"Mostly the same thing," I shrugged. "Usually with less sports and more menopause."

Evie laughed. "And your midlife crisis?"

"Oh, that's easy. I got a family and then became an interdimensional being of immeasurable power," I shrugged. "What can I say? I'm an overachiever. But there is another reason, one I haven't really shared with anyone, as to why I became a Titan."

"Better sex?"

"Dunno yet. We'll see when school is over."

"What?"

"Never mind," I said. "No, dearest daughter, I became a Titan for you."

"Oh bullshit," she laughed. "I love you, Dad, I really do, but there's no way you did that for—"

I reached out and took her hand, silencing her. Despite being in this young body, I tried to convey the weight of my age and experience through my eyes as I spoke.

"Dad, you're hurting my hand—"

"Sophia came for you before you were even a day old," I told her in a cold, flat voice. "I was holding you in my office while your mother rested."

"I—I know."

I lessened my grip on her hand but did not let go. "Sophia wanted you, even then. She promised to forswear her vengeance against the Blackwell family if I just gave you to her. I couldn't do that. But it was clear, Sophia was already moving against me. She'd already used Randy to try and take me out twice. She helped your mother write a training program just to see what I would do if you were ever in danger. I knew my time was running out. Even gods have trouble fighting a djinn, and I was only a minor god. I had to evolve to protect you. Again, I am beyond sorry for the last couple years."

"Well, you're here now," she said.

"I know, and I'm scared."

"Really?"

"I still don't know what her plan is," I admitted. "And since we're tied in points, I not sure if I can beat her. I tell everyone I can because that's what they wanna hear. But I'm flying blind, kid."

I let her hand go and leaned back against the pillar.

"Thank you," she whispered.

"You're welcome," I whispered back, then found my voice. "As long as it's within my power, I'll be there to help you. To keep you safe. I want great things for you. But I want you to want what *you* want, not what *I* want. Does that make sense?"

"Yeah, Dad, it does," she said with a smile. "It doesn't explain why you're down here bellyaching to a kid about solitude and sadness instead of being up there kicking ass and getting more points."

I mocked being stabbed in the heart. "Ah, stabbed in my fragile ego by the spawn of my balls."

"Gross."

"No, gross would be if I referred to you as my walking nut butter."

"Why—why are you like this?"

"It's a curse," I shrugged. "But anyway, we've got a game tonight and then the Winter Dance tomorrow night. In the meantime, best to let the herd thin itself out. But enough about me. How're your midterms going?"

"They're pretty much done," she said.

"I assume you can't tell me about them?"

She laughed. "No, we just can't tell the freshies about theirs. It spoils the surprise. Second years have a week of the Mafia game for their midterms. Families form, infighting happens, everyone screws over everyone. They have it again at the end of the year for finals."

"And the third years?"

Her face darkened. "Betrayal. Each one of us must betray another student. The professors call it our final lesson. That sooner or later, we have to cultivate a relationship, then destroy it. The closer and better we do, the better our grade."

"Ouch… that's a good one," I said. "How do they raise the stakes for the end-of-year finals?"

"They don't," she said. "This evaluation is the audition for the final semester. If accepted, the last half of the third year is mostly self-study. Aside from limited classwork, our interactions with the professors are mostly to help set up our exit careers. Those that don't make it have a chance to repeat the season, or they're cast into the Nothingness."

I shivered at that thought. I had no doubt that Evie would make it. Still, I changed the subject lest we dwell on darker thoughts.

"So, you ready for the game?" I asked.

"Of course," she said. "We get to beat up on the henchmen."

"And your mother."

Evie smiled.

I didn't. While we both looking forward to that particular part of the match, I had… concerns.

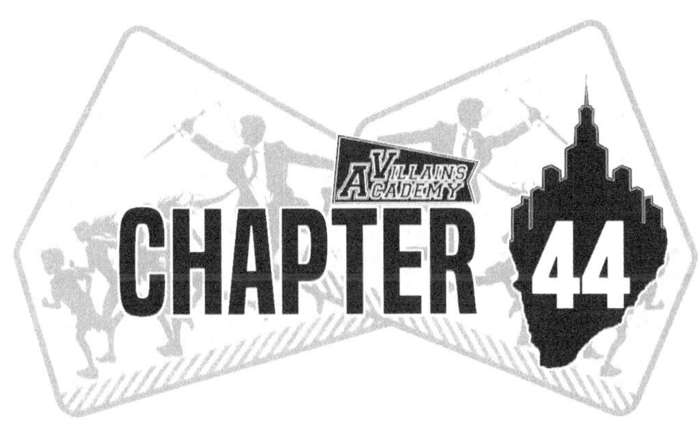

CHAPTER 44

WHERE I EXPLAIN THE OBVIOUS, USE MY H-PASS, AND CHAMPION ABUSIVE RELATIONSHIPS

Evie grabbed my pads and jerked me towards her so that we were practically eye to eye.

"What the shit, Dad?! Are you sandbagging?"

"No!" I snapped back, slapping her hand away and pulling free. "What did you think was going to happen?"

"Magic? Explosions? Freaking victory?" Emily said from her perch on the sideline bench.

I looked down at the augmented koala and despite being incredibly pissed off, I smiled. I mean, just look at her. Barely three feet tall and wearing sport pads? That's bloody adorable.

Still, our team was breathing hard. The late nights had grown colder, and winter was upon us. The field lights illuminated the steam billowing off our overheated bodies. We were tired, ragged, and worst of all... losing.

To henchmen.

Yeah, you heard it right, folks. By the end of the first half, Those in Loyal Service were beating us, the masterminds, eighteen to ten. And each of our ten points had been a war. And just like our game against the Veil Walkers come halftime, my teammates were looking to me for answers. And sure, I had them, obviously. But they wouldn't like them.

"Why do you think we're losing?" I asked aloud.

"Because you're scared of getting killed," said Janna Hatchet.

"Excuse me?" I said, squaring up on the second-year student.

The pirate smuggler girl glared down at me. "Well, aren't you? You're playing it safe out there. I know your class's midterm is still going on, but come on!"

"What are you getting at?"

"Jackson," Evie said, addressing me by name in front of the rest of the team. "When we were up against the Veil Walkers, you found a way to undermine gods and demons."

"And?"

"And are you doing that now?"

"No? Why?"

"Because now that we're playing against your *ex-wife*," Hatchet snapped, "you're doing nothing!"

I looked across the field to where Those in Loyal Service celebrated. Lydia had been having the time of her life as she giddily stabbed kids.

Great motherly instincts.

Wraith Knight, on the other hand, hadn't been going for the kill because he didn't need to. With the combination of his shadow shifting powers and tactical mind, he simply outplayed the nerds who made up the Mind Fire Calling's slaughterball team.

After our first win, my team had gotten a bit cocky. Historically, the MFC and the henchman path had been bottom-tier teams. But one taste of victory, and they thought this was a new era. Ironic, as they played like a team bereft of a game plan. The whole first half had been my teammates basically chasing the henchmen around, trying and failing to capture the Screele. Sadly, even geniuses sometimes need to have things explained.

"Why do you think we won against the Veil Walkers?" I asked my teammates on the sideline.

"Because you had a plan," Dieter said.

"Well, I did, that's true," I said. "But that's not what's happening here."

"What are you getting at?" Evie asked.

I almost laughed. "We won because the gods, demons, and otherworldly schmucks didn't expect to lose."

They all looked at me like I'd just spoken gibberish.

"Oh, for shit's sake," I growled. "This isn't rocket surgery, people. Despite routine gym sessions, when it comes to athletic prowess, we're basically Stephen Hawking, and Those in Loyal

Service are his chair. Do you see the symbiosis yet? In the real world, we think and they do. But we're not in the real world. We're here. So what they are doing is pounding our brains with their boots, grit, and determination."

"But... they're henchmen," someone in the back muttered.

"I swear to all the gods above and below, it's like I'm talking to a comments section on the internet," I sighed. "Listen up, you self-proclaimed experts and delusional geniuses. Because you apparently can't see the bigger picture, I'm going to have to spell it out for you in crayon."

"Don't be a dick," Emily said.

"Then be smarter!" I snapped back. "The reason I don't have any cool magic tricks to pull off is because they're not fucking wizards, gods, or monsters. They're *henchmen*."

The blank stares spoke volumes.

"Henchmen are morons," one of my teammates said.

"Yeah!" another person yelled out. "They're basically NPCs."

And there it was. Villainous racism.

Or was it classism? Eh, doesn't matter. It was clear that my teammates still ascribed to the... *ahem*, "separate water fountains" mentality when it came to the distinction between masterminds and henchmen.

Gods above and below, can you believe that? Good thing I wasn't that way.

Well, okay, sure, I may have spouted off the occasional demeaning thing about—or to—my henchmen. And back when we all lived in my dimension, I frequently made Wraith Knight and Myst eat in separate rooms, but I let them live in the house. So that's good, right? Oh yeah, and occasionally I slept with Myst, so that clearly means that I'm not—

Yeah, never mind. I just heard myself.

Um, wow... I'm not coming off any better here, am I? I'm feeling very—um, what's the term? Uh... very *third U.S. president* right about now?

Well, just like modern Americans and all political talking heads, I will briefly, but barely, acknowledge my faults and then pivot to point at the other side and how they're doing it worse. Because clearly, my teammates were way more guilty than me. They looked down on henchmen, while some of my best friends were henchmen. And I was pretty sure that meant that I got the H-pass.

That's right, my henchers. I'm here to represent you.

Hmm. I'm not sure if that is or isn't supposed to be a hard "r."

"Okay, listen up, you dearly deluded pack of intelligent morons," I barked. "Yes, some henchmen are disposable, nameless dweebs who wear ski masks and zebra-striped shirts and carry old timey sacks with the dollar symbol painted on the side. But we're not dealing with them. We're dealing with elite, named arch henchmen who made it into Sablestone Academy. The ones dedicated to villainy, who tend to be physically fit and who frequently display incredible adaptability in carrying out the mastermind's plans. The kind of henchmen who sit at a villain's right hand and who, if properly organized, can move mountains."

"Do you really see them that way?" Emily asked.

If she weren't so cute, I'd punt her furry ass across the field.

But if there was any hope of salvaging this game, then my team needed to know the dark secret, the one thing that truly separates the named henchman and the mastermind.

"The only reason named henchmen haven't taken over the bloody place," I said to my team, drawing them in close, "is because they haven't realized they can."

Everyone except Evie looked at me if I'd just shat myself.

"He's right," my daughter said. "I've seen it."

"Is this whole family delusional," Dieter asked, "or is this because she's half hencher?"

I have no idea where Evie got the gun, but she drew, aimed, and fired in the blink of an eye. The bullet split the lacrosse helmet's cheap plastic and blew Dieter's brains all over the players who'd remained sitting on the bench.

"Yeah motherfucker, that's our word!" I said, then stood over the body and assumed the teabag position.

"Jackson?" Evie said, stowing the weapon.

"Right," I said, getting my youthful self under control.

"You were saying?" Evie pressed.

Well, as setups go, that wasn't bad.

"None of you have seen the power a good minion can bring to the equation," I said. "While most henchmen have the self-worth of a bulimic teen—"

The glares from more than a few of the teammates were palpable.

"Right, bad example. Mathematically, that's a few of you. Oh, I know. Think of named henchmen like a hot girl's best guy friend, okay? The friend-zone fella who's 'always there to listen.' With me so far?"

"*Ugh!*" Emily grunted. "What's your point?"

"Don't you get it?" I said, looking these so-called geniuses over. "*We're* the hot chick in the dynamic! Who else is gonna hold my hair while I puke or drive me to the abortion clinic so my dad doesn't find out?"

Everyone was looking at me, but not in a good way.

"Metaphorically," I said, giving a dismissive wave. "Throughout all recorded history there have been people of renowned ability and talent. The only thing holding them back from domination was belief in themselves… and of course, the lack of familial wealth and connections. But there are also the cunning motherfuckers willing to exploit the talented! The managers, the coaches, the producers, and the agents. The person willing to pat the talented on the head, give them a makeover, and profit from their labor. That's us!"

I jumped up on the bench, continuing my rallying speech.

"We, the mastermind villains, are the gods damned equivalent of a Motown record deal gone bad. We're the Joker to Harley Quinn, the Mr. Burns to Smithers, the Emperor to Anakin Skywalker, Count Dooku, Mara Jade, Maul, and few other EU schmucks. Say what you will about ol' Sheeve—the bastard had an eye for talent. But the point is, the reason the named henchman sticks with us is the same as in any abusive relationship: The fear of leaving is greater than the fear of staying. And despite our abuse, they come to love us. It's our job to use them before they start thinking for themselves."

"Then why are we getting our asses kicked out there if we're supposed to be the ones in charge?!" Emily demanded.

"Because, you adorable murder bear, they aren't afraid of us. And, much offense intended, you all are as scary as… well, an adorable murder bear! You never cultivated the vital relationship between mastermind and henchman, choosing instead to look down on them. It's why the moment the game started, they immediately went after Mentalax."

Everyone looked over to see Dr. Moreau once again taking the alien's pulse. But seeing as he had nearly two dozen Lydia-provided stab wounds, and Keith was sucking down blue extraterrestrial blood, I had a feeling Mentalax wasn't going to pull through.

"As for my 'sandbagging,' I've been watching them and trying to get a feel for their strengths."

"And?" Emily pushed.

"And we go out there in the second half and show them why we're their future employers," I said. "Scare them, belittle them, make them feel like the garbage they are. Deep down, every henchman craves to be controlled. So be the one holding the bloody leash!"

There was a round of cheers as the team formed up and began making plays.

I just shook my head, hopped down, and went to the water bucket.

"So what's really going on?" Evie asked as privately as she could.

"Oh, I'm fairly certain that one of the players on their team is hunting me for the midterm. And I'll be damned if I'm gonna get blindsided by a fucking hencher."

"You're willing to throw away a win just to keep yourself safe?"

"Duh," I said, downing my water. "*Ah*. Let's be real, kid, I wasn't bullshitting. You know that henchmen are freaking dangerous."

"Yeah, they are," she agreed. "With Mom and Uncle Wraith leading them, we never stood a chance of winning."

"Exactly," I said. "At least not this game."

"*Hmm*?"

"Some plans are for the game. I plan on winning the war," I said, then downed another cup of water. "If nothing else, see if you can kill your mom. Trust me, it feels great."

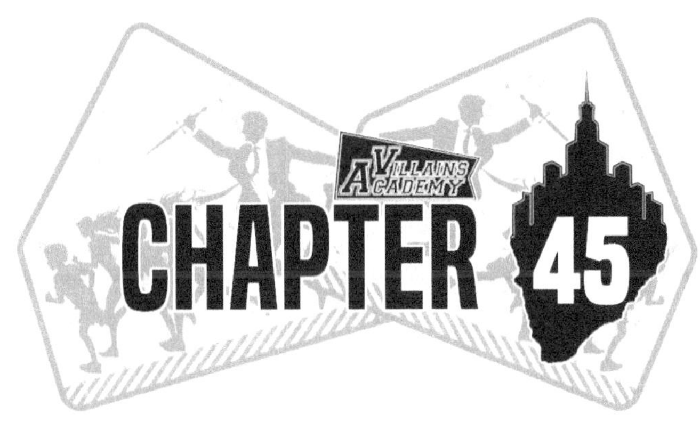

CHAPTER 45

WHERE I CATCH UP WITH WRAITH KNIGHT, TOUCH HIS NO-NO SPOT, AND NOTICE SMALL DETAILS

I ran as hard and as fast as I could with the Screele tucked under my arm. I heard my teammates cheering me on. But even with all the improvements I'd made to my body, there was crap-all I could do about the looming shadow just behind me.

Jumping onto the hood of a junked car, I went to vault over the obstacle but spotted Maureen Sparx lying in wait. The steampunk henchman popped up and swung a cog-bejeweled baseball bat at my ankles. I had no idea how bolting brass gears onto a wooden stick made something "steampunk," and I didn't care.

I had a bigger problem on my ass.

Somersaulting over the swing, I landed on my feet and kept running for the scoring platform. Unfortunately for me, my much larger and faster former employee easily followed.

"Sorry, boss!" Wraith Knight said just as the big bastard grabbed me from behind, twisted, then slammed me down hard.

With as much grace as a fat ballerina with an inner ear infection, I twirled, half tossing, half fumbling the Screele towards my nearest teammate before impact. Gasping for air, I pulled a clod of dirt out of the helmet's face mask but watched in dismay as Lydia intercepted the ball.

Damn it.

Wanna know the worst part? I was actually trying.

Gassed and nearly done, I collapsed on the field.

"You nearly had it, boss," the bigger guy said. His hand started to go out to help me but then stopped.

I didn't take it poorly. He was part of a team, and that team didn't need to see him showing kindness to me. We were villains, after all.

"Yeah, thanks," I grunted, forcing my legs under me while I fought back the overwhelming urge to vomit up a testicle. "My multiple bone fractures are soothed by your good sportsmanship."

"Sorry."

"Eh, don't be," I told him, inclining my chin towards the scoreboard. With mere minutes left in the match, it was Those in Loyal Service's thirty-one to the Mind Fire Calling's piss-poor twenty.

Lydia lateraled the ball to Eris, who spun around the anime kid, leapt over some field debris, and hauled ass up my team's ramp to the scoring bucket.

"She seems to be improving."

"Yeah," Wraith Knight said. "Last few weeks she's come out of her shell."

"Good for her."

"Hey, boss, you know—well, about the whole midterm team-up thing, I—"

"Don't," I said, waving away the thought. "Just don't."

"No, Jackson," he said, using my name. "It sucks. I know it. We all know it. But we—the rest of us, we don't know what we don't know."

"Wendell," I said, returning the first name favor, "it's…*ugh*, okay. I'm not sure what's going to happen after this school year's over. Even if I win, who knows what me being a Titan really means for us down the line."

"You—you said if."

"*Hmm?*"

"You didn't say *when* you win, you said *if.*"

"Did I? Huh."

"If you wanna talk, you know, like after the game?"

"I'm fine," I said, shutting that shit down. "Besides, how do I know this isn't a ploy to get me alone and kill me for the midterm?"

"Because I died yesterday," Wraith Knight said. "Woke up this morning."

I looked up at him. And I saw in his big, dopey eyes he was telling the truth.

"Who was it?"

"That werewolf girl, Ella," Wraith Knight said. "Hairy bitch got me when I was on the toilet. Not my finest moment."

"Who else is left for our group?"

"I dunno for sure," he said. "We all kind of promised to stay out of one another's way."

"Even your girlfriend?"

Wraith Knight looked away. "Well… you know."

"No worries, big guy. I assumed Myst was still in it," I said. "She's way more devious than we give her credit for. I'm guessing that Eris and Lydia are out."

"How can you tell?"

"Because they're both playing like champs," I said. "Like the stress is over."

"What about Sophia's side?"

"I have my suspicions," I said, watching as both teams met at midfield.

Once again, both sides fought like hell to gain possession of the Screele. On one hand, the whole exercise was futile. With barely three minutes left, what was the point? With both teams having similar power levels, but imbalanced physicality skewed towards the henchmen, there was literally no way to score enough to win.

But on the other hand, fuck 'em.

Sure, we were going to lose, but that was no reason not to go down fighting. Which was why the moment I spotted Evie scramble away from the scrum, Screele in hand, I turned, pivoted, and kicked Wraith Knight as hard as I could in the crotch.

Cup or not, momentum transfer of energy hurts like hell. Plus, if you know how to point your toes properly, you can really dig into the taint.

"Why?" he squeaked before falling over.

"Sorry," I said, then took off running for the henchmen's scoring platform. "A villain's gotta do what a villain's gotta do."

I threw up my hand, signaling that I was open. Evie hauled back and launched the Screele. The ball spiraled through the air, whistling as it got close. Tracking the Screele from over my shoulder, I altered my speed, positioned myself, and caught the ball mid-stride.

Oh yeah, it felt as cool as you'd imagine. Some people play catch with their kids. Evie and I played blood sports. And even though we were probably going to lose, I wanted to score once more just to show that we could.

The only thing between me and that goal was Maureen Sparx and her cog bat.

Dashing to intercept me, the steampunk villainess brought her bat up and swung for the fences. She wasn't going for a disabling blow to my knees or ankles this time, no. Maureen wanted to knock my head out of the park.

In a move born of panicked desperation rather than skill, I dropped into a slide and threw my head back. I heard the *whump* of the hefty bat slicing through the air as it missed my chin by a fraction of an inch. FYI, you can't get into the villain afterlife if you get killed by anything steampunk related.

Even the Never Realm has standards.

Popping up, I dashed for the endzone. Leaping onto the ramp, my legs pumped. Atop the platform, I held the Screele high, then brought sum'bitch down, dunking the ball into the scoring bucket for my first goal of the half.

And that's when I saw it.

A little black box, no bigger than a deck of playing cards at the back of the bucket. And the only reason I noticed it was because the floodlights gave off the barest glint of a short, curly copper wire antennae, superfluous brass accents, and a singular, quarter-sized cog wheel.

Motherfucker.

I didn't see Maureen hit the button on her transmitter in time. The bomb went off while my hand was under my false belly, touching the proper metal in an attempt to cast a shield spell.

I didn't quite make it.

The blast blew me off the field.

I tumbled through the air and hit the ground, ragdolling end over end. By the time I stopped, I had no idea where I was. I only knew pain.

But pain meant I was still alive.

Maybe there hadn't been enough of explosive in the bomb, or maybe my spell had mitigated some of the damage, but I didn't give a good gods damn. Broken, bloody, and with one remaining eye, I tried to get a feel for where I was. Through the ringing in my ears, I heard a familiar voice saying my name over and over.

"Jackson?! Jackson?! Can you hear me?"

"K—Keith?" I muttered through a mouthful of broken teeth.

My blurry vision focused on my roommate looking down at me. The pig boy smiled.

"T-take me to your d-dad's lab."

Keith gave me a reassuring smile. "Don't worry. I will."

I blacked out with an overwhelming sense of dread.

Keith—Keith doesn't talk that way.

CHAPTER 46

WHERE I REALIZE I'LL NEVER PLAY THE PIANO, CONNECT A FEW DOTS, AND WISH FOR MORE DRUGS

I woke to the sound of beeping machines and a whirring buzz. But there was only a distant awareness of pain.

I opened my one remaining eye and hazily watched while Dr. Moreau used his surgical saw to remove my left hand. There was only a minimal spurt of blood when the appendage fell away and *thumped* into a plastic bucket.

Huh. Shouldn't that have, like, hurt more? And like, bled more?

Ah, never mind. I spotted the IV port in my chest and followed the tube to the bag of goofy juice. That took care of the pain. Leather tourniquets wrapped around both arms and both legs took care of the bleeding. Made sense, as both hands at the wrist and both legs from the knee down had been removed.

Dr. Moreau had done some fairly messed-up stuff to me over the school year, but he always did so in his lab. Now admittedly, my brain was still fuzzy from the drugs, but this place looked more like an old, forgotten storeroom in the castle more than anything. At least, that's how it looked at first.

The longer I studied the cramped space, the more it resembled a generic torture chamber from one of those cheap body horror flicks. It could only be more cliché if my severed limbs were in display in front of—nope, never mind. There they were. My legs and other hand were mounted on the wall opposite my bed.

Well… that sucked.

Not only was I a quadriplegic, but my torturer had also gotten all their flair from bad movies and hack writers. "Dr. Moreau" picked my left hand out of the bloody bucket and hung it on the wall next to my other amputated parts.

"This—this isn't our usual dance, is it?" I said, my mouth dry.

He turned slightly, noticing that I was awake, and smiled. "No, it's not. Sorry, Jackson."

"It's okay," I said, laying my head back down on the pillow and closing my remaining eye. "It was just a matter of time before something like this happened."

"Oh?" he said. "You expected me to betray you?"

"Not at all," I said. "*Dr. Moreau* and I had great arrangement. I let him pump me full of knockout drugs to do his vivisections and kill me almost every night. That way I woke up healed and refreshed without losing points. I in turn kept an eye on Keith and made him feel good about who he was. You are not him. But pro tip, next time you impersonate the little guy, you gotta remember that Keith always refers to himself in the third person. I'd chastise you for sloppy work, but you're not my problem anymore, are you… Myst?"

I opened my eye and watched as "Dr. Moreau" let out a small chuckle before shifting back to the teen version of the femme fatale form I knew best.

"Thanks for the advice," said Myst, my former minion.

"Welcome."

She narrowed her eyes, clearly frustrated. "You're not even the least bit surprised, are you?"

"Nope. Sorry if that ruins your big reveal."

She sniffed. "So how long have you known?"

"Known?" I repeated. "Not until this moment. Suspected? Well, that started day one. Right after you were placed into the Forbidden Tome."

"You'll say anything to seem like the biggest brain in the room, won't you?"

"I told you then, magic types, wizards, witches, and warlocks are all power-hungry star fuckers," I said. "If they can't do it on their own, then they cozy up to a powerful, external force and leech everything they can. Just like you did with me for years. That might have explained why the Sablestone bumped you up from minion. But it was that 'Oh, Jackson, whatever is going to happen to us?' line of crap you were spouting that had me questioning your loyalty. After that it was just watching your patterns of behavior while doing a little reflection. Seriously, how long did you really think you could get away with using your powers before I realized?"

She let out a small, cold chuckle. "Heh. Normally you're so far up your own ass you miss the obvious until the end."

"Fair enough," I said with a shrug. "I'll admit that after coming back as a Titan, things were… hectic. But you, along with the rest of Sophia's crew, gave me time to think. And that's always a mistake."

"You truly do love the sound of your own voice," she said, checking my vitals on some monitor.

"Of course," I said. "About the only time I hear actual intelligence."

"Fuck, you're arrogant."

"And you're quite stupid, *Doris*," I said, using her real name just to watch her wince. "You of all people should know that the higher on the food chain one is, the more preoccupied they become with all manner of tasks and obligations. The lower one is, the more self-centered they become. It's why kids and minimum wage employees think the world is about them."

"Now you're just making excuses."

"No, I'm explaining what's going to happen to you in the very near future, but you're too blind to see it."

"Enlighten me, then."

"Gladly," I said. "I know that King Stanley was never there to give Lydia asylum. Which means he was looking for someone else. Seeing as you two had sweet gigs in his manga version following my death, odds are it was you. My guess is that when he first started sniffing around, he told you that my downfall was on the horizon or some such crap. But I don't think you jumped ship, at least not then. You likely rebuked him, at least initially, for Wraith Knight's sake if nothing else. But then I was beaten. I died. You had no idea if I was coming back. So you did exactly what I taught you: If you see an opportunity, you take it. But then I showed up, alive and empowered. Y'olly and King Stanley had made it very clear that our contract had expired, and that you two were products of his universe. But after I reclaimed the pair of you, I never issued new contracts. Yet somehow, you both have your powers. How? Well, the only answer is that you were, and still are, his thralls. If nothing else, I applaud the villainy."

"Is there a point in all that?" she asked.

"Heh, yeah. A big one, and I'm amazed I have to spell it out," I said with a small sigh. "When you worked for me, I ran a smaller operation, so you got personal attention. But working for him means you're just the flavor of the month. Once all this school setting crap is over, he won't rely on you anymore. He'll go back to juggling cosmic-level toys, and you'll be the discarded hunk of plastic he doesn't play with."

"I'm so looking forward to shutting you up… permanently."

"Settle down, girl who watched *The Craft* one too many times and thinks she's a boiling cauldron of gothy rage," I laughed. "Got a question for you, princess. Does Wendell know?"

She didn't have an answer for that one.

I did, though.

"I'm betting he doesn't. You likely made a deal for the pair of you, but as far as Wraith Knight is concerned, I'm still his patron and power source. Which is why he was placed in Those in Loyal Service. But when I get out of here, I'm going to tell him. And no matter how good you are in bed, which I know firsthand, he's going to hate you."

Myst roared, her body transforming into some kind of bug-eyed Lovecraftian nightmare. Wet, slick, and with thorned tentacles, she lashed out to strike me dead.

But stopped.

I looked up at the barbed, quivering mass but remained unmoving.

I was tied to the bed and all. Still, I smiled at her.

"You can't kill me, can you?"

"It isn't out of love for you," she said, shifting back into Myst form.

"Well, you got me at a weak moment, identified my assassin for the midterm, and did your job. Kudos. But Stanley's world is still going to die unless he either returns as soon as possible or formally renounces his position. I really was going to give it to you and Wraith Knight. You two would have been gods."

"You know," she said, stepping over to the various machines she pilfered from Dr. Moreau's lab, "my job was to capture you, keep you from escaping, and prevent you from being able to call for help."

I watched her press a few buttons. And in the span of only a few heartbeats, I felt pain.

Four amputations' worth of pain.

"No one said anything about keeping you happy," she said. "Don't worry, you won't die from shock. I kept the drip going just enough to prevent that from happening."

Without another word, Myst turned and walked out the door and clicked the light switch as she went, casting the stone room into darkness. I heard a locking sound from beyond the door.

The next sound was the scream of agony that tore its way free from my lips.

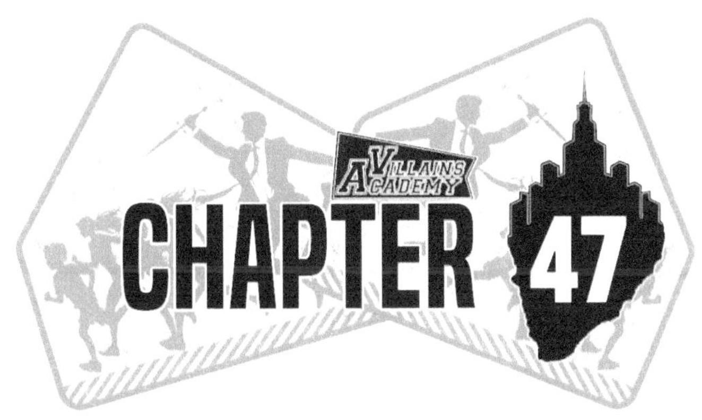

CHAPTER 47

WHERE I THINK ABOUT CERTAIN WORDS, POSSIBLY HAVE A CHANCE, AND CALL FOR HELP

There were three words that kept popping up and circling round and round within the ol' noodle.

Pain.

Bitch.

And dick.

Now to be fair, they weren't the only three words I'd been thinking on repeat. I'm not crazy. But they were just the bullet points that I kept coming back to.

Let's start with pain, as that one should be obvious. Let's see, it's been… gods above and below knew how many hours since Myst had left me in this state. But she had been right about one thing, there'd been just enough drugs flowing in to keep me from going into shock. But not nearly enough to grant me sleep, thus keeping me awake and in a perpetual state of agony. This brings me to the second word, bitch.

Myst was a bitch.

Everything hurt like a bitch.

And I was crying like a bitch.

If you've ever been the victim of unwanted amputation by a former minion-slash-occasional lover who possessed no medical training whatsoever, then you can confirm that it's not pleasant. Aside from the—oh, let's just call it—"general discomfort" of severing skin, muscle, bone, and tendons, there were also the phantom pains. My brain was constantly sending signals to the parts of me that should have been there yet was getting no response. As such, all of me was suffering from a biological "Mayday."

By the way, did you know that incontinence is a possible side effect of amputation? I didn't until now. Boy, nothing brightens my day like spasmatic loss of bladder and bowel control. And all that is before I even mention the tourniquets and how leaving them in place for too long causes bad things to happen.

My arms and legs looked like swollen hot dogs that had been left in the microwave for too long. There was no doubt that I had nerve damage and early onset tissue necrosis. Which is a fancy way of saying my limbs were starting to rot away.

Yay.

Which brings me to the last word, dick.

I was a dick, and as such, my dickish actions likely brought a lot of this on.

Calling someone a bitch, or referring to my crying like a bitch, was inherently sexist, which made me feel like a dick.

Oh, and while we're talking about sexism, why are there no expressions where "dick" is something good? Whiskey dick, dick around, limp dick, pencil dick, and so on are all negative. Even "big dick energy" is supposed to be positive, but it still often portrays a cocky (ha!) douche. And even douche is a—

Sigh, sorry for the stream of consciousness crap, folks. Letting the mind wander is a time-tested way of dealing with pain. Compartmentalization is crucial in times like this. You have to imagine two *you*s if you will. There's the you-you, the one who is suffering, but let's not focus on that asshole—

Huh, asshole. See, the butt does its job. Sure, it stinks, but the butt is working diligently to—

Oops. Again, sorry.

Anyway, aside from the you-you in pain, imagine another you that's standing outside of the suffering you. This new you—let's call them You Two, but not like the pretentious band—is free to think anything they want. The things you could have done better in life, the things you still want to accomplish, or even dumbass nonsense, it doesn't matter.

The longer You Two you can think, the longer You-You can hold out. Which was exactly what I was doing. Holding out.

That's right, dear reader. Jackson had a plan.

Heh heh, no, it wasn't a good one. Gods above and below, it was a freaking long shot. But based on my current situation, it was all I had. So I needed to keep my mind wandering. Now, what were my thoughts on universal basic income in relation to how the poor and stupid breed like bunnies, thus impacting climate change through carbon footprints?

Enough! the voice rumbled. *There's only so much inane babble I can take.*

"Took you long enough," I said with a sigh of relief.

While Possibility's voice echoed in my mind, their direct presence brought me a momentary reprieve from the pain.

I thought a TiT like you would've given up and left by now.

"I'm not a Titan in Training," I said, correcting Possibility. "I'm The Iconoclast Titan. I am the one who tears down beloved institutions."

Still a TiT.

"Sadly, yes, the acronym was an oversight on my part," I admitted. "But while we're on the subject, why do we get to say something is 'the tits' and mean it's good. But if I say, 'man that movie was balls,' it means the opposite."

Because balls power dicks, and dicks serve only two functions: expelling waste and fucking things up.

"Yeesh," I said with a roll of the eyes. "Save it for your BlueSky manifesto."

Why are you still here? Possibility asked.

"In this bed? Well, I don't really have the hands to untie myself or call for help. And in case you haven't noticed, I don't have the legs to walk out of this place. Read the room, pal, and stop blaming the victim."

Possibility sighed. *No, why have you remained in this farce? You could have left long ago.*

"Ah," I said. "Because you made it very clear that if I used my powers on campus, then you'd keep Evie."

But I would also keep Sophia, Possibility countered. *You would've won.*

"I'm still going to win," I said, then added, "probably. I just need to do it my way. Provided I can reliably navigate your bullshit."

Excuse me?

"Oh, don't act surprised," I told the Titan. "You've been intentionally obtuse about your rules. If I win, does that mean just me or my whole team? Do I have a team anymore? Can people switch teams? What exactly are the terms here?"

Play the game and find out.

"*Play the game and find out,*" I repeated in a mocking tone. "It's hard to play a game when the game master has their thumb on the scale."

I've done no such thing, Possibility said, sounding offended. *To do so would be anathema to all things chaotically possible.*

"Oh, sure, right. Yeah, I believe you," I scoffed. "It's clear that you're always watching and listening. There's no way you're not influencing events for a desired outcome."

The lights didn't flicker so much as the room itself sorta… glitched.

Do not mock me! Possibility snarled. *I've had countless eons to perfect myself. Even as I transitioned from Chaos to Possibility, I held firm to the core of me. I set the impossible into motion and watch the results. I observe all that transpires within my vast realm.*

"So uh, what you're saying is that you're watching kids?"

Stop trying to make it weird.

"Dude, this whole genre's weird," I said. "People who drool over coming-of-age sexuality and child murder stories are all freaks as far as I'm concerned. I'm just looking for a straight answer. Are there teams based on their allegiance or is this a free-for-all?"

Possibility refused to answer.

"Fine," I said. "Then at least tell me if this is even possible to win. I know I can use my powers and leave, but as I said, I'm not leaving my daughter behind. Despite this being a school for villains, is our deal legitimate?"

I swear that I have not and will not change the scenario. Those who survive the school year may leave in peace while those who fail will feed my deepest hunger.

"I see," I said. "Then I only have one more question while I have your attention."

Possibility sighed. *Which is?*

"What time is it?"

What? Why?

"I just want to know what time it is within this construct."

It is a little after six in the morning, Possibility said. *Six-oh-nine, to be precise.*

"Excellent," I said, leaning my head back.

There was a pounding on the door and a rattling of the knob. When the lock refused to yield, I heard the sound of stone grinding against stone.

"Right on time," I said.

What is going on?

"You tell me. You're the one always watching," I said with a hint of amusement. "I just wanted confirmation that you weren't playing favorites. After you swore you weren't, I knew my plan had a better chance of success."

What plan?

I laughed. "What? You thought I was waiting for you? Oh, gods above and below, no. I just needed to think as much insane shit as possible for you to show up and ease the pain bit. This kid form you shoved me into sucks when it comes to pain tolerance. No, my elder Titan friend, I was waiting on someone who can actually help me."

You've got to be shitting me, Possibility sighed. *Well, this should at least be amusing to watch. Good luck, Jackson.*

"Thanks," I said, then yelled as loud as I could. "In here, Keith! Help!"

A loose section of the stone wall fell away. It wasn't overly large, but it was big enough for a short, pudgy pig boy to squeeze through. Once inside, my roommate ran over to me, tears in his eyes.

"Keith is sorry!" Keith squealed. "Keith was—"

"It's okay," I said, cutting him off.

"What going on?" he asked. "I died at game!"

"I figured," I said. "You were killed last night so that you couldn't search for me. But my enemies didn't account for you being able to sniff me out, even deep within the castle. I knew I had to make it until after you rematerialized at five fifty-seven. It was just a matter of minutes for you to get here. And here you are."

"Keith tried to call you on rocky-talky, but Jackson no answer."

"Yeah," I said, nodding at my limbs on the far wall. "Myst made sure to take that ability away."

"Myst?! Keith kill Myst!" the porcine child seethed with surprising hatred.

"No, not yet," I told him.

"Then what can Keith do?" the pig boy asked, looking me over. "Keith can go get doctor-daddy?"

"No," I said, shaking my head. "Your dad can kill me, but I wouldn't come back until tomorrow. I can't do that."

"Why?"

"Several reasons. For one, I've been here since last night, so it's just under twelve hours, which means King Stanley will be coming for me after he wakes up to get the kill and my points. But the midterm ends tonight at midnight, during the dance, and I have a lot to get done between now and then. Plus, I have a date. You do *not* want to piss Beatrice off."

Keith snort-laughed. "She scares Keith."

"Yeah, I think that's what makes her cool," I said. "But I have a very important job for you. Are you up for it?"

Keith nodded.

"Good," I told him. "There's no way this would work for me. But with your help, I think we've got a shot. So, I want you to kneel, put your hands together, close your eyes, and repeat after me. Can you do that?"

Keith did as instructed. I took a breath and said a small prayer of my own.

This better work.

"Please, hear my words," I said with reverence. Keith then repeated them with the same level of gravitas. "Justice can be cruel as it cleaves the bad from the worse. And in a domain as this, that blade must be keen. A great injustice has happened this night and even the wicked, perhaps them especially, deserve justice."

Keith repeated my words. I took one more breath to steady my nerves.

"If there is to be any light in this school of sin, then it must come from the person who acts out of love. For this reason alone, I implore you to hear my prayers. Please Valliar, High God of Justice, you're my only hope."

Keith finished the prayer, a tear in his eye. There was a flash of blue-white light and the teenaged elvish god of Caledon stood there in my room. He beheld my broken body… and laughed.

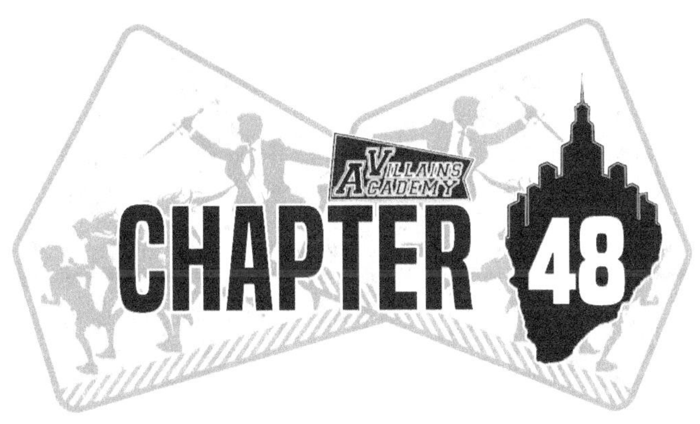

CHAPTER 48

WHERE I SELF-DIAGNOSE, GET GODLY HEALTHCARE, AND GO FOR A HAT TRICK

I'd always considered Valliar to be something of a prick. Most goody-goody types in genre fiction were. They're just as opinionated and confrontational as villains but think that a few "selfless deeds" gives them a pass.

Or does it?

Hmm… Anakin killed a lot of innocent trade federation people and slaughtered an entire tribe of indigenous Tuskans before taking up the name Vader. Then he murdered a whole crop of Jedi younglings, killed his wife, killed countless Rebels, tortured his daughter, was culpable in the Alderaan genocide, killed a defenseless Obi Wan, and so much more. But he saves a son he barely knows from the Emperor and he gets into Jedi Heaven? Yeesh.

Philosophers—the real ones, mind you, not the dimwits who read freshman PHIL101's syllabus and argue online like they're enlightened—have argued the validity of altruism. Perhaps it's my villainous nature, but I have a hard time believing that any self-aware being is capable of being "all good," or of constantly acting in a selfless way that provides the most benefit for all.

Take Superman. With his hearing, he'd be aware of countless people in need. So every moment he's chilling with Lois is him *not* helping those in need. He has the ability but chooses not to. And he's a hero?

But you know what isn't up for debate? Positive narcissism.

Look it up if you don't believe me. Also known as adaptive narcissism or healthy narcissism, positive narcissists often have a sense of self that is in alignment with the greater good while exhibiting traits like self-confidence, self-sufficiency, self-worth, empathy, and assertiveness.

Ahem… sound like anyone you know? Aside from "the greater good," which is debatable.

Anyway, as a self-diagnosed positive narcissist, I found this elf-buggering high god to be like all people who says that goodness is its own reward: a fucking dildo.

"Will you stop laughing?" I asked him for what felt like the hundredth time.

"I—I can't stop!" Valliar said, clutching his sides.

"It's not that funny."

"You—you used this simpleton's innocence to bring me here… to heal you. *You?*"

"Yes," I said, then looked over at Keith, who sat in a corner playing with my fake pregnancy belly and my hidden equipment. Either he didn't realize he was being mocked or didn't care. "I want you to use your godly magics to restore my body. I believe it's in your power set to do so."

"Oh, it is," Valliar said, confirming my assumption. "But why would I?"

"Because it's what you good guys do, right? You help those in need."

"We help those in need who are worthy of help."

I looked at my nubs, then back at him expectantly.

Valliar shook his head. "Myst's betrayal was something you set into motion by your dark actions. Stanley coming to claim his prize is well within his rights. You're hardly worthy. And all that is beside the fact that we're on opposite sides."

"Gods above and below," I said with a sigh. "Look, you pious prick, I may not be the protagonist you want, but I'm all ya got. What do you think is going to happen if Sophia wins? Do you think she's going to take care of your realm?"

This caused the high god of Caledon to sober up real fast.

"And you will?"

"I don't care that you don't like me. Hell, there are times that I don't like me. But the bottom line is that I own your realm and I fight like a pissed-off badger when people come for my stuff. Despite having a sister, I never bought into that whole 'sharing is caring' bullshit."

"Sister," Valliar said, clearly keying in on the wrong word. "That's an excellent point."

"Ah crap, no," I said. "Please no."

Valliar tapped the stone in the back of his hand, activating his rocky-talky. "Sister, are you there?"

"*Whaaat?*" Khasil's groggy voice said over the communication device. "I'm sleeping."

"You need to come to me," he said. "Now."

"Piss off," Khasil said. "There is nothing worth getting out of bed early on a day when we have gym."

"I'm with Jackson," Valliar said.

"So?"

"So, he's strapped to a table and his arms and legs have been cut off."

There was a flash of greenish-black smoke, and the teenaged queen of darkness stood there in her pajamas. And like her brother, the bitch started laughing.

"Oh, well done, brother!"

"Wasn't me," he said. "Myst betrayed him. He's been like this since last night."

Khasil laughed even harder.

There was a lesson in all this somewhere. But I refused to acknowledge it.

"Ya done?" I asked. "Because believe it or not, this is not pleasant for me."

"Then let us kill you and be done with it."

"Ah ah ah," I cautioned the dark deity. "I'm still active in the midterm. You kill me and it will hurt your points."

"Then what are we doing here?" she asked. "While I love to see Jackson in pain, we have a class starting soon."

"He wants me to heal him," Valliar said.

"Seriously?"

"Yes," he said. "Should I?"

"Why?" she asked. "For as long as we've known him, he's invaded our world against our wishes, absconded with our people, and wreaked havoc on our narratives."

"If you call those narratives," I muttered under my breath.

"See?" she said. "Even now he mocks us."

"You weren't acting so uppity when you came to my private classes for help."

"And I am beginning to regret my decision," she said. "Look at you."

"Oh no, villains get betrayed, who could have ever seen something like that coming?" I said in mock frustration. "The point is to have a backup plan or two. Which I do. Hence him being here."

"Your grand plan is what then, to beg?"

"If I have to, yes," I said. "Somone must stop them and keep my—your—world safe. And just because I'm a villain doesn't mean I should be denied aid. Isn't that your kind's core tenet?"

"For those who are *worthy*," he repeated.

"Jackson's worthy," Keith said, standing up from his spot in the corner. "Keith has been in school for many years and Jackson is Keith's only real friend."

"He uses you," Valliar said.

"Duh. Friends use friends," Keith countered. "Move stuff, get jobs, listen to sad stories of breakup. Friends always use friends. That's why they friends. Jackson uses Keith to get stuff. Keith uses Jackson for sucking off."

All eyes turned to me.

"We really, *really* need a better term for that one, bud," I sighed, then looked up at the Caledonian gods. "I let Dr. Moreau kill me almost every night. That way I heal back perfectly, and I don't lose points. Keith here gets to—"

"Suck Jackson off. "

"*Drink my blood and fluids through a straw*," I corrected. "And you know he's right. Of nearly everyone here, he's the most innocent. Which is why you answered his prayer."

"Damn you," Valliar said as he approached my bed.

"Brother?"

"He's right," Valliar said. "I have existed here, in this place, fighting against my nature for too long. I detest this man, truly.

But this innocent being sees him as a golden light. And as much as it sickens me, I must be true to myself."

Valliar unbuckled my restraints and laid a hand on my forehead.

"By my hand, be healed, Julian Jackson Blackwell."

My body was suddenly whole, and all the pain that had once been was now gone.

Oh, and so was Valliar.

"What?!" Khasil hissed, looking around in confusion. "Where did he go?!"

"*Hmm?*" I said, pulling out the IVs and undoing my now-unnecessary tourniquets. "Oh, that. Yeah, he's gone."

"Gone where?"

"Dunno," I said. "The rules on expulsion aren't exactly clear. I have my hunches though."

"Expulsion?!" Khasil repeated.

"Keith, buddy," I said. "You've been here long enough to know most things. What's the student handbook say about our school's Code of Conduct?"

"All students at Sablestone Academy must uphold the highest standard of villainy at all times," Keith said, affecting a tone of eloquence while reciting the book perfectly. "Any student who displays true and earnest acts of morality, altruism, or heroism will be stripped of their academic privileges and be cast out to find higher learning elsewhere."

"Thanks, bud," I said, disappointed to see a new stone in the back of my reformed hand. "Damn, I was kinda hoping to find a loophole in all this. Alas. So anyway, the short of it, Khassy, is that I pulled off a two-fer. One, I got rid of another of Sophia's agents, and just as importantly, I eliminated my target in the midterm."

"Valliar was your target?"

"Heh, yeah," I laughed. "I wasn't exactly sure how I was gonna pull that one off. Good times. So what's it going to be?"

"Excuse me?"

"Come on, Khass. I know you hate me for whatever reasons. But that was in the past. Villain to villain, it's time we had a real talk," I told her in an as earnest a voice as possible. "If you join me, then I'll do everything I can to ensure you come out of this place in the top ten and return to Caledon."

"Do—do I have to abdicate my position?"

"As a high god? Sadly, yes," I told her. "It's unfortunate, I know, but I wasn't lying. If I'm taken out, then there's no telling who or what will take control of your worlds. Regardless, you'll either be out, or your world will die. As of right now, I have caretakers in place maintaining Caledon's existence, but it won't last. Abdicate now, and Vammar the neutral will become the new high god."

"*Ugh*, Vammar? Really?"

"I know, I know," I said, going to the corner of the room and picking up my fake belly. Instead of strapping it on, I slung it over my shoulder like a pack. "But Vammar's taken your GameLit thing and is running with it. From my latest reports, he's working on something kinda cool. When this is all over, I'll put you back in under the same title as Goddess of Cold and Darkness. The only thing that changes is for you is that you no longer have to go to the high god meetings and provide update reports to The One."

"I do hate meetings," she said, chewing on a nail. She then shook her head in frustration. "But even if I did, Valliar would never—"

"I don't need him," I said, cutting her off. "I never did. I needed you. You, Khasil, are the elder twin. Nyx was kind enough to point out that night and darkness always come before the dawn. Which means that you own fifty-one percent of Caledon, and that's all I need. Just say the word and all is saved."

"He didn't return home?"

"No, I'm almost positive he did not," I said. "Y'olly was a special case. Valliar, well, he got eliminated under the rules of this construct. If I had to guess, he is still inside Possibility, but not Sablestone. Which ultimately means the choice is yours. No matter what happens, I'm a Titan and will likely get out of here. The rest of you? Eh?"

Khasil thought about it for several moments. But then I saw a smile creep onto her green, scaly face.

"It's been so long that I don't know why I hate you as much as I do," Khasil admitted. "Maybe I don't like competition. Maybe you're an asshole—"

"I guarantee that one."

"But," she said, holding up a finger. "I think I can let it all go under one condition."

"What?"

"Say that it isn't stupid."

"Come again?" I blinked, afraid of where this was going.

"My decision to make Caledon a GameLit world," she explained. "Admit that it wasn't a stupid idea."

"What's it matter if I do or don't?"

"You're doing it, right?"

"Doing what?"

"You're somehow recording all of this for one of your book adventure things?"

I narrowed my eyes. "Perhaps."

"Excellent," she said. "Then admit that my idea to transform Caledon into a GameLit world was, in fact, a smart move."

"Now I didn't say anything about—"

"Those are my terms."

Gods… damn it!

"Fine," I said. "It was the smartest move you could have made. Caledon was pretty generic before, and now it has the chance of being something special. You happy?"

"And say that you like GameLit and LitRPG books."

"That's going too fucking far!" I snapped. "I've made my stance very clear. The bulk of the genre is sad, numbers-based, power fantasy jerk-off porn for sadder nerds."

"Say it or no deal."

Again, I sighed. Come on, Jackson… you can do this. It's just like a first date. You lie and say whatever you have to for a chance of getting lucky.

"A few—*very few*, mind you—GameLit and LitRPGs have merit. And the ones I like, I really like. When done well… *ugh*. Those books can truly be enjoyable."

She put out her hand. "Then I abdicate Caledon to you, The Iconoclast Titan."

I took Khasil's right hand in my own, sealing the deal.

And with my left, I jabbed my recovered scalpel into her throat, killing her. I watched her body hit the ground, her eyes wide with shock. I then looked over at Keith.

"You wanna get in on this before the body fades away? Snake juice breakfast? Eh? Yum yum."

Keith didn't need to be asked twice. My porky pal scrambled over to her body and dove in, gorging himself as much as possible before the body dissolved. Keith burped, then wiped at his face with the sleeve of his pajamas.

"Why you kill her?"

"Three-fer," I said, holding up the back of my hand to show my connection to the Sablestone. "Apparently Valliar's target was his sister, and he was either willing to wait or refused to kill her. Either way, more points for me."

"What will Jackson do now?"

"Now?" I said with a smile. "Now I have a whole day to plan the downfall of my enemies, and a winter dance to attend."

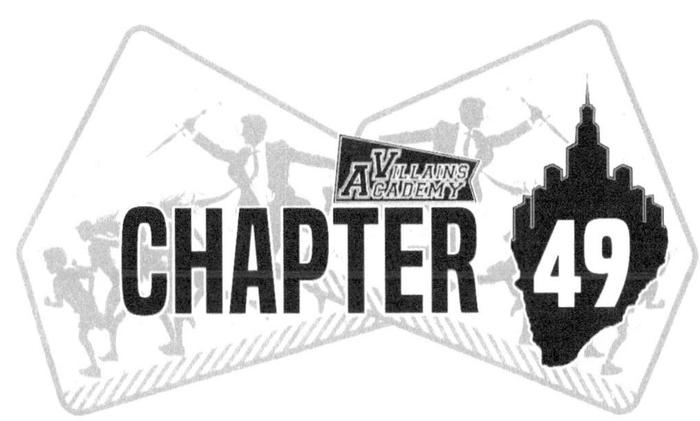

CHAPTER 49

WHERE I COMPARE THOSE WHO BLOW, AVOID BEING PLACED ON A WATCHLIST, AND SEE AN OLD FRIEND

"M'lady," I said, standing up from the stone bench and extending my arm.

"Really?" Beatrice said, stopping where the bridge from They Who Hunger's dormitory tower met the quad. "That's the line you're gonna use?"

"Yeah, it felt dirty in my mouth," I said, shaking my head with self-disgust. "Like a triple-chinned neckbeard with a fedora. My apologies."

"Speaking of clothing," Beatrice said, looking me up and down.

"Yeah," I sighed. "It's a choice."

It wasn't.

Without a shopping budget or access to store, I'd been forced to use magic to convert my school uniform into a youthful adaptation on the classic Shadow Master suit. A fitted smoky-gray coat with wintry-silver floral print, an off-white shirt, a black vest, and matching black slacks.

But the moment I'd donned the ensemble... *Sigh*. The slacks had turned to short pants.

"Well, it's on brand for you," Beatrice said as she took me in. "But how did you lose so much weight?"

"I have my ways," I said with a smile.

There was no longer a need to fake the fat. Myst knew the truth, which meant those who stood against me knew. I still had my magical tools on me; they were just less convenient to reach. I just had to make sure I grabbed the right item and not the baggy of snacks I packed.

Don't judge. Kid me gets snacky.

I was gonna miss the fake belly, though. It had been comforting and warm—the latter being the most germane to the moment, as there was a light snowfall that evening. The quad was covered in a thin layer of white, and it was rather beautiful.

As was my date.

Beatrice wore a playful one-shoulder dress that showed off her muscular left arm. The form-fitting sparkly black design flared out from her waist to her knees in those ruffle things that likely had a name. But because I was a guy, I didn't know—or care to learn—what they were called.

"You still active in your midterm?"

"Yes I am."

"Aren't you nervous about being spotted?"

"Nah," I told her. "I spent a shitload of the day casting a very powerful ritual."

"What kind?"

"I'm invisible," I said, then corrected myself, "or at least, not noticeable. Unless I want them to, most folks won't even realize I'm there."

"Cool."

"Thanks," I said. "It won't fool the faculty, trust me on that one. But for now, Sophia, Myst, and the rest won't know I'm here."

"Well then, shall we?" she asked, offering me her arm instead.

"Certainly," I said, linking my arm in hers.

"So," she began as we walked across the quad. "That shapeshifting bitch betrayed you, huh?"

"*Mm-hmm.*"

"And since they didn't find you in the basement of the castle, they're bound to do something tonight?"

"Almost certainly," I agreed as we approached the entryway.

"Good. I like it when things get interesting."

Once we were in the castle, we followed the herd-like migration of incoming students. It was a time-honored tradition for schools to host such events in either the gym or the cafeteria.

The distant, dull roar and thumping bass from deep underground confirmed the cafeteria. Which… kinda sucked.

Sure, our gym classes were outside, and it was winter. But space heaters are a thing. I woulda gladly traded a bit of shivering for some fresh air. The downside to this many kids in one enclosed location was a pungent funk that's impossible to ignore. Parents, teachers, and anyone else who legally spends too much time around the parasitic entities we call kids knows what I'm talking about.

Sometimes it's the onion and ass scent of the unwashed. Maybe it's the overpowering, eye-watering assault from those who haven't learned that less is more when applying colognes or perfumes. Perhaps it's that lone mint desperately trying to deodorize teenage shit-breath.

Sucking my last few breaths of clean air, my date and I headed into the dance. Instead of tacky balloon archways and crepe paper streamers, the partygoers were metaphorically transported to the dance's theme: Winter in Hell.

The cavern's stalagmites and stalactites had been coated in a substance that glowed a silvery-blue under the hidden blacklights, giving off a cold, glacier-like feel. A fine gray fog roiled ankle-deep across the floor, and a light magical snow wafted through the air. The stone walls had been covered with sparkly black fabric to enhance the expansive dark ambiance. The tables had been pushed to the perimeter to create a space for dancing. And the main lights had been turned off to set the mood, while overhead laser lights created that schlocky "disco" effect.

Looped chains and barbed hooks hung from the ceiling, many of which were used to support rectangular cages containing go-go dancing demons.

"Huh," I said, pausing to look at the caged hellspawn. "Are those real demons or illusions?"

"They're real," Beatrice said, pointing over her shoulder to a table far in the back corner where Headmaster Nyx and several of the professors sat as chaperones. "Baba Yaga summons a bunch up from the Never Realm to work as staff for these events."

"Cool. Cheap but reliable labor."

"Yeah, cool," Beatrice said, bobbing her head to the music.

Ah, the music. I'm sure you're asking, "What kind of music do villains listen to?" And that's a fair question. I'm sure some of you out there think the answer is classical. And why wouldn't you? The imagery of the sophisticated big bad villain listening to or performing Beethoven or Mozart has been ingrained in our collective minds for as long as there have been tales of villainy. But it's complete bullshit.

There is only one musical genre that perfectly encapsulates a villain's self-absorbed mania, narcissism, and need for attention.

Ska.

For real, we go nuts for that shit. And why wouldn't we?

A bunch of self-centered twats in outlandish, color-clashing costumes who are armed with an armada of the worst instruments in creation? *Mwa*! Perfection.

Oh, before you ask, I'm talking about brass instruments. They are, as we all know, the most aurally abusive of all musical instruments. Brass, and those who play them, suck. They're shrill, they hurt the ears, and to be frank, they have a lot in common with a Victorian age prostitute.

Sigh… please stop making me digress even further.

Fine, I'll explain.

Brass instruments and their players, like the whores of yore, are covered in slobber, molds, yeast, and bacteria. They're both worried about "embouchure," which is the way one positions their mouth around an… *instrument*, and all that's before we talk about their fingering techniques.

Now, I could go on. I've got this great bit where I mock high school jazz band kids who wear sunglasses while "wailing" during pep rallies. But my editor scolded me. They claimed I was being malicious while belaboring the point. Oh, get this, they argued that I was… how did they phrase it, *"alienating people who were talented or dedicated enough to learn an instrument?"*

Uh, yeah… that's the point.

Hi there, Jackson Blackwell, positive narcissist and hypocrite, nice to meet you. Anyone who can do something I can't is immediately stupid and prime for ridicule. How dare they try? But on the other hand, if someone *can't* do what I can, which is a lot, then obviously they're lazy, weak, and undeserving of love. Probably a little racist too.

Duh.

But fine. I'll be the bigger man and keep those thoughts to myself.

Word to the wise, folks: Don't get on the wrong side of an editor who suspiciously has a music background.

"Cool band," Beatrice said, breaking me out of my ranting fugue state.

I could just make them out at the far end of the crowded dance floor. If I was reading the name correctly on the bass drum, they were called The Rejected Wildelings.

"Yeah, cool," I said, looking them over.

Checkered blazers, purple skinny ties, cargo shorts, top hats, and bug-eyes sunglasses. Yup, a ska band or a fraternity disc golf team, which was basically the same thing. But... they weren't kids.

"Those aren't students."

"They're not," Beatrice said, tapping her foot to a cover of the Stones' "Paint it Black." "They're the substitute faculty."

"Substitute faculty?"

"Yeah," she said, moving her hips a little. "The backup professors who live at the base of the mountain in a village. Sometimes professors go away, take breaks or whatever, and the school needs alternates."

That's when it clicked. The goth woman playing bass was Carmilla, the hunchback drummer was Igor, the hyperactive guitarist bouncing around was Spring-heeled Jack, and the too-pretty front man was Dorian Gray. The brass section was... eh, who gives a shit. *Hmm...* that did give me an idea, though. I looked back at the demons and wondered if I could pull it off.

"For being a mastermind, you're pretty dense," Beatrice said, raising her voice to be heard over the music.

"What?" I said, breaking my train of thought.

"I wanna dance, idiot," Beatrice half-shouted while moving her shoulders and hips to the music. "See this? It's called dancing, it's what you do at a dance. And this is where you, my date, ask me to dance."

I laughed. "Do you really want to dance with me? Look at me. Compared to you I'm a fun-sized Snickers bar."

"Oh, get over yourself," Beatrice said, dragging me onto the dance floor.

Now, was the Shadow Master much of a dancer? Yes, yes I was. It was a necessity in my line of work. Plus, you don't want to look stupid when celebrating on the graves of your enemies. So, your pal Jackson cut loose a bit and had a little fun. Which shocked my date.

"You're not bad."

"I know," I said with a smirk, matching her moves. "But what's wrong with your face?"

"What?" she said, her hands going to her stitching.

"It's weird," I told her. "It's like you're almost… smiling?"

"Dick," she said before giving me a hip bump that sent me sprawling.

I'd earned that.

Beatrice and I boogied our way through a slew of up-tempo songs. But even while dancing, the Shadow Master is on duty. While we strutted our stuff, I scanned my surroundings. First thing, I checked the middle of the dance floor, confirming that my mental map of the castle had been accurate.

Perfect. With that bit of foreshadowing out of the way, I turned my attention to the crowd.

Lydia was getting down and dirty with Mikayla while several onlookers cheered them on. Dropping it low, those two knew what they were doing and enjoyed the attention. I didn't worry about the pack of pervs doing anything or crossing a line. Between the two of them, those gals had more than enough experience to spill blood and not lose a step.

Not too far away, Myst and Wraith Knight danced. He looked like he was having a good time, while she looked nervous. Neither really had much natural rhythm, but they were kinda adorkable. Then I remembered I was supposed to be mad at her.

Damn it, Myst. Why'd you have to go and ruin everything?

Because it'd been her only real option. Sophia and her crew had made good on their threats to kill me. Now she was in too deep.

Speaking of Sophia, where was she? I didn't see them among the people on the dance floor. Scanning the seating areas around the massive cavern's periphery, I didn't see her. My eyes fell on Evie, who looked, if I may say as a father, stunning in a simple black dress and minimal makeup. She was sitting with friends, laughing, and having a good time. I allowed my spell to slip for her. She caught my eye, smirked, and subtly pointed to a dark recess at the furthest corner of the cafeteria.

It took me a moment, but I spotted what she'd meant. Sophia and King Stanley were sitting at the furthest table away from people. Sophia had on some kind of multi-layered, multi-colored ensemble that looked like a belly dancer's bedlah outfit. Stanley had turned himself into one of those tall, lanky, duster-clad bad boy superheroes with a ponytail. The real shitty ones from the late 90s who were designed to make proto goth girls damp and future edgelords hard.

The only good thing about this type of superhero was their eventual death in the animated reboot.

Still dancing with Beatrice, I spotted Eris. It was clear that she'd come to the dance solo and was, sadly, the third wheel on Sophia and King Stanley's date. *Woof*, bad look. I get that being alone sucked, but no one wanted to be *that* friend.

And of course, there was Keith. The little piglet was doing the skank dance by himself and having the time of his life.

Just look at his little checkered suit I made for him! I had no idea where he'd gotten the bow tie, but he was rocking it! Gods above and below, if I could get him and Emily the koala to dance together, I might just die and go to weeb heaven.

Returning focus to my date, I enjoyed the moment of feeling young and free. When the band shifted gears into the obligatory slow song, the couples started doing that weird, full-body hug and shuffle dance thing that kids do.

Beatrice and I gave one another an awkward look.

"Do you—"

"No," I said too quickly.

"You don't?"

"Oh, it's not you," I said, "I just—"

"No, it's okay," Beatrice said. "I'm a little tired now anyway and—"

"Stop," I said, then sighed. "Look, I'd love to dance more with you. But considering that I'm an adult in a very short kid's body and you're a very tall teen girl, it means that your boobs would be resting on my head. And while I have zero problem acting like an adult with the others like me, *this* is something I'm not comfortable with."

She laughed. "Okay, cool. I get it."

"Would you like some punch?"

"*Yes*," she said a touch more enthusiastically than necessary, but I got it. Anything to end this awkward conversation. She looked over her shoulder and pointed.

"My friends are over at that table and they've got snacks. Grab the drinks and meet me there?"

"You got it," I told her.

Weaving through the throngs of swaying teens, I kept a sharp eye out. Even with my quasi-cloaking spell in effect, it was best to be on the move and not present an easy target. And while I was thirsty, there was one person I'd spotted that I definitely needed to talk with. Walking up to the refreshment stand, I nodded at the demon attendant.

"Two punches please," I said. "And maybe a few moments to chat? You know, for old time's sake."

A much smaller and greatly demoted Y'ollgorath sighed, hung his head, and poured some punch.

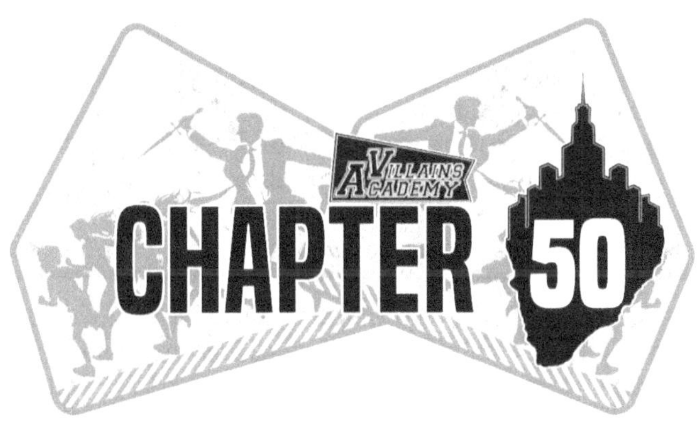

WHERE I LEARN ABOUT GEN-"Z'EMONS", SENSE DREAD, AND FEEL SEEN

The Y'olly that I'd worked with for all those years had been a hulking, near-fifteen-foot-tall behemoth. The juvenile "teen version" that'd bullied me the first few months of school, while smaller, had still been bigger than Beatrice. So to see this shrimpy, imp-like version was a shock.

Funny? You're gods damn right it was. It was fifty-fifty as to who would beat who in an arm-wrestling match between us.

"So, um, how ya been?" I asked, looking him over.

He handed me the drinks. "Just go away, Jackson."

"Aww, don't be like that, bud."

He sighed. "Make your jokes, take your bloody drinks, and go away. Please?"

"Jokes? Now why would I do something like that?" I asked with a smirk. "We're old friends, aren't we? It's a party, lighten up. So what happened?"

"What do you think happened?" he snapped, setting the punch back down. "My bosses were pissed. Not only did I take an unapproved leave of absence, but I also failed to defeat you. Thanks to that dick move of banishing me, I got demoted back to the first circle of the Never Realm. You have any idea what it's like to have all this experience and be stuck dealing with piss-ant kids who all think they're the next big thing?"

I blinked several times at the stupidity of that question.

"I swear, demons these days know nothing of what it's really like out there. They have no work ethic, and it seems like all they care about is anime, short-form videos, and gaming. Every damn one of them claims to have some kind of phobia, allergy, or mental issue that keeps them from doing… anything. The little pricks are demanding mental health days. Mental… health… days? *For demons?!*"

"Is it really that bad, or are we just getting old?" I asked, playing the Never Realm advocate.

"They all wanna work remotely, Jackson. *Remotely.* How do you torture souls remotely? Seriously, fuck this generation. When I was coming up, my superiors would beat me until I couldn't stand up and then kick me for lying down. We learned grit the hard way."

Yeesh, was this what I sounded like?

"I tell ya, there are days when I'm ready to hang it all up and join the other side. Things can't be worse up there, you feel me?"

"Well, before you put in your application with the side of the angels, I have a business opportunity for you."

"Dude, look at me," he said. "I've been demoted to imp status. It'll take centuries before I can broker any contracts."

"And hypothetically, how many circles would they jump you if you were the demon to land a contract that revolutionizes the future of villainy?"

"Don't piss on me and tell me it's raining," Y'olly said.

"On your leg."

"What?"

"The expression is 'don't piss *on my leg* and tell me it's raining'."

"Don't kink shame me."

"Whatever," I said, waving away water sports imagery. "Point is, I'm not bullshitting. I've got an idea, and I need the Never Realm to pull it off."

"What is it?" he asked. "You tell me, and I'll see what I can do. I still know a few people down there who are willing to talk to me."

I shook my head. "Not now and not here. Too many ears listening. Over winter break, that's when I'll want a sit-down. You tell whoever is willing to listen that I have a big deal on the table. But I'm gonna want something up front."

"What?"

"Nothing major," I said. "Just a little insurance policy for next semester. If things go the way I think they're going to go, then I'm gonna need it. Can you do that?"

"How do I know this isn't a setup for yours truly?" Y'olly asked.

"Demon, please," I scoffed. "You went up against me and failed. You plan on trying that again? At least so soon?"

"No?"

"Then we're cool," I said. "I'd never fault a villain for doing the job. You made it a bit personal, so I smacked you down. You keep making it personal… then so will I."

We looked at one another for several long seconds.

This moment could go a couple of different ways. But no matter how it played out, our relationship would forever be redefined.

Y'olly opted—smartly—to work in a way that best helped him.

"I'm open to business negotiations," he said, extending his skinny arm.

I took it, *Predator* style. We locked eyes again, this time playfully flexing in the saddest recreation of the Arnie and Carl Weathers meme. But after a few moments of straining, I managed to force his arm over.

It felt good.

"Dick," he cursed.

I chuckled. "So, now that you're not all team Sophia, anything you wanna tell me?"

"Would that I could, man. But she really kept things close to the vest. All I know is she'd been planning something to hurt you as deeply as possible," he said, then looked into the sea of students. "But something tells me you currently got more to worry about than just Sophia."

I glanced back. The imp was right. There was tension in the air. My Shadow Master senses told me that this had everything to do with the second-year students and their ongoing Mafia game midterm. Even now I could see it. Small groups forming, whispering, and casting glances.

Shit was about to go down.

"Winter break," I reminded Y'olly, then grabbed the drinks. "I'll reach out for a meeting. Make it happen and we'll get you back on top."

I turned to leave, but Y'olly stopped me with a hand on my shoulder. I turned back and he offered me two new drinks.

"Then you might want these instead."

I looked at the offered drinks, then gave the two in my hand a quick sniff.

I rolled my eyes. "Really? Nightshade?"

Y'olly shrugged. "Demon's gotta demon, you know?"

"Yeah, I get it," I said, then handed my drinks off to two passing students before accepting the poison-free drinks.

I still gave them a quick whiff to be sure.

Satisfied, I returned to Beatrice, who was at a table with her girlfriends, Annie and Melina, the cyborg and fly girl respectively, and their dates. Annie was sitting next to a knock-off Transformer in a sport coat. Based on his relative size and wheeled chassis, he looked like he could turn into some kind of motorcycle or ATV.

And he seemed to be a bit of a horndog.

"Come on, babe," the robo-changer said, all but pleading with the cyborg girl in a red party dress. "I'm just saying that blue gears are a real thing in my culture."

"Uh huh," Annie said with an eyeroll.

"Seriously," he pressed. "If we don't get our… oil changed regularly, our gears literally freeze and lock up."

"I think you'll be fine."

"Or you can change your own oil," Melina said from the other end of the table.

The fly girl was canoodling with a blob of sentient ooze.

"It doesn't feel the same," the robot jock sighed.

"You hungry, baby?" Melina asked the ooze, which quivered in what I assumed to be the affirmative.

The fly girl vomited up some stomach acid onto a finger sandwich, dissolving it, which the ooze then absorbed.

Gross.

"Punch," I said, handing a cup to my date.

"Thanks," she said, patting the chair next to her. "You all remember Jackson?"

"'Sup," the robot said, giving the dude chin lift.

"You look great," Melina said, noting my "weight loss."

"Thanks."

"You're just in time for the show," Annie added.

"Mm," I grunted. "Second-year shenanigans about to start?"

"Good eye," she said.

"It's what I do," I said, taking the seat next to Beatrice. "So who're the major players?"

Beatrice pointed at several different tables. "Out of the five families in the beginning, only two are left. The Vipers and the New Kings."

"What happens to the students who were in the other three?" I asked. "Are they out of the midterm?"

"No," Beatrice said after taking a sip of the punch. "The second-year tests aren't about elimination."

"They're about adaptation," Annie said, pushing her date's hands off her knee. "Five families start. A few wars and some infighting later and most families collapse. After that, the students are absorbed into the families that survived."

Made sense. The stereotypical "mafia game" was an analogy for how villainy operated in the field. Powerful organizations—or companies—constantly destroyed or absorbed their competition, stole the proprietary secrets, and profited.

"So what then? Students are graded on how they adapt to the events?"

"More or less," Melina said after slurping up some more of the dissolved finger sandwiches. "It's a test of teamwork and personal resilience. If a kid's family falls, then how far do they climb within the new organization."

"And it always turns into a huge shitshow at the end of the semester," Beatrice said. "Winter Dance and Prom are never boring."

That simple statement gave me pause. "Never?"

"It's tradition," Melina said. "Freshman year, we watched the second years turn this place into a bloodbath."

"And we did the same when it was our turn," Annie added.

"Yeah, but we were *way* more brutal!"

The three girls laughed and high fived. But while they were jovial, my blood ran cold. Second-year students, under the cover of darkness, moved through the crowds to get into positions at opposite ends of the dance.

"And everyone knows this?" I asked, shifting focus from the opposing mafia kids to Sophia and King Stanley.

"Oh, everyone knows," Beatrice continued. "Even the professors and the band are in on it."

Sure as shit, Nyx and the rest of the professors at the teacher table bore a look of eager anticipation. Were they… betting?

Gods damn it.

That was when the band switched up the tempo, dropping into that softer, more generic rhythm bands do when the front man wants to talk to the audience.

"Hello, Sablestone!" Dorian Gray said into the mic, getting some "woo"s from the crown. "Midnight is nearly upon us, and I've just been informed that the final two remaining mafia families, the Vipers and the New Kings, are here tonight."

As soon as he said that, the band smashed out a few bombastic notes while the overhead lighting shifted, casting the mafia family tables in green and purple lights, respectively.

The band then shifted back into that same droll rhythm so that Dorian could keep talking.

"Good luck to our second-years. But we also have the freshman final four here tonight. Sophia, Stanley, Jackson, and Myst, where are ya?!"

The moment painting pansy punk said our names, a spotlight shone down on each of is. When the light hit me, I felt the spell I'd spent hours on shatter. Every student could now see me. Which included every person I'd been avoiding.

Bloody hell.

"So how 'bout we just get on with it?" Dorian said before turning to his bandmates and asking, "You all ready?" in that fake-ass, stage performance way.

Sigh. I always suspected Dorian was a theater kid.

Igor began laying out a very familiar beat on the drums while Carmilla and Spring-heeled Jack dropped the iconic intro. When the band broke into "Ballroom Blitz," the entire dance broke out into chaos.

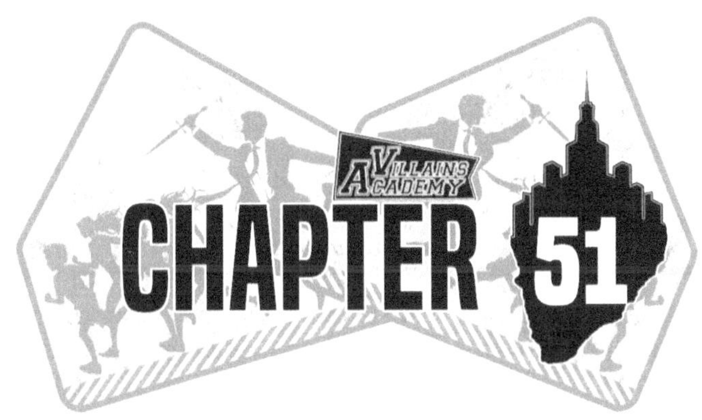

WHERE I TAKE A DIVE, MOUNT A MAN, AND RECREATE AN UNDERAPPRECIATED MOVIE

"Down!" Beatrice yelled, grabbing me by the back of the neck and hauling us both to the ground.

The energy blast missed my head by inches, but the bright light in the dark space had been close enough to fry my eyes. I blinked like crazy, trying to get my vision clear while willing my pupils to adjust. Blurrily, I watched Annie and Melina work together, flipping a series of tables over to give us some cover.

What had been a dance was now a war zone. The cafeteria was a cacophony of teenage aggression backed by an on-the-nose soundtrack.

"What that crap is that supposed to do?!" I shouted to Beatrice. "This isn't the movies, it's a bloody table!"

My date smirked when several shots slammed into our makeshift shelter. Instead of blowing huge chunks of splintered wood into our bodies, the blast ricocheted off in a fine, sparkly cascade of cooling plasma.

"Huh?!"

"Enchanted tables," Annie said by way of explanation. "They're designed to survive anything,"

She and her horny GoBot of a date extended the futuristic blasters from their forearm housings and began blind firing.

"Okay, *why* are they enchanted?"

"Villain students equal a lot of collateral damage, duh," Melina added before she popped up and spat corrosive bile onto a charging second-year's face.

The... ah hell, I couldn't tell what he was anymore due to his freaking face melting off. Well, whatever he was, he tried to scream, but the sound that came out was more like a gargling whimper. Melina's date, Blobert, for I had no better name for it, was apparently still a bit peckish. Ignoring the blasts of magic, gunfire, and energy beams, he oozed out and engulfed the melted second-year kid.

It was... very gross.

The parts of Blobert that were blown away filled back in as he dissolved his food. Huh. I reckon that being made of sentient goo has its perks.

Well, you know, except for the whole no genitals thing.

Or maybe that was a plus? Mine seemed to get me into more trouble than they were worth.

With my eyesight more or less restored, I dared to peek over the table to get the lay of the land and hopefully see if I could spot the asshole who'd taken a shot at me. Amid the child slaughter, I tracked a pair of figures skirting the periphery and moving into a flanking position. When they passed a glowing stalagmite, I clearly saw Sophia. I assumed the other one to be King Stanley. It looked like the high god of the comic realms had transformed again, this time into a generic spit-curled and square-jawed bloke with a cape and tights.

King Stanley spotted me, and his eyes glowed red with an intense charging energy. I ducked back down, easily dodging his shot. Comic book blasts, for whatever bloody reason, seemed to follow the same laser logic as *Star Wars*. Energy beams did not move at the speed of light, but rather clocked in at around the average fastball.

With a sense of earned smugness, I popped back up to give King Stanley the finger. He in turn used that moment to shoot once more. The blast disintegrated my outstretched middle finger on my right hand.

It did not tickle.

"Shit fuck titty ass balls!" I cursed, dropping back down behind the table, cradling my cauterized stump. "That was my favorite flicking finger!"

Oh, he was gonna pay for that.

Eventually.

The problem was that King Stanley wasn't my target. And if my logic was right, he never would be. After killing Khasil, I'd received my next target, and it was Myst. With her as my target, and King Stanley getting my name after taking out Maureen, that left Myst going after Sophia, and Sophia targeting King Stanley.

Ugh, this was giving me a headache.

Regardless, I wasn't sure if Myst had it in her to make a move against Sophia. I damn sure knew that the only reason King Stanley was still in the game was because Sophia wanted it that way. To what end, who could say. But it was clear that I was the next to go, and they'd planned on using the sophomore's mafia slaughter as the perfect distraction.

"Why don't you just come out and get it over with," I heard Sophia say over my rocky-talky. "Final four isn't anything to be ashamed of. Unless, of course, you're afraid of me?"

Bitch was taunting me.

But she'd given me an idea.

"You, Gobotron!"

"My name's Phallax," the bargain bin transmorpher said while popping off a few shots.

"Don't care. I got an idea and I'm gonna need your help."

"Why in the name of the dark spark would I help a freshie?"

"Because if you want Annie to *change your oil*, then you're gonna need to do something cool to earn it. Right?"

Annie nodded. "Yeah, pretty much."

Like many teens of his age, Phallax was motivated by sex and was willing to do whatever for a chance.

"Fine. What do you need?"

"Speed," I said. "I assume you're fast?"

"Seriously?" he snickered. "Bro, I'm the fastest thing here."

"Sucks for you there, Annie," I chuckled. "Okay, Blobert, I need your help too."

The quivering mound of goop wriggled and bobbed.

"He asked how you knew his name," Melina said, translating snot to English.

Holy shit. "Um, because I… cared enough to learn it?"

"Then why didn't you know my name?" Phallax asked.

"Because you're a huge tool," I said. "Look, Blobert, can you like choose to not dissolve something, or rather someone, *inside* you?"

The blob wiggled and twisted.

"He said 'yes,' but wants to know why," Melina said.

"Because we're gonna wreck shop and become legends at this school," I said, then added, "Probably. Maybe. Look, don't know what kind of shenanigans past kids have pulled. But this shit will be memorable."

The mound of yellowish-green gelatin shimmied.

"He wants to know if he's allowed to eat anyone else?"

"Dude, if we do this right, then you're going to chow-town."

Blobert bobbed up and down in an excited motion.

"He's in," Melina said.

"Awesome. Okay dude, do your change-o-form thing, and let's roll out!"

"You better be right about the oil change," Phallax grumbled before shifting configurations.

Phallax's body went through a series of unnecessary twists, turns, and sound effects before settling into a futuristic-looking four-wheeled ATV. Now, why did a silicon-based lifeform from a techno robotic universe transform into a facsimile of a vehicle made popular by rednecks, monster truck enthusiasts, and children with unironic rattails? Who the fuck knew. The multiverse is a mysterious and often stupid thing.

I mounted up, throwing one leg over, and I swore I heard Phallax grunt in pleasure. Ignoring every implication, I gestured for Blobert to join us.

"You envelop me, don't—I repeat, *don't*—eat me," I told the sentient goo-ball. "You keep me safe, anyone else we pass is free game. Oh, and do your best to look scary, cool?"

Blobert quivered in response, then oozed his way up my leg and spread across my entire body. It wasn't *unpleasant.* In fact, it was warm, gushy, and kinda comforting.

Kinda like being born in reverse.

Once he settled into place, Blobert was kind enough to open a little window for my face so I could see and breathe.

"Thanks dude," I told him, then twisted the throttle, revving Phallax's engine.

And no, that imagery was not lost on me. I was just doing my best to ignore it as we were most likely crotch-to-crotch. Tapping my rocky-talky, I opened a line to Sophia.

"You know what, you're right. Maybe I have been a little afraid of what you're going to do. We might as well come out, right?"

"We?" I heard her say.

And that was my cue. Popping the clutch, I hit the… gas? Fusion juice? Whatever it was that Phallax ran on, I opened that sum'bitch wide open. The three of us shot out from behind the table barricade in what had to be either the coolest—or dumbest—looking way possible.

I'll let you be the judge.

Imagine a twelve-year-old boy inside a bubble of living snot riding a cyber version of a trailer park Cadillac. Oh, and said snot bubble was waving at least a dozen goopy tentacles in an attempt to look "scary."

Eh? Thoughts?

Sigh… yeah, I already know the answer. From how almost everyone stopped and stared, we not only looked like Jake Gyllenhaal in his greatest role, *Bubble Boy*, but we were also clearly the cringiest thing that Sablestone Academy for Villains had ever produced.

But hey, at least we got their attention. Which was all I needed.

Let them think I was funny, cute, or harmless.

Everyone thinks Pac-Man is adorable right before he chomps a motherfucker.

CHAPTER 52

WHERE I CREATE A NEW WORD, EXPLAIN THE IMPORTANCE OF ATTENTION, AND INVITE A GUEST TO THE PARTY

I can practically hear you asking, "Why are you doing this?" And that's a great question. Why should I, a Titan stuck in a boy's body, ride a sentient ATV, indoors, *through* a dance, while wearing a flesh-hungry ball of acidic goo? Well, dear reader, there are two answers.

One, because it's freaking cool.

And secondly, I had a plan. What kind of plan requires an ATV and a gooball? Let me answer your question with a question: You ever see a streaker hop the barricade at a sporting event and run across the field? World kinda stops, doesn't it? Hard to carry on when unexpected tits-n-dicks are flapping across the turf.

Now I wasn't nude, thankfully, but the stratagem was the same: be so gods damned bizarre that you take the attention away from the conflict and replace it with a new target. In this case, me. For what reason? Well, we'll get to that.

Rocketing across the dance floor was admittedly fun, what with Blobert absorbing all the damage. When too much of his gunk had been blown away, my gooey shield plucked another unlucky schmuck off the dance floor and chowed down, replenishing himself. With a working system in place, the three of us literally plowed a path.

Some partygoers died due to shocked stupidity, Blobert's appetite, or the really, really cool energy weapons built in

Phallax's ATV form. Initially I'd been afraid to press any of his buttons for fear of activating an ejector seat—or an erection set, for that matter. But then I noticed something that looked like a trigger on his steering column, then the laws of villainy dictate that when you see a trigger, you pull that sucker.

And pull I did. Heh heh, man, you shoulda seen 'em die. Just chunky bits of kid everywhere. Now, I'm not advocating child murder. But I'm not *not* advocating for it either. It's YA, so you know what I'm talking about. Right?

Okay, folks, now's not the time to get morally righteous or squeamish on me. Considering everything we've done together over these recorded adventures, a little bit of—of...

Huh, what's the word for killing teenagers? Pedicide? No, that's killing children in general, but more like little kids. Infanticide, of course, refers to killing kids one year or younger—wait, why the fuck do we even have that word? You know what, never mind. I don't wanna know what Dark Ages practices happened to give me historical context. I'm a villain, not a psycho.

But I'm not talking about killing kid-kids, I'm talking about shitty kids. Teenagers. The "okay boomer" arrogant little shits who've never really suffered but constantly whine like they have. The little pricks who live in a bubble of insurance and cellphone coverage while consuming influencer prankster vids or eating detergent on a dare. The kids who'd be lost at best and dead at worst if they grew up in *any* generation prior to this one.

Wow, there really isn't a word for specifically killing teens, is there?

We've got words for killing family members, animals, and leaders. Gods above and below, we have words for the killing of intangible things. Did you know that linguicide is intentionally causing the death of a language, or that famicide is the killing of another's reputation? Yet we don't have a word for killing teenagers?

Fuck it, let's pull a Bill Shakespeare and create a new word for the killing of teens. Stands to reason it should exist, especially for Y-bloody-A, i.e., the genre built on fear, death, and a whole gods damned mountain of teen corpses.

Let's see, "Pais" was a gender-neutral Greek word for the young, but that also referred to a slave, so that's out. "Neo" means more new rather than young. "Hebe" was an ancient Greek word that meant youth in the prime of life. But, come on, we're not calling it "hebicide" for obvious, anti-Semitic-sounding reasons.

Ah, I got it. Delinquelate! To eradicate delinquents. Perfect! That's what I was doing, I was delinquelating the ever-living shit outta these little pricks with extreme prejudice.

And it felt good.

Huh. Unless your question was "No, dumbass, why are you riding around like an idiot and ranting about murder words this deep into the third act instead of, you know, finishing the gods damned book?!"

If that was your question, then… um, *shut up?*

Things may seem murky and chaotic to you, but there's a method to my madness. See, I needed all eyes on me. One of the things they don't teach in villainy, or hell… maybe they do at this school? Anyway, when you're the center of attention, you get a good look at who's *not* looking at you.

Stick with me.

When one is up on a stage, literally or metaphorically, you're not looking at the spectacle since *you are* the spectacle. As such, when someone isn't paying attention or turns away, it's way easier to spot. Now why is that important?

Because, class, when you spot someone not surprised, shocked, or following herd mentality, that tells you that they are the people who need to be watched and monitored. If the government, social media ads, and big retail corporations do it, then who am I to argue?

So as we sped through weapons fire and magical attacks, I got a good look at the crowd. And man… I wish I could say I wasn't surprised; I really do. But seeing what I saw, well, I think I knew how things were going to go down. Gods above and below, this is the one time I hoped to be wrong.

I realize you don't understand, but I'm sure we'll get there soon.

Locking up the front brakes, I whipped Phallax's back end around so that it slammed into a pair of partygoers. Idling the engine, I plotted my course, then checked the clock. Yup. Definitely time to get on with it.

"Blobert, you good bud?"

My slimy shield manifested a tentacle, fished out a half-digested arm, and flicked the corpse's hand into a thumbs-up.

"Good enough for me," I said before opening the throttle.

This time my path wasn't a random dash of destruction, but rather a calculated route. I had places to be, and timing was crucial. Roaring the engine, I zigged and zagged through the throngs of teens, shifted hard, and then went straight for the stage. The backup professors-slash-band clearly didn't wanna deal with my crap, so they dropped their instruments and wisely fled.

"Barricade, Blobert!" I instructed the goo, who oozed off me and created a translucent wall.

Hopping off Phallax, I dashed for the mic, then reached for the lynchpin of this whole farkakteh plan…

My copy of Coach Mother's magic whistle.

While not as powerful as the original, and already sporting a crack from having been used once earlier in the day, my copy had a few good uses in it before completely shattering.

I blew the whistle into the mic. The shrill burst pierced the ears of every attending student and staff member. A second, deeper crack appeared along the item.

"Everyone stop!" I commanded.

And like… well, magic, everyone did. The roar of combat and teenage bullshit suddenly ceased, granting me, an older person in spirit, blessed silence. I took a moment to appreciate the relative calm before giving the whistle another blast, which caused a third crack to form.

"Summon the Sablestone," I commanded.

The crowd of kids suddenly began talking again, as the new command overrode the previous one. Once free, the partygoers looked confused, as none of them had the power to summon the stone.

But Headmaster Nyx did.

The Titan smirked but complied. Nyx raised her hand in a beckoning gesture and the room rumbled. The circular iris in the middle of the stone dance floor opened as a stone column carrying the villainous relic rose like an ancient, angry god. Realization crashed over the silent room.

If the Sablestone was here, then so was death. Real death.

I heard hundreds of buttholes clenching. Don't ask me how I know that sound.

The student body stood there frozen more from fear than from my command. Which, of course, was the point. It's almost like someone—*ahem…* me—had an awareness of the castle's layout and realized that the stone was designed to appear in the two places where students gathered in the greatest numbers. The amphitheater directly above and the cafeteria. And as I said earlier, the cafeteria and the gym were traditionally where most schools held their dances.

I told you there was gonna be some foreshadowing.

Now that I had their attention, it was time to see if the Shadow Master still had a flair for the dramatic.

But like, in a cool way. Not in a theater way.

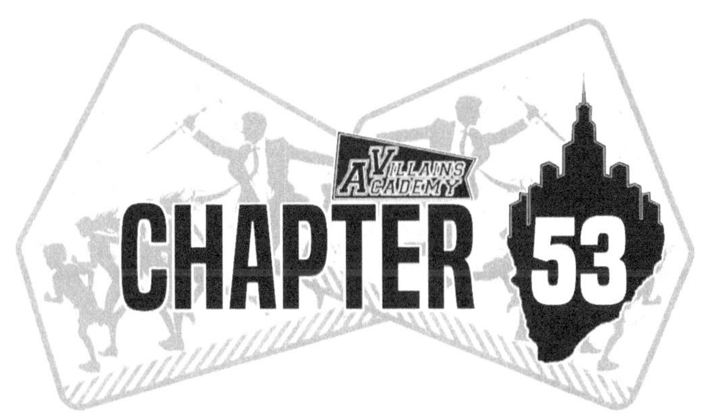

WHERE I PERHAPS MAKE A MISTAKE, VILLAINSPLAIN MURDER FANTASIES, AND REGRET BRINGING A KNIFE TO A LASER FIGHT

"Pop quiz, class. What happens if you die while in proximity to the Sablestone?"

The question was obviously rhetorical, so no one spoke.

Well, almost no one.

"You gets dead for real!"

Sigh. "Thank you, Keith, for stating the obvious."

"You's welcome!" he said, snapping off a pair of finger guns.

I never should have taught him that.

"Now, I'm sure a few of you think of yourselves as badasses. Soon-to-be legends of villainy. Well, here's your chance," I said, daring the class to action. "Go on, go for it. Kill your target. Kill an enemy. Be *ruthless*! But, like real life, your safety net is gone. The moment you strike, you're gonna leave yourself open for an attack from the person you didn't even know was gunning for you. Villainy. It's a bitch. Any takers?"

Just as I predicted, no one moved.

If I may brag a bit, I used everything the faculty taught me over the semester. I displayed proper physical conditioning and villainous planning while using my magical skills and resource management to put myself into this position. Along with knowledge of lair construction, manipulation, and… *ugh*, theatrics, I had the entire school shaking in their dress shoes. Now, was this because I was the best student?

Yes. Clearly. A thousand times yes.

I had a captive audience frozen in fear. And it was delicious. In fact, I was willing to bet that everyone was so scared of real death that no one would dare—

"Die, you sanctimonious undead fuck!"

Before I knew what happened, Renfield had pulled a wooden stake from inside his jacket, spun to his left, and drove the point into Dracula's heart. The vampire icon unleashed an unearthly howl of pain as a gods damned geyser of blood erupted from his chest and he fell out of his chair. Springing to his feet, Renfield reached up the back of his dinner jacket and drew a big ass knife.

Folks, when I say, "a big ass knife," I'm not referring to the overly ornate fantasy blades some D&D dildo displays in their nerd cave. I'm talking about them Walmart special kind of machete knives. The kind that rednecks give their kids as stocking stuffers. You know, the kids who grow up to be the guy who flips the sign from "Stop" to "Slow" at roadway construction sites.

With a manic war cry, the lanky professor brought his weapon down, beheading Dracula in a single blow. The bespectacled madman grabbed the vampire's head, jumped onto the faculty table, and held it high for all to see. But the professor didn't stop there. The crazy coot punted Dracula's head it into the crowd and then opened his coat to reveal a staggering number of incendiary devices and sharp, stabby things.

"Let's fuck these fucking kids up!"

Huh. I wonder what he was—

As if they'd been waiting for that particular dinner bell to be rung, most of the professors looked at the students with wicked glee in their evil eyes. The staff here had over a thousand years of combined literary existence. Stories that detail dark hearts and darker deeds. Emboldened by Renfield's call to action and the presence of the Sablestone, our beloved educators suddenly realized not only that murder is fun, but also that kids are tender and tasty.

Oops.

Folks, your ol' pal Jackson may have miscalculated. When I'd planned to summon the Sablestone, it was to keep the peace until midnight and thus my points. While I'd accounted for teen bravado, those who say "fuck around and find out" are mostly smack-talking cowards.

But—and this is a big but—I *may* have forgotten to consider another factor: the animosity most longtime teachers have for students.

What? You think that kindly old Mrs. Finkleman back in the fourth grade liked you?

HA! Mrs. Finkleman *hated* you.

Dear reader, there isn't a seasoned teacher out there who doesn't feel beaten down by a system that no longer supports them. There isn't a year that goes by when teachers are tasked to do some new thing that should be handled at home. But teachers tend to take it on the chin because, as in most abusive relationships, they're there for the kids.

After a couple generations of fuckwits breeding more fuckwits, teachers are now burdened with fuckwit parents along with their fuckling brood.

These are the parents who think their "special child" is beyond reproach. They blame teachers when the kids screw up instead of holding themselves accountable for this new breed of unlovable twats.

Yes, I'm talking about your kids.

If you've ever uttered something even remotely close to, "No, you must understand, Mrs. Finkleman, our little Ashleigh is not like other kids. She's special and has quirks that you must account for," then you are, in fact, the problem.

Lemme break it down Barney style so that there's no room for confusion: If twenty-plus kids in a classroom of thirty-two have "quirks" that require additional attention, then you all either have weak seed, or you're indulging in some new-school, woo-woo bullshit.

It's okay, the truth hurts. Just like how public schools have morphed into day care under the guise of education. Oh, it might've been a place where kids learned… once. Back when class sizes were small, teachers had actual authority to educate, and parents worked *with* teachers to curb disruptive behavior.

Unfortunately, school boards are now infested with fuckknuckles who insist on being addressed as *Doctor* Fuckknuckle while they replace education with inclusion, standardized test prep, and… I dunno, emotional support ferrets or some such shit.

Leading from the back are the new generation of lawsuit-averse principals, an armada of assholes who support board-backed politics and policies instead of supporting teachers. If you don't believe me, go to YouTube, search "teacher quits," and watch a few. See if you can spot the repeating theme.

Overworked, underpaid, rarely appreciated, and sometimes assaulted by kids, is it any wonder why pretty much every broken teacher has a "purge" fantasy or two? And the staff at Sablestone weren't any different. Well… they were a bit different, at least in one key way.

They were villains. And I'd just provided them with a consequence-free environment.

Again, oops.

Nyx had said that all the professors sought a way out of this construct within Possibility. And while I was legitimately working on one, they clearly had another option. A rather simple one.

No students meant no reason to be there.

The staff would rather face oblivion than deal with another semester. At least that's how I read the look Nyx was giving me. But on the bright side, it was kinda cool to see experts in action, you know? The professors of Sablestone Academy weren't a bunch of dadbod couch quarterbacks. They were the icons of villainy for a reason, and amazing to watch.

Captain Hook swung his namesake wide, snagging a fleeing teen in the spine. Eager to make up for the lost time of killing Lost Boys, the good captain gave a quick, hard yank, spinning the kid around and plunging his saber up hilt deep. The dying child vomited blood and bile while Hook whispered, "Tell Peter I'll see him in Hell."

Gods… *damn*, that got dark.

A flash of motion followed by the screams of children caught my attention. Tracking the falling bodies, I spotted the Cheshire Cat, who blinked in and out of existence. He appeared atop a teen just long enough to tear out eyes or rip out a throat. He preferred to see his victims suffer before eating them.

You know… like a fucking cat.

Coach Mother had gone bloody primal when presented with a chance to unleash her pent-up frustration. The brutish ogress was covered in scorch marks. Remnants of broken weapons jutted out from her thick, calloused flesh. But she showed no signs of stopping. A severed arm in one hand and a ripped-off leg in the other, Grendel's mama brutally crushed whatever was in front of her. When her improvised flails were no longer serviceable, she'd rip off fresh ones and repeat the process.

Ooh, a robot leg. That's gonna do some damage.

A group of magical students tried forming a defensive line, defending the emergency exit. Unfortunately, the doors were only so wide and only so many could flee. While I applauded the junior wizards' desire to defend the bottleneck, they weren't prepared for the arcane powerhouse that was Baba Yaga.

The old crone skillfully scratched an eldritch sigil in the air with her crooked wand. The world seemed to shimmer and twitch before a bloody thundercrash of unseen force descended upon her students, shredding their pitiful defensive magics like tissue paper. She then did what every D&D caster class does when presented with such a prime opportunity. I believe the meme goes something like, *I don't care how many orphans there are! I said I cast fireball!*

A massive crackling conflagration of light and flames burst into existence. The students trying to get out the door were transformed into ash. The only thing left of them was their blast shadows on the walls.

Heh, cool.

Lucky for me, I was safe because I was behind Blobert. As long as he and Phallax were with me, I was ready for any—

"Hey!" I snapped when the sentient ooze slithered away, retreating into the dark corners of the cafeteria. "Where the shit are you going?!"

"We're getting the fuck outta here, freshie," Phallax called out, dashing off to join the retreating goop.

Bloody hell.

Y'olly was right. This was why the new generation was never gonna make it in the real world. I mean, look at 'em. One little massacre and they run for the hills? Yeesh. Sixteen-year-olds lied about their age to fight and die in World War One. Now? Kid gets a mean Insta-comment and they're double-dosing Zoloft due to "cyber-bullying."

But I didn't have time for hyperbolic musings. While I was no shrinking violet when it came to slaughter, I had something more precious to worry about.

Evie.

Scanning the chaos, I spotted my daughter… and my blood ran cold.

Sophia, Eris, and Myst had grabbed her and were dragging Evie away. She was fighting and kicking like hell to break free, but Myst had transformed into gorillapus to subdue her.

Just as I was about to dash off the makeshift stage to help, a male, muscular, square-jawed, and exceedingly handsome bloke blocked my way. I pulled a vorpal scalpel from my jacket's inner pocket.

"If you don't get the fuck out of my way, Stanley, I'll kill you."

King Stanley laughed once, then fired his eye lasers at me.

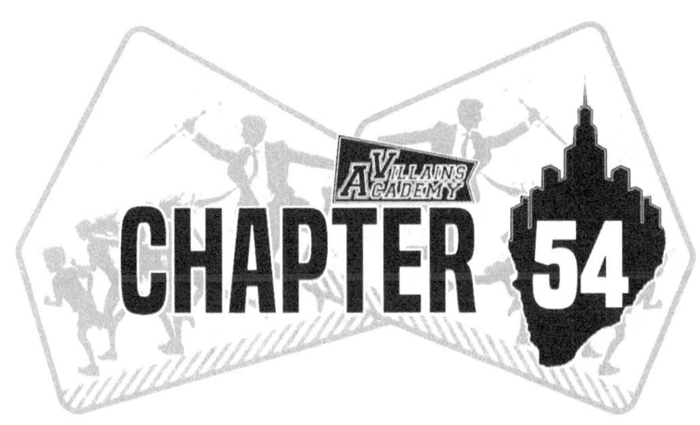

WHERE I EXPLAIN GENRE FATIGUE, HAVE A KILLER SET OF TITS, AND ACCIDENTALLY OPEN A BACK DOOR

Dropping the scalpel and stuffing the whistle down my pants, I quickly brought my hands up, deftly weaving a shield spell. It wasn't my best work, but it was done just in time to deflect the beam. Again, I have to thank the gods of contrived writing for limiting the speed of light in sci-fi fantasy genre fiction for the sake of narrative. Otherwise, I'd have had an instantaneous hole in my head.

The red laser *pinged* off my orange arcane shield with a shower of yellowish-white sparks before ricocheting off somewhere into the crowd. Based on the screams, I'd ballpark that the errant beam killed at least three more kids.

"Wow, I wasn't even trying to do that," I told the god of superheroes. "Man, YA really likes dead kids for the sake of drama, doesn't it?"

"Do you ever stop talking!?" King Stanley roared, swinging a super-strength punch down on top of my shield.

Magic studies and fitness regimen aside, I was still in the body of a five-foot nothing, hundred-pound kid. Diving to one side, I narrowly avoided the pseudo-Kryptonian blow that shattered the stage risers.

"Stand still and die," King Stanley seethed.

"Bite my tween ass," I spat back, diving for the scalpel.

But just as my right hand touched the enchanted blade, Stanley's boot came down on my wrist, breaking the bone.

"Gods damn it!"

King Stanley growled slightly, twisting his heel just to inflict a bit more pain. "Nothing smart to say now?"

"Wha—what's your problem with me?!" I blurted out through my clenched teeth. "What have I done to make you hate me this much? I honestly don't get it."

"You have the audacity to ask me that?" King Stanley said. "After what you did?"

"Did what?!" I said, genuinely confused. "If anything, I helped out when you and Valliar were trapped by Randy!"

"Exactly!" King Stanley seethed. "I am one of the elder gods, and you made me, and my comic universe, look stupid. Ever since then, the entire genre has been on the decline."

I looked up at the pissed-off deity and laughed. Hard.

"Are you kidding me?" I said. "You're blaming me for superhero fatigue?"

"Superhero fatigue's a myth!" he snapped. "There's no such thing!"

"What? It's totally a thing."

The old god took a step back and wagged his finger at me. "No! It isn't. Superheroes have existed since the beginning of time. Tales of the extraordinarily powerful confronting the powers of evil have always been—and always will be—part of storytelling! But you and your venomous ilk live to arrogantly deconstruct the works of better minds!"

"Oh, come on," I said, backing away and wincing. "As much as I'd love to take all the credit, the truth is that tearing things down is at the very core of mankind's corrupted soul. When something is too good for too long, people can't help but eat their idols. Everything that is loved or popular has a ticking clock. It's a question of when, not if, people barbecue their sacred cows."

"No no *no*! You're not talking your way out of this one," he said, his eyes once again glowing as power built up. "You poisoned what was beautiful!"

I stared right back into those red eyes. "You don't see your own culpability, do you?"

"Me?" he said, blinking just for a second. "What—what are you blathering about?"

Gods above and below, I didn't think I was going to have to explain something so simple to one so old and powerful. Alas, power can blind us all.

"Superheroes had their renaissance," I said, confidently herosplaining to the comic book god. "The media's skull-fucked our eyes with wave after wave of superhero shows, movies, and books for over twenty years. So yeah, people got tired of it. I'm just lucky *Villains Pride* hit when it did."

"No," King Stanley said, shaking his head as if trying to avoid the reality. "No, that's not true!"

"You know it is," I said, really channeling that manipulation and social engineering course. "Look, remember back when the bulk of paranormal fantasy was all chick-lit? Coming-of-age stories for the girls and vampire masturbation, shifter sex, and fairy fucking for the women?"

"Yeah?" Stanley said, slightly confused.

"Great. You remember what happened next, right? The subgenre exploded into the mainstream thanks to YA blockbusters and male-skewed, action-adventure redesigns. Demand became higher. But instead of a careful drip feed of quality content, we got every wannabe writer who could glue two sentences together trying their hand at urban fantasy. Which meant the market was flooded with mass-produced copycats all trying to outsnark one another."

"So?"

"So?!" I spat back. "It meant that the fans, the people the gods need to keep their worlds afloat, got sick of it and walked away. Action-inclined guys switched to space combat stories while the hornball gals begging for bodice-ripping spice shifted to dungeons and dildos... er, romantasy. Gods above and below, with all the mainstream success that LitRPG is getting now, how long until the market is overflowing from the metaphorical toilet water due to all the shit clogging the pipe? What's your guess, eighteen months or so until we're up to our tits in Carl and Donut clones?"

Still cradling my wrist, I got to my feet and looked up at the muscular elder god.

"You want to know what killed superhero fiction? You did," I said defiantly. "You had a hit, so you rammed it down everyone's throat. But just like the last zombie craze, you couldn't help yourself."

"But—but the people demanded more!"

I shook my head. "You stupid—ahh, never mind. Listen, anything without an end will eventually just become an annoying noise or a hollow husk. Stories, book series, or even people. Things are beautiful because they end, not because they go on forever, you dumb fuck."

King Stanley smiled. It wasn't wicked or cruel. It was a contented kind of smile. The involuntary expression that comes with a deep sense of satisfaction.

"Thank you, Jackson. Truly, thank you," King Stanley said as the power in his eyes continued to swell. "You made this decision so much easier. Sophia wanted to keep playing these infuriating little games with you. A push here, a nudge there. But I'm done."

I backed up, but stopped when I bumped into the stone wall at the rear edge of the stage. There was nowhere else to go. I could only watch while the destructive power in King Stanley's eyes swelled to epic levels.

"I know what will happen to my world if I don't return, which is why I'm done fucking around. You made a mistake bringing that stone here. Your last one."

"Well, then I want you to know that you've taught me a lot," I said. "More than you're ever going to know. So thank you. Also… finger titties."

The crimson-eyed superhero blinked several times in confusion. "What?"

"Finger titties!" I said, a lot louder this time.

"Is that supposed to be funny?"

"Fucking *finger titties!*"

King Stanley sighed. "Goodbye, Jackson."

"One hundred deathmerits to King Stanley," a new voice said.

The Deified Creator of Marvelous Imaginations Who Rides Upon a Dark Horse collapsed on the spot. Dead.

No wind-up, no pretense. The elder god of the comic universe fell and would never rise again. For Possibility had given me the tool to destroy my enemies.

"Thank you, Professor," I said.

Professor James Moriarty shook his head as if coming out of a daze. "Blackwell? What happened? What did I just do?"

"Exactly what I programmed you to do," I told him. "You were the first person I went to see this morning after casting my invisibility spell."

"You used that whistle copy on me, didn't you?"

"A hundred percent," I admitted.

"With a codeword trigger to activate me."

"Yes sir."

"… Well done."

"Sir?"

"Elegant yet simple. Good work, Blackwell."

I wasn't sure how to take the short but earnest compliment. "Um, thank you, sir?"

"You are welcome," he said. "Now there are two of you I hold in my esteem."

"Boss, you okay?" Wraith Knight boomed.

The big man was followed by Lydia, Mikayla, and Beatrice.

"Jackson, what's going on?" Lydia demanded. "Where's Evie?"

"Pardon me, Professor," I said, excusing myself. "Come on, I'll explain on the way."

"On the way to where?" my ex-wife demanded. "Where did they take her?"

"Just move!"

I didn't want to explain that I'd messed up. That like me, Sophia had found a loophole. Normally, the Sablestone resting room required a person to enter willingly while stripping them of their powers.

But only when the stone was present.

By summoning the stone here, I'd removed that safety measure, at least temporarily. If Sophia and her allies were fast enough and got there before the stone returned, then they'd be able to enter the room and theoretically *keep* their powers. We, on the other hand, would have to give up our abilities to enter a room where death was permanent.

Unless we got there in time. If we hauled ass, then maybe we'd have a chance to get there before the whistle's compulsion magic wore off—

The loud grinding sound of the stone pillar retreating into the floor told me all I needed to hear.

Possibility claimed not to have his thumb on the scale, but I was becoming more and more convinced that the antient Titan had a hard-on for YA tropes and plot escalation.

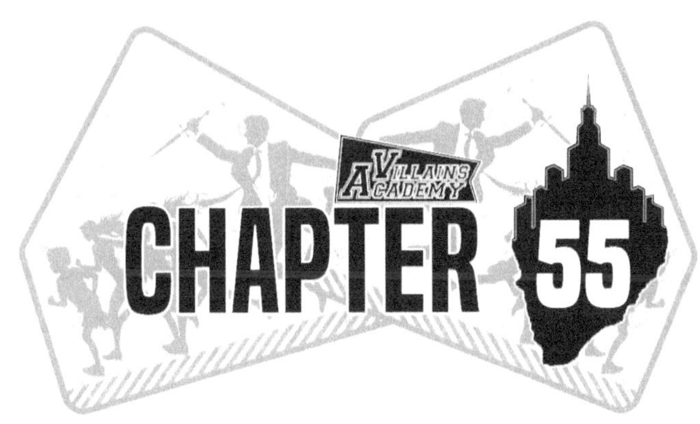

CHAPTER 55

WHERE I HEAR ABOUT A HORRIBLE DISEASE, WITNESS A COMEDY OF ERRORS, AND CLARIFY A PROMISE

Wraith Knight stopped and rounded on me. His big hand slapping across my chest halted me in my tracks.

"She did what?!"

Lydia spun, pulling two knives from—shit, I don't know where. Considering how form-fitting her dress was, they had to have been…

You know what, never mind.

I like to tell family-friendly stories with these recorded adventures, and I refuse to debase this tale by even alluding to her wielding a twatana.

I have standards, damn it.

"Get your hands off him and keep moving," Lydia said, making it clear she wasn't going to give Wraith Knight a second warning.

"No, we need to talk about this *now*," WK said to Lydia, keeping his eyes on me. "What are you accusing Myst of exactly?"

Great. We were deep in the catacombs, getting ever closer to the Sablestone's resting spot and mere moments away from our inevitable confrontation with Sophia. But instead of getting on with it, these chucklefucks wanted to stop and have a conversation-slash-pissing contest. Why?

Because that's what all gods damned YA books, manga stories—and too many indie authors, if you ask me—do to draw out the drama. They build tension, inch up to the final confrontation, then stop and talk about whatever drama that, for some reason, had to be dealt with right then. Shonen anime fans know what I mean. Antagonist and protagonist are about to clash, but the story chooses that moment to shift and have a nine-episode arc about some D-tier side character and how they overcame something.

It's bloody annoying, and I for one will not stand for it. So I paused my little floating ball of magical light and addressed the others.

"Myst abducted me after the slaughterball game," I said, repeating myself. "She then drugged me, chopped me up, and left me incapacitated. Okay?"

"Heh, cool," Mikayla nodded, her demon side approving.

"Boo hoo," Beatrice said, holding out her stitched and stapled arm.

I glared at her. She winked back. Clearly she was having a little fun at my expense.

"Wait," Wraith Knight said, looking me over. "Then how'd you come back?"

"Keith," I said, filling in the blanks. "He came looking for me and I got him to pray to Valliar. Once the old bastard showed up, I played on his righteous nature and got him to put me back together. Which then got him immediately expelled."

"What about Khasil?" Mikayla asked. "I didn't see her at the dance."

"I got her to abdicate control of Caledon… then I killed her," I said. "But she'll be back tomorrow morning."

The succubus gave me an approving nod. "Not bad."

"Yeah yeah yeah, you're great, whatever, but back to Myst helping to kidnap Evie," Lydia growled. "How'd you miss something that big?"

"What?"

She glared at me. "I didn't stutter. How did you, of all people, miss that? Wendell I get, but you?"

Wraith Knight looked at Lydia with a mix of anger and confusion. "What that's supposed to mean?"

She rolled her eyes. "You're a nerd banging a girl who's out of his league. Doris might be a four, maybe a five with good lighting, but *Myst* is a nine. Which means you're vagina blind."

"It is a medical-grade condition," Mikayla said, agreeing with Lydia. "It's also known a Genital Obfuscation Syndrome."

"I'm not… vagina blind."

"Then *you knew* she was a traitorous piece of shit?!"

Oh, for the love of—why didn't Lydia see that turning this powder keg of a moment into an explosion was a bad idea?

Sigh. Because despite her many, many flaws, she was a mom. A mom who was scared for her child and was looking to take it out on anyone. And since Myst and Wraith Knight came as a package deal, he was the next best thing.

"None of us saw it coming," I said, slowly peeling WK's fingers off my chest, "because when you care for someone, you don't think rationally. You tend to think the best of them while ignoring the signs that a more rational, detached mind would see. Turning on one another is not gonna help. So why don't we all stow our attitudes and fucking focus on what's important, which is getting Evie back."

Wraith Knight looked down and let out a breath. "Yeah, okay."

"Whatever," Lydia said.

Beatrice looked thoroughly disappointed. "Man, I thought someone was gonna stab someone."

"Give it time," Mikayla snickered.

We continued along the corridors in relative silence. I flexed the four remaining fingers of my broken right hand. It hurt like hell and the wrist was swollen, but I'd make it work. I didn't really have a choice.

"Is—is she going to be okay?" Lydia whispered as she came to my side.

She'd torn a high slit up her dress, allowing her freedom of movement. But even being "ready for action," my ex-wife looked nervous.

"If Sophia wanted Evie dead, then she would've done it while the Sablestone was at the dance," I said as the various scenarios played out in my mind. "King Stanley was a diversion. Sophia snatched Evie in such a way that she was seen doing it. She wants us to follow."

"Why?" she asked.

I started to say something, mostly some bullshit to pacify her, but I held my tongue. It was her daughter too, and she deserved to know the truth. Even if it made me look like a schmuck.

"Because Sophia planned for my move," I admitted. "She may not have known exactly what, but she knows me well enough to predict my intentions. With the stone at the dance, it meant the resting room was empty. She and the rest could grab Evie, rush down, and get into place before the stone returned."

"Which means they get to keep their powers and we have to give up ours if we follow. And since it's Evie, we were coming regardless of the consequences," Lydia said, seeing the picture. "Damn it."

"Yeah."

I waited for her to berate me for being stupid, blind, or arrogant. But she didn't. She just turned and asked, "Did you really kill King Stanley?"

I looked her in the eye. "He got between me and Evie."

Lydia took my hand and gave it a reassuring squeeze.

"Then we'll do this next part together."

Bolstered by our union, we silently crept along the passageways for a few more minutes. Getting closer to the nexus hub where the Sablestone rested, I held up my fist to silence and stop my team.

I got down low and crept a bit more forward to where the path opened into the circular stone room. I carefully peered around the edge of the wall, inviting Lydia to do the same. This close to one another, I could smell a mix of her perfume, sweat, and natural pheromones. It reminded me of all the adventures we'd had together.

And how they were over.

Sigh. Head in the game, Jackson. Stuff your emotions back down into the black, abyssal core of your being and focus on the job.

Evie was seated on the ground and bound by ropes to the Sablestone pillar. Eris was at the far end of the room, checking the other passages while Myst stood guard. Sophia had her back to the others, studying the door that led to "the Nothingness."

"What're they doing?" Lydia whispered, her voice barely audible.

"We're waiting for you to arrive," Sophia said, raising her voice while she continued studying the door.

"Damn that djinn's hearing," I growled.

Lydia and I exchanged a frustrated look, then stood up, motioning for Mikayla, Wraith Knight, and Beatrice to join us.

"Dad! Mom!" Evie called out as she fought against the ropes.

"It's okay, baby," Lydia said, stepping fully into view but not crossing the threshold. Not just yet, anyway.

Sophia slowly turned away from the Nothingness door to face us. Once she held my gaze, her eyes deliberately glanced over at the Sablestone and then back at me. The unspoken message was clear.

"Please come in, Jackson," she said. "We have a lot to discuss."

"What do you want?" I said, standing my ground instead of entering.

"No no, that's not how this works," she said, shaking her head. The djinn floated over to the Sablestone and ran a hand over Evie's hair. "You come in and we all have a nice talk about the future."

Lydia looked at me for guidance. "Jackson?"

"Smart move," I said, ignoring my ex for the moment. "Waiting for me to summon the stone."

"You always did need to be the center of attention. And the more I thought about it, nothing else but the real presence of death would capture everyone's attention," she said, then laughed a little. "Heh, it's funny if you think about it. In another life, you would've made an excellent theater kid."

"Take that back!" I snapped. "I get that we're enemies, but there's no reason to be hurtful."

"I don't think you realize the severity of the situation," Myst said. My former minion came from behind the Sablestone plinth while transforming her hand into a claw. Kneeling down, Myst placed a sharp finger to Evie's throat. "We hold all the cards."

"Doris!" Wraith Knight practically shrieked. "What're you doing?!"

"All he has to do is come in," she said, pressing down ever so slightly.

"If you even harm a hair on her head, I'll gut you!" Lydia hissed.

Myst sniffed, then flicked a finger, severing a small lock of Evie's hair.

"Oops."

Gods damn it.

Knives out and with a cry of rage, Lydia charged in… then ate a face full of stone floor a half second later. By crossing the threshold, she'd given up her supernatural rogue skills, and I'd already witnessed clumsy Lydia firsthand.

Well, at least she didn't stab herself in the throat.

Groaning, Lydia tried to stand, but Eris dashed in and slide tackled my ex-wife, taking out her ankle. When Lydia tried to get up, Eris lashed out with a low, circular kick that swept Lydia's support hands out from under her. Reintroduced to the floor, Lydia spat a string of curses, but Eris wasn't done. Grabbing Lydia's arm, Eris performed a complex jiu jitsu roll that not only disarmed my former wife but also locked her into a position that promised to pop her shoulder out of socket.

I shook my head.

Was I the only one who remembered when Eris singlehandedly took on Lydia and Wraith Knight back in *Villains Defeat*? Unlike my baby mama, Eris's skills were earned from hard work and dedication, not from having high fantasy stats. And it was clear that she'd spent these last couple months of school refining said skills. It was something I wished Mikalya had considered before she rushed in to help her girlfriend.

Alas, she did not.

Remember just a few moments ago when I mentioned how caring for someone can lead to irrational thinking? I mean, I remember, but I bloody well said it.

Lemme ask you something, dear reader. If a normal human girl is robbed of her superhuman dexterity and then falls flat on her face, wouldn't that raise suspicion? It might even urge you to show a little caution, right? Well, Mikayla either didn't notice or didn't care.

Yeesh. And Lydia called Wraith Knight vagina blind.

Another question for you. What do you think happens when a winged, bespectacled, gawky, and top-heavy teenage succubus from the Never Realm loses control of her powers *and* her demonic coordination? Why, that's right. Said succubus resembles a spastic moose on ice skates.

In her defense, I'm one hundred percent certain that Sophia was cranking up her probability mojo, which contributed to Mikayla's demise. But the long and short of it happened thusly: Blinded by vag—love, Mikayla dashed in and her cloven hoof immediately tripped over a raised stone. But she didn't fall right away. Her windmilling arms and now independently flapping wings worked incongruously. This in turn led to a comically long, tap-dance-like attempt to regain control. The entire room watched as the demoness staggered across the circular room, smashed her face into the far wall, and knocked herself out cold.

Elapsed time: Eight-point-nine seconds.

"And then there were three," I grumbled.

Myst stood up from Evie and transformed into gorillapus. She stared at the rest of us, waiting for us to make our move.

I looked up at Wraith Knight. "You ready for this?"

"No point in waiting," he said, lowering his center of gravity for a charge.

"Right behind you," Beatrice said.

"On three," I said. "One, two . . . *three!*"

Wraith Knight shot into the room, aiming right for his girlfriend. But the moment the big man reached Myst, he stopped, pivoted, and swung at me. Or rather, where I would have been had I followed him into the room.

Which I did not. Because I'm not stupid.

The big man stood there, a mix of confusion, regret, and shame. I nonchalantly crossed my arms and leaned against the stone entryway, refusing to cross the threshold while glaring at my former minions standing side by side... on the wrong side.

"Boss, listen. I—"

"*Shh*," I said, shaking my head. "Save it. I don't wanna hear it."

"Boss—Jackson, please," he said. "You gotta—"

"Shut up!" Sophia hissed. "It doesn't matter. He's beaten. Come in here and face us here you will die. If you don't, then she dies. And if you use your Titan powers, then you automatically forfeit your child. So choose, Jackson. Choose how you want to go out."

"Daddy?" Evie said.

"It's going to be okay, sweetheart," I told her in as soothing a tone as possible.

I said it in the way all good parents should, with the unspoken promise of hope and safety. Kids didn't need to hear us promise or brag that we'd crawl across a mile of knives straight into Hell for them. They should already believe it.

Evie damn sure did.

Which was why it probably came as a surprise to her when I turned to leave.

"*Daddy?!*"

"It's going to be okay for *me*, sweetheart," I clarified, leaving my daughter to the mercy of my enemies. "Good luck!"

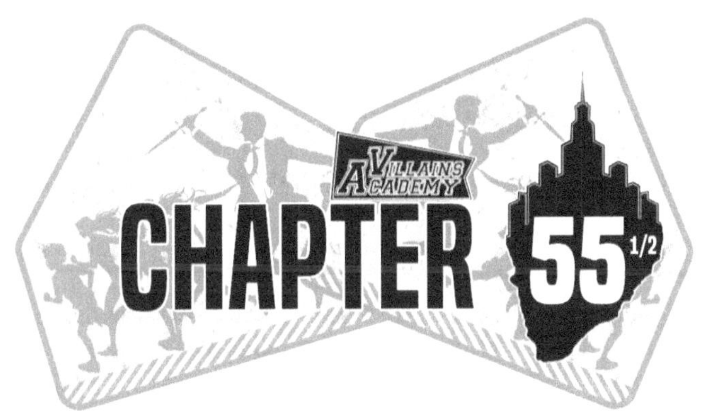

WHERE I WIN YOU BACK BY MOCKING MISSISSIPPI AND PROMOTE PICKLEBALL

Waaaaait, wait wait wait, don't go closing the book just yet. How about we all take a breath and talk it out? Well… I'll talk. Feel free to talk back if you like, but I'm not gonna hear you.

Aside from the listening software that's on all your phones, computers, and every Bluetooth device in your house, that is. You're welcome for all the targeted ads.

Now let's be real with one another—I've done way worse. Remember that time in *Villains Defeat* when I adopted an entire orphanage to bribe Frau Kinderfresser, then abandoned them? That was like two books ago, and you're still here. So abandoning Evie shouldn't be anything new.

Besides, I can make another kid, duh.

Hah! No, seriously. Get back here. I just needed to see your faces. You see, dear reader, it only looks like I'm abandoning my daughter in need. But I'm not, I swear. I'm abandoning *Evie*.

Yes, there's a difference.

You may be confused, but you're gonna have to trust me. I'm a villain, not a guy from Mississippi.

Seriously, that's not me talking shit. Reportedly, Mississippi has the highest number of absentee fathers and fathers abandoning their families. And I can't believe that an unapologetic capitalistic prick like me is saying this, but ya gotta do better, dads of the Magnolia State. Mississippi is already at the low end of women's health, labor force participation, education, and perhaps the greatest sin I could dig up… you're way behind in adopting and playing Pickleball.

Pickleball!

Dude, have you tried it? It's a stupid amount of fun and it's the fastest-growing sport for a reason. Mississippi's in forty-nineth place in play adoption and *barely* ahead of Louisiana, but that's not saying much. Those voodoo jazz enthusiasts are too full of Cajun-fried crawfish and laden with titty-beads to play. Even they did, you'd never understand whatever they were trying to say.

Where was I going with all this? Oh, yes, abandoning Evie.

I'd *never* abandon my daughter. But *Evie?* Heh, that asshole doesn't deserve me sticking around. Which is exactly why I'm gonna walk away and—

SLAP!

Ow.

Turns out, I wasn't leaving. Not because of a sudden sense of parental concern for Evie, but because I'd momentarily forgotten that Beatrice was with us. More importantly, behind me.

She didn't charge in with Wraith Knight, did she? So either she also suspected something was up with my former minion, or she was an ace card for my adversaries.

Based on the thunderous hit she'd placed on my face, I was leaning toward the latter.

Well, I normally have a trick or two up my sleeve.

And sometimes a knuckle or two in the butt.

Well, it's not always a knuckle.

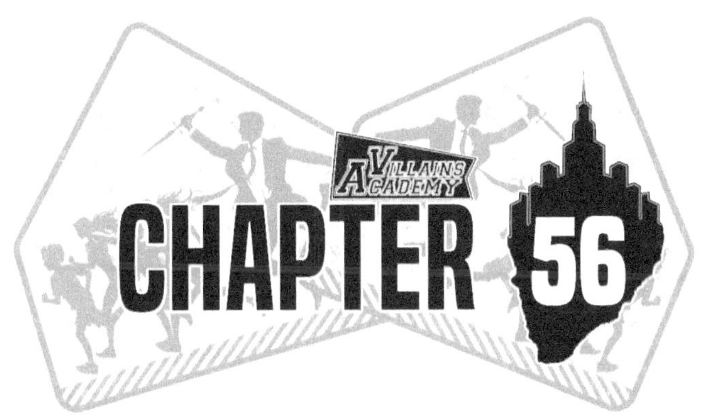

WHERE I FEEL VIOLATED, EXPLAIN THE COSMIC LAW CONCERNING PIZZA, AND TOOT MY OWN HORN

"Oh, you've gotta be kidding me," I groaned.

My head was ringing and my vision was blurry. But since Beatrice only slapped me stupid instead of ripping my head off, she wanted me alive and aware. Still, she coulda left me with a little dignity. But no. Clearly, she had her orders.

Stunned as I was, I couldn't stop my date from ripping off my jacket, shirt, pants, and shoes. Now, if this had been any other situation… I would've been into it. But it wasn't any other situation. On top of us both being kids, it was a betrayal and a literal shakedown.

Hidden contraband piled up as Beatrice continued to shred my clothes. Crafting components, magical trinkets, several of Dr. Moreau's vorpal scalpels, and one baggie of apple slices lay at her feet. She tossed the rags away and glared down at me.

"Where's the whistle?"

"Up my butt, you wanna look?" I sneered back at her.

I felt the static electricity in the air increase. She was charging up her electric field and was fully prepared to taze me.

"Settle down now," I told her. "I lost it in the chaos. Or maybe you missed the part where I was trying like hell to stay alive while King Stanley was trying to laser my face off?"

I slowly reached for the pile of my stuff, but her foot came down hard, nearly breaking my other hand.

"Stop!"

"Will you please chill?!" I snapped back. "You got me. I am just freaking hungry."

I gently placed my hand on the bag of apple slices. She growled.

"Relax, they're just sliced apples," I said, opening the baggy. "Granny Smith. See?"

"Why do you—"

"Ever since I got into my fitness regimen, I need to eat heathier and more often," I explained. "So I prep mini meals for on the go. And since I never got to any of the finger foods at the dance, and seeing as I'm about to die, I'd just like a snack."

"Whatever," she said.

"This—mm, this is your midterm betrayal, right?" I asked, munching on the fruit.

The large girl nodded. "Bring someone into close confidence, use them, and then turn on them when the moment's right."

"All things considered," I said, popping another slice into my mouth, "is this even gonna count? We both know that *she* came up with this idea, not you."

"There's nowhere in the rules where it says the idea has to be your own," Beatrice countered. "I'm the one who approached you when you were vulnerable, ingratiated myself, and got you to teach me. I even made myself available to ask out. Not too bad for a brute."

Well, she had me there. I'd had so many things going on, I'd let my guard down and allowed another blind spot. I could make excuses, but I was the one sitting there nearly naked.

"Well earned," I conceded, finishing off the last of the apples. "So, how are we doing this?"

"You enter the room on your own, or I press your skull against the barrier with ever-increasing force," Beatrice said, popping her knuckles. "Either you give in, or you die painfully. We're close enough to the stone that it might actually stick."

Shit. I never really tested that hypothesis, did I?

Was I already within range of the Sablestone's death field, or was it contained to that room alone while it rested? I didn't know for sure, and I wasn't certain that I wanted to find out.

Beatrice stepped up into my personal space. Without my weapons and magical implements, I didn't stand a chance.

"Fine," I said, throwing up my hands in resignation.

With what dignity I had left, which was next to none considering I was a Titan in Darth Vader Underoos, I willingly gave up my personal power, crossed the threshold, and entered the Sablestone room. Walking into the proverbial lion's mouth, I adjusted my junk while scanning the room for every detail.

Evie was still bound to the plinth. Eris still held a struggling Lydia in a joint lock, while Myst and Wraith Knight watched me with caution. Beatrice remained behind, standing guard just beyond the threshold. Smart.

And of course, Sophia had all four of her cat eyes trained on me. A wicked smile split her face, displaying the braces on her needle-like teeth.

I just rolled my eyes and shifted my underwear a little more.

"Everything okay?" Sophia purred.

"I wouldn't say that at all," I said, finally satisfied with how things had settled down there. "But I'm here now. So what's next?"

"Simple," she said. "One of you two is going to die. Permanently. Either you give yourself up willingly, or I kill your child."

"Did it really need to come to this?" I asked her, shifting my body weight from one leg to another.

"Djinn law demands that—"

"Ah, bullshit," I said. "This is way past djinn law, if that's even really a thing. You swore vengeance on my parents for using you. You'd crush their children and their children's children, or some such shit. But you also promised to forswear vengeance if I gave you Evie. Gods above and below, you once said you'd forswear vengeance if I gave you the last slice of meat-splosion pizza during that one office party."

"Which you didn't do."

"Hey!" I snapped. "You're the douche bucket who wanted the Hawaiian pizza."

"So?"

"*So?!*" I scoffed. "There are some fundamental, unbreakable laws of the universe. And chief among them: Thou canst order a specialty pizza and then expect to eat another kind of pizza until the specialty pizza is fully consumed. That's just scripture."

"Oh, for the love of—what's your bloody point?"

"The point is that you're so gods damned liberal with the forswearing that none of this has *anything* to do with your djinn vengeance. It's personal and you know it. You're pissed at me for some contrived crap. So how about we just stop? Huh? Finish out the next semester in peace, let Evie graduate, and then go our separate ways?"

"You're not getting it," she said. "There is no next semester. This is the end. Either you die, or Evie dies. That's it."

"Fine," I said. "Kill her."

"Daddy?!"

"Jackson!" Lydia hissed.

"Oh, don't you *Daddy* me, young lady," I scolded. "You're in big trouble. You had me going for a bit, you really did. But this farce is over."

"Don't push me, Jackson," Sophia said, trying to get my attention.

"I'm not pushing you, Sophia, I'm calling *her* bluff," I said, my eyes still on Evie.

"Look, I'm serious," Sophia pressed, "I will—"

"Blah blah blah, just—just shut the fuck up, will you?" I said while rubbing my head, which still hurt like unholy hell. "Can we just drop the act, please? I think we're all past the ruse at this point."

"J—Jackson, what in the nine hells is going on?" Lydia grunted, still trying, and failing, to free herself from Eris's joint lock.

"Huh, maybe it isn't clear to everyone?" I said, looking around. "Well, I guess it's time for the parlor scene. Normally I love this stuff, but not when I'm the victim. But fine, for the sake of all the dumb shits—er, the loyal fans—following along with the book, as well as my clueless ex-wife, we might as well do this."

And that's when I farted.

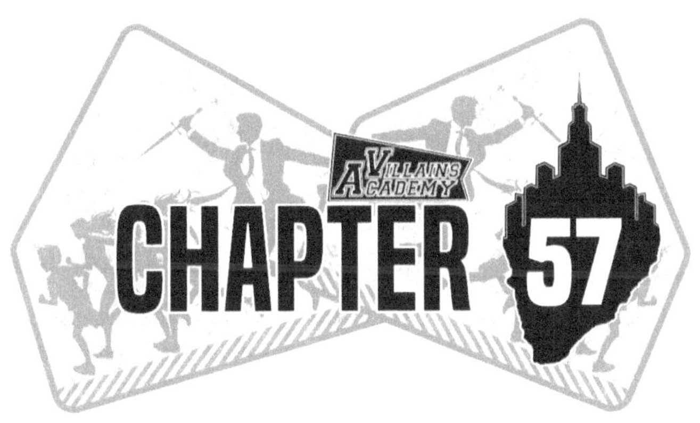

CHAPTER 57

WHERE I COMPLIMENT MY BUTT, EXPLAIN HOW OTHERS SUCK, AND STOP BELABORING THE POINT

The fart was not terribly loud or long. It wasn't wet or squeaky. If anything, it was a short, bland, run-of-the-mill flatus. Now, that's not to say that the fart was unimportant. The rectal expulsion was critical to my plan. For it was through the fart that everyone present heard the sharp, if slightly muffled, trilling whistle that emanated from my ass.

I think you see where this is going.

I didn't lie to Beatrice. Well, not completely. I kinda told the truth, then redirected the conversation and added a misleading fib. Eagle-eyed readers will have spotted me stuffing my copy of Coach Mother's magic whistle down my pants just before King Stanley came for me with his eye lasers. And I'm sure at least a few of you are now realizing what all that crotch shifting and adjusting was all about.

Yes, my loyal fans, I blew a magic whistle with my butthole.

Your move, Shakespeare.

"Everyone freeze," I proclaimed with all the confidence in the world.

And to my surprise… it worked.

"Okay, holy shit you guys, uh, wow," I laughed. "Full disclosure, I only gave that like a thirty—no, *twenty* percent chance of working."

"Wha izz hahnnening?!" Sophia tried to say through unmoving lips.

"What's happening," I said, reaching down the back of my underwear, "is this."

With a small pop, I pulled the whistle free and held it out for all to behold.

You see, folks, I hadn't been lying about the apples all the way back in chapter nineteen. They really do make me gassy. Not terribly or embarrassingly so, but something about the fibrous nature of the fruit gets my guts churning. However, when life hands you lemons, you make lemonade. Or in this case, flatulade.

Which, now that I say it, sounds like the worst flavor of sports drink.

"When the Sablestone is in place, one must relinquish their personal power to enter this place," I said to the frozen people in the room before settling my attention on Sophia. "The very rule you were banking on to protect you and give you an upper hand. But did you really think I wasn't going to find a way around a rule? Do you even know who I am?"

I ran the whistle under Sophia's nose, and her eyes watered.

Was it gross? Well… yeah, it had been up my butt. However, when one is given the opportunity to be a child, one is obligated to do childish things. At least I didn't draw a poo-moustache on her.

I have standards.

"The power in this whistle, copy or not, isn't my power, now is it?" I said, looking the fractured object over. "The real magic whistle, and the vorpal knife used to make the copy, are things that Possibility created. I brought *his* power in here, not mine."

"Jjahshun," Lydia muttered.

"Yes dear?" I said, looking over at my ex.

"Wwwa da fuuh?!"

"I think you're asking me what the fuck is going on?"

"Yyyh, ahhshul!"

"Ah, well, I'm getting to that, dear," I told her. "Now time is limited, and I have a lot to get off my chest. So…"

I cracked my neck and cleared my throat.

"None of this was Sophia's plan. How could it be? Moriarty practically spelled it out in our first class with him. Djinn are great at chaos but piss-poor at planning."

"Fffk yuuh!" Sophia said, sounding more than a little offended. "I vhuz uh grrt plnnr!"

"A great planner?" I repeated. "No. But you were an excellent *personal assistant*. I miss that. The mind-boggling mental prowess it takes to master Microsoft Office aside, your plans to take me down were always half-baked at best."

"Uhnill I killd yuh azz," she sneered, or tried to.

"Yes, until you killed my ass," I agreed. "But like Beatrice out there, that wasn't your plan, now was it?"

I stepped away from my former secretary and looked down at Eris still holding Lydia.

"And no, sadly, it wasn't your plan either," I told my former nemesis. "The idea to reach out and use you to bring me down was, in fact, genius. But Sophia doesn't think like that. Sure, when given orders, our favorite djinn here's a powerhouse of villainy. However, the kind of lateral thinking it takes to search my recorded adventures in order to weaponize my mistakes requires mastermind levels of thinking. Something the Sablestone proved that neither Eris nor Sophia had or were. But we'll come back to that."

I got up and went over to where Myst and Wraith Knight were frozen and shook my head.

"When this is all over, you two really need to work on your communication skills already, okay? Yeesh. From the moment you argued over *The Princess Bride*, I knew I never had to worry about you two being on the same page."

Frozen as they were, I could see in their eyes that they were confused.

I sighed.

"Myst worked very hard to use my biases against me. I'd theorized that she was in league with King Stanley, that he was your respective patron, and thus the source of your superpowers. Problem came when he died."

"Hhhes duhhd?!" Myst said, trying to flick her eyes in WK's direction.

"Oh yeah," I said, laughing a little. "Dead dead. And while Wendell here did a great job not using his powers to sell the lie, he forgot to tell you to do the same. My guess is that he didn't realize that you'd already left the dance. At least I hope so. Otherwise, he really dropped the ball. Regardless, you using your powers down here after Stanley was dead was... pardon me, a dead giveaway. Details, my minions. Details are key. Something we masterminds thrive on. Which brings me back to the main point, the brains behind this whole operation."

I returned to the center of the room.

"While trying to figure this all out, I'd briefly entertained the notion that I was wrong. That I was asking the wrong questions. Turns out, I was asking the right questions, but asking them of the wrong people. Y'olly, Valliar, Khasil, Mikayla, Eris, and even the late King Stanley were all smokescreens, red herrings, distractions. I'd spent so much time learning the rules of this place and how to take Sophia's crew down, or flip them to my side, that I missed the obvious. Despite living in one, I allowed the genre setting to elude me. Y-freaking-A. The wish-dot-com of literature. And what does this genre love besides dead kids, love triangles, brooding hotties, and simplistic writing designed to make dim adults feel smart? Why, hiding the antagonist in plain sight, of course."

I knelt in front of my daughter.

"Heya, sweetie," I said, licking my thumb and then rubbing away some imaginary schmutz. "How ya doing?"

She said nothing verbally, but as I already told you: When you have the center of attention, where and *how* people look speak volumes.

I crossed my legs and looked into my daughter's smoldering eyes.

"Moriarty said that there'd been only one student born with power that he respected. I, like everyone else, took that to mean someone from the Veil Walkers. Maybe a student from the past? But that's the problem with assumptions. It makes you your own unreliable narrator. When you're wise enough to step back and let go of your biases, one can see the bigger picture. As such, I was able to see that I should've been looking for a mastermind whom Moriarty adores, who was born with power, and who also had enough inside information to use my history against me. And with that in mind, it was easy for me to find a person who could easily hide in my blind spot. Someone who not only claimed that my love was a weakness, but also told me that if there was something of mine she wanted, she'd just take it. Little did I know that she'd already taken my minions and my djinn."

I got really close to my daughter and let my patented smarmy, shit-eating smile cross my face.

"Isn't that right, Evie?"

My smug look lasted all of two seconds before Evie lurched forward and headbutted my face.

WHERE I DEFEND MY MISTAKE, GET PUT ON THE SPOT, AND GIVE SOME ADVICE

I know, I know. It's so cliché and frankly bad writing to have the villain's monologue be their undoing. But… and I hate to say it, some stereotypes are true. Now, I'm not gonna go into racial consistencies, certain demographics, and their patterns of behavior, or which country's citizen behave in which predictable way. I mean, I very much want to. But my legal team has advised me to steer clear for as long as I want to keep taking your money. *Sigh.*

What I will say on behalf of we villains is that we bloody *love* the monologue. It's half the reason we got into the business. Since most of you are—let's face it—sheep, the closest thing you'll ever get to the monologue is a poorly constructed and confrontation- free internet post. Special cringe for you dweebs who later brag within your respective echo chambers about how you "slammed," "owned," or "destroyed" the opposition in your misspelled manifesto or selfie video rant.

Until you've physically stood over a fallen enemy, one put down by your actions, you'll never truly know the joy of the monologue. But keep on dreaming, you glorious keyboard warriors, it's cute.

It warms my heart knowing that people like you end up serving people like me.

In this case, "people like me" means actual *me*. And actual me's face really, really hurt. A concussion-inducing slap followed by a headbutt does not make for happy times. Thank the gods above and below I played slaughterball and built up a bit of grit.

Rolling back, I spun away to create distance while blinking away the pain. Clearly the whistle's magic had faded, and everyone was free.

"Nice speech, Daddy," Evie said as the rope that had bound her suddenly came loose. "But, like, come on. That could have been an email."

"And if your mom had given up the butt that first night, none of this would have happened," I said, shaking off the cobwebs. "Yet here we are."

"*Eww*. You are… so gross," Evie said, then made a flicking gesture.

Waves of unseen power crashed into my chest and flung me across the room. I hit the stone wall and hung there a few feet off the ground. A second later, Lydia, Eris, and Mikalya *thudded* hard against the wall in rapid succession. All four of us were held there, pinned by Evie's power.

"Why?" Eris asked, shaking her head. "I helped you!"

"You thought you were helping *me*," Sophia said calmly. "I know you were on the fence as to which side to join. We're making that choice for you."

"But—"

"Let it go, Eris," I sighed. "You helped steal a kid who turned out to be the one calling the shots. But you didn't know that. No way was she going to keep you on staff. You got played and screwed over by a manipulative djinn. Welcome to the club."

"Will you two shut up?" Lydia grunted, thrashing her arms and legs, desperately fighting to get free. "Since—since when does Evie have powers?!"

"Uh, since like, *always*, Mom?" our daughter said. "I was born of a god in an otherworldly dimension, duh."

"Don't be shitty, young lady," I said. "It's not your mom's fault she's kinda dim."

"Dick!" Lydia snapped. "I know she *was* a demi-goddess, but I thought that was only in your old dimension and when you were a god. Didn't Frank say something about that just before we came here?"

"Yeah… he did," I said with a shake of my head, damning myself. "I was so caught up in the plot and trying to save Evie, I hadn't considered the prick may have been lying from the start, just to create more chaos."

"Just because someone says something, that doesn't make it so," Evie said by way of explanation.

And she said it with a smirk, which really pissed me off.

No, not for the reasons you're thinking. Smarmy kid being smarmy is on par for that age. No, I was mad about something way more important.

"Where in the Hell was all this power during our slaughterball games?!" I spat. "Here I am carrying the team on my shoulders while you could've been helping more? Bad form, dear. Bad form!"

It was Evie's turn to sigh. "What's first rule of having power, Dad?"

I rolled my eyes. I hated being schooled by my own spawn. "Once you show people what you can do, they can then plan for it."

"That's right," she said. "And how many times did the Emperor use his power in your beloved *Star Wars*?"

"The good movies or the shitty ones?"

"Doesn't matter," she said.

"*Doesn't matter?!*" I repeated. "Now see here, young lady—"

"Palpatine barely used them at all because he didn't need to," she said, cutting me off. "Instead of being flashy, he discreetly pushed the people where he wanted them to create the outcome he desired. But when necessary, he had more than enough gas in the tank to run those Jedi chumps over."

"Wait, wait wait wait, I'm the *Jedi* in this scenario?"

She shrugged. "More or less."

That little bitch.

Wraith Knight, Myst, and Sophia took up position beside Evie. Beatrice, who'd been standing guard, crossed the threshold and came into the room to join them. This little quintet practically did the superhero team pose. Evie with my minions, my djinn, and my date. I wasn't sure if I was supposed to be pissed or proud.

"Good job, babe," Beatrice said, leaning down and giving Evie a quick kiss. "You did it."

Babe? Huh, did that mean that—ah… shit.

"Seriously?" Lydia said, looking over at me. "You took your daughter's girlfriend to the dance?"

"I didn't know!"

"That's not an excuse," Mikayla said, shaking her head at me.

Me. A sex demon was scolding *me* for being inappropriate. Gods above and below, save me from this contrived irony.

"How am I the bad guy in this?" I asked.

"That's disgusting," Eris said, adding to the dog pile.

"Okay, enough of this shit," I said. "I'm not some Florida man headline. I knew Evie was secretly seeing someone on the side, but I didn't know who. This was part of their plan. I'm the victim here."

"*Men*," Lydia, Mikayla, and Eris said in unison, as if I'd dug up and defiled Ruth Bader Ginsburg's corpse.

You know what, fuck it. They all deserved the bear.

"Oh, Jackson," Sophia said. "You should see the look on your face. I know the 'turning your allies against you' thing is kinda cliché, but it's a classic for a reason."

"Him I get," Lydia said, "but why punish me? Or Mikayla for that matter?"

"Way to be a team player, hon," I said, scolding my ex.

"But I'm her mom!"

"Myst is more like a mother to me than you are," Evie said.

Ouch. Kids… am I right? They know exactly where to twist the knife.

"Excuse me?" Lydia seethed.

"Mom, please," Evie snickered. "Auntie Myst delivered me, then you went drinking immediately after without even naming me. Uncle Wraith taught me to walk when you two were out on a mission or a Never Realm party orgy. Neither of you were really what normal people would call hands-on."

"Evie," Lydia said, trying to defend herself, but our daughter held up a hand, silencing my ex-wife.

Gods above and below, I've wanted to do that so many times.

"Parents don't give kids enough credit," Evie said, making sure she caught my eye as she explained herself to us. "They always think their words and their rules are what kids absorb. No, it's their actions. What a parent does is infinitely stronger than what a parent says. And kids see way more than everyone realizes. You two had always been a pair of self-serving narcissists. And this was clearly illustrated when you were freed from the burden of motherhood, Mom."

Evie walked over and stood in front of Mikayla.

"She loves you, and I think you love her. But is that a good thing? You jumped through a lot of hoops just for a chance of happiness. Was it worth it? Should I hate you for helping to break my parents apart or should I applaud you for it?"

"Yeesh, kid, I know teens are dramatic, but this is pushing the limits."

"Something to say, Dad?" Evie asked, stepping up to me.

"Just there are other ways for parents and kids to have a constructive conversation," I said. "Ones that don't require the rock of certain death."

"Is everything a joke to you?"

"I could explain, but you're too ignorant to understand."

"Jackson!" Lydia hissed.

"What?" I said. "I can only foot stomp this so many times. Children lack the lived experience of an adult. They don't have same context."

"Is this the same adult who confided in *a child* that they were, what was it you said, scared?"

"Heh heh, well, I never said I was—"

"Scared because you didn't know if you could beat Sophia," Evie continued.

"Yeesh, kid," I grumbled. "That was between us."

"And that while you told everyone they wanted to hear," Evie pressed, "you were basically flying blind."

"Evie once licked her mother's vibrator!" I announced to the room. "It saw it happen. I didn't tell her because little kids put things they find in their mouths. But since we're sharing secrets, yup, she did that."

"See," she said. "Everything's a joke."

"No, that really happened," I said. "But the reason I use humor, *kid*, is because the only other option is to curl up in a ball of anxiety and stress. But since I'm not a day drunk trophy wife, I pop my Zoloft, laugh at tragedy—especially my own—and move the fuck on. Because that what a functional adult does."

"And how should I *move the fuck on* then?" Evie asked.

"Evie, dear," Sophia said, whispering over her shoulder. "I think it's time to do what we're here for."

"Hey, we just said we were going to defeat him," Myst said.

"Yeah," Wraith Knight agreed. "Trap him inside Possibility for a while so that you could take over the business."

"Shut up, fools!" Sophia hissed. "Do it, Evie. You know what love does to all great villains."

I'd always given Evie a lot of credit. Teenage moodiness aside, she'd always had a good head on her shoulders. And clearly, Sophia had been using her influence to poison Evie's mind. Pushing her while using my daughter's intellect for her own gain. Still…

Evie had a certain level of unhinged detachment brewing behind her eyes. It'd easy to simply diagnose and dismiss her vibe as typical teenage hysteria. But I knew better. I'd been advising villains for far too long not to know that look.

For us villains, there's a spot right between mastermind and madness we know not to cross. We all walk up to it, maybe dip a toe or two over. But the longer we teeter on that edge, the easier it is to peer over and wonder…

What if—what if I just burn it all down?

"Babe?" Beatrice said, a look of concern on the girl's face.

For you normal folk, there's a phenomenon known as "the call of the void." If you've ever stood atop something incredibly high up and looked down, there's this weird moment when your brain panics and screams to move back. But for whatever bloody reason, it's interpreted as thinking about jumping. You ponder the idea for several heartbeats too long before moving back. Or at least, that's what's supposed to happen.

Evie? She'd just taken the plunge.

A burst of raw, angry power erupted from my daughter and slammed into us. Lydia's and Eris's screams merged with my own. Each second was agony, and part of me wished to die. But another part hung on out of spite. While Evie looked conflicted, Sophia looked giddy. The assault ended as soon as it had started.

"What are you doing?" Sophia said. "Finish them."

Evie ignored her.

"What am I supposed to be, Dad?" my daughter asked. "Cruel and cold? Or should I allow loved ones to be my weakness, like you?"

The question had not been rhetorical. My child wanted to know if it was better to have loved and lost or to have never loved at all. And it was clear that my life, perhaps all our lives, were dependent on my answer.

So I took a breath and gave her the best—and only—piece of parental advice she'd ever need.

"Fuck it, do what ya want."

Yup. Totally earned that "Father of the Year" coffee mug.

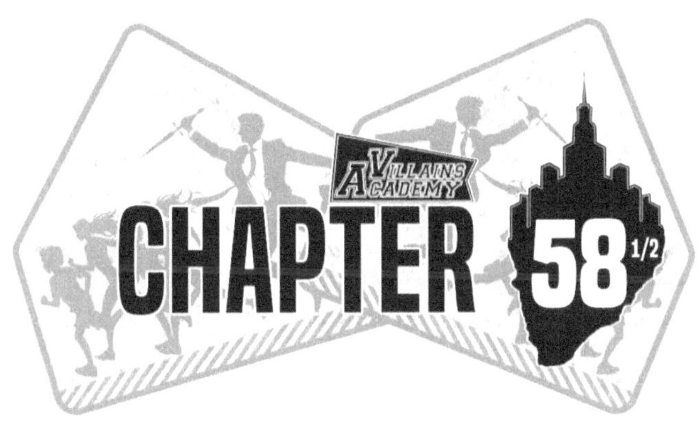

WHERE I GET MY "KAREN" ON AND METAPHORICALLY PACK A HOBO'S BINDLE

I can literally hear you wondering, just what in the fresh hell was I doing? Telling a ticking timebomb of teenage trauma to do whatever she wants? That's not only the worst kind of parenting, but it's also dangerous.

Well first off, this is my kid, not yours, so don't tell me how to parent. My kid goes to an exclusive private school and is educated by the top minds in their respective field. Yours are almost assuredly the pale, bug-eyed, little gen alpha freaks who say shit like "sigma," "Ohio rizz," and "skibidi." The kids who, thanks to screen addiction and vitamin D deficiency, have the bone density of a baby penguin with terminal cancer.

Secondly, there was simple fact that had been eluding everyone… myself included. So allow me to spell it out.

Evie… is a kid. *Ta-dah!*

No no, you're missing the point. She's not a standard teen. I mean, she's actually *a kid*.

Frank, the agent of chaos that he is, screwed us all with that bit of misdirection about Evie and her powers. But while taking with one hand, he was offering with the other. Remember what else he said? Lemme refresh your memory: No matter what she looked like, Evie was, biologically, about seven years old.

Let's let that sit for a moment.

All this time, I'd lamented my situation—being trapped in a child's body. But as a self-diagnosed positive narcissist (callback), I was able to empathize with others. In this case, Evie. I was an old—well, seasoned—man in a kid body. The opposite was true with her. Evie suffered from Shazam syndrome. A kid in an older body. Despite an approximate *physical* age of near seventeen, Evie only had around seven years of life experience. That's a deficiency of *almost a decade*.

No memories, no loves, no losses, no friends, no sleepovers, nothing. This isn't the same as some sweatpants-wearing suburbanite who's actively repressing their childhood. No. Evie never really had a childhood.

Damn it. Sophia strikes again.

But this brings me back to Evie's question, her threat to kill me, and my response. Parents out there, please back me up on this one. What do you say to a pouty seven-year-old who throws a tantrum and threatens do something stupid, like run away?

That's right.

You look them in the eye, shrug, and say, "Well, bye."

You can add a "good luck," for flavor. Or, if you wanna be playfully shitty, offer to help them pack. Regardless of execution, the parenting tool remains the same.

Call their bluff and hold your ground.

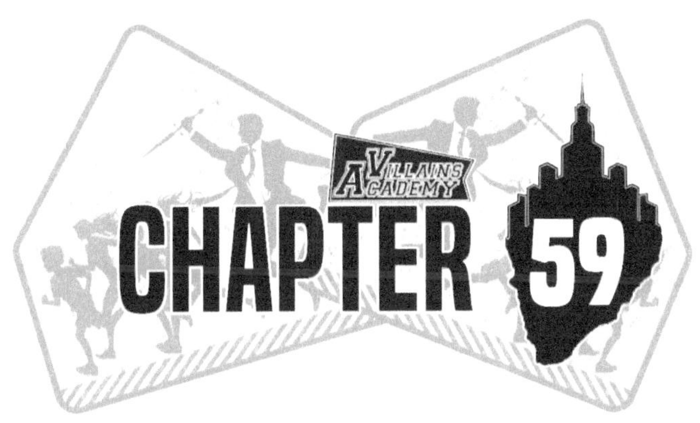

WHERE I PERFORM MENTAL GYMNASTICS, ADVOCATE FOR BUDDHA-CIDE, AND YEARN FOR A MENTOS

"I mean it," Evie said. "I'll do it."

"Yup, I know," I told her.

She held her ground, and her body language was aggressive. And while that might fool some people, I've had a lot of practice studying villains. Twenty-plus years of watching warlords, wizards, and wretches who came seeking my council. And when they sat on the other side of my desk to give their spiel, it was always with confidence and conviction. As the counselor, my job was to poke holes in their façade and call bullshit on everything they say. It might sound cruel, but there's a purpose. A client wouldn't be there if they were fine; they're there because they need help.

Huh. More I think about it, I basically acted like that self-destructive person on a first date. The brusque, abrasive prick who refuses to just go with the flow and later complains that they're single.

No, the irony is not lost on me.

Regardless, Evie looked like a rock, but the vibe underneath was anything but solid. She was a mix of fear, anxiety, and anger.

Perfect.

"Well… we had a good run," I said. "Do what you gotta do."

"*What're you doing?!*" Lydia hissed.

"Awaiting my untimely end," I told her, then dramatically squinted. "Just—just promise to remember me from time to time."

"Jackson!" Lydia snapped.

"*Sigh*… fine. Us," I amended. "Remember *us* when we're dead and gone and you're all alone."

Evie narrowed her eyes at me. "You don't believe I'll do it, do you?"

"Oh, honey, you don't get it," I chuckled. "I don't care."

"What?"

"While the specifics are different, none of this is new to me," I said. "People have been wanting to kill me since I was your age. So all this comes down to you. Either shit or get off the pot."

She wavered… just like I knew she would.

But leave it to Lydia to not see what I was doing.

"Honey, he doesn't mean it!" my ex said, undermining the lesson.

Gods… *damn it,* woman!

Well, if I needed further proof we weren't on the same page, there it was. Clearly Lydia never had a mom threaten to leave her in a JC Penney after throwing a tantrum and refusing to leave the toy aisle. I guess it's time to switch gears.

"It's all our fault, really," I said, as if musing over a stray thought with a just touch of theatric melancholy. "We're her parents and we shoulda seen the truth sooner."

"What're you talking about?" Evie asked.

"Don't," Sophia said, putting a hand on Evie's shoulder. "Don't let him talk, just finish him—"

"What truth?" Evie asked, pushing Sophia's hand away.

"We chose to be villains," I said, looking her directly in the eyes. "Your mother and I chose to be the bad guys. To live this life. Myst, Wraith Knight, and Mikayla all chose to work for a villain. Eris chose to go up against one. Sophia… well, she was born a bitch."

"Hey!"

"But we never gave you the option *not* to be a villain," I continued, "and now you're getting all the wrong advice on a career path you might not be suited for."

Evie paused there and looked like she was puzzling something over. I used that moment to press my point.

"Honey, there's no rule in villainy against letting love into your life."

"Yeah, there is. Your rule," she said, as if catching me in a lie. "The Fourteenth Rule of Villainy. 'Trust leads to relationships. Relationships lead to betrayal. Betrayal is your own damn fault. Ergo, trust is dumb'."

Bloody hell, why is it that kids can't find the fucking ketchup in the fridge, despite it being the big red bottle right there in front of them, but they can remember anything you've ever said, done, or promised if it helps their argument?

Farsighted fucking pettifoggers, every one of them.

"That was written years ago," I deflected.

"Yeah, when you were successful," Sophia countered.

"Hey now," I cautioned, "I'm still successful."

"Uh, Dad?" Evie said in that snotty tone that kids adopt when they think they know more than their parents. "Look at where you're at?"

"Sure, things aren't going my way at the moment, I'll give you that," I said, recognizing that I was pinned against the wall like a bug on display. "But I'm a Titan now. That's the big leagues."

"But it wasn't your goal," Sophia said, "it was a reaction to our plan. And as a Titan, you don't counsel villains."

"Plus, sorry Dad," Evie said, "but you're not really a villain anymore either."

"*Now see here, young lady!*" I said, putting on the dad voice.

Well, I tried. Sadly, there wasn't a whole lotta bass in this body.

"And it's all because you allowed love into your life," Evie pressed. "All the professors here agree with the old you. Love is a weakness."

"Oh, what do they know?"

"Uh, *everything?*" she said, raising her eyebrow in that shitty way.

I fought the urge to glare at Lydia.

"They're all icons immortalized in history," she said, then added, "while your recorded adventures are barely indie darlings for nihilists."

Ouch. Bloody ouch.

Well, she hit me with the truth, so I guess it was my turn. There was one more weapon in my arsenal, the one we hold back for just the right moment. The time-tested "big gun" of parenting: tough love. But it was gonna have to be tough love with… *yuck*, honesty.

"Fine, Evie. You want a real answer from me?" I asked. "Then here it is: I don't know."

This caused her to blink. Hell, everyone in the room blinked at that one. Those were not words I uttered often… if ever.

"Just before we came here," I began, "I made a comment about how 'I was wrong' are the three hardest words for a person to say. 'I was wrong' means one is admitting to being fallible, which is stupid because we all are. However, 'I don't know' is far worse. 'I don't know' doesn't just admit ignorance, which could be overcome with education, but it also evokes a sense of personal deficiency. To say those words means that despite a lifetime of experience, there isn't enough data to accurately see the present, let alone predict the future. Those words are an admittance of fear. Which is why I really try to say 'I'm not sure' instead. Here it is, kid, should you let love in or be a loveless villain? I don't know because there is never a way of knowing what 'the right' move is. But I'm gonna break villain code and be completely, one hundred percent honest. You ready? Your parents, all parents, are idiots."

"Yeah, I know that," she said with all the unearned authority of youth.

I shut that shit down immediately.

"No, you'd assumed that," I told her. "I'm confirming it. We, your monoliths of maturity and experience, are making shit up as we go, the same you. When it comes to raising kids, it's all guess work and improv. What works for one kid might not work for another. And since children don't come with a manual, mistakes are inevitable. If parents can make mistakes, then what does that mean for a kid who's questioning everything? Gods above and below know how much long-term damage we're doing daily. But we blindly march on. So what's the best path for you? I—we— have no bloody clue. But I'm not going to my grave without setting a few things straight."

"Like what?" she asked.

"First, screw your professors," I said. "They're anthropomorphic manifestations of literary characters that only work because the hand that penned them played both sides of the field. When one controls both the protagonist and the antagonist, then there is no real greatness to admire, only the illusion. Plus, and let's be real here, most of these motherfuckers got beat or killed by some real chumps in their own stories.

"Secondly," I continued, "Hero worship and admiration are the bane of potential. Following someone else's path guarantees that your name will never be chiseled into the bedrock of history. There's a reason that Buddhist sage guy said, 'If you meet the Buddha on the road, kill him'.

"Lastly," I said, then took a breath, "it takes real strength to not only see your fears, but to embrace them. Love was never a flaw; it was what I feared more than being alone. And when you fear a thing, you give it power over you. So again, if you need to kill me, us, for whatever reason, then do it. But trust me when I tell you this, if you kill us, then you'll be repeating history. And it will be years before you realize the same lessons that I had to learn on my own."

Evie took a step towards me. "What're you talking about?"

"Enough of this," Sophia said, coming to Evie's side. "You have him, here and vulnerable. Just do as we planned and finish him off. After that, you'll have everything you ever want—"

The blast of Evie's power sent Sophia flying across the room. The teenage djinn laid on the floor, moaning but alive.

"Explain," Evie said. "What history will I be repeating."

I took a breath then allowed my deepest feelings and regrets to be temporarily free. Conjuring up more than a few painful memories, I next spoke to Evie not as my daughter, but as a person.

"Sophia took my father, Malcolm Blackwell, quickly," I said, recalling the car accident. "My mother, Suri Farahmand 'Jackson' Blackwell, lingered for years, fighting her sickness before passing. Their guidance, their love, was taken from me by that fucking djinn and her need for vengeance. But she'd also convinced a very young man that it was necessary. That it was for the best. Because being alone, with as few attachments as possible, was the path to greatness."

I paused a moment and let the tear roll down my cheek.

"She used my intellect to spread what I thought was my influence across the multiverse. But it was hers. I think you're bright enough to see the pattern. And if you let her, then Sophia will do the same to you. So, Evelyn Farahmand Blackwell, you have a choice to make. Is it okay for a villain to love, or not? I know my answer, but you have to find yours."

Having said my peace, I closed my eyes and waited.

I did not die.

I did, however, fall to the hard stone floor and nearly break my ass bone. But before I could complain, my daughter was there, hugging me.

"Daddy, I'm sorry!"

"*Shh*," I said, hushing her in soothing tones. "It's okay, it's okay."

"I—I don't know if I want to be a villain," she said.

"Honey, it's okay," I repeated.

"Really?" she said, wiping away her tears.

"Oh, baby," I laughed. "Private school and higher education are a classist scam concocted by trustee boards designed to steal as much money as humanly possible from people dumb enough to give it."

"But, like, all this schooling," she said. "What's the point of it if I don't become a villain?"

"Sweetie," I chuckled. "Less than half of college graduates work in a job directly related to their major. You know how many art school kids become working artists? Like ten percent. Regardless, the lessons you learn here are applicable everywhere. But no matter what you do, I'll love and support you."

"*We* will always love and support you," Lydia said, adding to our hug. "Always."

"Boss?" Wraith Knight said, looking down at me.

"Jackson?" Myst added, unsure of what to do in the moment.

I wasn't happy with Myst and Wraith Knight, but I didn't plan on killing them.

At least not yet.

I didn't know the full story of their betrayal, but abandoning me to support my daughter? That's a gray area of villainy that I could possibly overlook.

Possibly.

"Just get in here," I told them, opening the circle of love.

Beatrice stood to the side for a moment, before reaching out a hand to Evie. My daughter took it, but there was a moment that passed between them that I couldn't read. All that talk about not being sure about letting love in made me think that Evie had been keeping her "secret girlfriend" at arm's length, which was never healthy for any relationship. And at the risk of sounding sexist, I know dick-all about teenage girls. Despite their higher levels of executive skills, they were all varying levels of crazy to me. Best to let them work it out.

Eris didn't look pleased to have been used, but the look in her eye told me she was done being a pawn. I'd given her until now to decide which side she was on. And based on the nod she gave me, I had my answer.

Mikayla just shook her head. This little family was pretty messed up. But that's the way of villains. And considering that she hadn't taken the chance to run away screaming, it meant that she really did care for Lydia and was willing to tolerate… whatever this was.

Yup, everyone seemed to be in a better place.

Well, almost everyone.

"Okay, I've had just about enough of this Hallmark Channel crap!"

I looked up and saw Sophia standing in the center of the room, next to the Sablestone pillar, awkwardly wrapping the rope around herself.

It was as if she couldn't use both hands—

Ah… crap.

She was holding my butt whistle.

"You wanna back out of our deal, little girl? Fine. If all of you have to die, then so be it."

"Sophia, don't!" I yelled to her. "You don't want to do this. And, well… that's been in my ass."

She looked at the item, considered it, then shrugged.

"Worth it," she said, and blew.

The whistle let out a cracked yet distinct final tone before it finally shattered. But Sophia didn't need multiple uses. She only needed one.

And perhaps a breath mint.

"Open the portal to the Nothingness!" she commanded.

And the ever-listening Possibility, compelled by his own power, reluctantly obeyed. Each passageway's portcullis dropped, sealing the room off while the door to the Nothingness cracked open.

CHAPTER 60

WHERE I PREDICT MY FATE, USE PHYSICS TO MY BENEFIT, AND GIVE A FINAL COMMAND

"Hold on to something!" I roared.

"On to what?!" I heard Lydia yell from somewhere.

"Anything!"

There was no up or down in this maddening cacophony of rushing wind and chaos. Swirling dirt and debris blinded us while the gale force winds slammed our bodies against the ceiling, floor, and walls. The unfathomably powerful suction had created an irresistible vortex. We looped the room in a clockwise pattern, but it was only a matter of moments until the door to the Nothingness was wide enough for our personal Charybdis to swallow us whole.

There was a very real moment when I almost gave into the base desire to succumb to forces beyond my control, accept my fate, and die.

Almost.

I'd be gods damned if I was going out like this. If I've said it once, I've said it a thousand times: Jackson Blackwell is going to die of heart failure, in bed, during marathon sex with at least three incredibly adventurous and extremely flexible women with daddy issues.

And maybe one extra guy.

Pushing myself beyond my limits, I focused through the insanity and my pain to find a way to survive. And by the grace of whatever gods still found me amusing, I crashed into a closed portcullis. Before I even had time to think, I pushed my arms though and held on for dear life.

Hanging there with my scrawny legs dangling uselessly behind me, I foolishly looked at the slowly opening door and what lay beyond. I expected howling madness or eldritch horrors.

But it was worse.

Past that border to the Nothingness, there was only the horrible sense of finality. Void. The end of all things. And as stupid as it seemed, I laughed.

I mean, you gotta admit that it was hard to not see this room like a toilet. And we were the turds circling the drain for a final flush.

While I could hold on for the moment, the suction was intensifying with each passing second. Once again, my weary and beaten body considered letting go and allowing this to be my end. But a flash of motion and a scream overrode all that selfish shit.

"Daddy!"

"Evie!"

My left hand shot out on its own, snatching Evie's wrist before the cyclone pulled her out of reach. Her sudden added weight caused my support hand, my already broken, four-fingered right hand, to slip.

Adrenaline and instinct took over.

Through rage alone, I willed my injured hand into a makeshift claw. My fingernails scraped along the steel lattice, desperately searching for purchase. Twice lucky, I caught a joint in the gate's metal mesh and held on, if only for the moment.

The unending vacuum twisted and pulled Evie, threatening to tear my child away from me. With each shift and rotation, I felt my bloody nailbeds threaten to rip away.

But I would not let go. I refused to let go.

"I got you!" I yelled, mentally putting my pain in a box and ignoring it.

"My powers are gone!" I heard her yell.

Of course they were. I knew that Nyx used the Sablestone to channel the extradimensional force into a nullifying field. But with the door opening, all the safeguards were gone. But there was no point in screaming all that exposition. Not while I was trying—and failing—to pull Evie closer to me.

Please. I begged any entity listening to give me strength.

"Daddy!" Evie cried out in panic.

I looked down to see Sophia sling around the room like third-rate Spider-Man and grab onto Evie's leg.

That gods damned djinn had planned this, or at least something like it. By having Evie theatrically tied up, she'd have a safety line in case things went tits up. With one end secured to the Sablestone plinth and the other around her waist, Sophia was able to ride the whirlwind, as it were. And now, she'd latched onto Evie like a rabid pit bull and was trying like hell to yank her from my grasp.

"I told you!" Sophia bellowed over the maddening wind. "One of you is going to die today!"

"Jackson!" I heard Lydia scream from somewhere. "Use your Titan powers!"

I could. I knew I could. They were there, just past the membrane-thin barrier that kept me in this form. All I had to do was reach out and let me, the Titan me, flood back into this reduced version of me.

But I wouldn't.

Despite Lydia's slew of raw-throated motherly pleas, Possibility's edict was still in effect. If I used those powers, then I'd condemn Evie.

I'd be gods damned if I'd let that happen. But I couldn't hang on any longer, either. This body, despite all the work I'd put into it, just wasn't strong enough.

However, that didn't mean my mind was weak.

"Hang on, baby, this is gonna get wild," I told her, then let go of the portcullis.

"Daddy?!"

It's weird, you know? That in moments of crisis, the mind speeds up to impossible levels thanks to our fight-or-flight instincts. For most people, turning into danger instead of away seems counterintuitive to the body's self-preservation protocol. But sometimes you must risk everything for the people that matter.

The moment I released my grip and gave up my bodily autonomy to the vortex, I felt every adrenergic receptor in my brain light up. With my mind rocketing like a jet engine, for just a blip of time, everything seemed to freeze.

Which was exactly what I needed to make this bat-shit crazy plan work.

That and a shitload of adrenaline.

I saw it. I saw the plan. I knew what to do. The question was, would I be able to do it?

Heh heh… yes.

I have always been and always will be the motherfucking Shadow Master.

And I don't fail.

Pivoting in freefall, I rolled up Evie's arm like an inside-turn dance move. Once we were face to face, I wrapped my legs around her waist, bent as far backwards as I could, and clamped down on Sophia's hands and wrist.

"Heya!" I screamed, then twisted.

Sophia screamed. It honestly doesn't take a lot of strength to break the small bones in a hand. Just the right technique and the willingness to inflict pain.

"What—what are you doing!" Evie demanded.

"Just hang on!" I said, trying to sound as chill as possible while trying not to crap my pants.

I hadn't been embellishing that story I told Evie from my youth, the one with the spinning carnival ride and troublesome classmates. I did know just enough about centripetal and centrifugal force to be dangerous. And at this moment, we were very close to being a human pendulum.

Or rather, a human hammer throw.

You see, dear reader, the pillar at the center of the room was the fixed-point constant that acted as the axis. The rope was the connector, and the three of us were the load. Now, I don't know all the actual details and formulae for calculating the conversion of mass, potential energy, and kinetic energy, and I likely never will.

That's what nerds are for.

Long story short, when swinging an object, the load at the end of a connector gets way heavier as it travels faster around the axis.

Free from friction and caught in the Nothingness's vortex, the three of us spun around and around the room. Each revolution wound the rope around the pillar, which shortened our line and sped us up. It didn't take long before our combined weight was more than Sophia, and her injured hand, could handle. The second I felt the djinn's grip on Evie's legs release, I tightened my grip on Sophia's wrist and my legs around Evie's waist.

I knew I wasn't strong enough to hold onto her either, but I wasn't trying to.

I was just aiming for my comrades.

Pissed off at them or not, I knew my old team—and enemies—were capable people. Not as capable as I am, mind you, but capable nonetheless. During that initial freefall after letting go, I spotted the others. Like me, they'd managed to latch onto one of the closed portcullises and were waiting for me to make my move.

Which was now.

With a cry of defiance to all who'd ever doubted me, I let Evie go. She screamed, sailing in an arc towards the others. With Wraith Knight and Beatrice as anchors, Myst, Mikalya, and Eris held onto Lydia, whose outstretched arms reached for Evie.

I wasn't betting on her rogue skills to catch her. That'd be idiotic under the circumstances.

I was betting on a mother's love to save her child.

Like a viper, Lydia snatched Evie's hands and pulled her in close. The second she was safe, the others switched from rescue to survival.

Which just left me and Sophia.

And maybe—maybe—that's how it was always meant to be.

The pair of us were a dizzy, tangled, injured mess, wrapped around the Sablestone pillar. Secured by the rope, Sophia had the advantage, while I was just hanging on as best I could. Sophia used that opportunity to reach out and clamp her hands around my throat.

"It was supposed to be us!" she screamed. "You and me—you and me against the who gods damned multiverse! That was our agreement!"

"You killed my parents!" I yelled back. "You made me a villain!"

"And you liked it!"

She was right. Part of me, a real part of me, always knew that villainy was my destiny. And with her as my guide, there wasn't anything that could stop me.

But sometimes, the hero and the villain *aren't* all that different after all. To truly move on, to reach your potential, you have to let your guide, your mentor—your best friend—go.

According to Campbell's version of the Monomyth, the hero's mentor sometimes dies during the "Approaching the Inmost Cave" or the "Ordeal" phase. But the passing of villain mentors isn't given the same level of gravitas as losing Obi Wan, Gandalf, or Dumbledore. And maybe it's better that way.

It's best you never see us cry, lest you see us as people. It's better you instead see us as those who are capable of incredibly dark deeds.

"K-Keith?" I choked out after tapping the stone in the back of my hand. "You there?"

"Keith is here!" he called back. "You okay?"

"No," I wheezed. "You… ready?"

"Keith is ready!" I heard the little pig boy call back.

"Operation: A-COUP-DEMIA is a go!"

With the line still open, I heard Keith huff as he ran in what I assumed to be the bloody wasteland of the cafeteria above us.

"Headmaster Nyx!"

"Keith, I don't have time right now."

"Jackson want Keith to give you something."

"What?" she sighed.

"This!"

The line went dead just as the suicide vest I'd rigged up in Keith's suit—the one I made from several pounds of alchemically created explosives and dozens of his father's vorpal scalpels—exploded.

And the moment he, and more importantly Headmaster Nyx, died, I felt the sudden, *titanic* shift.

It wasn't power, exactly. Rather a sense of absent guidance. With there only being one currently living Titan inside Possibility, the Sablestone sought direction. And I was there to give that blasted hunk of murder rock its orders.

"Up," I commanded. "To the top of the castle. And fast!"

As soon as the words were uttered, the pillar began to rise.

"What—what are you doing?!"

"What I have to."

"Come on," she said as realization hit her. "No… not like this. Come on, Jackson, I attack you, you attack me. That's our dance. I had so many things planned for next semester."

"I'm sorry, but you already said it. There is no next semester."

Reaching up between her arms, I easily broke the chokehold. Free from her grip, I scrambled down the rising column like a squirrel with ADHD, thankful for having watched all those lumberjack competitions on TV. Still wound up in the rope and powerless, Sophia was unable to stop what happened next.

The iris in the ceiling was only large enough for the stone and the pillar to pass through. Which meant my former assistant was smushed against the ceiling while the rising pillar shredded her body along with the ropes. Her screams were…

Damn it, they were horrifying.

Free of her literal lifeline, the bloody and nearly pulped remains of Sophia Rose DeVrille were taken by the howling winds and sucked into the Nothingness. I watched my oldest friend, my best friend—my only real friend—fall into oblivion. But as she passed on, I saw the strangest thing.

She was smiling. The bloody buck-toothed bitch was smiling.

And as she faded away, Sophia winked at me. It wasn't a goodbye wink. It was an "I know something you don't" wink.

I did not like that.

But I bloody well didn't have time to dwell on it either, because I was quickly running out of gas. There's only so long a person can work a pole before succumbing to exhaustion. Yes, all stripper and/or sex worker jokes intended.

"Come the fuck on!" I called out. "I beat her, she's gone! Close the gods damned door!"

Fine, Possibility said in my head, then sighed. *Just as things were getting good.*

The door to the Nothingness closed far faster than it had opened. As it did, the winds died down, and we all fell to the ground.

Scared, breathing heavily, clearly exhausted… but safe.

I didn't know what would happen next. Something in the way that Sophia had left this world left me with a little ball of anxiety. But for the moment, it was over. I looked to my… well, my family.

Yuck.

There was a silent, unspoken promise between us. One that meant, at least for now, all hostilities were on hold.

Mostly. I still had a bone to pick.

"Dad," Evie said as she got to her feet. "I just want to—"

"Stop," I said as coldly as I could.

"I was just gonna—"

"Stop... *talking!*" I said through clenched jaws.

Getting to my own feet, I stood there, nearly naked, and looked up at my child with all the burning rage that only a pissed-off parent can have.

"Do you have any *gods damned* idea of what you've done?"

"I just—"

"That was *not* permission for you to speak!" I snarled. "This is a one-way communication, little lady, and you will bloody well *listen!*"

Evie blinked in surprise, but she didn't move or say anything further. Hell, her knees wobbled a bit.

Now, I don't know why I said what I said next. Maybe because it's part of this great cycle of dysfunction we call parenthood. If I've gotta carry these scars, then so do you. Regardless...

"I'm so mad at you right now, *I don't want to even look at you!*"

She sniffed, her eyes pleading.

"Now... *go to your room!*"

WHERE I GIVE A POST-COITAL CATCH UP, HAVE RENEWED FAITH IN THE YOUNG, AND PREPARE FOR A WHOLE LOTTA NOTHING

"You ready?" Nyx asked me.

"In a moment," I said, enjoying my cigarette, my adult body, and the afterglow of angry Titan-on-Titan sex.

Heh heh, like Nyx and I hooking up was ever in doubt.

You'd think we would've done this earlier, but believe it or not, even at a school for villains there are rules against impropriety and perceived favoritism. However, graduation day was upon us. And while the school year wasn't officially over, point totals and grades were locked in. And as such, there was nothing stopping us from bending the rules… and her over a desk.

Hey oh! That's right, high five me!

No? Eh, I wouldn't either. While I'd had relations with mortals, gods, and all manner of deviant demons, this had been my first foray into relations as a Titan *and* with a Titan. So, let's just say that when we started, I was… um, quick to answer the teacher's questions?

But because I'm still relatively young in Titan terms, there were things I had yet to learn. Things Nyx was very willing to show me.

And take out on me.

Apparently, having a backup plan to kill her in case I ever needed to control the Sablestone not only netted me a buttload of points, but it really, really pissed her off.

While also turning her on.

I regret nothing.

Still, there was a lot to do today. So I sat up, flicked my smoke away, and stretched.

"Is everything in place?"

"Yes," Nyx said, sitting up next to me. "The staff is informed and ready."

"Good," I said, hopping off the desk and picking up my clothes. "Do we have a time frame for when this is all supposed to… dissolve?"

"No," Nyx said, adjusting her voluminous hair so that it once again resembled a professional women's suit. "With Evie graduating and this being the technical end, I don't know how or when it will happen. So everyone's on standby."

I nodded, slipping on my pants and tucking in my shirt.

"How did you work out the relocation logistics?" she asked, passing me my socks.

"Mm, thanks," I said, accepting the items. "I used Y'olly."

"Really?"

"Yeah," I said, putting on my socks. "He needed a way to get back in the good graces of his superiors, and I needed a contact who owes me. Since the Never Realm touches all planes of being, it was simple enough to pitch them the idea of housing the multiverse's premier villains' academy. The only tricky part was creating portals large enough to shift an entire mountain community. That's a lot of resources on their end."

"It didn't hurt that we beat the hero academy in the intramurals," Nyx said. "The Never Realm should be honored to be the home for such a prestigious institution."

I smiled at that memory while putting on my shoes. "Indeed."

"Won't your—what is it you call them, 'dear readers'?—be upset that you terminated transmissions for the second semester?" she asked. "A lot happened in last half of the school year."

"Yeah, they might be," I said, but ultimately shook my head. "But I didn't see a point. Sure, I could've dragged this out and made this entire school year into a two-part adventure. But why?"

"Don't you think they'd want to know that Valliar ended up in a corner of Possibility that became the Lightbridge Academy for Heroes? And that the two academies clashed at intramurals?"

"Maybe," I said, putting on my jacket. "But other books have done that story."

"But you were instrumental in defeating Lightbridge," she said.

"So?"

"I thought you'd like a chance to gloat, perhaps?" she said. "Maybe let them know how you also helped lead the Mind Fire Calling to their first slaughterball Championship."

"Gloat? Please. I'm a humble person."

She stopped and stared at me.

Yeah, I wasn't buying my bullshit either.

"Sure, I could bilk those chumps who buy my schlock for another book," I said. "It isn't all that hard. Run around, do some zany things while ranting and telling butthole jokes. They eat that shit up."

"But?"

"But," I continued, "at a certain point, you're just stringing something along for the sake of having more, not because there's more story to tell. Gods above and below, I can think of countless book series and TV shows that should've just ended long ago. But some creators are afraid of what lies on the other side. Or they just want money. Regardless, dragging an idea past its expiration date destroys what was once loved. Things are beautiful because they end."

I lit another cigarette and took a deep drag.

"There's more," Nyx said, clearly not satisfied with my half-truth.

I let out a little wistful sigh.

"Without Sophia… my heart just wasn't in it," I admitted. "Moriarty was right about me in that way. I never had a real antagonist, not in the traditional sense. But I did have a best friend who was my nemesis."

Nyx put her hand on my shoulder. It was meant to be comforting, but it only made me put my walls back up.

"But let's be honest," I said, affecting my normal smartass persona. "Aside from some teenage shenanigans and some angsty drama where I reconnected with my old minions, this semester wasn't really a problem for me, so it wasn't worth sharing."

"Well, negotiating with the Never Realm for your own *Portrait of Dorian Gray* mechanic so that you couldn't die was cheating," she said, but then added, "but in a good way."

"Exactly," I said, straightening my suit. "It was, for all intents and purposes, boring. My readers don't like boring. They like it when I'm clever, or at least when I appear to be. Besides, I truly only stayed on this semester for my daughter."

"Speaking of," Nyx said, looking up at the clock in her office. "I don't think we can procrastinate much longer."

"Agreed," I said, not looking forward to being back in my child body. "See you out there."

"And in fourth place," Headmaster Nyx said into the lectern's microphone. "Bloberto DeUzeman."

Those gathered in the castle's grand amphitheater politely applauded while the yellowish-green ball of goop undulated across the stage. Towards the front where the parents and family were seated behind the graduates, I spotted a pair of similarly colored sentient globs slapping their tendrils together in support. Ol' Blobert paused for a picture with the headmaster before rolling off stage.

How he kept the robe and cap on was beyond me.

"Do you think it's cruel or fair?" Lydia asked.

"What do you mean?

"Having the students graduate according to rank," she said. "Last place to first."

"It isn't a school for feelings," I said. "This is supposed to remind them that in villainy, like life, there are people at the top. And if you want that spot, then you have to be better than the person ahead of you."

"While watching out for the people behind you," Myst added.

"Yeah," I agreed, keeping my tone neutral.

We… well, weren't good. Not bad, but… you know.

I couldn't condemn her and Wraith Knight's betrayal after having given Randy, Paige, or even Sophia for that matter, a few swings at my title. They'd—shit, they'd always remained loyal, just not to me. They'd been Evie's secret guardians for her entire life. Working with me, learning from me, using the power I'd bestowed upon them for their own gains. And when the time came, Evie had become their patron.

She may have had a crisis about family, but she'd already built one and hadn't realized it.

"In third place," Headmaster Nyx said. "Emily Bloodstainbear."

"She is stupidly adorable," Mikalya said from her seat next to Lydia. "Even with all the wires and augmentations, I wanna hug her."

"I wouldn't if I were you," Eris said.

"Why?" the demoness asked.

"Do you remember the chlamydia epidemic during spring break?"

"Yeah, so what—*oh*, oh you're kidding me?"

"Nope," Eris said with a shake of her head. "Turns out that Emily is a repository for a genetically engineered version that's a hundred times more potent."

"There was a lot of talk about oozing anal lesions," Mikayala said, nodding along. "But we're all inoculated?"

"Yeah, we are," Eris said. "But I didn't get the whole class."

"I don't care about the whole class," the succubus smirked.

I repressed a small laugh. Eris, my former nemesis turned quasi-ally, had really bloomed over the second semester. Once she'd accepted herself and applied that intellect and aptitude to Renfield's class, *woof*, Eris had become formidable. Despite her Ivy League education in business, Ms. Pence was something of a STEM polymath in both chemistry and mechanics. Her high-tech battle suits had been instrumental in defeating the students from the Lightbridge Academy for Heroes.

But again, dear reader, you didn't really need a sequel to this tale. I've said it before. If you want those long-form stories of heroes and villains, read a Drew Hayes book.

After buying all of mine first, of course.

"In second place, our Cruelatorian," Headmaster Nyx said, "Beatrice Volthammer."

"How do you think we would have ranked?" Lydia asked while we applauded.

"We're not far off it now," I said, looking down our row.

I was in the seat closest to the aisle, followed by Lydia, Mikayla, Eris, Myst, and Wraith Knight, with Khasil bringing up the rear.

The goddess of darkness had gone the opposite route of Eris. Without her brother, Khasil was listless. Their final fight during intramurals had been nothing short of epic. But after that… the fire had gone out of her. Without that sibling rivalry, or being a high god, there was little of the old Khasil left.

"There might be a minor switch here and there," I said, considering Lydia's question. "But I think we're fairly close to our final point totals."

"You might be right."

"I usually am."

"Ass."

"Also true," I said, then switched back to the golem walking across the stage to accept her diploma. "How uh—how are they?"

Lydia exhaled through her nose, pondering the question. "Evie hasn't said much on it. I think they're at least on speaking terms, maybe a little more? But she's hurting a lot since their official breakup."

"First heartbreaks are… difficult," I said. "But we all have to go through them."

"Yeah, but it still sucks," she said. "I liked them together."

"Like you knew they were a couple."

"Oh, and you did, Florida man?"

"Blah blah blah," I said, playfully ignoring her jibes.

Lydia and I'd been on much better terms since winter break. So much so that we felt like we could co-parent without being complete dicks to one another. Sure, there'd always be differences in our styles and approaches, but we were on the side that mattered.

Evie's side.

"So, how was banging Nyx in her office?"

I nearly choked when she asked me that. "Ex—excuse me?"

"Heh, please," Lydia laughed. "You smell like musk and you have starlight sprinkles in your hair. It doesn't take being the number one freshman to see things."

I looked down at my Sablestone Academy Freshman First Place award and smiled.

"You wanna touch it?" I asked. "It's the closest thing you'll ever come to greatness… other than my penis, that is."

"Will it be over in less than minute, like every other time?"

"*Two*," I said, leaning into the insult. "I'm feeling good."

"And last but certainly not least, this year's graduating class Viledictorian," Headmaster Nyx announced. "Evelyn Blackwell."

While everyone in the amphitheater applauded, I knew for a fact that I clapped the loudest.

Well, perhaps I was tied with Lydia.

We both stood and watched her cross the stage in her ceremonial black robes with swelling pride and misty eyes. Evie gracefully paused to shake hands with each of the path's professors. Coach Mother and Baba Yaga gave her respectful shakes. Renfield gave her a hug. Carmilla, having replaced Dracula this semester, gave a simple nod. Moriarty, though—that old bastard looked like he was about to cry. I could tell that he truly cared for Evie and enjoyed helping to shape her mind.

Yeah, I was a little jealous. He'd gotten two more years with her than I had. Two years of lessons, insights, and accomplishments.

Once she reached center of the stage, Headmaster Nyx extended her hand and gave Evie a firm shake before stepping aside. When Evie took her position behind the lectern, the applause died down and we all took our seats.

Before she spoke, I took a moment to marvel at my child and the sweeping mountain vista behind her. I swear the setting sun's rays existed to spotlight her and only her. To illuminate her raw potential and her accomplishments.

Maybe that's what all parents think.

They'd be wrong, of course.

There's only one top of class, and it wasn't any of your booger-chewing trolls up there. It was my glorious gods damned daughter. The rest of you can suck it.

"Graduating class, fellow students, esteemed faculty, and visiting family," Evie began, "I think I'm supposed to say something uplifting. Something about how we represent the next generation of villains and how we're going to shape the future. But that's all bullshit."

There was a murmur among the crowd.

I smiled.

"My father taught me that there are rules in this world. Sometimes they're created by a society or an establishment. Sometimes they're self-imposed. Rules, by their very nature, impose restrictions. They guide our thoughts and actions through limitations. But the very nature of villainy, and greatness, is to defy rules. While I will forever be grateful to my peers, professors, and my parents, I say this from the bottom of my heart: Fuck your rules."

All the students exploded in cheers.

The majority of the adult villains, parents, and faculty present… less so.

Ah, to be young and idealistic.

"So, to the gathered villains representing the past and present, we the future have a message for you," Evie continued with a wicked grin. "If you think I, or any of us, will be content with becoming another version of you, then you better guess again. We've studied your moves, we've learned your secrets, and we know your weaknesses. We're coming for you. And if any of my peers disagree with me, well… I'm up here and you're down there. Either take my spot or learn your bloody place."

Gods above and below, I couldn't be prouder.

"Third Year Class of Sablestone Academy for Villains," Headmaster Nyx said, retaking control of the lectern and the mic while Evie took her spot. "Prepare for graduation."

Each of the third-years stood, hands on their caps in anticipation.

"Congratulations," Nyx announced. "The world is now yours!"

Graduation caps flew into the air while the crowd burst into thunderous applause and deafening cheers.

But all that noise was nothing compared to the monumental eruption that freaking *broke* our world.

I—I don't know how to say it. Human words cannot describe the sound of reality shattering. Not in a way that conveys the magnitude of the event. It was something one felt as much as heard. A primal, primordial power that upon awareness of its presence forced all of us in that amphitheater, mortal and monsters, deities, and denizens alike, to our knees.

Out there, past the grand stage overlooking the mountains, a hand composed of nothing ripped through the fabric of existence. The hand was followed by another as the rift that divided reality widened.

In moments, a silhouette of void emerged, waist deep and laughing.

A very familiar four-eyed, djinn-like silhouette.

When Sophia spoke, her voice was like an indescribable number of cluster bombs detonating at once. The shockwaves of sound rippled across the cosmos.

"Guess who's back, motherfuckers?!"

I looked at this new, Nothingness-infused Sophia. And while I knew I should be filled with awe and fear at the atomic level…

I felt giddy.

"Now this…" I said aloud, my voice just above a whisper, "is a gods damn challenge worth writing about."

~ The End.

Jackson Blackwell will return in:
Villains End, The Shadow Master Book 7,
The **final** chapter of the Shadow Master Saga

THE FINAL NOTE FROM JACKSON

Hey there dear reader, you know who this is and you know what to do. It's time to rate, review, and tell everyone you know—or will ever know, about how much you love the Shadow Master Saga. Go on now, you have your assignment.

Hey… you watched me in my short pants. You owe me.

~JJ Blackwell

ABOUT THE AUTHOR

MK Gibson (Gibby to his friends) is an author, husband, father, retired USAF MSgt, semi-pro digital artist, and a lifetime geek. He's a member of the Authors & Dragons podcast/YouTube network and currently the DM for their main D&D game, The Dicey Bastards.

He lives in Hagerstown, MD with his wife, and first-line editor, Valerie, their son Jack, their beagle mutt rescues Luna & Stella, and their cats Grimm, Agatha, and Fawkes. When he's not writing, MK Gibson enjoys a good whiskey, bad movies, and just spending time with those he calls "family."

"Each of us has an amazing story to tell, if we only take the time to listen."

You can follow or contact MK Gibson via the following platforms:

Facebook - Facebook.com/Gibthewriter
Instagram - instagram.com/mikekgibson
Threads - @mikekgibson
Email - Gibthewriter@gmail.com
Website - MKGibson.com
Twitter (X) - @GibsonMK1

MORE FROM M.K. GIBSON

Technomancer Novels:
To Beat the Devil
Flotsam Prison Blues
Angels and the Bad Man
One Piece at a Time
Flesh and Blood

Shadow Master Saga:
Villains Rule
Villains Pride
Villains Deception
Villains Defeat
Villains Return
Villains Academy

The Hammer of Witches Series
She Dreams of Fire
She Wakes in Water
She Walks the Earth

Agents of MORTAL: Deicide

The Cape is a Lie: The Ballad of Kevin

www.ingramcontent.com/pod-product-compliance
Lightning Source LLC
Chambersburg PA
CBHW020319180726
47991CB00018B/45